North
TO
Home

CRISSI MCDONALD

North
TO
Home

CRISSI MCDONALD

Lilith House Press

Lilith House Press
Estes Park, Colorado

ISBN 978-1-7369673-7-9 (softcover)
ISBN 978-1-7369673-8-6 (ebook)
Library of Congress Control Number 2022903656

Cover and interior design: Jane Dixon-Smith/jdsmith-design.com
Editor: Susan Tasaki
Cover art: Carissa Sorensen
Author photograph: Lindsey A. Sutherland/lindseyasutherlandcreations.com

ONE

A four-day drive unraveled the remnants of my life, but not the knot of memories that has followed me from Texas to Puget Sound. I was finally on the ferry taking me to Camas Island, in Washington state's San Juan archipelago. I close my eyes and let the wet air lave across me, loosening the knot, softening the ropes around my heart. I inhale the salt and spice of old conifer forests, the scents welcome after the fug of exhaust fumes that engulfed me as I'd inched through Seattle traffic on my way to Anacortes.

From the deck, the wild wind whipping across my ears, I can't stop looking at the water, this Salish Sea, this harbinger of a new world. I take a photo and text it to my daughter Abbie. It's May, a year since Nathan and I divorced. Shoving the phone back in my hip pocket, I'm determined to enjoy this new chapter of my life.

The breeze is damp against my skin, so unlike the Texas air that rushes by in dry bursts, impatient as tumbleweeds. I brush wisps of hair out of my face and look down at the railing I'm leaning against. The orange life preserver hanging on the railing is marked with the ferry's name, *Samish*. It seems to be unused, which loosens another knot of anxiety, as does the sight of green water unfolding against the prow. I inhale until my ribs creak.

The air. In it, I feel the promise of serenity to come—in walks on island beaches, in the alien wonder of the Resident pod of fish-eating killer whales that spends part of its year near these islands.

An animal shelter on the island accepted my online volunteer application, and I planned to call them and arrange a time to meet. Trading in my thriving Texas dog-training business for a volunteer gig at an animal shelter makes perfect sense to me in this bold new life. With my half of the sale of our family home nesting in my bank account, I'm set for at least

a year. I reckon if I can't change my life in that amount of time, my clients, and my daughter, will welcome me back to Texas.

Looking away from the emerald water, my mind drifts back to the last days I spent in my Texas home. I'd packed my belongings, the heartache of leaving behind half of my library greater than the loss of my marriage. The tears I thought I'd cry while signing the papers that transferred my family home to a young couple from Tennessee never filled my eyes.

Spending my last sleepless night in an empty bed, I looked through the window, wondering what the silver moon would look like on Camas Island. My old and tattered Texas life was done; the house was sold, and I was moving as far away as I could, to a place where I wouldn't see pity or judgement in anyone else's eyes. Bad enough, according to my circle of friends, that Nathan cheated on me. I could imagine them at their favorite Odessa café, "Nolee Evans is now Nolee Burnett, bless her heart." But that was my first step to reclaiming my life, and I wasn't going to budge. Nolee Burnett at fifty was a different woman than she'd been when she married Nathan Evans at twenty-nine. The tears I thought I should be shedding refused to gather in my eyes, then, and now.

The view in front of me comes into bright, sunlit focus. The ferry glides across the dark, glassy-green sea, and the forested islands dotting the inlet round up above the water, giant whale backs furred in pine trees. I had thought I would live and die in West Texas, a wrinkled wife and content grandmother, but life had other plans for me. As did my ex-husband Nathan, who left me last year, for the man he'd been having an affair with.

In the end, it didn't bother me that my silent husband had fallen in love with a man; live and let live is my motto. It was the three years of secrecy, years in which I blundered along in happy-enough ignorance, running a successful business and visiting Abbie in Austin, wondering if Nathan would ever warm up to me again—the subterranean current that ran beneath my denial that anything was wrong.

The affair began when Carlos hired Nathan's accounting firm. Carlos showed up as a new client with questions about how to grow his construction business, which had stalled. Nathan was excited about this client and the challenge of helping him increase his business. Within a year, Carlos's business had jumped two tax brackets, and Nathan had jumped into bed with Carlos.

These thoughts and the familiar anger glide in tandem inside my head, much like the ripples that follow along in the wake of the ferry. Trying

to see into the water's depths, I realize I'm tired of shouldering the twin burdens of shame for my ignorance and my self-righteous anger with Nathan. Instead, I mutter out loud, "You can do this, Nolee Burnett." The words are whipped away from my lips, as much a reassurance as a prayer sent out to whatever forces watch over our small lives.

I wonder what adventures await me. The house I've rented in a remote cove on Camas Island is one I've never seen. My thoughts drift backward again, hearing Abbie's shock when I let her know I was swapping a life of Texas pride for the much wetter lifestyle of an island in the Puget Sound.

Abbie didn't want the changes that I knew would set me free. I'm old enough to know that we take ourselves wherever we go, but I'm also a dreamer. I want to believe that it's possible to drop our past. It's dead, yet I'd spent so much time doing my best to resurrect the corpses of my dead choices. Or rather, the corpses of the consequences of my choices.

The house in Texas held memories but was not the place I wanted to get to know myself at fifty. Half of my life was over. Nothing could shake the sensation that I was changing yet again, a snake sloughing off the old skin to reveal a shiny new one. A life of my own choosing. To get up when I wanted and not mince around someone else's mood. No more wondering if they were halfway out the door (in Nathan's case, that was a yes) or just tired. Or tired of me. Would I learn to cook? Would I turn the music on and dance until I was out of breath? Could I take long baths without worrying about who wasn't waiting for me? What would it be like to be visible to myself, I wondered?

It was my fault for believing that Nathan's attitude defined me. In a moment of nastiness, I'd started calling him "Silent Nate," though never to his face. I'd lived with eyes that didn't see me, ears that didn't hear my voice, and a heart that grew cold to me. Keeping his attitude toward me alive wasn't a part of the plan for rebuilding my life.

I make my way from the deck to inside the ferry; people are reading and mugs of something hot steam in the cold air. The smell of coffee is strong, but I order tea. Coffee has always smelled better than it tastes, I thought, even when it's loaded with milk and sugar.

Holding the steaming cup in my hands, I inhale the sharp tang of what must be cheap black tea—any port in a storm, I tell myself—I turn and see an older man holding a small, trembling dog against his chest. They're sitting in a worn booth by the window, the sun glinting of the dog's blond coat. She *(or he, Nolee)* is wearing a pink nylon harness with gold crowns embroidered on it. I'm drawn toward them, walking with measured steps on the moving floor, the warm cup in my hand forgotten.

We make eye contact and I smile. "Your dog is adorable," I enthuse. "What breed is she? Or he?"

The man looks away from the window. He glances down at the trembling ball of fur in his arms, gently stroking the dog's head.

"She's half Corgi and half Pomeranian." His voice has a slight tremor, but he gives me a quick grin before looking down at her again.

"I had a dog too. A Border Collie named Luna."

He gives me another flash of a grin, petting his dog.

"What's her name?"

"Willow. The Queen of England had a Corgi with that name." Willow trembles, and I feel stirrings of the same frenetic movement in my gut. I take a step closer, but neither the man nor Willow seem to mind.

"That's a perfect name for her. Do you mind if I sit down?"

He shakes his head and motions to the seat opposite him. I put out my hand.

"I'm Nolee. Moving here from Texas." His grip is warm and dry, and he releases my hand without looking me in the eye.

"Gerald. Visiting a friend on Shaw."

I want to ask him which island that is, but the trembling moves from my guts to my head. I blink, putting the tea on the table and my hands in my lap because they're shaking too. Both Gerald and Willow look at me. I take a deep breath, and another one, closing my eyes.

"Ma'am? Nolee? Are you okay?"

I open my eyes and smile. "I am, thank you. Not used to being on the water."

He makes a comment I don't hear, because in that moment, my ears are filled with howling and whining that bounces off a windshield in a car with all its windows rolled up. I feel as though I'm on a ship in the ocean during a storm. My heart is beating against my ribcage, my teeth are shredding fabric. I shake my head, clearing my vision and glance out the window where the sun is shining on the calm, viridescent water.

"Does Willow get anxious in your car? Tear things up?" I'm used to the shock that moves across people's faces when I say these things, and Gerald isn't any different. I take another breath, focusing on Willow, who is now squirming in Gerald's embrace. It looks like he's holding on to her more tightly.

"How did you know that?" He shrinks away from me.

"Just a guess. I saw a lot of dogs in cars when I came up to the deck. Most of them were curled up asleep. She seems a bit more worried."

Gerald gives me a wary glance. "She gets anxious. She chews on the seats and has even destroyed a kennel, so I bring her up here with me."

I nod. Give him another smile. "Have you tried letting her sit next to you up here?"

His bushy eyebrows, already raised, go even higher.

"I couldn't risk that!"

"Oh. It's just—" I dart my eyes away from his glare. "--she's on a leash and I thought maybe she would feel better on your lap. Or walking around."

There's silence then, and enough of it that I regret scaring this kind old man and his dog.

"I'm sorry. I'm a dog trainer and unsolicited advice just pops out sometimes. It was nice to meet you and Willow."

We both stand at the same time. He turns away from me and, stoop-shouldered, leaves.

An announcement over the loudspeaker shouts me out of my embarrassment. "Please return to your vehicles and prepare for departure at Camas Island." Jogging down the steep metal stairs to my car, I can feel the knots tightening again. As I'm sitting behind the wheel, my hands clenched, my stomach flips, and my brain joins the party. *What in the hell are you doing, Nolee? You don't know anyone here. You're too old to change your life. If you wanted to move, you should've moved to Austin to be closer to your daughter. Hell, most of your clients are there. All your life is in Texas. This is nuts!*

There's a bump and a sliding-sideways sensation, then another announcement tells us to drive off the ferry. In front of me is a truck loaded with a variety of flowering shrubs. I inch closer, thinking that the voice that ran me down sounded way too much like Nathan's for comfort. I give the steering wheel a bang with my fist, uttering, louder this time, "You can do this, Nolee Burnett!"

The line of cars exiting the ferry is slow-moving. The road forks, and some head right, and some left. I can see the ocean through the buildings and trees. Elation fills me as the road curves up and around hills. This is how a dog who's lived most of his life tied up must feel: no more tug at the neck, no more measuring steps by the length of a chain. As I pass the green valleys where I spot sheep and barns, it's hard to believe that the ocean is just beyond the ridge of the green mountain slope, not just another valley. Rolling the windows down and turning up the volume, I sing "*Goodbye yellow brick road*" at the top of my lungs.

Passing the car in front of me, I notice the speed limit sign and ease my foot off the gas. When I glance at the speedometer, I see I've been flying along at sixty through a forty-mile-per-hour zone. As I slow, I check my rearview mirror. The driver doesn't flip me off or honk at me. It sinks in that I'm not in Texas anymore.

I enter a forest so dense that I have to take off my sunglasses to see. The car bumps along a dirt road that meanders down a steep hill, doubles back on itself, then flattens out. I think I'm seeing the sky through the trees, then realize it's the sea. Mountains still covered in snow rise in the distance, and the sheer rocky faces of evergreen islands cut down into the dark water. As I park the car and get out, stretching, I see wooden chairs and a picnic table in front of the A-frame cabin I've rented. I walk down to the rocky beach, and all thought is erased by an unlikely landscape of the forest at the edge of the sea.

From the photos online, I'd thought my cabin was the only house in the small cove. It isn't. I see another house to my left, which is where the road I came in on dead-ends. There are trees between us, the sun-dappled ground showing patches of spring green grass. My cabin is the smaller of the two. It has one loft bedroom, a bathroom with a clawfoot tub, and a kitchen and dining area with large windows that frame the cove, and the ocean beyond it. I couldn't have found something more perfect if I'd built it myself.

Osprey Bay is shaped like a small crescent moon, and a gentle tide pushes and pulls against the rocks, making a susurration similar to ones I'd heard when the wind swept through prairie grasses. Although I could tell the sun would come up around the bend of land on my right, I could also see from the mountains and islands in the hazy distance that sunsets would be spectacular. I take a deep breath, the air going into my lungs a counterpoint to the waves whispering against the shore of this calm inlet. I exhale, watching as a small boat speeds by out in the channel beyond the buoys. A plane passes overhead, its engine the only human-made noise

I hear through birdsong and the waves. The air is cool and damp on my face.

Walking to the porch, I see a weathered rocking chair, wood stacked to the left of the door, and a welcome mat that says, "Wipe Your Paws," with dog prints scattered around it. I smile, and once again feel the grief of losing my Border Collie, Luna. She would have been out on the beach, doing her best to herd the waves into her sense of order.

My landlord, Ava, had texted me yesterday. *Welcome to Camas! The house key is under the mat. Let me know if you need anything.* Bringing my suitcases from the car, I open the door, seeing the boxes I'd shipped ahead stacked inside. The tower they formed would have fallen over were they not filled with books. As I look around at the bare living area, I notice a small bookshelf with a smaller television perched on top of it. A potbelly woodstove squats close to the door I'd just come through. I unplug the television, walk it over to a coat closet, and set it inside on the floor. Who needs it, when there is an entire world to discover? Who wants to watch other people living an exciting life when your own life is on the brink of becoming exciting and new? I pick up one of the suitcases, carrying it into the bedroom upstairs.

The sliding glass door on the far wall allows light to fill the room and opens onto another spectacular view of the beach and sea. The double bed is covered with a white quilt stitched in blues, greens, and the black of the orcas that swim around otters, gulls, and seals. I run my fingers over the smooth threads, marveling at the skill of the artists needlework. A dresser, a lamp, and an overstuffed chair take up the rest of the triangular shaped room. The advertisement had said "shabby chic," and I smile at the euphemism. "Shabby chic" wasn't too far a stretch to describe my own personal style.

After carrying the rest of my bags to the bedroom, I thump down the stairs and wander into the kitchen to make a list of the food I would need. The nearest grocery store is in Northsound. Besides books, I'd brought what little there was from my kitchen in the trunk of my Honda. Some cast-iron skillets that my grandmother used to make jalapeño cornbread. Silverware from my mom. Dishes from my marriage. I'd also brought a couple of pots and pans and things that I hoped still worked.

The rhythm of cleaning and unpacking replaces thinking too much about what was next. As the day coalesces into darkness, I walk out to the porch and watch the sun set through the clouds over the hazy islands. I'd need to look at the map I brought and learn all their names.

At first, I think the gray cloud that appears from the water is the beginnings of evening fog. Then I hear the rush of an exhale and see a tall black fin rise above the surface. My first sighting of a killer whale. I stand on my tiptoes, scanning the horizon before walking to the beach. I don't see a fin, but the exhale floats up into the last light of the sun, evaporating like the killer whale.

I find a log softened by the ocean and bleached by past summer days. Sitting down, I look out at the now-dark cove, noticing a line of distant lights on the islands across the channel, their presence the only way I know there is anything beyond the deep dark. I counted time in the wind through the arms of the trees and the sea drumming against the beach. Then there was nothing except the waves, and me, and the sea filled with my dreams.

TWO

The male orca sucks in air before submerging again, shutting his eyes against the rush of water as he dives. The sea here is murky on top, fading to black as the land drops off. When he sounds, the squeaks and whistles fall off the edge into a deeper canyon, barely tickling his jaw when they return, faint pictures forming behind his eyes. It's a cloudless sunrise, the time when dark and light are indistinguishable from each other.

The whitecaps decorate the sea in the cove, and he finds joy in the water's silk brushing along his flukes. He stays under the surface, his great heart beating more slowly, the thrill of the freedom of the sea filling him as much as the air he just took in. He sounds again, sending out the same low- to high-pitched whistle, feeling for the returning answer of his pod.

The orca rotates, gliding upside down underneath the surface, his white belly seen only by the gulls that fly above, keeping their shiny black eyes open in case he feeds and leaves fish scraps floating on the surface.

As he makes his way through the channel, he feels the vibration of a boat nearby. Diving deeper and slanting away from the sun, he avoids the menace and deafening roar of its propellers. He pushes toward the open water with powerful strokes of his tail. This water bathes him in a landscape of kelp and the distant squeaks and whistles of his pod. Their song tells him they are near the far bank on the land's sun-side. Their grunts and clicks give him a picture of them feeding on salmon. The change in the water's taste and the warmth on his black skin cause him to point his nose upward and drive as hard as he can against the weight of the water, freeing himself above the waves, freeing his lungs with an inrush of air, before crashing down and diving. Again, he pushes upward, and this time, clears a wave in a great leaping arc.

The orca swims on, surfacing to take another breath before gliding just under the waves, scanning the ocean for his pod. He sends out his own clicks and rumbles, although he knows this section of land and water as he knows his own cousin, who's now feeding with his mother's help. As he rises for another lungful of air, his dorsal fin sluices through the water, revealing the notch on its trailing edge at the tip.

He dives again into the deeps, the sight of his pod clearer with his eyes closed than open. They share a slipstream of thought, one that moves beyond tides and out of the range of even their own hearing. Its tendrils connect all members of The Pod, like the night wind on their flukes or the songs of the singing cousins who travel through these waters twice each season.

All ocean creatures inhabit this slipstream, though the singers and other fluke-bearers bear it along in their own bodies. It's like a long strand of kelp and attached to it is each member of The Pod, strung along its wide green surface, unable to ignore the whistles, clicks, groans, and muttering of the teeming ocean, unable to separate their own hearts from those of their kin.

When men went from shooting at them with guns to capturing them and ripping them from their ocean family, the male orca's pod hid, finding safer waters to live in. For many seasons, they stayed as far north as they could, only going in search of salmon when the nagging thrum of boats died down. He and his pod weren't unscathed; several of them have scars or notches from propeller strikes, and a bullet took a chunk out of his dorsal fin when he tried stealing salmon too near a fishing boat.

Experts at appearing and disappearing, the male orca and the matriarch, his grandmother, guided their pod to distant coves, never staying in one area for more than a sunrise and moonset, growing fat on salmon in the summer before traveling to colder waters and safety once again.

The orca feels the welcoming calls of his family ripple through his lower jaw, his heart, and his belly, as a picture of them swimming through the kelp appears. He sends back his song before leaping out of the water and diving to join them. On its surface, the ocean is filled with music of the water folding into itself. As he dives deeper, he hears the rhythmic bass throb of the deep sea, a serenade that pulses through his blood and bones in time with his heartbeat.

Although I forced myself back inside at midnight, I'm up the next morning when the soft gray light of dawn slips into the bedroom. I stretch in the bed's warmth for a moment, then throw back the ocean quilt and sit up.

Dressed in sweatpants and a down jacket, I jam my feet into boots caked with dried Texas clay and open the door to calls of the gulls and morning birdsong. A sense of alien wonder is still with me as I inhale the air's weighty salt-spice. The morning sun illuminates the bright green of new needles glowing in the dim recesses of the forest and the rocks crunch under my feet as I walk to the log I'd spent half the night sitting on or leaning against. As I listen, I understand where the low booming sound that had crashed its way into my dreams in the early hours of the morning was coming from. The bay, quiet and tame last night, has transformed into a loud and untamed beast.

I can see the high-tide line along the cove, new pieces of driftwood, damp rocks and sand, and dark green of kelp exposed on the still-wet beach. Tendrils of foam trail behind each wave as it pushes up to the shore. I can't see any shiny heads or the high vapor of an exhale. Only waves crowned in white, bobbing logs, and a sea as blue as the sky. A consortium of screeching gulls gathers on the surface outside the line of buoys. Everywhere I look, nothing is familiar. It's all as different from Texas as it could get, a yin-yang pull of opposites.

I wonder if this new life will change me into someone different. If I'm being honest, I wouldn't mind a change. Fifty years of living with the same voice in my head, the same set of opinions and quirks, was wearing on me. New thoughts would be as welcome as this new scenery. A new life, even more so. I'd spent so much time reshaping myself to be someone I thought Nathan would like that I'd lost track of who I was.

"That's enough of that," I mutter, channeling my Aunt Tulip as I turn away from the ocean to walk back to the cabin. I smile at the memory. Aunt Tulip didn't approve of indulging in too much thinking. She was famous for haring off on adventures whenever she felt the notion. This move from Texas to Washington would have pleased her. Her favorite saying has become my mantra: "Make up your mind, then follow your heart." I climb the steps to the porch, toe each boot off before slipping on some thick socks, and wander into the kitchen. The cereal box is still on the counter from last night, and I figure it'll be as good for breakfast as it was for dinner.

Taking a cup of tea out to the porch, I look at my neighbor's house, a blue that might be gray, or gray that might be blue. It has peeling white trim and a deck, gray and dull, that wraps around the front. A stone chimney runs between windows that stretch from the roof. A floating dock slopes down to the water. I notice two sea kayaks pulled up on the beach. One is bright blue with two seats and the other is an orange single-seater. The space around the house is tidy, but also seems empty. Of the owner, I can't see a thing, though there is a black 4Runner parked in the driveway. *Serial killers prefer things tidy,* I think. Then, *Nolee, you read too many murder mysteries.* Sighing, I reassure myself that if there was a risk of dying at the hands of one of my neighbors, my landlords would probably have let me know.

As I turn my gaze back to the ocean, reflecting watery diamonds from the sun now high above the waves, it occurs to me I was still doing it. Still letting my thoughts carry me away from the moment I was in. It'd become a habit in a marriage so empty of companionship that I ended up being my own companion. When I was helping people with their dogs, I didn't have any trouble relating, making small talk (about their dog), and feeling competent. However, once my hand was away from a leash, or a dog's warm, furry head, the gray mist of doubt would always slink back into my body.

Taking a sip of tea, I close my eyes and inhale deeply. Maybe I'll knock on that gray-blue house's front door and introduce myself. Life's background is no longer the haven it once was, I realize. From here onward, I want to live in the foreground. I will let the sea air chase away the suffocating fog of my old life.

Opening my eyes, I steal a quick glance at the house again, hoping no one's watching me from the porch or the window. But the windows are dark, and it looks as though the occupant isn't a morning person. I get it. Mornings usually aren't my thing either, but if I'm going to wake up near the ocean at least for the next year, that's another thing that might change.

I open the door again and step out onto the porch, feeling the air on my face, this air made of ocean mist and forest peat.

The morning passes in a wash of birdsong and the sound of the ocean clicking against the rocks. I walk the small stretch of beach. The tide's going out and the air's rich with the vaguely fishy, salty smell of the sea. It's both like and unlike the smell I recalled from the Gulf of Mexico, where we sometimes took summer trips when I was a kid. I think about sitting down on the log again but glancing back at my house reminds of the reality that I still need to unpack. A small, white, speckled stone catches my eye, and I pick it up. Rubbing my fingers together, I notice they're sticky with salt water. I walk back toward the cabin, feeling quieter than I have in years.

Inside, I look at my phone and a text from Abbie. *Are you out there?* I smile. Typical Abbie; a little worried, a lot my daughter. I reply *Couldn't be better. Pictures later.* She answers, *I didn't think you'd be up early. Glad to hear you're doing great. xo.*

After starting a fire in the small woodstove to chase away the chill in the air, I hear a knock on the door. I leave the box of pots and pans and look out the window. A teenage boy stands with his hands shoved into too-small jeans pockets, his shoulders tense under his oversized hoodie, bleached-blond hair in a ponytail under a baseball cap. I open the door and smile at him.

"Hello."

"Ms. Burnett?" he asks.

"Yes. Call me Nolee. What's your name?"

"I'm Pete and Ava Zhou's son? Alex?"

"Hi Alex. I was wondering who I needed to thank for bringing in all those heavy boxes. Is it you?"

Alex smiles in return and nods his head. His shoulders drop and he stops fidgeting.

"Mom and Dad wanted to be sure everything was okay, so they sent me over."

"Everything is perfect. Do you want to come in and have some tea? Coffee? Or maybe you don't drink that yet?"

"I'm older than I look, and yeah, I like coffee. But I'm meeting some friends down at the marina to go sailing, so I'll catch you later." As Alex was talking, I wondered if this was another sign I was getting old. Everyone who was young looked *so* young. "Where's the marina? Maybe I could take a canoe out sometime."

Alex laughed before saying, "I don't think you'd, like, want to canoe around here. You'd be better off in a kayak or a boat."

"You can tell I come from Texas, I guess."

"That and the accent. There's a private marina close to here–that's where I go. You'll want to check out the rentals there."

"I'd probably better take some lessons first. Have a great time, and thanks for checking on me. Say hi to your mom and dad."

Alex nods again and turns away, but before I can close the door, he turns back. "Mrs. Burnett–Nolee? I forgot to tell you something from my mom."

"What is it?"

"The other thing she wanted me to let you know is that your neighbor? The one in the blue house? He isn't dangerous or anything, and he's super private, but Mom's heard some funny things about him."

That got my attention. *Serial killer, after all?*

"What kind of funny things?"

"Well," Alex shoves his hands back in his pockets, "like, the people who used to rent this place swore he would dive off the dock into the sea at night, naked, and literally never came up again."

"I'm sure it was because it was dark, or the water tricked their eyes." I knew I was reassuring myself, sure there was a rational explanation. "I haven't seen anything like that. I did see a big killer whale yesterday evening, though."

"Yeah, talk to my mom about that. She's got some stories about him too."

I wave as Alex walks away, then go back inside to have another cup of tea while I unpack the remains of my old life. My stomach rumbles, reminding me that I also need an actual meal. Slinging my backpack over my shoulder, I close the door and walk to my trusty car, patting its gray hood and saying, "Hi-ho, Silver, it's off to Northsound we go."

As I'm putting away my haul from the local market, I hear a door slam. Looking through the window facing my neighbor's house, I see a lean dark-haired man dressed in black emerge. He pauses by the front door, and sun sparks silver off the key ring he's holding. He strides over to his 4Runner. *Who wears black jeans anymore?* I snark to myself. He gets in, swinging easily into the seat. From what I can see of the interior, it's also black. "If he were in Texas, that thing would be hotter than the hinges of Hades," I mutter to myself. The red lights pop on, but he doesn't move. I hear the thump of drums and bass accented by a scree of higher-pitched notes. Stepping closer to the window, I wonder if what I think I'm hearing is right. Bagpipes? I'm only guessing, though, since I've never actually heard bagpipes before. He backs up slowly before pulling forward to the road and driving away. He doesn't look that weird to me.

That night, asleep beneath the ocean quilt, I wake up to the thump of drums and bass. I glance at the clock and see that it's almost midnight. Once again, I get up and look through the curtains, watching my neighbor unlock his door and go inside. A light flicks on in the front windows, but I can't see anything other than the reflection of the dark cove. He must have privacy film on his windows. Probably a good thing, given that neighbors like me are taking an inordinate interest in his life. I shake my head and climb back under the quilt. My last thought before I fall asleep is that I need to find time to go over there and introduce myself.

The next morning, after calling my landlady Ava to invite her over for tea and a chat, I take a walk on the beach. The neighbor's vehicle is gone. So much for introductions.

Ava pulls in as I reach the porch. Her rusty pickup truck creaks to a halt, and the door squeals when she slams it closed.

"I like what you've done with the place," she says, standing in the living area and turning slowly. "I don't think I've ever seen these many books in here before."

"If I'd packed my car with all the books I wanted to bring, there wouldn't have been room for anything else."

We sit at the oak table, and Ava runs her hands over it, admiring the warm golden glow I'd coaxed out of it that morning. Not much older than I am, she has permed and dyed black hair and a round face that beams good humor. She smiles and nods as I talk, encouraging me to keep going. She's on friendly terms with talking too, and the afternoon light slants through the windows as drink our tea and get to know one another.

"Your son mentioned that the neighbor in that blue house was a bit of a loner? Something about jumping into the ocean at night naked?" I can't help smiling as I say this. "It sounds odd, but different strokes and all that."

"Well," Ava began, leaning toward me as though she didn't want anyone else to hear. "It's only secondhand information. Everyone who has lived in this house has hardly heard a peep out of him. He owns a boat and takes people out on it—whale-watching, hikes to other islands, even for marriage proposals."

"That doesn't sound too odd. What's his name?"

"Keet Noland. Jumping in the bay naked is weird, but the really odd thing is that the water around here averages about 48 degrees year-round. If you or I tried that stunt, we'd last ten minutes before serious hypothermia set in." Ava takes a sip of tea and leans back in her chair, which emits a loud creak.

"Have you ever asked him about the swimming stuff?" I swirl the tea around in my cup before finishing it.

Ava laughs. "I did. Once. He said he was used to it because he swam all the time as a kid up in Sitka, where the water is even colder. But I didn't hear about any more naked midnight swims from people who stayed here after that."

"Shy about it, you think?"

Ava gives a small shrug. "I don't know. He's quiet. Keeps to himself. Maybe he just likes his privacy."

I sat for a moment, thinking, and then asked, "Alex said you have some stories about the killer whale who hangs out here sometimes."

"He's much more sociable than your neighbor," she laughs, excitement lighting her eyes. "That killer whale has been around these waters for decades. He spends a lot of time with his pod, but the folks who stay here see him in this bay regularly. It must be peaceful for him, away from all the boat traffic in the channel."

I hadn't really considered what the world must sound like to the animals living underwater. I'd thought it would be quieter, but now that Ava mentions the boat noise, I get a better idea of how loud it must be for the local killer whales.

"He rescued a dog once," Ava says, bringing my attention back to the moment.

"A dog?" I lean forward, picking up my mug before remembering I'd already finished my tea.

"Yes, a tiny Chihuahua on a boat a couple rented. Apparently, it got so excited when it saw the killer whales it ran and fell right off, yipping, into the water."

"The owners must've been terrified," For all that Chihuahuas were brave, they were also so small that water this cold could've killed it, even if the killer whale hadn't.

"They were . . . they thought their little dog was about to become a whale snack." She puts her empty mug back on the table and pauses, knowing I won't interrupt.

"Well, the pod circled the boat, then retreated some distance away from it. The big one, though, the male who hangs out here–you can tell it's him because of that cut out of his dorsal fin–he swims over to the dog, puts it on his nose, and delivers it to the boat it fell out of."

"That's amazing! What did the owners do?"

"They wrapped the dog in one of their jackets. By the time they turned to see where the killer whale who saved their dog had gone, the pod was already swimming away."

"Is that kind of thing usual with killer whales?"

Ava stands up, pulling on her jacket over her broad shoulders. "It can be. They mostly ignore people, though. It's against the law to go chasing after them or try to touch them."

As she starts through the open door, she turns around and says, "You should go out on a whale trip with that Keet Noland. Then you can tell me what he's all about." Giving me a wink and a smile, she closes the door with a bang behind her.

I didn't tell Ava that I've never been out on the ocean, or on a boat. Not even a kayak. The closest I'd come to the sea's wild waters was as a child, at the Gulf. I'd sit on the shore, my feet curling into the wet sand, and let the waves lap over me, pulling up shiny rocks and shells, watching the dance of water and sunlight on my round legs. I remember my mom laughing from the front seat of our car on the way back, telling my dad that it was the first time she'd seen me so quiet. I can still see the profile of his face as he replied without smiling, "Maybe we could get some peace if we moved closer to the Gulf."

As I wash out the mugs, I look out the window facing the gray-blue house and notice that the 4Runner is back. The taillights flick off as the driver's-side door opens, and my neighbor steps out, holding a paper bag under one arm. He has his back to me as he shuts and locks the door, then he turns and looks in my direction. I can't tell if he's seen me or not, so I look down and rinse the mugs out. When I look up again, the door to his house is closing.

THREE

After a week of unpacking, I now have my new home organized. Books are arranged by topic, and then by size. A small oak dining table has a locally made pottery bowl on it holding a small collection of gifts from the sea. The bowl's glaze reminds me of the color of the land in Texas. All the curtains and windows are clean. Nothing comes between me and that view of the wide and endless sea. The sound of the water carries through my open front door, hypnotizing my busy brain into silence.

Of my mysterious neighbor, I still don't know a thing. Private is one way to describe him. Personally, I would say reclusive. I'm not sure why I seem to be obsessed with him, unless it's because I can't stand an unsolved mystery.

The room's oversized chair is decorated with claw marks from a previous cat. I think about Luna and how much I miss her. Maybe it's time for another dog. A walk isn't quite the same without a dog running after a ball.

I pick up my phone, find the webpage for the local shelter, and start scrolling for adoptable dogs. They're all male, and either very young or very old. "Too soon, anyway, girl," I say to myself.

I walk out the door with my phone, taking photos to text to Abbie. Searching the bay for the notched dorsal fin, I see only the sun throwing its light onto the waves. It makes me feel as though I could catch the rays in my hands and hold them close to feel their warmth.

A dark, shiny head pops above the surface of the water and drifts with the current, then disappears, leaving almost no ripple in the surface. A moment later, the head pops back up, this time closer to shore. I think I've just seen my first seal.

I walk along the sunlit beach, noticing that the blue of the sky is different here than in Texas, where sky seems to prevail over everything. I take photos of the rocks and driftwood, a selfie with the ocean in the background, and the bowl-like curve of land that holds the sea within it.

Another shiny head pops above the surface. It's small and before I can figure out what it might be, it dives, a long and flat tail following behind. I watch as, moments later, a long sinewy body of an otter makes its way to a log, crunching on the crab it holds in its dexterous paws.

"Great morning for a walk, isn't it?"

The voice behind me is rich and slow, a baritone current that strikes my ears and snakes down my spine. I turn to see the owner of this voice, and there's my neighbor. The lean man with black hair, wearing jeans (*not black today*), a black jacket over a black t-shirt, and hiking boots. His chocolate-brown eyes tilt up at the same angle as his high, broad cheekbones, his skin light brown. Although I hope I'm not looking at them directly, I'm surprised by his full, smiling lips. There are gray strands running through his hair. The wind blows it into his eyes, and he uses a graceful and long fingered hand to brush it back.

Sliding my phone into the back pocket of my jeans, I grin. "Yeah, around here, it would be a great day for anything."

I stride toward him with my hand out. "Nolee Burnett, nice to meet you."

His dark eyes crinkle at the corners as he takes my hand in his and, with a gentle squeeze, says, "Keet Noland. Your neighbor. Glad to meet you, Nolee. Is that a family name?" His voice is deeper than I imagined.

"Sort of. All the women on my mother's side of the family have flower names. My full name is Magnolia, but since that's a mouthful, I go by Nolee. My daughter is Violet Abbie, but she doesn't see fit to use the first name. Maybe she got her rebellious spirit from me."

I stop talking, even though Keet is smiling and seems to be listening. I look at the ground, and then back up. "I had a great-aunt named Buttercup, but she hated the name so much that she went by Bee." Keet is still watching me, thoughtful and silent, waiting for the gust of my story to blow itself out.

"Sorry. I can get a little chatty sometimes."

"It's not a problem. I enjoy listening."

I hear the cry of the gulls and the wind through the pines. Then, pushing his wayward hair out of his eyes, he adds, "Your daughter, Violet Abbie Burnett?"

"No, I divorced her father a year ago. Her last name is Evans." He's watching me, still silent.

Between the ocean, the breeze, and Keet's way of talking, I feel the tension of the last ten years drain into the rocks. I'm also short of breath, and I'm not sure why. Anxious to fill the void, I ask him, "So, what about you? Is yours a family name? I don't believe I've met any Keets before."

He smiles and looks out to the horizon. "No, not a family name. My grandmother raised me. She lives up in Alaska, in Sitka."

I want to ask about his mother and father, but he doesn't look like a man who easily talks about personal subjects. I smile again and try a safer topic.

"Noticed that you have a couple of kayaks. Do you have time to get out very often? There's not much call for kayaks in West Texas, but I'm thinking of taking some lessons so I can get out on that water."

"It's pleasant, out on the sea. I own a business—a private charter company, taking people out on my sailboat to see the local wildlife."

He has a stillness about him. Or maybe I only notice this because I feel like such a tornado myself.

"Well, now, that's something else I'll need to add to my list. Do you have room for one more?" I smile, hoping I don't sound as awkward as I feel.

Keet pauses, then says, "Sure. Call the office and we'll book a day and time for you. I keep odd hours."

I wait for him to tell me the name of his business. He smiles and waits for me to say something. When I can't stand it anymore, I say, "Great, I'll do that. Do you want to text me the information?"

"I don't text. Let me go back to the house and get a card for you." He turns, and I notice that he walks as though he's a part of the land, not on it.

Old school, I think as I watch him go inside his house. Turning back to the sea, I see the wind and waves have both picked up. When I hear the crunch of his boots on the rocks, I turn and smile again, and take the card he holds out to me.

"Thanks, Keet. I'll give your office a call."

"I'll look forward to it. Enjoy your day, Nolee."

I nod, say "You too," and go back to my cabin, looking at the card as I walk. It's white with a black killer whale leaping from blue waves. The words "Camas Island Sailing Tours" run across the top in black, with a phone number beside it. No website. I pull my phone out of my hip pocket and tap on the Yelp app, curious to see if his business at least has any reviews.

Which it does—a long list of five-star reviews. One mentions that the captain has a degree in marine biology from the University of Washington. The reviewers rave about seeing tons of wildlife, as well as Captain Noland's vast knowledge of the area and its marine residents.

This may be worth checking out, I think. That Keet has caught my interest is a feeling I shove back into my pocket, along with my phone. The last thing I need is another emotional complication on top of all the confusion I'm sorting through. The last thing I need is even the prospect of a man in my life.

Keet watches her walk away, her auburn braid swinging against her back, its loose tendrils brushing her pale neck. He'd started to invite her out to kayak one morning, but stopped when he looked into her eyes, startled by how green they are; it's as though the Salish Sea was staring back at him. Her face was open and friendly, and he could see lines around her mouth that told him she smiled a lot. She wasn't much taller than five feet, with a curving figure and a grip that told him she was anything but soft. Her skin was pale, a faint pink blush rising in her cheeks when he surprised her. She was all circles: round face, round hips, large round eyes in a face that wasn't hidden by makeup.

For the first time in a very long time, he'd forgotten what he wanted to say. That's when he realized she was seeing him. Maybe into him. He was used to eye contact, but rarely did he have the sensation of someone taking him in quite so thoroughly. He'd been alone long enough to be out of practice with the thoughts he's having, much less trying to act on them.

As he walks back toward his house, he thinks about his ex-fiancée, who chose her career and Los Angeles over life on an island. Over him. Even though most of his customers are women—even some very attractive women—he hasn't felt like attempting to get to know them. Living alone was less complicated. He could be who he was, keep the hours he did, and do what he wanted. For the past five years, he'd filled his days and nights with swims, running his business, and making meals that were too elaborate for one person.

He used to find solace in cooking food and enjoying the flavors he'd coaxed out. Lately, though, he'd been having most of his meals at local restaurants. He'd even been considering selling his boat, selling his house, and choosing a different life, one that wasn't so isolated. Experience had taught him that any intimate relationship is a near-impossibility, and he wasn't going to pin his hopes on a woman he just met just because she had great eyes. She might never show up on his boat. Despite trying to force himself to be rational, a feeling, small and shy, whispers that he'd like to see her again.

He shuts the door, locks it, and calls his office manager.

"Trish, hey . . . yeah, everything's fine. Can you do me a favor? If a woman named Nolee. . ." he spells it for her before continuing ". . .yeah, Nolee Burnett calls to book one of the excursions, can you let her know it's free? If she gives you any trouble, tell her it's a welcome-to-the-neigh-borhood gift. Thanks. See you soon."

He holds the phone in his hand, tapping it against his chin before putting it back in its cradle. Looking out the windows that stretch from floor to ceiling, he feels the sea's song vibrate through his body. It's hard to resist its pull. But since Ava asked him about his night swims, he realized that the people who used to live there had seen him, and he stopped all his swims from home unless the cabin was empty.

His next tour isn't for a couple of days, but that doesn't mean he'll spend those days chained to the land. Deciding, he picks up his keys and leaves the house, locking the door behind him.

Once at the marina, he spends the day on his boat, *The Salish See*, putting her in order. He checks that the bilge is dry, the charts rolled and tucked into place, the cushions and life vests are stowed, the sails are furled, the lines are secure fore and aft, and there's no sign of wear from rubbing. As the light drains from the sky, turning it from pale blue to gray, and the marina's lights go on, he sits on the bow, long legs dangling over the side. He looks out at the black water undulating around him and his breathing slows, his eyes close. He needs a swim. He needs the companionship of the water.

The water, which for so many of his customers is too cold to tolerate more than a couple of seconds, is to him a pleasant chill after the warmth of the air. He tires of the pull of gravity on his body when he's on land, the way he feels as though he's always pushing against an unseen and immoveable force. In the water, he's weightless, resting in its buoyancy the way he used to rest on his grandmother's lap in the pale gray of a summer Sitka evening. Unafraid. Not alone.

His stomach rumbles, reminding him he needs to eat. Nolee's face appears behind his closed eyes, frozen like a photograph, smiling at him as she takes his card. Her skin is pale, which surprises him. Weren't people in Texas always in the sun?

Opening his eyes again, he takes in a deep breath of salt air. He listens as the sea rocks the boats against the docks, the quiet knocking and creaking of the fenders punctuated by the bell-like ringing of halyards against masts.

For a moment, he considers getting takeout and going back home, but the thought of the same food and the same evening routine depresses him—it's such a strong contrast to the magnetic force the sea exerts on his heart and mind, to the symphony of sounds that surround him.

Keet stands up, then ducks his head as he steps down into the cabin. He removes his clothes, standing naked in the darkness, the only light illuminating an oval scar halfway down his spine. The cold air raises bumps along his broad shoulders, but the cold is welcome. He scratches his hand against his face, hearing the rasp of stubble. He looks out of the window, making sure no one's watching him or his boat.

The parking lot is empty, and no lights shine nearby. He watched the people from the nearest sailboat leave hours ago. The man toted a six-pack in one hand and had his arm around a woman who could be his daughter–though the way her hips swung in time with his as they walked said the chances of them being related were slim.

He smiles and feels the rough, no-slip material under his feet as he walks to the side of the boat. Taking hold of the rail, he swings over with ease, lowers himself into the dark silk of the water, and swims.

I wait a few days before calling the number on Keet's card. His office manager's name is Trish, and she's relaxed as she checks the sailing schedule; accompanied by the background sounds of a clicking keyboard, I chat about my move. I hang up, jotting down the date and time I just reserved. I wonder if I should feel flattered that he was giving me a free tour, and if I should give him some sort of gift. *Nolee Burnett, you need to stop* shoulding *all over yourself.* My therapist back in Texas would be pleased to hear I remembered something from our time together. I look out the window toward Keet's house. The driveway is empty.

I fill the rest of my day with the sea and sun. I lie down on the rocks, wondering how long the hard surface will be comfortable. Then I discover that not only do I feel the heat reaching into my bones, but I'm sleepy again. My eyes close to the cry of an eagle and the lap of the water. When I wake up, I feel more relaxed than I have in years. Maybe ever. I turn my head, groggy and wondering what time it is, then notice that the sun was dropping toward the hazy outline of one of the forested islands.

Sitting up, I brush the loose hair out of my face and glance at Keet's house. No car. No smoke from the chimney. Stretching, I feel my muscles glide loosely across my back. I walk inside, mulling what I can eat that's both easy and will appease my belly.

A dinner of cheese, crackers, and an apple is accompanied by phone scrolling, searching for kayaks to rent but also IM'ing with friends back in Texas. No one answers, so I send a photo of the sunset behind a distant island, the water black, the sky yellow-orange. It couldn't be more different from Texas, and I know suddenly that I'm happy to be here instead of there.

That night, I dream about Keet. He's facing me, standing waist deep in the black waters of Osprey Bay. Though it's night, the bare skin of his chest glows and I can see his reflection in the ocean, which is as still as glass around his hips. He isn't saying anything, just looking at me through dark and unblinking eyes. A breeze I can't feel lifts his black hair. I take a step closer, and he turns his back to me, raising his arms to a moon that is full and glowing.

I jolt awake, wondering if my nightgown is damp because of a hot flash or the dream of Keet. The night is growing dim around the edges. The morning is beginning.

I get up and open the curtains, and then the sliding door. The air doesn't help my lingering agitation about the dream; it sifts through my clothes, brushing against breast and belly, until I close my eyes, breathing in the now familiar scent of this island that is my new home. I wonder how I've lived so much of my life without being enveloped by the air as completely as I feel in this moment, in the approaching dawn.

FOUR

Keet spends the next week taking tours out in the mornings and swimming in the evenings. When his thoughts drifted toward Nolee, he redirected them, focusing instead on the endless needs of his sailboat, or the water he was immersed in.

Now, the morning is bright and clear, with a southwest wind that promises good sailing. Earlier, he'd seen Nolee's name penciled in for today's tour, along with those of four others. He smiles, taps her name on the paper, and makes his way down to the dock.

A few minutes later, he sees her get out of her car, slamming the door and tucking her keys into her jacket pocket. Glancing at the white analog clock face of his watch, he notices that she's fifteen minutes early.

Walking down the pier, gathering her hair into a ponytail, she looks up and he waves.

"Hello, Nolee."

"Hi there."

"Grab one of the life jackets as you come aboard." He motions to the pile of red and orange life vests. "The formal name is Personal Flotation Device."

"Not nearly as clever as the name of your boat," she smiles.

She takes the top one off the pile and adjusts the straps around her chest and waist.

"Hope I'm not too early; it's a compulsion."

"Not a problem. I think you've met Alex?"

Nolee makes a last adjustment to her vest and ponytail, looks up, and smiles. "Yes, we met when I moved in. How are you?"

"Good, thanks." Alex checks the lines, then stands up.

"Alex has been crewing for me for a couple of summers. He's quite a sailor."

Alex looks down and smiles. "Captain Noland makes it fun."

Keet sees his other guests ambling down the pier to the boat. "Alex, can you get these folks settled? I'd like to look at the weather and wind speed one more time." Alex steps off the boat to greet the customers.

Keet steps past Nolee, catching a faint scent of roses and citrus.

As he goes through his safety talk, Keet is aware of her gaze and how she doesn't fidget or glance at her phone every three seconds like the other couples. As he's letting his passengers know the rules of the boat, she tilts her head as she watches him, the green of her eyes reminding him again of the sea. Giving himself a mental shake, he focuses on what they'll see on their tour. After reminding the passengers that their baseball caps are likely to get blown off, he sees Nolee take a blue knit cap out of her pocket and fit it to her head, tucking the ponytail underneath.

After motoring out into the channel, Alex raises the sails. Keet watches as first the main sail and then the jib billow. Alex takes the last turns on the winch to tighten the halyards, the sails rippling and snapping in the wind. Their cracking reminds Keet of the power of the wind, and how it's best to embrace it in this age-old dance with the sea. Alex glances at Keet and nods, then adjusts the main and jib sheets to the bearing that Keet has chosen. The sails steady as they begin to glide toward open water.

Nolee walks back to Keet, who is cradling the helm with both hands. She looks up at the sails rising and falling against the sky and then looks at Keet.

"Beautiful day for this. Thanks again for the invitation."

"It's my pleasure."

"How long have you been sailing?"

"Since I was a kid. My grandfather taught me. We were in a smaller boat, one that we steered with a tiller instead of a helm like this." He pats the wheel, looking down at it. "It's a different feeling, using a tiller. There's a closer connection to the water."

He looks at Nolee, sees her nodding. Looking out at the horizon, he says, "A tiller isn't practical in a bigger vessel like this one. Rough water can throw you around on the end of it. But if you balance the sails, a little weather isn't a big deal. The boat sometimes can steer itself."

He sees Nolee doesn't understand what he just said, so he tries again. "A tiller is a lever that attaches directly to the top of the rudder. It's part of how we steer the boat."

"Ah." She's quiet, looking up at the sails rising white against a pale blue sky, then looks out over the ocean in front of them.

Keet isn't sure why he feels the need to keep talking. Maybe because not many people show any interest in what he does. Maybe because he's alone so much. Maybe because he sees in her eyes that she's listening, not distracted by anything else.

"A tiller makes a boat more responsive to adjustments, makes it quicker. The Salish See's helm is connected to the rudder by chains and gears, so there's a degree of separation between what I do here with the helm and what happens to the boat. But if I pay attention," he grins, "I can feel the water passing the hull and rudder, feel the boat trying to follow a point different than my bearing course."

"What then?"

"Then we adjust the sails to make things easier, give The Salish See what she wants so she can make way without fighting the water."

"So, you're telling me that sailing is about finding peace between the wind and sea?"

His own laughter comes as a surprise. It's the first light moment he's felt in a long time. He looks at her again, says, "I hadn't thought about it like that, but yes." Feeling a slight shudder under his feet, Keet corrects his course and steers to port. In the silence between them, the snap of the sails and the low conversations of the other passengers glide over them.

Nolee interrupts the silence. "I'm sure glad I don't feel seasick. You might've had to take me back to the marina."

"I'm glad too. It's not a big deal, though. You throw up over the side and I have meclizine if you need something for motion sickness. But we don't go back because people get a little nauseous."

The ocean parts a path as the wind fills the sails and pushes them across the emerald-green water.

"What did you do back in Texas?" He corrects his course after feeling a slight shudder under his feet, steering again to port. He'll sail through a channel between islands before heading west again.

"I was—well, I suppose I still am—a dog trainer, and also had a small boarding facility."

He nods, wondering what it would be like to have a dog. He has nothing against cats or dogs but including pets in the life he has wouldn't work, for him or the pet.

As if she read his mind, she asks "Do you have a dog? Or cats? An iguana?"

He laughs, shaking his head. "No, I was just thinking that my life hasn't ever had the space or time in it for a pet."

"Well, I'm going to volunteer at the local shelter. If I see a dog who needs a sailor, I'll let you know."

"I'm more likely a sailor who needs the sea rather than a pet, but thanks."

She watches him, her eyes squinting against the wind. "Got it. I'm going to need a dog before long, though. I miss Luna too much to keep knocking around that cabin by myself."

"Luna was your last dog?"

Nolee smiles at the memories, and looks away from him, out over the sea. "Yes. A little black-and-white Border Collie. I think she would have loved sailing, too. We did everything together."

"She sounds like a nice dog to have around."

"She was all of that."

They're quiet then, the wind and the sea and the conversations of the other guests rolling past them. Keet steers west, toward a cove where he knows a pod of orcas often spends time. On the way there, he points out seals and harbor porpoises, gulls, and kelp beds.

He watches as Nolee makes her way to the bow. He begins his talk on the animals of the area, and the names of the islands they're passing, mentioning that he provides trips to Sucia and Patos Islands for sunset picnics and day-hikes. Keet feels the boat slicing through the waves, the bow rising and falling on the morning chop. The sails snap in the breeze, and a faint scent of roses drifts back to him.

He shifts his gaze from his passengers once again to Nolee, who smiles at him, then turns and chats with the couple sitting near her. Tilting her face to the sky, she closes her eyes and rocks back and forth, then opens her eyes and gazes up at the sails. He's surprised to realize that he's glad she's his neighbor.

As they glide around the gentle curve of an island, Keet spots the black dorsal fins of a pod of orcas. He heads into the wind, watching as Alex sheets the sails, bringing them in and slowing the boat to a crawl. When he's dead to wind and stopped, he looks up, double-checking that the sails are tightly sheeted, which in these conditions will let him sit without the use of a sea anchor. He glances back out at the undulating water, noticing dorsal fins cutting through the condensation of their exhales. They're surfacing and swimming at a regular pace. Not hunting, then.

"Folks, this is a pod of what we call Transient killer whales. These days, they're more accurately known as Bigg's killer whales, after the scientist who first studied them, Michael Bigg. They usually hang out here this time of year. They eat other mammals, including seals, sea lions, harbor porpoises, and whales. You'll notice that the seals we passed earlier were staying close to shore, even though that was miles back." He sees his passengers raising their cameras and phones to capture the whales' backs and fins. "Dr. Michael Bigg noticed that each has a distinctly shaped dorsal fin, and the white patches behind the fin, the saddle patch, are also different. When compared to the local orcas, who have open saddle patches that are white and usually patterned, Bigg's killer whales' saddle patches are closed, and more gray than white." He notices that Nolee is the only one who put her phone down after taking a couple of photos, now standing apart from the group of shutterbug tourists, watching the orcas.

"We can't get any closer. They're a protected species, and the law requires us to stay far enough away to not interfere with them. It looks like they're cruising through this area. Right now, we're at the border between the US and Canada."

As the excitement of finding the killer whales calms down, the air is filled with the sounds of water against the sides of the boat and and the cries of the gulls overhead. He takes a deep breath and continues his talk.

"Orcas, or killer whales, are more accurately the largest members of the dolphin family. Their scientific name is *Orcinus orca*. This group has a long history of being documented in these waters, and we've had the opportunity to see new calves grow up, as well as how each pod structures itself."

The faces that had turned toward him now turn back to the water, some eyes shaded by hands.

"They're coming this way!" a bald man shouts. He points to the dorsal fins and shiny black backs rising and falling through the water. Keet sees that Nolee hasn't taken her eyes off them and has moved farther away from the small knot of people. He watches her lean forward, as if trying to get closer.

"Would these killer whales eat people?" a woman asks.

"No, there have no reports of wild orcas attacking humans. Even though they'll kill and eat whales, seals, dolphins, and even moose who dare to swim between the islands farther north, the likelihood of them attacking and eating a human is almost nonexistent. We're not on their menu."

There's silence again as they listen to the pod's powerful exhales. Other boats are in the vicinity as well, bobbing on the surface with their motors idling. More black dorsal fins slice through the water, from small and triangular to the large fin that towers over the surface of the sea. Keet points him out.

"That one is the pod's adult male. Orca pods are matrilineal, meaning a female—his mother or grandmother—calls all the shots. Orcas stay together for their entire lives, with the males only leaving briefly to mate with a female in a different group."

"God," says the bald man, his belly stretching the limits of his cotton t-shirt. "Can you imagine having to stay with your mother for the rest of your life?" There's laughter among the group, but Nolee isn't joining in. She's watching as the killer whales turn and swim back the way they came.

"We'll stay her another fifteen minutes or so. Now would be a good time to take any photos before we turn about."

He looks to weather and sees the line of the wind made visible as it skitters across the water's surface. Shifting, like fans laid upon the water by Neptune himself, they point out the best course home. Feeling a strong shudder in the hull as they cut through the channel's cross-current, he steers off the wind and gives Alex a thumbs up after he loosens the sheets of main and jib, preparing to give his customers a smooth ride back to the marina.

After making sure everyone's safe on the dock, he turns around to see Nolee still on the boat, leaning against the rail and looking out at the expanse of water.

"What did you think about sailing?" he asks her.

She turns and smiles at him. "Oh, it was all right."

They both laugh, then she says, "It's funny, you know?"

"What's that?" Keet double-checks the lines securing the sailboat to the dock.

"Some dogs I work with, I can feel the wolf in them. The wildness. Not all dogs, and not all the time, but there's something . . . unclaimed in those that have it. No amount of training can bury it or erase it."

Keet's silent, thinking about what she's sharing with him.

"When I was watching those killer whales—orcas, I mean—I got the same feeling. They're wild and unclaimed. But that's what makes them so beautiful. They don't need a thing from us, do they? We could disappear off the face of the earth and they would get along just fine."

She's looking at him as he stands, a line in his hand. He lets out a breath and says "They need nothing from us. And if we disappeared, honestly, they'd be better off. 'Unclaimed' is exactly the right word for the wildness in this world. I appreciate you understand orcas like that."

Nolee laughs, sliding the cap from her head. "It's difficult to miss. I can see why you love your job so much. I'd be tempted to stay out there, in the company of orcas and the sea."

Keet smiles. "There are many days when I give in to that temptation."

I'm still enjoying the rocking of the boat, reluctant to leave, watching Keet tie *The Salish See* to the dock. I don't realize I'm humming the song I was listening to in the car on the way here until he says, "Fleetwood Mac fan?"

"What?" I try to remember the name of the song but can't. The sea air and the boat trip have reduced the noise in my normally loud brain to a peaceful hum. That I haven't even made it off his boat yet tells me this is a good place to be.

"You were humming 'Sweet Little Lies.' I thought you might like Fleetwood Mac."

"Is that who sings it? I thought it was Abba."

Keet pauses with a rope—which he tells me is called a line—in his hand, and looks at me to see if I'm serious, which I am. He then throws his head back and laughs.

"That's the funniest thing I've heard in a very long time. Abba did 'Dancing Queen,' by the way."

"I thought Queen did that one," I regret saying it as soon as I see him break out laughing again.

"Okay, funny guy, who sang 'Me and You and a Dog Named Boo?'" I cross my arms in front of me, knowing there's no way he's going to guess that song from my childhood. I actually had a dog named Boo, and it's one of the few bands I know.

"Lobo, 1973." The wind catches his hair, and his eyes are alight with humor. I still want to strangle him.

"You know, if you get within any distance of me, I'll be tempted to give you a pinch." I'm only half joking, and Keet, obviously a smart man who knows when to not push his luck, shrugs, then finishes tying off the boat to the cleats on the dock, still smiling.

I sing again, a song from a cartoon when I was a kid.

"*On the mountain was a treasure/Buried deep beneath the stone . . .*"
But before I can finish, he interrupts me.

"'One Tin Soldier,' Coven, 1971."

I look at him from the deck, but as though he's expecting blows to rain on him from above, he's walked to the back of the boat to tie that end off with a second line.

"How in God's good name can you even know that?"

Keet shrugs. "Just a talent. I can't play an instrument, but my brain is like a card catalog for sounds and words. All I have to do is access the right index card and everything's there."

"And that," I laugh, "pretty much shows your age. I haven't thought of index cards and card catalogs since I was in college. Which was before the internet was a thing."

"Yeah, kids these days have it easy." The boat secured, he climbs back aboard, approaching me warily as if I'm going to make good on my promise of violence.

"Don't worry. I don't stay mad for long. Besides, it's just envy. I love music but am no good at it."

In the silence, I can hear Keet putting his boat in order. A gust of wind picks up, galloping across the sea, making whitecaps.

"*She's got it/Yeah, baby, she's got it . . .*" my voice travels out over the water, and I'm sure he won't know this '80s tune.

"'Venus,' Shocking Blue, 1970."

"Ha!" I laugh, pointing at him. "Gotcha! That was an '80s hit." Keet throws me a pitying look and sighs.

"The Bangles did a cover of it, but Shocking Blue did it originally."

I yank my phone out of my back pocket and wait for Google to load. When the answer on the screen is exactly what Keet said, I jam it back into my pocket and finally get off the boat.

"Thanks for the beautiful tour, Keet," I say over my shoulder as I walk down the dock to the parking lot. "I'm going home to find a song you don't know."

I hear him shout "Good luck with that," and I smile to myself.

FIVE

I don't see any sign of Keet for several days, though I tell myself I'm not looking for him. After our conversation, I guess he gave in to temptation and went out on his boat until he felt like coming back.

As I'm unloading groceries from my car, I see him pull into his driveway, step out of his black SUV, then turn back to grab something off the front seat before slamming the door shut. He sees me and waves before going his cabin. Both arms full of bags, I wobble up the steps and get inside, where I drop the bags on the kitchen table. I'm stretching my back when I hear a knock on the door I'd left open.

"Hey Nolee."

I stop the stretch halfway and turn to see Keet. He's wearing jeans, but today, his t-shirt is gray, and from a place called Langley Whale Center. Under the line art of a gray whale are the words Whidbey Island, Washington. I turn back to the bags, thinking how well his shirt fits his torso, and how his jeans sit on his hips.

"Oh, hey, Keet. What's up?" I nudge a tilting bag upright. There's no way I'm going to let it fall over and have him see three boxes of cheese crackers and five bars of chocolate. Though the apples might redeem me.

"I thought we could try kayaking one day. I have a tour tomorrow, but maybe the day after? If you're not busy?"

I turn toward him again, wanting to see his expression when I say, "Well, I'll check my calendar, but that would be great." I can tell he's not sure if I'm serious or not.

"If you're too busy . . ."

"Keet, this is the least busy I've been in the whole of my adult life. A kayak lesson would be the best thing for me. Keep me from bingeing on Netflix and eating one of those boxes of cheese crackers I just bought."

He gives me a quick smile, brushes his dark hair away from his face, and says, "Neither of those sounds all that bad. What time do you want to meet?"

"Does one o'clock work? Or do we need to be on the water at a different time?"

"One's perfect. See you then." Through the window, I see him stride to his house and go in. Idly, I think to myself that it's a big house for one guy, and wonder if he owns it. Putting the crackers in the small pantry, I also wonder where he was for almost three days.

Then I remind myself that Keet's whereabouts are none of my business, and that figuring out what I'm supposed to do with myself now was more important. Dismantling my life in Texas and moving west, I didn't think much beyond getting here and moving in. Now what?

My cell phone rings. On the screen I see a Texas number, and the initials SN. Silent Nate is calling again. Two more rings as I consider what he might want. Then I answer it, but what I really want to do is hit "ignore call." And my ex, who is making it.

"Hey."

"How's it going out there on the wet coast?" He thinks he's being funny, but I can hear the tension in his voice, and he clears his throat twice before I can answer.

"Couldn't be better. What's up?" I turn so I can see at the ocean through my still-open front door. The waves remind me that everything is temporary. Even calls from ex-husbands.

"Abbie made me promise to call you and invite you to our wedding. Carlos thought it would be a nice gesture. So, you're officially invited if you want to come back. Save the date, September 29th."

These are the most words Nathan has strung together for me in ten years, so not only am I shocked by the sound of his voice, but that he kept a promise to our daughter. He's been on the flighty side of life for a while, and him committing to anything, much less his own word, comes as a shock.

"That's kind." I take a breath, reminding myself to be polite, at least for Abbie's sake. She may be twenty-two, but we're still her parents, and at some point, I'll have to face events where we are all together. "Why don't you email me the details and I'll give it some thought."

I can hear him release a big breath; maybe he expected a much different reaction from me. He had reason to, after all. The quieter he got during our marriage, the more vociferous I became. The more I pushed and hollered, the more he withdrew.

"Thanks. I'll send the invitation to you later today."

"Will do. Bye."

I tap the red button on the screen, shaking my head. Would wonders never cease. Maybe Carlos is good for Nathan, and I can give up on the one-woman war I've been waging against them both this past year.

I tap out a text to Abbie. *Your dad called and invited me to his wedding. I'm thinking about it. xo Mom*

The floating dots appear, and then her message: a thumbs-up emoji and a heart.

That night, I close the laptop, put it on the table beside my bed, and roll over to go to sleep. It seems like I'm dreaming immediately. In the black water of Osprey Bay, I see a standing cloaked and hooded figure. In my dream, I know that I'm dreaming, and I also know that it's Keet, wearing the cloak that shimmers like obsidian silk. He turns and lowers the hood, and I wake with a jolt, sitting up and rubbing my eyes, trying to remember what was underneath that startled me. But the dream has vaporized, like warm orca breath hitting cold air.

By the time I wake up again a couple of hours later, I've forgotten everything but the uneasy feeling in the pit of my stomach.

～～～

They meet on the beach later that morning, as he's pulling the double kayak closer to the water. It's a gray day, the sun hiding behind thick clouds that promise rain later.

"Good morning, Keet," she smiles.

"Good morning!" He stands up straight and puts his hands in the pockets of his black shorts. "Is that your alma mater?"

She looks down at what she's wearing—a navy University of Texas sweatshirt—like she's forgotten what she had on.

"This? Oh! No. Abbie goes there. She got it for me."

"What's she studying?"

"Architectural engineering." Nolee shakes her head. "I don't know how my ex and I made such a bright young woman, but Abbie is the smartest of us."

"She sounds like it."

"I read on Yelp that you have a degree in marine biology?"

"Well, not exactly. Someone must've misunderstood my orientation speech."

She smiles. "Yeah, it was pretty detailed, all right."

"Has to be. I don't want people dying on my boat. Or off it." Although his words are hard, he smiles as he says them. He'd like to avoid putting her on edge before they even get in the kayak.

"Tell me about this 'degree.'" Nolee says, tilting her head. He can hear the quotes around the word.

"I left Sitka–that's where I grew up, with my grandparents—and went to Washington State. I'd started college courses my last two years in high school. When I got to the university, I wanted to major in Marine Biology. I was miserable. It was loud and busy all the time, and I felt like I'd landed on another planet. I stuck it out for a couple of years, and then one summer, when I came back here to work, I stayed."

"I get it. I've never been to Sitka, but I can imagine what a shock it must've been for you." She gives him a thoughtful look. The wind lifts her ponytail, and some auburn strands come loose. She tucks them behind one ear.

"It was. The courses were fine . . . lots of math and science. It was the people, and the noise. I couldn't cope. I missed being with the ocean."

Nolee nods, looking out to sea before she says, "If I'd grown up with this kind of silence all the time, the rest of the world *would* be too much. It's growing on me, this quiet."

They're both silent, listening to the waves and their own thoughts. Then Keet bends down and grabs the short rope at the front of the kayak. "If you'll get that line at the end there, we'll take this closer to the water." Nolee looks at the end of the boat, and, finding the short black line attached to a metal ring, she lifts, and they carry it with quick shuffling steps before putting it down at the water's edge.

"I have a degree in philosophy, with a minor in English lit," she says, out of breath. "Sounds like you enjoyed school."

"I did, but that degree basically qualified me to become a teacher, a lawyer, or to sling fries at a fast-food place."

Keet laughs and says, "I notice you aren't doing any of those things."

"That's exactly what my dad said. I didn't really want to go to college, but he and Mom said I needed a degree. So, I chose the one that let me do the most reading."

They're silent again, Nolee watching as Keet sets two paddles down beside the kayak.

"I've always loved dogs like crazy. I began training our ranch dogs when I was a little girl." He looks at her as she gazes out to sea. "Reading is all well and fine, but even books are better when there's a dog around."

"It sounds like you miss having one," Keet says.

"I do. Know of any female dogs who need a good home?" The green of her eyes seems more intense, and he realizes she's looking at him through tears that she's holding back.

"None so far, but I'd be happy to keep an ear out for one."

The wind picks up, and the waves reach out for the kayak. He shrugs into his black life vest, cinching it around his waist. Nolee watches him before asking, "We should be safe to go out today, right? It won't rain or lightning or anything?"

He looks at the sky again. "Don't you have a weather app on your phone?"

She blinks before giving him a slow grin. "How do you know about apps?"

He laughs and leans down to readjust the strap running to the rudder, which had twisted.

"I called Trish at the office, and she checked for me. Rain later this evening, no thunderstorms in the area."

"Great. Tell me about this kayak."

Even though he's naming the parts of the double kayak he and Nolee are taking, he's distracted every time he looks at her. *If I were a dog, I'd behave too*, he thinks, aware that the green gaze she gives him is direct and level.

"Here's your life jacket." He hands her the red vest and watches as she straps it on and adjusts the fit.

"I feel less nervous already."

Keet adjusts his vest, then grabs the paddle. When he looks back at her, she's running her hands through her hair, pulling the ponytail through the back of a baseball cap.

"I'll sit in back and take care of the rudder," he points to a thin black piece of plastic that looks like a huge knife. He unsnaps it from its folded position.

"Which leaves me in the front," Nolee says. "You won't splash water down my back when I'm not looking?" Underneath her attempt at flirting, he senses she's nervous.

"I'm harmless." He can't break his gaze from hers and wonders how long this statement will remain true.

She tilts her head again and laughs, "Somehow, I very much doubt that, Keet Noland." She follows this with a half-smile.

He clears his throat and hands her a paddle with a black shaft and orange blades.

"Put your hands here and here," he shows her, using his own paddle. "See those words on one side of the blade?" Nolee nods.

He continues. "Those go toward you so that the water is scooped as you paddle. To check your hand placement, hold the paddle above your head, and make sure you bend your elbows so that each arm is at a ninety-degree angle to the shaft. You don't want to white-knuckle it. Your hands need to hold the shaft, but not grip it. It's easier for the ocean to take it from you that way. Plus, your arms will get exhausted."

Nolee raises the paddle, looks up, and shifts her grip.

"Great! You look like a pro already," Keet says. "When you use the paddle, it's in an infinity pattern: circular, left down, right up, with the middle as the center of the movement."

She tries out the paddle, moving it up and down, at first more like a teeter-totter than the infinity symbol. He says nothing, watching as her shoulders relax. She takes a breath, and the sideways figure eight appears.

She smiles, and then chirps, "Let's stop talking and get out on that water, Keet!"

He glances at her feet. "Your sneakers and jeans are going to get wet. You might want to look around for some water shoes."

She looks down at her sneakers, then at the black mesh and rubber shoes he has on his feet. "Well, a little water won't hurt." She rolls up her jeans to her knees. They step into the water, and he hears her gasp at the cold when it hits her bare legs. Guiding the kayak out into water, he motions for her to get in first. Holding the paddle in one hand, she puts her leg into the kayak and plops onto the seat, stretching her legs in front of her before repositioning the paddle.

Keet gives a push, then slides into the back seat of the kayak, holding his paddle in both hands.

"Nolee, you set the rhythm and I'll match you. Remember, it's an infinity symbol, and you're going to twist through your waist."

She slaps the blade down into the water like she's chopping wood, and the kayak rocks to the left. Keet rows against the tide, trying to avoid drifting back to shore.

She tries a dozen more strokes, but her inexpert handling means they aren't going to get very far unless Keet helps.

"Keep after it, Nolee. This is your first time, no big deal."

Frowning with concentration, she lifts her right blade into the air, twists her torso, and lowers the left end of the paddle into the water in slow motion, with hardly a splash. She repeats the process on the other side with the same success, her head moving back and forth as she uses her eyes to adjust how she's paddling. He can see her relaxing.

Keet matches his strokes to hers. She's silent, concentrating on feeling the water with her paddle and keeping the same rhythm. Her shoulders relax more, and she looks out at the water that they're gliding across. As their blades push through the water together, he sees a trickle of sea water run down the raised paddle, dampening the cuff of her pullover.

"I can see why you love this so much," she says over her shoulder.

"I've been on the water in one way or another my entire life."

"So far."

He's quiet for a moment, and then her joke registers with him.

"Right! I'm not quite done yet, it seems." But in his mind, he wonders if that's true.

There's silence again, except for the wind through the pines on land and the sound of their paddles meeting the ocean in tandem. Keet relaxes into the feeling of harmony that exists between them, and between the kayak and the sea. He can't remember the last time he felt peaceful around another person. This feeling usually happens when he is in solitude with the water, the sky, and the islands calling him their own.

They glide around the bay, staying close to shore. Keet's thinking it's time to let Nolee know they can call it a day when he hears her singing.

"Just like a paperback novel/The kind the drugstore sells . . ." Nolee's voice carries on the wind back to him, a sweet and clear alto above the sound of the waves lapping at their kayak.

"'If You Could Read My Mind,' Gordon Lightfoot, 1970," Keet says.

"Here's the thing—I still wouldn't know if you're right or wrong!" Nolee laughs, leans over and splashes water back at him. It drips from his face as he answers her laugh with a wide smile.

"Google it. Besides, how many of these is it going to take before you know I'm right?"

"Oh ho-ho—he knows about Google." Nolee tries to look at him, but can't fully turn, instead looking over her shoulder. She splashes him with water again and says, "Did Trish tell you about that too?"

"You'll just have to trust me. Or trust your own memory." He dips his hand in the water, and flicks water on the back of her neck.

"Hey!"

"You started it, Nolee Burnett."

Nolee answers the smile in his voice with one of her own. The day may be gray, but he feels like he has the sun on his back and a horizon full of blue possibilities.

They're pulling the kayak above the tide line, their feet cold and shoes soggy with salt water, when Keet turns to face Nolee.

"I make a great salmon dinner. Want to join me some night?"

Trying to brush the sand off the legs of her jeans, she says, without looking up, "That sounds amazing. More amazing than cheese and crackers, which is what you'd get if you came to my house."

"It'll be a welcome-to-Osprey-Bay-and-your-new-life kind of dinner. Six o'clock tomorrow?"

She smiles, giving up on removing sticky sand from denim.

"Perfect. What can I bring?"

"Do you drink wine?"

"Can't stand the stuff. How about Scotch?"

Keet's surprise shows on his face before he says, "Scotch it is. Bring your favorite, and I'll try it. I haven't had it before."

"What?! How can you have gotten this far in life and not tried Scotch?"

"I'm not a big drinker, but I've always enjoyed wine, or martinis. Never thought of anything else. Are there special glasses?"

Nolee chuckles and nods. "I'll bring two glasses as well. Thanks for the kayak lesson, Keet. I think I've found my new calling."

"You're welcome. It was fun."

He watches her walk back to her cabin. Halfway there, she bends down and takes off her shoes and socks, then stands back up and waves. He waves back, hoping she didn't notice that he was admiring the curve of her hips. She walks through the sand, then into her house. He smiles and makes a list in his head of the food he'll need to buy in Northsound.

SIX

I lean against the door and look down at my jeans, sticky and wet with sea water, rough with sand, and clinging to me more tightly than ticks to a dog. But that's not what's bothering me. What bothers me is how elated I'm feeling at Keet's dinner invitation. He made it sound casual, and it most likely is. Then why am I so giddy?

Closing the curtains in the front room and shimmying out of my jeans and underwear, I pull off the rest of my clothes and leave them in a heap by the front door. Shivering, I jog down the hall to the bathroom and turn on the shower.

As I'm watching the grains of sand wash down the drain, it occurs to me that Keet is just being friendly to his neighbor. Maybe even he tires of being alone in that big house. I close my eyes and let the hot water wash across the top of my head.

By the time I'm out and dressed again, I've decided that today I'm going to that animal shelter and finish my volunteer interview. Maybe work with some dogs, maybe even help with the cats.

After calling the shelter and finding out I can come in later that afternoon, I sit down with a cup of tea and a book. My eyes are following the same words on the same page for the tenth time when I realize I've been thinking about Keet. I wonder what his hair would feel like in my hands. I wonder what his body would feel like against mine, and if I'd have to be on my tiptoes to kiss him.

The book falls to the floor with a thump when I stand. I drink the rest of the tea, pick up the book and close it, and stand looking out at the water I was just on. With Keet.

Get hold of yourself, girl! Even though I'm not due at the pet shelter for another hour, I need to get out of this house and give myself something to

43

think about other than my mysterious neighbor. I grab my phone out of my backpack and search for pet stores on Camas Island. I see one called Chena's Doghouse. That's as good a place to go as any. Besides, I need to shop for the dog I'm going to find soon.

I look for my keys, throw the phone in my backpack, and drive away from Osprey Bay before my obsessed brain can say tall, dark stranger. Making sure my ancient iPod's connected to the USB port, I choose my Best of the '80s playlist. Then it's just me and Prince riding in a little red corvette all the way to town.

The ring of a bell follows me into the store. Ava's behind the counter, sorting through boxes of dog treats.

"Ava! I didn't know you worked here."

She breaks her gaze away from the treats, her pink cheeks beaming rounder as she smiles. Her perm is updated, and the dyed black curls bounce as she waves to me.

"Just helping my friend who owns the place. She's gone to Seattle for a couple of days, and I told her I'd be happy to mind the store. Gets me out of the house, too."

"I'd be interested in helping sometimes if she needs it. I'm not much use with cat stuff, but I could help anyone with dogs."

"I remember you used to own a dog-training business." She tilts her head at me, reminding me of the birds that used to hang out at the feeder in the spring, when the bluebells burst out of the warming ground.

"I did. What's your friend's name? You can give her my cell phone number. I'd be happy to chat if she's interested. I'm spending way too much time in my house lately, too."

"Chena Petrovna. I'll let her know. Are you shopping for a new dog?" She walks out from behind the counter, the floor creaking as she steps on wooden boards worn smooth by years of feet and paws.

I turn to follow her, walking past shelves of dog treats and toys. "More like shopping for a future dog. I'm heading over to the shelter in about half an hour so I can start volunteering."

"Well, here's where we keep the food. The raw food is in the freezer." She turns to me again and I notice again that she's shorter than I am. It's a rare day that I can look someone in the eye without tilting my head up.

"I don't think I'll buy any food yet. Maybe you could point me to the dog beds, though?"

She walks around shelves that are stacked high with various dog foods and points at another set of shelves, with dog beds and crate pads of various sizes and colors.

"Knock yourself out, Nolee. Let me know if you need any help."

I find a large dog bed shaped like a sofa and prop it on the counter by the computer Ava is using to ring up the sale.

"I want to get a couple of bowls too," I say, looking around.

"Go to the wall with the collars and make a right—they're next to the treats." With a click of the mouse, Ava adds the dog bed to my bill.

I find the bowls, sorted by plastic, stainless steel, and some pottery crocks that I haven't seen anywhere else.

"Hey, Ava, where are these ceramic dog bowls from?"

"A couple of local potters made those. People love them."

I can see why. They're thick, with a solid bottom and wide opening. I hold one in my hands, looking at the blues and greens that remind me of the waters of Osprey Bay. I pick out a smaller bowl in matching colors and a mat to put them on, then go back to the register.

At the cabin after my time at the shelter, I feel more like myself than I have in months. Cleaning dog pens, taking the dogs on walks, and even playing with the cats feels like the sun has come out after a long and dark storm. I put the bowls in the sink with a little soap and some hot water, then place the mat on the floor at the end of the counter.

When I try to find a place for the bed, I realize that it's too big for my room. I move the sofa a little, trying the bed between it and the wood-stove. It occurs to me that if I find a puppy, I'll most likely need a crate, not a bed. Oh well. I go back to the sink, scrub the bowls, rinse them, and put them in the dish drainer.

Looking out the front window at the ocean, I can hear the waves thrumming on the shore and can't resist going closer. I walk out to the log that has become my favorite spot to sit and let the breeze tangle my hair and nudge my eyes close. Breathing evenly, I can feel the warmth of the fallen tree under my hands. I hear a loud exhale and my eyes pop open.

The killer whale is back. His dorsal fin cuts through the sea, melting into the dark water and then rising through his exhale. He waves his tail flukes back and forth, then sinks under the water. I move closer, feeling the spray of the waves on my face, scanning the bay for his dorsal fin.

There he is again, this time gliding closer to shore. His head juts out of the water, the bright white of his eye patches made more luminous by his dark body and the water that laps around him. I wonder if he can see me. He disappears, then reappears, leaping out of the water and crashing back into it. He leaps three more times before I see his dorsal fin heading out of the bay. I stand on the shore and think about what it would be like to be that big, that free of gravity. I never much took to swimming, but after seeing how easy it was to get the paddle to glide through the water, I wonder if being in the sea might be simpler than I think.

The chill of the evening air drives me back inside. I build a fire, open my laptop, and read through an email from Abbie. I'm still reading when I hear the loud exhales again. This time it sounds like there's more than one killer whale in the bay.

Grabbing my jacket, I open the door and look out into the dusk. There they are, a pod, their different-sized dorsal fins slicing the surface. They circle, appear, and disappear, heading in a zig-zag pattern closer to the beach. The setting sun's orange and red streaks are reflected on their black skin, making it look as though the ocean has transformed from liquid into whale, then back to liquid once more. I watch them until I can no longer stand the cold.

The next morning, drinking my tea and checking the calendar on my laptop, I see that it's almost the end of May. I feel so at home it seems I've been here longer. I look around at my cabin. There's dust on the furniture, and a basket full of dirty laundry needs to be dealt with.

By the time I finish my housekeeping, the light is harder and brighter. A look in the newly polished mirror tells me that I could stand some cleaning as well. As I go through my routine—clay mask, hair conditioner, nails—I tell myself I'm just making myself presentable.

Another dream about Keet woke me up early, adding to my free-floating anxiety about this evening. Surely if he was some sort of perv, I'd have seen it by now. Maybe walking into his house alone wasn't the best idea, but he really didn't seem to be dangerous.

My phone pings. I swipe it open to see a text from Ava. *Chena says she'd love to talk with you about working at her shop part time.* I send a smiley face emoji, then *Please let her know I'll stop in tomorrow.* After pausing with my thumbs over the keypad, I type in *Having dinner with Keet Noland tonight. Forgot to tell you that the whale watch was superb. Seems like a nice enough guy.* Three floating dots appear, then *Good to know. Have fun at dinner!*

There. Someone else knows what I'm doing tonight.

I glance at the clock and note that the mask and conditioner have ten more minutes to work their magic. While I wait, I pick up the British murder mystery I've been reading and remind myself to Google where Norfolk is.

After rinsing everything off, I sit on the bed and look at my closet. How did I ever get such a collection of blue jeans and sweatshirts? I pick out the jeans that look the least beat-up, then search through my collection of sweaters, which are far outnumbered by hoodies, pullovers, and fleeces. I pull out a dark blue cable-knit sweater, and a t-shirt to layer underneath it. And shoes. Of which I have not even a half-dozen. Luna was always more excited about shoes than I've ever been. The tan leather flats will have to do.

My hair glides smoothly through my fingers. I don't expect anyone else's hands to be in my hair tonight, but I like the shine, the auburn coaxed back to life. Pulling it away from my face, I secure it with a silver barrette, leaving the back down. At least it's a change from my usual ponytail or braid.

Then it hits me. I'm fifty years old and behaving like I'm going on a date. I remind myself that he's being a friendly neighbor, and that I need to stop trying so hard. Although I find it gratifying to pay attention to myself again, I also know that if I'm not careful, I could end up with some sort of one-sided infatuation. And I'd lived in the land of one-sided for too many years to fancy going back again.

Without another glance in the mirror, I put on my jacket, grab the bag with the whiskey and glasses and head out the door.

SEVEN

Keet hears a triple knock. He strides over, opening his door to see Nolee standing with a bag in one hand. She smiles as she hands it to him. "Let the whiskey tasting begin."

"Come in, I'll get this poured. Any special instructions?" He looks at her again, thinking she looks beautiful, then says, "You look nice."

She looks down, straightening the hem of her sweater. "Well, it's been a while since I've been invited to dinner, so I thought a sweater would be better than a sweatshirt."

"Excellent choice. Good color for you, too."

They're silent, and Keet realizes they're still standing in the doorway. Was he staring? He steps aside so she can get by him, closes the door and lifts the bag.

"How much, and do I put anything else in the glass?"

"For you, a dash with a little water. For me, two fingers"—she holds up two fingers sideways— "and neat. No water, no ice."

"Hardcore, huh?"

She grins. "I prefer to taste my Scotch."

"I'll try your way then."

"Daredevil, huh?"

Keet smiles, then turns toward the kitchen.

"What did you do today?" she asks from behind him.

"Cleaned this place up a little. Went to the marina and took *The Salish See* out by myself. Grabbed a couple of extra things at the market. Came back and started cooking. You?"

"The same, except for the sailing, going to the market, and cooking things. I need to do a store run soon, though. I'm out of cereal." He turns and sees her hanging her jacket on one of the hooks by the door.

"You're a big cereal fan?" He pulls out the bottle of Scotch and reads the label. Balvenie. The plain glasses are larger at the bottom than the top. He likes the way their roundness feels in the palm of his hand.

"I eat it probably more than is healthy. But my grandma was right: cereal is good for supper too. This will be my first proper dinner since I moved here. By the time the end of the day rolls around, I can't be bothered to think about cooking."

Keet pulls the cork out of the top, waving the bottle in front of his nose.

"You might not want to get too close to that . . ." Nolee begins. Keet squints his eyes and puts the bottle back on the counter.

"Whew!"

"Yeah, it's not a delicate aroma like wine. More like a smoky punch in the nose."

"Here's yours." He hands her the glass, and watches as she holds it to her nose and sighs.

"Nectar of the gods."

He pours himself the same amount and raises his glass to Nolee. "Cheers."

She eyes the amount of Scotch in his glass and replies, "Sláinte."

"What language was that?" He enjoys the alcohol's smoky flavor, and the warmth it creates as it hits his stomach.

"Gaelic. It's the only word I know. There's a family story about a red-headed Scotsman who was a farrier. He stopped in the town my great-grandmother lived in, and they had a torrid affair. He moved on two months later, but seven months after that, my grandmother came into the world. With a head full of red hair. She gave it to my mom, and my mom gave it to me. Mine isn't as red as theirs, though. I also found out that the Burnett family motto is 'Courage grows stronger at the wound.' I've always liked that idea." She takes another sip. "What do you think of the Scotch?"

"I wasn't sure about it, but I can see why you like it. This is good." He takes another sip, now noticing its subtle layers of peat and cinnamon before he swallows it. "That's quite a family motto."

"Well, hand it to the Scots to not mince words." She raises her glass and takes another sip.

"I'm seeing that you got more than just the red in your hair from your Scottish ancestors."

He sets his glass down, still admiring the way it bells out at the bottom, like a woman with luscious hips. Checking on the sweet potatoes, he sees they're oozing a thick syrup. He takes them out of the oven, wrapping them in foil and putting them in a separate compartment of the stove to keep warm.

"Oh yeah . . . I did something else yesterday. Went to the pet food place in Northsound and got a dog bed and a couple of bowls. You know, to be ready for a dog whenever she arrives." Nolee takes a breath and smiles at her glass. "And I volunteered at the animal shelter. Even cleaned the cats' litter boxes."

"Didn't bring a cat home?" He removes the foil that covers the salmon fillets and layers then with butter and lemon, then sprinkles them with garlic. He slides the pan in the oven and sets a timer.

"Not a cat fan. They're cute enough, but I only want dogs."

Keet reaches for a blue bowl and sets it on the counter. From the refrigerator, he takes mixed greens, pears, goat cheese, and almonds before closing the door.

"That pottery looks like the dog bowls I just bought."

He glances at the bowl. "I think the local potters have been here forever. I got this as a gift from one of them after they went sailing with me." He adds the washed greens to the bowl, followed by the almonds and chunks of goat cheese, then tosses everything.

"Can I help at all?" Nolee is watching him, absorbed by his putting together of their meal.

"Sure. You can cut this pear. It needs to be sliced thin."

She takes the pear and the small knife from him, halves the pear, then halves it again, cutting out the center out and chopping off the ends.

It's quiet while he takes the sourdough bread out of its wrapper and places it on another baking sheet, sliding it into the oven with the salmon. He glances at Nolee, seeing that she's concentrating and slicing the pear with caution.

"You okay over there?"

She sets the knife down. "Yes. I've been known to almost chop my fingers off when I cut something, so I'm always careful."

"You don't have to finish it—I can do that." He moves to take the knife and the other half of the pear, but she waves her hand at him, shooing him away.

"I'm fine!" And she goes back to slicing.

Only partly convinced, he turns and takes a scratched glass measuring cup out of the cupboard. He pours in olive oil, adds in some apple cider vinegar, salt and pepper, chopped garlic, parsley, and a spoonful of local honey, then whisks it all together before pouring it into a glass cruet.

He notices that the sound of the knife hitting the counter has stopped. He glances over at Nolee. She lifts her eyes from the cruet to him.

"No bottled dressing?"

He shakes his head. "It's easy enough to make. It tastes better. The bottled stuff is too expensive."

He gathers the slices of pear in his hands, and then places them in the salad. He tosses it, adds a pinch of salt, and then tosses it again. Lifting the bowl, he asks, "Can you take that over to the table?"

She puts her hands around the bowl, and the tips of her fingers meet his. Smiling into his eyes, she turns and places it on the table, running her fingers over the smooth wood. The dark brown surface is nicked, and shows the swirls where branches used to be. Despite his ambivalence about his life, he oils and cleans this table every week. The ladderback chairs are stained the same color with dark gray cushions.

"Did you have this table made?"

"My grandfather Jack made it. When my grandmother moved into an apartment in town, in Sitka, she asked if I wanted it. I couldn't turn her down."

"It's a beautiful table, Keet. What a wonderful way to remember your grandfather."

He nods, then takes the salmon and puts it on a wooden board, laying it into the concave oval cut into its surface; the bread goes on a faded circular cutting board. He grabs a knife and turns toward the table, but Nolee is there, hands out. The board with the salmon goes into her hands, and he carries the knife and the bread to the table behind her. He notices the silver clip in her hair.

He goes back to the kitchen, takes two shallow white bowls out of the cupboard, then places a sweet potato in each. Placing them on the table, he says, "I put knives out, but this salmon is so tender I doubt you'll need one."

"Keet, this looks like a meal I'd get at a fancy restaurant in Austin." Standing behind her chair, she's smiling at the food, then turns toward him, still smiling. The light in her green eyes makes him forget about the meal he just made.

"I haven't been cooking this way recently," he says, moving around to the opposite side of the table and sitting down. "It feels good to put together a meal, and to share it." He raises his Scotch glass. "Here's to good meals and good neighbors."

Nolee raises her glass, takes a sip, and then puts it down and begins eating.

After a few minutes, she looks up from her plate and says, "This is the best meal I've eaten in years."

Keet smiles at her. "Good! I'm happy to hear that. Wait until you taste dessert though."

"Dessert too? What is it?"

"A lemon custard tart with raspberries."

"You made that?"

He shakes his head. "I'm not much of a baker. The local bakery in town is amazing, and they make superb desserts. You can thank them."

"Well, I can thank you for thinking of dessert."

"I have a bit of a sweet tooth. Any chance to go by the bakery is one I'll take."

Keet notices that Nolee's glass is empty.

"Do you want more?" He motions to her glass.

"Hell, yes."

"Done." He pours a generous portion of the dark amber liquid into her glass and sits back down.

"Thanks," she says, and then takes a large mouthful. While she's savoring the drink, he tells her, "I took a private charter for a husband and wife from Los Angeles about a week ago."

"Yeah?" Nolee breaks off a piece of bread and spreads a thick layer of butter on it.

"They argued almost from the time we left the marina to the time we got back."

"Okay, spill," she smiles, leaning forward. "What were they fighting about?" She takes a bite of the bread, closing her eyes and humming while she chews. He stumbles on the first words, surprised by the sight of her face and the sound of her voice.

"It was their tenth wedding anniversary, and he loves to sail, but she gets seasick. In between the yelling and her throwing up, he's running back to me asking for water, then anti-nausea medicine, then asks how far we were from Sucia, the island where he'd arranged a romantic picnic dinner. He wants me to make the wind blow harder, or my boat go faster."

"Ha!" Nolee laughs. "So did that dinner get eaten? And if it did, did she keep it down on the way back?"

"She did, but she was half asleep most of the return trip. She woke up when we docked, and then asked where the killer whales were, since that's all she wanted to see. Last I heard, they were arguing all the way to their car."

Nolee laughs again, then spears the last of the salmon and pops it in her mouth. She closes her eyes again as she chews.

She swallows and wipes her mouth with a cloth napkin. She looks at him, and he swears the green in her eyes has deepened along with her voice. "Keet! How do you make food taste this good?"

"Just practice, I guess. Plus, that salmon came straight out of the sea today."

"Mm. This is amazing. What can I do to thank you? You've treated me to an amazing sailboat tour, and now an amazing dinner."

"You can come out on the boat with me again. This time, I'll take you to a part of the islands that few people know about."

"Wait a minute. *I'm* supposed to be thanking *you*," she leans her head on her hand, smiling at him in a way that he'd normally take as an invitation. He stands instead, thinking she's probably smiling like that because of the Scotch, and takes their plates to the counter by the sink.

"Okay, those kayaks and the paddles need to be cleaned. Want to help me tomorrow?"

She stands up. "Count me in."

"But first," he says, opening the refrigerator and reaching in, "dessert."

Her eyes light up again, and Keet thinks maybe he was wrong about the Scotch. After placing each tart on a plate, he hands one to her and they sit down. The only sound is the ocean outside, and the clink of forks as they eat.

After finishing dessert, Nolee helps him clear the table. She asks, "Can I do anything else to help clean up?"

He shakes his head. "Nope. It's practically done already."

He sees her looking into his living room, amazement written all over her face.

"When I first came in, Keet, I thought those were books. But they're CDs, aren't they?"

He looks at the far wall of his living room, the floor-to-ceiling shelves holding not only his CD collection, but his stereo system as well.

"They are. I've been collecting for a while. I have a bunch of vinyl records up at my grandmother's place in Sitka, but I've moved on from that. CDs are easier to store."

Nolee smiles at him, pointing to the wall of music. "Can I look?"

"Be my guest."

She walks slowly along each shelf, running her fingers along each spine, kneeling to see the music closest to the floor.

"You've got everything here. I would call your tastes eclectic."

"Well, not everything, but definitely eclectic. I can't get enough of music. My only regret is that I won't live long enough to listen to it all."

She turns, eyes smiling before her mouth follows. "I feel the same way about books. Do you have any favorites?"

He dries his hands on a muslin towel, then folds it and places it on the counter. "No favorites. It really depends on my mood. Also, I'm not much good with music if it's past the millennium. My interest waned about the time all the popular music started to sound the same. "

She laughs. "My daughter would disagree with you. She played me song after song, a game where I had to guess who was singing. I never got it right. Though," she laughs, "as you've seen, I don't get much right when it comes to music."

He laughs too. "Do you listen to any folk music?" Nolee shakes her head. He continues, "I'd like to know more about it. A friend gave me a CD by a group called Mandolin Orange that's amazing. Almost good enough to get me to the mainland to see a show in Seattle."

"Almost?"

"It would take being close to unconsciousness for me to put myself in a crowd of people. I don't care how good the music is."

"You might change your mind if the Eagles were playing."

"Oh?"

"It was the best concert I've been to in my life. And I've been to a lot of 'em."

She walks to the door, where she grabs her coat off a hook and pats each pocket. "Oh, hell."

"What's wrong? Forgot your house keys?"

"No, I don't lock my door. I was going to bring a flashlight, but I was so focused on the Scotch, I forgot."

"Speaking of . . ." he walks over to the counter and puts the Balvenie back in the bag, along with the two clean glasses. Handing the bag to Nolee, he takes a flashlight from another hook.

"You can borrow mine. Bring it back tomorrow when you come over for kayak cleaning. I'll call you when I'm ready."

"You're a gem. Thank you again for dinner, and dessert." She smiles and opens the door, flicking the flashlight on and shining it in front of her.

He watches until she goes inside her cabin and turns on the lights, then closes his door and snaps the deadbolt into place.

The next morning I'm sitting on the porch with a cup of tea and a book, watching the sun turn the pines from black to deep green when I hear the land line ring inside. When I pick it up, I hear Keet's voice, still rough from sleep.

"I'm getting ready to clean those kayaks, if you'd like to help."

"Sure. Be right over." I hang up the phone with a clatter, pull on my rubber boots, and close the door behind me.

When I get there, Keet has the two kayaks up on sawhorses. He smiles when I wave. He's wearing his standard uniform today, a black t-shirt and black shorts. How he can walk on these rocks with bare feet is a mystery to me.

He drags out a hose and a bucket.

"Good morning, Nolee." His face crinkles into a smile as he takes a step toward me. I reach up and give him a quick hug, and he briefly returns it, then steps back, looking surprised.

"I'm not good at being the stand-offish type. Hope I didn't surprise you?"

"Only a little," he laughs. "I've been working so much that I guess I've gotten out of the hugging habit.

"Sounds like we both may need to get used to it again." I wince at how that comes out, curse my quick tongue, and try to deflect my embarrassment by asking, "So do we wash these guys down? Wax them?"

Keet walks over to the bucket and picks up the sponge.

"Nothing that complex. We basically wipe them down with some warm water, then spray it off. These newer kayaks really need little in the way of maintenance."

I take the sponge from him, and our eyes lock the moment our fingertips touch. I don't know I'm moving closer to him until he says, "I'm going to go get another sponge. Be right back." He lets go of the sponge

I'm holding on, which is when I breathe again. *What has gotten into you, Nolee Burnett?*

I wipe off the blue kayak, scrubbing at a few bits of dried-on kelp. I'm halfway down the first side when he comes back with another bucket and sponge. We work in silence until I can't stand it anymore.

"How long have you lived on Camas Island, Keet?"

He stops working on the orange kayak and puts the sponge in the bucket. Pausing, he then says, "I guess it's been more than thirty years. Between eighteen and twenty, I came here in the summers. Then, when I dropped out of WSU, I moved here."

"That's a long time. It must suit you?"

He shrugs. "It's easy enough to like. Everything is close, and there aren't many people most of the year. How long did you live in Texas?"

"I was born in Abilene and then we moved to Odessa when I was five. I basically lived there until I moved here. So, fifty years."

"Did you like it?"

"I did. But I also think I knew nothing else. It took the divorce to get me thinking about going somewhere different. But I'm glad I did."

"How come Camas Island?" He wipes his hands on his shorts.

"Because it's not Texas." I can tell by his smile that he's waiting for a more thorough explanation.

"Because I didn't feel like I could find out who I am at this stage of my life while staying in a place that already knew how it defined me."

Nodding his head, he says, "I get that."

"I'd heard about Camas Island from my friend Shelly, who used to come up here during the summer. She loved it. Shelly's in New York now, but when I told her about the divorce, she said I needed to see Camas Island. I researched it, found Ava and her rental cabin, and here I am. Must've been meant to be. Everything fell into place when I needed it."

Keet bends down to grab the hose. "Be right back; I need to turn this on."

I finish wiping down the kayak and toss my sponge back in the bucket.

"So, you didn't visit before deciding?" he asks me, spraying the orange kayak.

"No, I looked at everything I could online. YouTube videos, Airbnb, blogs, Instagram, Google maps, satellite photos—you know." Keet stops spraying the kayak and is squinting at me, his eyebrows drawn together a slight frown.

"Something the matter?"

"I know you were speaking English, but I don't have any idea what those last things are, other than they have to do with the internet."

"Wow." I can't hide the incredulity in my voice, or the judginess. "I use the internet for practically everything."

"And have you found this to be what you expected from your internet searches?"

"Now that you mention it . . . some of it, yes. A lot, no."

"In what ways?" He goes back to spraying the kayak, and I notice the water running in rivulets down the muscles of his dark calves.

"The air. No one told me how the air here almost feels like you can eat it. I wasn't ready for how the sea and sky and pine trees are all crammed together. The biggest insight was how fast I was living, inside and out, and how slow everything here seems by comparison."

He hands me the hose and I turn and rinse off the blue kayak, feeling the splash of the cool water on my legs. I may not have water shoes yet, but I packed a whole box of shorts.

"Nathan, my ex, was the most opposed to me moving. It made me crazy; we weren't together anymore, and yet he was still trying to control my life. I would've moved to Shangri-La just to rile him up more. As it was, Camas Island made him mad enough for my satisfaction."

I hand the hose back to Keet, turning before I can get distracted by his eyes again.

"Do you mind if I ask why you got divorced?"

This time I look at him. His face is calm, and he's asked the question in a low and soft voice that melts my resistance to reveal an answer.

"Nate fell in love with someone else."

"Oh. Well. I can see why that would have been a problem."

"Yeah. They're getting married. His fiancé's name is Carlos. It bothers me that he kept it a secret from me for so long."

There's silence then, and Keet walks around to the paddles lined up in the sand.

"Let's put these kayaks down and rinse off the paddles."

I help him take the double kayak off the sawhorse and he brings the single orange kayak over next to it. He places three paddles crosswise on the sawhorses and hoses them off. Just when I'm thinking I've revealed too much, Keet says, "I used to be engaged."

"Oh?"

"Sascha Quint. She moved here with her parents when she was twelve and grew up working at their family restaurant. After she turned eighteen, she spent her summers in Los Angeles doing modeling gigs. I met her when I was thirty-two and she was twenty-four. By then, she was deep into a full-time modeling career, and I couldn't believe someone like her would go for someone like me. We were engaged five years later."

"What happened?"

"She wanted to live in LA full time. I couldn't do it. We tried the long-distance relationship thing, and I visited twice, but it felt just like when I tried to go to college. Horrible. Too much noise, too many people. She didn't want to be on the island anymore, said there was nothing for her here. We broke off the engagement and she moved."

"I'm sorry to hear that, Keet."

"Yeah. Exes, right?"

I smile at him. "Well, without them we wouldn't be where we are, would we?" I wipe my hands on my t-shirt.

"I hadn't thought about it that way, but you're right."

He's done rinsing the paddles and leaves them on the sawhorses to dry. I watch as he lines them up, shuffling them back and forth. He seems to come to some decision, because he flashes his quick and bright smile, and says, "I feel like sailing today. Want to join me?"

My mouth goes dry. I blink. "Yes. Do you have any place in mind?"

"I'd like to see if we can track down an orca pod I've been watching for a while. I want to check on them and make sure they're all doing okay."

"Definitely count me in. At this rate, though, I'll be cleaning kayaks from now till doomsday."

Keet laughs. I like the way the laugh lights up his face, the way his light brown skin crinkles around his mouth.

"No, you won't. You seemed to enjoy the tour, and it's different when there's no one else on the boat—better, I think."

"I'm honored to be included."

"I'll head over there now and get things ready. Want to come by in about an hour?"

"Sure. I'll stop by the market and pick up something to eat."

"I wouldn't turn down lunch." He smiles again and steps toward me, then enfolds me in a hug. I don't know if he feels it, but a frisson of excitement bursts inside my chest. He's warmer than I expect, but before I can completely embarrass myself yet again, we step apart.

"Any sandwich requests?"

He thinks for a moment. "Tuna."

"Not a turkey fan?"

"Not much of a meat fan, actually. I like all kinds of seafood. Some chicken. No beef, lamb, or pork. Though . . ." and here he pauses, giving me a guilty smile.

"Yes? Spit it out–I'm a rabid carnivore, you won't shock me."

"I do really like bacon."

"Who doesn't?! Tuna it is. I'll see you in about an hour."

When I get to the marina, I park my car and grab the paper sack that holds our lunch. As I walk down the floating dock, I can see him checking the sails, moving back and forth on *The Salish See*. His hair's tucked into a black knit cap and his hands seem to caress the sails as he adjusts them. He sees me and waves, and as I wave back, I think about hugging him again.

I step on board, putting the sack down on a seat. I don't see any life vests.

"Keet, do you want me to wear a—what did you call them? Personal Flotation Device?"

"Only if you want to. I think we'll have a smooth trip." He leans over for another hug. I smile and close my eyes, this time more relaxed. He smells like the sea, and cedar, and a deeper musky scent.

"Thanks for bringing lunch. Let's get to where we're going so we can eat."

"Sounds great." As I set the bag into a cooler he brought, I realize that in the past couple of hours, I've received more affection from a man I hardly know than I did from my ex-husband in a decade.

EIGHT

Bobbing on the low tide, we're tucked into a cove away from most of the boat traffic in the channels. I put our empty lunch containers back in the bag and take a last sip of tea from my thermos.

"Are you sure they're here?" I ask Keet.

"They will be. This is a quiet spot. It's also where plenty of fish hang out. Don't let the secret out to the fisherman though." His smile is relaxed as looks first at the island we've anchored close to, and then the horizon.

"Need any help? I'm not Alex, but I take direction well."

"All's well. Look off the port side, though."

I see them, at first two dorsal fins, then three more, then a small one, riding in the slipstream of a larger orca.

I point, unnecessarily, because Keet's already looking. An unexpected delight washes over me—it's been so long since I've felt this innocent wonder that I'm speechless. I can't take my eyes off them, their dorsal fins cutting through the waves, their black-and-white bodies rising to breathe before twisting and diving, disappearing into the green depths.

As we stand elbow-to-elbow at the bow rail, watching, Keet points to the smallest orca.

"The baby is a little under a year old. That's his mom next to him. He's the newest member of the pod, which also includes his sister, grandmother, cousin, and auntie."

I see the baby gliding by his mother's side. His eye patches and belly have a faint pinkish cast. He rolls away from her before popping up close to the boat, then swimming its length with his dark eye pointed up at us. As I catch his eye, I wonder what he's thinking, and then it hits me that looking into the eye of an orca isn't anything like looking into the eye of a dog. The baby orca bumps alongside the hull and then his mother is beside him, guiding him back to the pod.

I watch as they dive, then come up for air on the other side of the boat. The exhaled scent of rotting fish wafts across us, and I'm rub my nose to disperse the scent.

Keet says, "You can tell them apart by the shape of their dorsal fins, and the saddle patch—that light gray area behind the dorsal fin."

"That one, with the largest dorsal fin. Who is he? Or she?"

"She's the grandmother, the eldest of the pod. She's taught her family where to find fish, the best places to rest and sleep, where the sea is the most fun to play in."

His dark gaze makes me consider how it would feel to stand closer to him. When he speaks again, I break away from his look to watch the pod. "All the local orcas, both the Residents and the Bigg's we saw the other day, are identified by a letter and a number; some of them have also been named."

"Just for fun, let's name them ourselves. We can call the eldest Nana."

"Very creative." He gives me a wink, then points to another orca whose dorsal fin rivals that of the grandmother's. "See how she has a curve, just there at the top? And how her saddle patch goes across her back, then looks like an inverted comma? That's her daughter."

I'm admiring the way the sun reflects on her wet black skin when he says, "Would you like to name her Daughter?" Hearing the laughter in his voice, I smile and shove his elbow with mine.

I watch the pod moving underwater, rising at frequent intervals to breathe. Their movements are synchronized, and from the spacing of their dorsal fins and heads, it looks like they stay close, both on the surface and underwater. The combined mist from their exhales hangs low across the green surface.

"Okay, funny man, let's name her Atma. If you've spent any time meditating—which I haven't—you'll recognize it as the Sanskrit word for 'breath' or 'spirit.'"

Nudging me with his shoulder, he says, "It's perfect. But how do you know a Sanskrit word if you don't meditate?"

"I had a client in Austin who changed her name to Atma. I told her one day what a beautiful name that was, and she told me what it meant, and that her parents had named her Kelly. No idea why she wanted to change it. Where I'm from, you stick with the name you're given. I'm lucky my mom was into flowers and not famous women outlaws. You could be talkin' to a Calamity Jane right now."

Keet chuckles and leans into my shoulder again. Still looking out at the water, I return the lean. "Who's next?"

Keet points to another orca, who's floating on the surface, giving us more time to look at her.

"What do you see?" he asks.

"Her dorsal fin is shorter than Atma's, and straighter. Oh! It has a large, jagged piece at the top."

"Yes, probably a boat accident. She's lucky that's all she has to remember it by. She's Atma's younger sister." He's silent then, and I notice he's breathing in time with her.

Then I realize what I'm really seeing, and feeling.

"You like her. You like all of them."

He rests his elbows on the bow rail and, still gazing at the relaxing orca, says, "Yes, I do. I've been watching them for a long time. I feel like they're family."

"I get that. My dogs have felt like family to me, too. You're lucky—you know where to find them so you can keep in touch."

Each orca floats like a slick, black log on the surface. The sounds of the sea lapping at the side of the boat, the whales rising and falling like the sea they swim through, and Keet's soft breathing beside me lull me. I feel sleepy, even though I woke up today well rested.

"What are they doing?"

Keet stands up and lets out a long, slow breath. "They're sleeping." He sits down on the deck, crossing his long legs and pulling his cap off.

"Should we go?" I ask, sitting down next to him. I know I don't like to be bothered when I'm falling asleep.

"We will, soon. You have the rest of the orcas to name, remember. So, who is she, this sister to Atma?"

"That makes her the baby's aunt, right? Tia, then. It's Spanish."

"I can see we have an international pod here," Keet smiles.

He points, "Next to Tia, there is another female. Her dorsal fin is unmarked—"

I interrupt him with a laugh. "Does that mean she's smarter and stays out of the way of boats?" My quick mouth has gotten me into trouble yet again. I just insulted his family.

Keet takes a breath and says, "It's got nothing to do with intelligence. Orcas have the second largest brain on the planet, next only to sperm whales. Their brain outweighs ours, is more complex than ours, and has areas we have no clue about how they use. For all we know, their consciousness is so expanded, we can't imagine what they know or how they experience their world."

It's the most I've heard him say at one time, and the most impassioned.

"Sorry. My mouth sometimes gets ahead of my clearly slower brain."

"Apology accepted. As penance, give Atma's daughter the most beautiful name you can think of."

"No pressure," I say, before looking again at the resting pod again, and her rounded saddle patch and shiny black dorsal fin.

"How about Bellisima? Belle for short?"

"Is that Italian?"

"It is. It means 'beautiful.'" I'm relieved to see his smile is back.

"Really? That's the best you've got?"

"Just for that, you get to name the baby. He's a boy, right?"

"Yep, and his name is George," Keet leans back on his hands, basking in his own cleverness.

"George? George?"

"Say it one more time and then ask me why." He's playing with me now, his tone mocking but his brown eyes bright with the same self-satisfaction I see when he names some obscure song I'm trying to stump him with.

"All right, I'll bite. Why George?"

"Because he's curious, like the monkey."

Then I remember the books my mom read to me when I was a kid. The Curious George series was my favorite. When I was being cantankerous, my mom would shout "Magnolia George!" as though that were my given middle name.

"I don't see the male orca. Didn't you say this is his mother's pod?"

"Yes, it is, but he doesn't spend all his time with them."

"Which one is his mom?" I look out over the black fins bobbing above the sunlit water, trying to remember their markings.

"The one you call Atma. Nana is *her* mom, Tia is Atma's sister. Belle is Atma's daughter."

I smile at the thought of this family—together for such a long time, resting here as though they don't have an entire ocean in which to roam. Human families could take notes from orcas.

"Do you have a name for the big male orca?" he asks.

"You know, I can't seem to find it. Maybe if he swam by, I could think of something." I can picture the big male, the large notch in the middle of his dorsal fin, the heft and bulk of his back as he surfaces for a breath. But of his name, I don't have even a whisper of an idea.

I point to the last female we haven't named. George is bobbing next to her, letting his body bump into hers as the waves move them both. "Her dorsal fin is rounder than the others. I can't see her saddle patch."

"It's thinner across the top. When she leaps, you can see it swoops toward her eyepatch. It's grayer than it is white. She's Tia's daughter."

I think for a minute, no longer distracted by the way Keet's knee bumps into mine each time the boat rocks.

"Poppy?"

"A flower name," and he shifts closer to me, and now I feel his shoulder and his knee against mine.

He must've seen something in my face then because he then says, "Am I too close?" and moves away.

"No. I mean yes. Oh, hell, I don't know what I mean." I pat the recently vacated space next to me and say, "You're all right . . . come on back over here."

Keet shifts closer. "I don't mean to make you uncomfortable. Tell me to back off if you want to." He looks at me, searching my eyes with his. "You rarely let your expressions give you away, Nolee. But when I was close to you, you seemed . . . alarmed, maybe?"

The honesty of his gaze and the rich sound of his voice are a type of sincerity I haven't experienced in a long time. This is a new sensation, a man being open with and to me. All those years with Nathan's secrecy and guile left me with the unhealthy expectation that I was always being kept in the dark.

"It wasn't because I'm afraid of you, Keet. I mean, I don't know you very well . . . yet." *Hush girl*, I tell myself. "But it's been a long time since a man has paid any attention to me. I spent a lot of years being invisible to the one person who was supposed to see me the most clearly. Turns out, feeling visible scares me, even though it's what I think I want."

In the silence, I listen to the breathing of the whales as they bob away from the cove.

"I thought they were sleeping?"

"They are, but they can swim and sleep and breathe all at the same time."

"How is that even possible?"

"Only half of their brain's asleep; the other half takes care of business." Keet nudges me with his shoulder and smiles. "Deflect much?"

I laugh and brush a strand of hair away out of my face. Keet waits for my answer.

"Oof, I am *so* out of practice with stuff like this," I mutter.

"Stuff like what?"

"Talking about something that not the weather, or my horrible marriage, or . . ." I stutter, frustrated that I can't articulate it.

"Nolee, you don't have to talk about anything if you don't want to. I'm happy just sharing this day with you."

I gulp back my frustration. "Well, that's one way to make me speechless."

"How's that?" He's leaning back on his hands so that only our outstretched legs are touching.

"Give me a compliment. You know," and I can't stop myself now, "these patterns I developed with Nathan, they're still there. I have a new life, new friends, new environment, new house, and none of it seems to matter. I'm still tied up in them." I thump the deck of his boat with my palm, frustrated that I can't change my way of seeing the world.

Watching the horizon bob up and down, I close my eyes so the swaying in my belly doesn't turn into an embarrassing episode of heaving up lunch over the rail. I slow my breathing and try to match it to the receding breathing of the orcas, as I saw Keet do earlier.

"Nolee? You okay?"

"Finer than frog's hair, as my Great-Aunt Bee would say."

"That's Buttercup, right?"

I open my eyes and nod, feeling as though I'm cutting through a dense web of silence, one that I'd wrapped myself in.

"I fought so long to be visible to Nathan, and I never was, no matter what I did or said or who I tried to make myself into. When I realize you see me, and not only that, but that we get along so well, it really knocks me for a loop."

Keet takes this in, smiling, then nudges my booted foot with his. Looking into my eyes, he asks, "What does it feel like to be visible again?"

I dart a quick glance again to his face, so near mine, and say the first word that comes into my head. "Terrifying." He nods turning his gaze out to the horizon. I feel the gentle rocking of the boat in the sway of my body, up and down and side to side, holding without pushing.

"I get that. Probably more than you know." His shoulder bumps into mine and when I look at him again, I see flecks of light brown in his dark eyes.

"It's just that," I give a nervous laugh, "for so many years I thought I was okay on my own. But you know what makes loneliness worse?"

"Tell me."

"When you're with someone and they don't even know you're there. Or who you are. Even after years together . . . maybe even *because* of years together." I knuckle the tears away from my eyes, determined not to bring all the darkness of my past to this bright day on the water.

His voice, when he answers me, is low and close to my ear. "I understand that kind of loneliness." He pauses. "Do you think he was lonely too?"

I can feel anger boiling up in me, the fibers of my self-spun web strong and tempting me with their protection. After taking a deep breath, I reply. "I would guess so, since he started having an affair."

The boat rocks and bobs. Looking out at the shifting horizon, I realize that all the black fins are gone. The pod has drifted away. I get up and stand gripping the rail, rubbing the tears from my cheeks and trying to get a grip.

Keet joins me, standing close and staying silent. As the sea breeze dries my tears, I realize that it had never crossed my mind that Nate's rejection was about him being lonely as well and doing something about it. The anger still burns, however, anger that he couldn't be honest with me about what was going on.

I turn to Keet, the profile of his face chiseled and dark against the afternoon sky.

"At the risk of sounding like I'm taking sides—which I'm not—it seems to me that affairs are about something lacking between two people, whether it's communication, or trust, or honesty."

"Are you saying I had a part in his affair? Because I'm not seeing it."

"I'm not saying anything, because I wasn't there. You and Nate were. But I can tell you that Sascha and I—" He stops, glancing at me. "We dealt with this same thing. She was in LA, a beautiful and well-known model. Of course, men tempted her. And she gave into those temptations. More than once. She used to tell me that if I moved in with her, she wouldn't need to have sex with other men."

"She blamed you?"

"She did. I did, too, after all my anger and hurt ran out. After that, I beat myself up for not being able to live in Los Angeles. I tried, and I couldn't. Then I realized that the easiest solution was to not be together. If our being far apart was that difficult, the logical thing to do was break up. Save us both the pain."

"I don't honestly know what I would've done if Nate told me about his affair early on. Looking back, I had two responses to anything he told me: silence, or yelling."

Keet, his eyes on the horizon, leans closer to me.

"But," I continue, "we were both definitely lacking in the honesty department. Still. I wish I would've known sooner."

"Maybe he was as scared as you were lonely."

"Hmm. Keet?"

"Nolee?" There's the smile again, the one that reaches his eyes. There's no pity or doubt in their dark depths. He's not taking back his remarks or second-guessing what he said.

"How is it you can just . . . I don't know . . . *be* with all that garbage I just came out with?"

He folds his hands and leans his elbows on the rail, putting himself closer to my eye level. "Because it's not garbage. It's just emotion. From what little you've told me, it doesn't sound like emotion was allowed in your marriage. It's got to come out some way, Nolee. You can't hold all that energy inside and expect it to disappear. To me, it's like sailing. To get somewhere, you've got to have a good wind and a strong sail. When you block your emotions, it's like trying to hold back the wind."

"You helped me more in ten minutes than my therapist back in Texas did in six months. Sure you're only a sailor?" The corners of his mouth quirk up at my weak attempt at humor.

"Just someone who pays attention."

I watch as he raises the anchor, moves to the sails, then to the helm. We begin to glide away slowly from the cove and back out to the channel that will take us to the marina. I hear him call to me over the wind.

"Poppy's a great name for her."

I turn my face to the sea spray, happy that the wetness on my face isn't of my own making.

Once we're back at the marina and he's tied off the boat, I step on to the dock. My legs and brain still think we're on the boat. It's not an unpleasant sensation.

"You might feel as though you're still on the water for a little while," Keet says from beside me.

His voice breaks through my insight, and I realize my eyes were closed as I enjoyed the back-and-forth sway.

"Is it that obvious?"

"It happens. Some people like it, some don't." He turns and finishes tying off the line to the dock.

"Put me in the former category, then." Shopping bag in one hand, I give him a one-armed hug. "If I say thank you again, you'll think I don't have much of a vocabulary."

"There's nothing wrong with your vocabulary, Nolee. Besides, I'd forgotten how great it is to share sailing, and my orca pod, with someone who gets it. All of it."

We step apart, and he says, "I'm going to be gone for a bit, but I'll call when I get back."

"Going sailing for a while?"

He pauses and then turns away from me. When he turns back, he says, "Something like that."

"Okay. No more nosy questions." I smile at him again and flick my wind-whipped braid over my shoulder. "Have a great trip and call me when you can."

I take the stairs up from the dock and walk to my car. Putting the bag on the front seat, I turn and see Keet watching me. I wave, he waves back, and I get into the car and drive home. The pleasure of the day is dampened by knowing I won't see Keet for a while.

Back at the cabin, I stand on the porch, still feeling the sea's rock and sway. Out of habit, or because it makes me feel good, I look over at Keet's house. He's not there, and he won't be for a while. It's time for me to focus on what inhabits my own life, rather than using Keet to discover what excites me.

I walk in the house and close the door with a slam, then grab my phone to Facetime with Abbie. Just as I open it, I see a text from Nate.

Coming to the wedding, or not?

Typical. No *Hello*, no *How are you?* I get ready to fire off a peevish text, then remember that it's been more than a month since he asked. I erase what I'd typed and start over. *Thinking about it. When do you need a firm answer?*

Putting the phone down on the table, my gaze is again drawn to Keet's house. I turn so I can look out the window at the ocean instead, watching the movement of the waves in the late afternoon sun. The thumping of my heart softens, and I unclench my jaw. My phone pings. Nate again. *It would be good if you can make up your mind sooner rather than later. Our caterer is having fits.*

I sigh and walk out of the cabin, straight to the log. I can still feel the heat of the day captured in its white, water-softened surface. Thoughts of Texas, Nate and Carlos, and the expectation that I'll be the gracious ex-wife pull me down. I think about what saying yes to Nate would require: taking the ferry away from the island, driving for two hours back into a crush of cars and people, getting on a plane, then getting in a car again. All to be around friends and family, many of whom haven't answered my texts or emails.

That's when I see it. The woman I was when I got here is gone. Maybe she was the woman who'd been invisible for so long, she couldn't even see herself. In the two months I've been on the island, I've done and seen and thought so many things that were new to me. My new life was adding muscle and bone and skin to the skeleton I'd made myself into. Being invisible had been a choice, and I could choose something else if I wanted.

I did want. More than the travel, or the awkward interactions that every social event brought, I didn't want to go back to a place and to people who'd convinced me to believe I was something I wasn't. That part of me could rest in peace.

My first text is to Abbie. *Hi, honey. I wanted to let you know I won't be coming to your father's wedding. I hope you have a great time! xo*

The next goes to Nate. *You can let your caterer know there's one less person to have fits about.* I read it before hitting send, and although the snark feels incredibly deserved and is almost too appealing, I erase it. *I appreciate the invite but won't be able to make it.* I hit send before the doubt outweighs my conviction.

Once back in the cabin, I take a can of soup out of the pantry. I open the refrigerator and sigh. Soup, cheese, and crackers for dinner—again.

NINE

The orca is a slow-rolling spiral of black and white, sending out low-to-high creaky-door calls that ricochets off the sea floor. In his mind's eye, he can see the slope of the land as it angles to the shore. The hiss of the waves on rocks accompanies his own clicks, crescendos, and bird-like sounds. The picture changes, and he bounces a series of quick clicks off the seal he now hears swimming away. Her progress is slow and unhurried, and he floats in the murky green, giving the seal the distance she needs.

He exhales as he seeks the surface, and the water is frothy with bubbles by the time he rises. Air, warmer than the water, envelops his dorsal fin first, then his back. He dives before flipping around and, with a powerful thrust of his tail, pushing his head out of the water. He's in the bay that he often frequents, but of the humans, there isn't a sound. The orca inhales a rush of warm air and dives deep, swimming first nose down, then rolling from one side to the other. The cold water caresses his body, and he slips through it, lovers enamored with the touch of one another. Gulls follow his flashing black-and-white form until it's clear he's not feeding; with a tilt of their wings, they soar closer to shore.

He swims with urgency, sending out a repeating cry, looking for his pod beyond the cliff that grows out of the water. Their song echoes from the deeper waters, and he tilts his body west, feeling the sound that binds them shorten, a bond that's unbreakable. He arcs above the dark water, his dorsal fin rocking in the air, his flippers and flukes connected to his lover, the sea.

After a week of snacks and takeout, Keet's invitation is not only welcomed by my stomach but also by my mind; I've missed his company. I'm making friends with the other volunteers at the shelter, and I enjoy my pet-shop stints with Chena. But besides them, there's no one else I see regularly.

I explain all this to Keet, thanking him again for the dinner invitation. He smiles as he places a thick handful of dark-green leaves on the counter.

"I've missed your company, too, Nolee."

The sound of Keet's scissors cutting through the large leaves brings my attention to them.

"Is that kale?" I can't keep the surprise from my voice.

"It is," he answers, moving the kale from the counter to a colorful pottery bowl. He drizzles olive oil over it, along with a pinch of salt from a bamboo salt cellar. After washing his hands in the sink, he plunges them wrist-deep into the kale and begins working it between his fingers.

I feel the air between us change as I watch the muscles of his forearms ripple under his skin. I clear my throat before saying to him, "You know what I think about food that needs a massage before it's edible?"

He glances up at me, not stopping his ministrations to the pulverized leaves. "Nope."

"Any food you have to massage isn't fit for the dinner table."

As soon as it's out of my mouth, what sounded clever now just sounds ungrateful. The man is cooking me dinner and I, in my discomfort, hoping to be witty, have insulted his choice.

But before I can apologize, he laughs. He sets his wrists against the edge of the bowl and throws back his head, then wipes one eye with the back of his wrist.

I smile uncertainly before saying, "And you know what I think about guests who insult the chef's meal-prep technique?"

Still chuckling, he shakes his head.

"They aren't fit for the dinner table either."

He glances at me, and I can tell he's not upset by my remarks, which is kind of a novelty. Not many people tolerate my humor; Abbie does, but otherwise, I try to keep it in check. My quick mouth has gotten me in trouble more times than I can recall. It certainly didn't endear me to Nathan, who was often on the receiving end of my sharp bite.

"I think you're fit for *my* dinner table, and I also think you're going to be amazed by this kale."

"I'll take an extra helping, then."

After we eat, I'm clearing the table and carrying the plates to the sink when he says, "I was thinking last week after our kayak lesson that if you wanted to take the single out by yourself, you can give that a try."

The plates go in the sink and then I turn and smile at him, feeling a rush of warm joy so intense I want to hug him. I've covered half the distance between us, drawn by his dark eyes and solid presence, before I stop. "You don't know how much I'd love that! Not that you aren't great company and a wonderful teacher . . ." I trail off, unsure how to fix what I've just said.

"I get it—solo kayaking is different than having company."

"Yes." I pause, rooted to the spot where I'm standing. "You know, when I work with a dog by itself, without having to talk to its owner, there's almost a different sort of reality happening. The dog and I have a mutual understanding, one that goes beyond language. Or even species."

I pause, trying to put into words something I've not tried to explain before, or even thought about consciously. "It's a meeting place where we experience something together that's more than dog or human." I look out the window at the light of a half-moon on the bay. "We are each of those things, but also more than. I feel like the dog and I become a living Venn diagram ." I shake my head. "Does any of that make sense?"

I look back at Keet, and he nods. "Yes. When I'm sailing, or swimming, there's a point where I feel like I'm not human at all—just water. And waves."

"When you let me join the tour, I noticed the way you held the steering wheel." When he lowers his eyes and smiles, I think, *Lord, will I ever get that right?* "Helm, I mean. You didn't grip it. You just rested your hands there, and your whole body went with the movement of the boat."

Keet nods. "Yes. The sea, the boat, and me. A watery Venn diagram."

"Exactly! I feel it a little now that I'm getting better at kayaking, and without a dog, I think I've been missing getting out of my narrow point of view. Watching you and Alex on the sailboat, seeing you both so at ease, it made me curious if I could feel that with the sea too."

I hear a new song playing in the background.

"Ok, human playlist, who, what, and when is this song?"

He smiles and says, "Mills Brothers, 'Cab Driver,' 1950-something."

"You don't have the exact year?"

"Not at the moment, no." I can't break away from the smoldering I see in his eyes. He takes a step closer and says, "Besides, I think the word 'jukebox' would be more appropriate."

"Only for you, Keet Noland."

I turn and walk back to the sink, intending to wash up before walking home. Doing something other than giving in to the urge to kiss Keet.

"You can leave it, Nolee."

"Rule is, whoever cooks doesn't clean."

"And whose rule is that?"

I turn on the hot water and add some dish soap, then start washing. "Mine. You're kind to cook us dinner. And you're tidy enough that there's not a lot for me to clean, anyway. A few dishes are my way of saying thanks."

"Then who am I to prevent you from expressing your gratitude." I glance at him and watch as he pulls out a chair and lowers himself into it. How can a man that tall be that graceful? I turn my concentration to the dishes.

"I'm taking a few clients out tomorrow. I'll be away for a couple of days."

"Thank you for trusting me in one of your kayaks." I put the plates in the dish rack to dry and start on the forks and knives.

"Promise me you'll stay close to shore, and not go out if the sea looks choppy." I agree, rinsing the silverware and turning off the hot water. The slick, soapy water runs over my hands as I wring out the dishcloth out and hang it over the edge of the sink to dry.

"Scout's honor."

I walk by Keet, putting my hand on his shoulder. "Thanks again for the amazing meal. It would've been an apple and peanut butter tonight otherwise."

He looks up at me and then stands, his eyes not leaving mine. Now he's close enough for me to give him that hug. Instead, I look up at him, losing my breath. He reaches over to touch my cheek and says, "Can I walk you home?" I nod and turn toward the door, finding my breath again.

Flicking the switch on the flashlight I had remembered this time, we go down the steps. I'm once again struck by how quietly he moves—much more quietly than me, and I'm quite a bit smaller. Then I laugh to myself as I realize that unless I'm with a dog, I walk like I'm mad at the ground.

What's funny?" he asks. He's walking close, hands in the pockets of his jeans.

"I was just thinking how you're so quiet when you walk, and I'm like a bull in a china shop. When I work with dogs, things get quieter, but otherwise I walk like I'm throwing a tantrum."

I hear a hum of amusement from Keet, but no reply. I imagine how I'd walk if there was a dog trotting on the other side of me. My steps lengthen and relax, and I move with the earth instead of on top of it.

The night is dark, and the light from the flashlight throws a glowing circle on ground covered by rocks and sand turned monochrome in its glow. The waves are thundering in the night, the tide coming in, and with no wind, it could be just Keet and I, walking between the worlds we both know, a Venn diagram in motion.

We're at my porch steps before I want to be. After we hug, he stays at the bottom as I cross the porch and open the door. I turn and see him standing, half shadow, half man. I freeze for a moment, my mind grasping for a memory that refuses to float to the surface. Then I catch myself and say, "I'll let you know how the kayaking goes when you get back. Thanks again for dinner."

"You're welcome. Food tastes better when there's someone to share it with, doesn't it?"

"It does, and especially when someone else makes it."

He laughs again. I enjoy making him laugh. His otherwise serious expression gives way to a quick and easy smile, as though he takes himself lightly.

"Goodnight, Nolee. See you in a couple of days."

I wave, close the door, flick on the light, and wonder what I can do for two days to keep from thinking about my neighbor. I pull out my phone and text Abbie.

I met someone. His name is Keet, and we've been spending some time together.

She highlights my message with exclamation points, and then I get a text.

That's great, Mom! More details!

I smile, wondering why I've not shared this with my daughter. She's far more accepting of another man in my life than even I've been.

My phone rings, and a photo of Abbie in a pink UT hoodie standing in front of the Blanton Museum of Art pops up.

We talk into the night. As much as I have to say about Camas Island and Keet, she has more to tell me about her classes and the guys she's dating. When I hang up, I'm still smiling. All talked out about Keet, I get ready for bed and fall asleep to the sound of the sea against the rocky shore.

A pale blue sky and calm waves greet me the next morning. While eating breakfast on the porch and looking over at Keet's house, I wonder at the dance we're doing. At this stage of my life, I'm aware that my past's getting in the way of my present. Enough of that . . . time to get out on the water and give thinking about Keet a rest.

After I push off and find the rhythm of the paddles, I point myself away from the sun, enjoying the warmth of the morning rays on my back. It's the middle of June, but the breeze is chilly and I'm glad for the extra layer of my life vest. I stay parallel to the shore, getting to know the sea's mood and how she wants to guide my little kayak. Then, turning the way Keet showed me, slow and steady, I point the kayak's orange bow toward the channel.

The rhythmic paddling—the repeating infinity sign that Keet goes on about—weaves its way into my body. My breathing slows, and I sense the ocean rowing through me, instead of the other way around. I glance over my shoulder, and seeing that I'm farther out than I intended, turn to make my way back to shore.

As I'm turning, I see a black dorsal fin, a fluid blade cutting through dark water. The orca's exhale sends vapor rising through the sunlight, creating a sundog before disappearing into the sky. An enormous head appears, the white patches above his eyes a startling contrast with his body and the water. The towering notched dorsal fin tells me that it's the male orca. I stop paddling and swallow, hoping my stomach stays in its rightful place.

He's closer now, rising and falling, changing course so that he's parallel to the kayak. From this perspective, both close and at water level, I see the wobble of his dorsal fin as he sinks into the water. Glancing toward land, I wonder if paddling would activate some ancient cetacean chase-and-catch instinct in him.

Girl, he rescued a Chihuahua. *You're fine!*

I take a breath and turn the kayak with slow strokes using only my left paddle and aim toward shore. The orca swims on my left (*port, Nolee*), matching my halting progress, which must be like an adult shadowing a baby who's just learning to walk.

He points the blunt mass of his head down and goes under the kayak, and I have a fleeting thought about being capsized. Then, with a flash of white belly and tail, he spirals upright and rises to the surface just out of reach of my paddle. Looking at him at his level on the water is so far out of my realm of understanding that I can't, for a moment, respond. I'm frozen, the paddle across my lap, the sea lapping at the kayak with soft knocks and hisses, the orca doubling back for another pass underneath me. The only thing between me and this thirty-foot wolf of the sea is a small kayak that feels flimsy compared to his bulk. I wonder if he can hear, or feel, the tremor that's taking over my legs.

He doesn't come close to touching the kayak, though. Instead, he pokes his head out of the water, "spyhopping" as Keet calls it, and blows an exhale before swimming by, first on the left, then on the right. *Port, starboard*, I think.

A memory from my childhood surfaces. During a road trip to El Paso, we passed a truck larger than any I'd ever seen. It towered above our compact car, blocking the sun. We saw other semis that day, but that first impression of an enormous beast never left me. I felt we'd narrowly escaped rousing the attention of a giant.

This sense of being dwarfed and insignificant in the face of something so alien is the same. The male orca has erased everything else but himself. In his presence, I feel freed, unmoored from an ocean of endless personal doubts. My trembling body grows quiet, and my death grip on the paddle loosens.

Not feeling silly at all, I call out to him. "Hello, you."

He swims toward me, his dorsal fin parting the waves in a thin V behind him. Stopping abruptly before hitting the boat, he rolls onto his side again, looking at me through a black eye that seems to hold the secrets of the universe. A singular stillness, lost and found again in the gaze of the orca, replaces my fear.

Leaning over, my hand on the side of the kayak, I could reach out and touch him, but I don't. He's too magnificent to treat like a petting-zoo animal. I can see his saddle patch, a gray and white pattern that reminds me of the symbol used for hurricanes: a circle with a strand of white swirling around it.

"You're stunning, you know." He blows bubbles and makes a sound suspiciously like one Nathan made after eating my mom's three-bean chili.

"Hey," I laugh, "that's not funny!" He floats just beneath the surface, lying along the length of the kayak, his tail beating lazily against the pull of the tide. One flick of that giant tail, and I'll be in the water with him. I can't remember if Keet said that he's one of the Resident fish-eating orcas, or a Transient that hunts other mammals. Another flutter of fear ripples through my stomach, then he makes the three-bean-chili sound again.

"Okay, it's a little funny." He exhales, then inhales, once more, then arcs away from the kayak. The last I see of him is his lowering dorsal fin, disappearing, pointed away from Osprey Bay.

I turn the front of the kayak (*the bow*, I remind myself) back toward the cabin, and practice re-establishing a steady paddle rhythm. The day seems brighter. I'm not trembling anymore, and there's a fizz of excitement in my belly, as though I've swallowed honeybees and they're swirling around, trying to escape. I laugh and tilt my face to the sun, pausing with the paddle across my lap, my joy as vast as the gentle rhythm of the sea.

Halfway to the rocky beach, as I try to raise one blade out of the water, it feels heavy . . . stuck. I look at the blade, only to see that the something it's stuck in is the big orca's mouth. Once he sees me looking at him, he exhales an explosion of water droplets, then gives a high-pitched squeak, releasing the paddle and making a graceful twirl before swimming away again. I wipe the salt water away from my face, watching the retreating dorsal fin knife between sea and sky. He was beside me and then gone so quickly, I wonder if I imagined it. But I know I'm not imagining the smell of his fishy breath drifting back to me on the breeze.

"See you later," I call out. Smiling to myself, I think that this has been the best first solo kayak outing in the history of kayaking.

TEN

Dragging the kayak onto the shore, slick kelp and small bits of rock caught in my water shoes, I shiver at the icy water washing over my bare legs. But if getting to be with orcas requires dealing with cold water, it's something I'll gladly do.

The rest of the day passes, the light long and easy, the waves quiet. I finish one book and start another. When the light softens and I've switched positions three times in as many minutes, I know it's time to get up and do something else.

I go in the kitchen, wondering what I can make for dinner that requires the least amount of effort. Cooking, and everything that's needed to do it, is such a nuisance. Momma was a fantastic cook, and she seemed to enjoy it. I smile at the memory.

Keet seems to like it too, his attention absorbed by the food and its preparation. I look out the window at the sea, growing darker as the sun sinks, and wonder where he is, and if I'll hear from him when he gets back. Or would the time away make him realize that he's fine without someone else, safer on his own. That thought has occurred to me, more than once. When I see him again, the resolve not to get tangled up with another man leaves my head as though I'd never thought it.

Watching the sky wash from pale gold to orange, I smile when I think of Keet. I'm going to be just fine, with or without Keet Noland. But I might like a chance to find out what "with him" would be like.

The answering machine's red light is blinking. Everyone I know has my cell phone, but only three have the landline number: Abbie, Ava, and Keet. I push the play button, not sure whose voice I hope to hear.

"Nolee. It's Keet. I'm back earlier than I'd planned. Wondering if you want to have dinner again tomorrow? I caught some salmon I'd like to make for you. I'll be home tomorrow morning. Check in with me then? Bye."

I play the message a second time just to hear his deep voice and realize that, of course, I knew who I wanted it to be. Of course, I'm going to keep an eye out for him and accept his dinner invitation. Of course.

"The light here plays tricks," Nolee says. "It looks like what would be seven in the evening back home, but it's almost nine. I can see why Ava hung blackout curtains in the bedroom; it never really gets full dark this time of year, does it?"

"No, it doesn't." Keet answers, placing the wooden platter of salmon on the table. "Can you grab the silverware?"

She opens a drawer and takes out two sets of forks, knives, and spoons, laying a hand on his arm before walking away. He smells a hint of roses, and citrus. He snaps back before he follows her, drawn like a ripple in her wake, and looks at the table instead. Salmon, black rice sprinkled with pine nuts, a salad made with greens he bought at the farmer's market, and the sunflower-seed bread Nolee picked up at the bakery. The cruet of pale-yellow salad dressing glows in the light that spills out over the table.

"Are we missing anything?" he asks her.

"Not that I can see. Did I tell you I found the last dark chocolate lava cake at the bakery? They even sent me away with raspberry coulis. What the hell is raspberry coulis, anyway?"

Keet laughs. "It's a fancy name for sauce. In this case, made from raspberries; you drizzle it over the cake. Have you had it before?"

"I don't think so. I would've remembered that."

After they sit down, Keet asks, "Tell me about your orca encounter yesterday."

Nolee stops putting food on her plate, bows her head, and when she looks at him again, there are tears in her eyes. Although he's not uncomfortable with her tears, it surprises him that the orca had such a profound effect on her.

"Where do I start, Keet? How do I even capture the . . . magic? Can't believe I'm using that word, by the way. I was out kayaking, and he was in the cove. I'd wondered if he was nearby; the seal wasn't around."

"His diet is salmon. Around here, only Bigg's eat mammals, and they rarely come in this far."

"Tell that to the seal." She lays her fork down on her plate. "He was huge, Keet. Not just his length, but the sheer bulk of him. You know," she continues, dousing her salad with the dressing, "one reason I don't like horses is because they're so big. My father wanted to make a horsewoman out of me, and I fought him every step of the way."

"Did you feel differently after you knew more about horses, or do you just not like them?"

"I knew enough—and cared enough—that I could get a job done and not trouble them too much. It never felt right, though, to sit on a creature who was so majestic. Riding them, ordering them around because we could. Once I grew up, I was the only one on the ranch who rode without spurs; that's one thing my dad could never change my mind on. But it was always a chore, being with horses. It never felt good. The thing that changed it was when we started taking dogs out to help with the cattle. I was eight, and it was love at first sight. By the time I was eleven, I was training them on my own, and only rode my horse to keep up with the dogs."

"So, what do horses have to do with the orca?" As he dips the bread in rosemary olive oil, it occurs to him that the meals he's shared with Nolee feel enjoyable. The realization brings everything into sharper focus: Nolee and the light on her hair; her face, animated by excitement; the way her hands trace pictures in the air as she talks. The way her sweater follows the curve of her shoulders and breasts.

"Well, his size, and how close he was. Even with the kayak, I'm small in comparison. I'm completely in his element, at his mercy. It took me back to those years on the ranch, riding horses. Once you're on their backs, you can only hope you're also in their good graces. When he was there, it was like . . . like time stopped."

Nolee places her fork on her plate and leans forward, looking at him as though she's trying to transmit what she's feeling directly into him with her bright green eyes.

"I sometimes get that sensation when I'm working with a dog—that time doesn't have a hold on me anymore. I was so afraid when I knew the orca was not only in the cove with me, but swimming closer. It made me shake, and the only thing I could do was try to stay still and hope that I was in his good graces that day."

She picks up her fork and continues eating. "This meal is amazing."

What he wants to say is that she's amazing, that in her presence he feels himself waking up, as though the sun is shining on his closed eyes, the light coaxing him to see. Instead, he says "Thanks."

She continues her story. "He swam up right next to the boat. I felt completely irrelevant. Not like I was unimportant, but more like a tiny part of an enormous universe. Looking into his eye was like touching that universe. Being with the orca made me wonder why we focus on outer space when there are beings here on earth that are so obviously intelligent and have such a different experience of life and this planet than we do. Why aren't we trying to understand them more?"

"I wonder that myself." He folds his napkin and places it on top of his empty plate.

"You know," she says. "If I really wanted to get woo-woo, I'd say he knew I was nervous and was trying not to scare me. He made a noise like a kid blowing bubbles in the water . . . well, it was ruder than that." She laughs and Keet laughs with her. "And instantly, the experience went from mystical to hilarious. We were communicating, in some odd and foreign way, but we were."

She leans forward. "Please tell me I'm not crazy for feeling that way."

"As you would say, you're preaching to the choir, Nolee." He smiles and reaches across the table to touch her hand. Their fingers intertwine, and he's surprised at how strong her grip is. She always uses her hands with softness, but their power tells him that her gentleness isn't because of a lack of strength.

"All these years of being with the pod, which I really think of as *my* pod . . . if I've learned nothing else, it's that communication can happen in all kinds of ways, not just with our five senses, or even just with their vocalizations. I've felt things and known things in their presence that I can't, even now, explain."

She gives his hand a squeeze and releases it. "Thank you, Keet. I had a hunch you'd understand."

He watches as Nolee finishes her meal, and she notices him watching her.

"God, have you ever seen anyone shovel food into their mouth like I do?" She finishes the last couple of bites, then takes both their plates to the sink.

As she washes the plates, she says, "I still don't have a name for him."

He smiles. "Maybe his name is how he makes you feel."

"I'm going to need a minute to chew on that one, Keet. What I *can* say is that you've done a rare thing."

"What's that?" She's got her head cocked to one side, and her mouth curves up in a small half-grin.

"You've made a Burnett speechless."

He laughs, and feels a jolt of recognition pass through him, the feeling that he's found someone he's always known.

Dishes done, she moves to the refrigerator and brings out the cake.

"I think we need to celebrate my first solo kayak outing with cake. And some raspberry syrup."

As they dive into dessert, she asks between mouthfuls, "Enough about me. You said you grew up in Sitka?"

"I did," he nods. "My mom and dad left when I was eleven; they moved to Nebraska, where my dad was from."

"That must have been hard on you."

"It was. I didn't understand it, but I think I've made my peace with their decision. Plus, I got to know my grandmother. She's a great woman. My grandfather Jack passed away when I was sixteen, but he was important to me as well. He was Tlingit and Athabascan. My dad, Charlie, was white."

"Was?"

"He and my mom died in a car wreck when I was twenty-three."

"I'm sorry to hear that, Keet. Is your grandmother still alive?"

"She is. Growing up, we used to live by the ocean, but now she lives in an apartment in town. Her son, my uncle, takes care of her. Grandmother is in her eighties now, and mentally sharper than I am most days."

Nolee laughs. "Do you see her often?"

"At least once or twice a year, when I head north for a visit."

"Do you sail up there?"

Keet pauses, chasing the last of the raspberry coulis and cake around his plate. "Sometimes. I play it by ear."

"I think I need to look at a map. I still don't know the geography around here."

Keet's grateful for the change in subject. He finishes the last bite of his cake, then stands up, taking Nolee's plate from her.

"My turn to wash. You want some tea?"

"I won't fight you for the dishes, and yes, I'd like some tea. Ginger?"

He moves around the kitchen. His hands are shaking, and he's surprised. He used to see his mother's hands shake just like this, when the battle of trying to stop herself from swimming in the ocean went on too long. He makes two fists, willing them to be still.

"Speaking of sailing, how did you get into the whale-watching business?" She stands at the end of the counter, watching him. He turns away from her to pick up the kettle and pour the steaming water into the mugs, blocking the tremble from her sight.

"One summer, when I came up here to work, I met this this guy, Todd Roberts. He and I were the same age, and we crewed together. Even on our days off, we went sailing. He came into some money a couple of summers after we met and asked if I wanted to go in with him on a boat and start a business. I thought it was a great idea. Gave me a good reason to leave the university."

"Where's Todd now? Does he have his own boat?"

Keet pauses, stirring honey into the tea. He can feel the heat of the mug against his fingertips. In his head, pictures of Todd flash: smiling as he sits at the helm, lying on his back looking at the sky, laughing as Keet dives into the water and comes up again, taunting him to jump in, too. And less happy ones as well: Todd's gaunt face, nose rimmed in white powder and eyes desperate as he begs Keet to give him a month to get clean, begs him to let him sail one more time to Canada to drop off "some product" for his friends.

He's brought back from his memories when Nolee says, "I'm sorry. I'm so curious sometimes—well, nosy—that I forget there are probably things neither of us wants to talk about."

He smiles at her. "We had a falling out, but that's a story for another time. The night is too good to waste it on revisiting ghosts."

"Does that mean he died?"

He shakes his head. "No, he isn't dead, though at the time, I was close to wanting to kill him. He's not in my life anymore, and I try to keep it that way. The past is a corpse; there's no use trying to bring it back to life."

He sees her eyes widen at his words.

"Was that too strong?" he asks, touching her arm.

"No, not at all. I startled because those were almost the exact words that ran through my head while I was on the ferry, thinking I could outrace my heartache."

"If it was heartache you were trying to outrace, you probably needed to be on a faster ship."

They laugh together, and the first tendrils of an emotion he's built a wall against push their way through the cracks.

Nolee takes her flashlight off the shelf by the door. "I must sound like a broken record, but I think you outdid yourself with that meal, Keet."

"Thanks. I think it's good because we're good company for each other."

She smiles up at him, the lines fanning out from her eyes and her nose crinkling. Her skin's pinker than it normally is, as though it's catching the sun that reflects off the sea.

He steps closer, wraps his arms around her shoulders, and feels her embrace around his waist. She rests her cheek against his chest, and he knows she can feel his heart racing. He's unsure, caught between emotion and the logic—the logic of not forming attachments. He needs to swim, is aching for it, yet it seems like background noise now. What has his full attention is how Nolee feels. Her soft curves. Her strong arms.

She steps away before he does and says goodnight. She leaves the pool of light spilling across his front porch, and he watches until she reaches her house and goes inside. Closing the door quietly, he leans against it, lets out a long breath, and decides to swim out from his dock, even if only for a couple of hours—to spend time in the womb of the sea.

The lights in Nolee's cabin flick on, and then minutes later, flick off again. He waits until the light in her bedroom is out, then turns off all the lights in the living room, stripping down to his shorts.

Barefoot, he walks across the rocks and out to the dock. The A-frame cabin is dark. He's almost sure that her curtains are closed and hopes she's in her bed. All thoughts recede as he steps out of his shorts and dives into the cold, dark water. The last thing he hears is a dog barking in the distance. And then the sea has him, and then he swims, no longer trembling, no longer separate.

ELEVEN

Half-awake in the dawn light, I replay the feel of Keet's warm hand on my back when we hugged goodnight. As I rub my face, I try to remember if seeing Keet dive into the black sea was a dream, or something I witnessed.

The sound of a dog barking and howling outside brings me back to the present. Swinging my legs out of bed and shivering at the cool air against my bare skin, I look out of window toward Keet's house. There's a dog on his porch, barking at the partially open door. As I watch, Keet tries to step out, and the dog snaps at his shoe. He pops back in and shuts the door.

The dog gets louder, and I can hear the fear underneath all the noise. Pulling on jeans and a sweatshirt over my nightgown, I bundle my hair into a messy bun and shove my feet into the mud boots. I head through the door and toward the barking.

As I get closer, Keet cracks the door open and shouts at me, "Can you make it go away, please?"

"Good morning," I shout back, hoping he hears me over the noise. The little dog is so incensed that each bark lifts it off its dirty white feet.

I give a whistle and walk closer, and sure enough, the dog rushes off the porch, teeth bared. The barking stops, but the growling begins.

It can't be more than six months old. The white mask on its face, the upright ears, now held stiffly, and the coyote-like slant of its eyes tell me there's Border Collie in there somewhere, but its head is wider, and its filthy red coat is short.

Rather than spend any more time guessing about our noisy intruder, it's time to help her turn down the volume—both literally and figuratively. I turn sideways and look away from her, and the growling stops, replaced by the same noisy volleys. I breathe into my belly, then into my knees, then into my feet. The barking is now unsure, an uneven staccato that's losing its conviction. The red dog circles counterclockwise and faces me again, still barking. Noticing that the mystery pup is probably a female, I turn again so my side is to her. I walk away and squat down, looking out on the bay and continuing to breathe. The barking gets louder, and then stops.

I hear her pad across the gravel, her steps uneven and hesitant. She rumbles a low threat of more barking. She sniffs deeply, taking in the air around me, then snuffles the back of my sweatshirt, and then my jeans. In slow motion, I wrap my arms around my drawn-up knees waiting to see what she does. A tangle of fear and agitation grips my chest, but I know these sensations aren't mine. I breathe into them; she won't bite, and it's my job to provide a calm and safe place for her emotions to go.

As her nose leads her to circle me counterclockwise, I drop my head and look at the ground, seeing all the different colors of the rocks I'm sitting on. One is poking me uncomfortably, so I move a little.

I lift my head up as she passes and refine my earlier guesses. She's probably a little older than six months, and thin. If she is someone's dog, she hasn't seen them in a long time. She passes by again, this time quiet as she walks and sniffs, then comes in closer. I can see the dirt in her coat. She has four white paws, a typical Border Collie cape, and a matching white chest, all of which are caked with dirt.

She stops in front of me again, and I look out to the forest, away from her amber gaze. Her nose lifts to the breeze, and I straighten out my legs and put my hands on my lap. Unsure about this movement, she circles to my back again, sniffing my sweatshirt, my hair, and the waistband of my jeans. *This must be a dog's olfactory buffet*, I think. I lower a hand to the ground, and she startles away, rumbling her disapproval. I'm still breathing deep when I feel her dry nose on my hand. She stalks around me, only going a short distance away, and sits again, not letting me out of her sight.

"Hey, Keet! Open the door!" I see the door open a crack, and his dark eyes squinting out at me.

"Bring two bowls out—one with water, and one with some of the salmon and rice leftovers." I don't turn my head, or move my body, but the young dog is watching the door, and me, alert to any threat to her freedom. I hear the door click shut, and then open again a moment later.

"Just come down the stairs and put them halfway between the house and me."

I see him throw me a skeptical glance and mutter something I can't hear before doing as I asked.

The red dog trots farther away, but isn't barking, though a low hum that might turn into a growl carries in the morning air. Keet closes his door. I'm certain he's watching through the windows, though. I give him points for not hanging around.

The breeze carries the scent of the salmon to me, but it reaches the pup first. She makes a wide circle, trotting for the food and water. She gulps the food down without chewing, then throws a slant-eyed glance over her shoulder before drinking the bowl of water.

"No wonder you're out of sorts. How long has it been since your last meal, red dog?" She cocks her head at the sound of my voice and sits again. I see both bowls are empty. I lean back on my hands, smelling the forest and the salty, fishy smell of the sea before looking at her out of the corner of my eye.

She lies down, her left paw folded under her body, watching me without agitation.

"I bet if I sit here long enough, you might just get sleepy."

Keet's door clicks open. This startles her, and she trots away from the bowls and lays down.

Keet stands on the porch. "She's making me late for work."

"You could've just come out; she's not going to do anything." I smile at the scowl crossing his face, thunder and lightning above a rough sea.

"No, *you* could've just come out. I thought I'd lose a toe. What do we do about her?"

"Let me see if I can convince her she's safe. Some more food and water would be good."

He turns back toward the house, before turning around again and in a voice now more the rumble of a passing storm says, "You've probably already named her, haven't you?"

I smile as I look at her. "Yes. Her name is Fae."

"As in Dunaway?"

I laugh, which startles the dog again, but after one circle she sits, closer to me by inches.

"No, as in the wee magic folk of myths. Kin to faeries."

Keet rolls his eyes and mutters, "Name her Bray–she's as loud as a donkey. Or name her Troll if you want something mythical." The door shuts and I'm left watching Fae, smiling at Keet's irritation.

He comes back out, bowls in hand, and sets them down. Fae gulps down the food, but only drinks half the water. Keet, sitting on the porch's top step, grumbles. "I'm going to have to boil those bowls in hot water now. Dog spit!"

"There's nothing wrong with a little dog spit, or dog hair. And look how beautiful her coat is. My hair used to be that color."

Fae lies down between me and the bowls. Her eyes blink slowly.

"Give her a bath and I bet it's even lovelier," Keet says. I think I detect a note of grudging acceptance before he says in a softer voice, "Your hair is beautiful."

This catches me off guard, and my face burns as I turn my head away from both Fae and Keet. Once I feel the blush recede, I turn to back to him. "Yours isn't too bad either." I change position, then stand up. Fae pops up to her feet, watchful but not barking.

"Come on, Fae, let's see what you think of my place." I walk away, listening for her steps on the rocks. Tossing a wave over my shoulder, I call out, "Thanks, Keet. I'll call you and let you know how we get along."

"You better make sure she's not someone else's. Though, with that charm and personality, I can see why she's on her own. Don't fall asleep with her in the same room, either."

"We'll be fine. Do you mind if I take the kayak out tomorrow?"

"Go for it. Be careful." He waves, shuts his door, and I hear the lock snick into place.

I smile, thinking how much more of *his* personality this stray dog brings out. "Fae" is exactly the right name for her; she's charmed me already. I'm sure at some point soon, she'll charm Keet, too.

I stop at my porch and turn, and there she is. I sit on the step, and she sniffs the air, walking toward me with her tail low and wagging at the tip.

"Well, look at you! Fae, you're going to be all right."

She climbs the steps as far away as she can get from me, circles behind me, and smells my hair again. When I turn toward her, her nose is inches from mine. I snuffle and sigh, and she breaks into a doggie grin and raises a paw. I reach out and give her chest a light scratch. She flops down on her side and shows me her muddy and weed-tangled belly, and I scratch that too. I think I have a new friend.

The gravel pops under Keet's 4Runner as he backs out of his driveway. I give a wave, but he's focused on something else, and he drives away without seeing me. Turning to Fae, I stroke her behind the ears and watch as she closes her amber eyes in pleasure.

TWELVE

The orca is swimming with slow strokes of his tail, his white belly to the surface. He's spent the night diving deep, disappearing from the surface so the motorboats passing overhead can't see him. He closes his eyes—silent, suspended in the cool water, feeling its ebb and flow, letting the sea take him where it wants. There are distant sounds of other boats. He hears the splash of birds and rolls lazily on his side, seeing their paddling feet and pale underbellies.

With a flick of his giant tail, he rolls upright and twists through the water, flashing black-and-white and back to black as he rises to breathe. The air on his dorsal fin is warm, a warmth that skims along his back, given to him by the summer sun. Hearing the whine of boat engines, he dives again, raising his tail above the surface and slapping the water. This time, there's no lazy rolling or feeling the sea's vibrations. He sounds, and pictures of the seabed and fish flash through his brain.

The orca knows exactly where he is, and where he wants to go. He hears the calls of his family, the faint vibrations tickling along his jaw and into his head. In those vibrations, he sees the underwater landmarks, and their swimming and feeding shapes. His answer is high and strident, and then crescendos down to a rumbling that bounces off the sea's floor. He sings a high cry, surfaces to breathe, and dives again, repeating his song, pulled by a force that rules him from rostrum to tail—an embodied longing. The orca knows that only the touch of his family, flippers and tails, sleek bellies and chins, can transform that longing into one of peace.

When he finds them, they leap and dive together, a moving ball of spinning black-and-white that coalesces and breaks apart, comes within a fin's length of each other, touching softly. He arcs above the water, dives, then rolls to watch the baby imitate his moves. They swim together, the smaller whale not tucked into his mother's side as usual, but instead, nudging the big male, nosing along his dorsal fin, rolling along his back.

After their games, they find fish and share with the baby before going to the surface to breathe. In the distance, the pod hears the whine of another boat, high and piercing. They cease their calling; the boat's vibration and noise make their heads ache. They swim in the opposite direction, once again searching for salmon. Each takes a turn sending out clicks, directing attention to distinct parts of the sea, until the male determines a shifting image of the fish below them. Then, they dive as one and herd the salmon toward the surface.

The male orca stops feeding, and hangs in the water, only the tip of his large dorsal fin exposed. He closes his eyes and sounds, and the faint, glimmering image of a kayak in the cove he frequents flashes behind his eyes. He swims away from his pod, sounding and listening, catching in the slipstream of thought, an image that the waves have carried back to him. In the bay he frequents is an overturned kayak. He feels, against his skin and mind, the thrashing person in the water. It's the woman.

The first thing I'm aware of is water sloshing across my face. I'm lying on my belly across something that's rising and falling with the current. My hair, once in a ponytail, is plastered across my eyes as I gulp for breath, then cough. I'm being carried at a slow and steady pace by what feels like a giant, warm inner tube. Shaking my head, coughing more saltwater out of my throat, and taking another breath, I hear the ocean hissing and drumming on the shore. I must be near land. I squint through stinging eyes and see a hazy outline of trees against the sky.

Propping myself up on my hands and barely able to keep my eyes open, I look down and what see snaps me awake. The giant underneath me isn't an inner tube. Though the shiny skin is dark and has a wet pliancy, it vibrates with life. To my left, a giant black dorsal fin rises like a monolith out of the water. I can't see the backside of the fin, but I guess it has a notch at the top. The orca rises, exhales his fishy breath in my face, and gulps air before ducking his head under a wave.

I cough again, collapsing against his solid bulk. I'm shaking so hard I think I'll fall off, lost at sea forever. But the orca swims on, and I feel him shift underneath me to keep me across his back. The life vest is still snug, which I'm grateful for, and even more grateful that I'm draped across the orca's back and not in his mouth.

I can't tell if I'm shivering with cold or terror. My eyes close, the need to sleep overriding my fear, then am doused by a wave as the orca sinks beneath me. I gasp awake. The beach is closer. A slow thought about the danger shallow water might present to the orca drifts through my drowsy brain, replaced by the need to be back on land. There's a sensation of gaining speed, and a giant push. The solid presence beneath me disappears, and my feet slide on the slippery rocks. I crawl out of the water and fall down so I can rest.

"Nolee! Wake up!"

The fog in my brain is thick, gripping me with wet claws. Was it hours or seconds that I'd been lying there? My eyes open, seeing the wet rocks, the strand of broken kelp waving at me in the foam of the retreating tide. I'm shaking hard enough to make my teeth chatter, but I can't stand, so I close my eyes instead.

Something pushes me onto my side, and a fist pounds between my shoulder blades, jarring me awake. I gag and cough up the last of the seawater. My awareness shifts again, a skip of several frames that shudders to a stop. Instead of a broad black back against my cheek and the protection of a dorsal fin touching the sky, there's a hard surface under my head and the smell of wood smoke. I feel my shoes and socks coming off, then my jeans, vest, and shirt. I mumble and try to roll over, not liking the feeling of being exposed and not knowing who exactly it is I'm exposed to. A heavy blanket covers me, and I'm aware of being picked up again and placed on a softer surface. I hear a low rumbling that might come from the heat of a fire, or a man's agitated voice. *Keet!* I drift to sleep once more.

I startle awake in time to see Keet's familiar shape kneeling in front of his fireplace, pushing logs into the flames. He's talking to himself, the bass of his voice a counterbalance to the staccato cracks and pops of the logs catching in the blaze. I start shivering again, muscles jumping in agitation. Keet stops muttering, turns, and strides over to me.

"Nolee, what happened?" His voice is pitched low, as though he's trying not to scare me. I can only chatter my teeth in reply.

"I'll make you some tea." He walks out of my line of sight. I close my eyes.

I hear the hiss and whistle of a kettle coming to boil. Moments later, a steaming mug is placed on the low wooden table in front of me, and I feel the fire's heat fill the room. The scent of ginger nips into my waterlogged brain, but I can't stop shaking enough to hold the mug.

"You need a warm bath," Keet says before he leaves the room. The shivering is lessening, and I'm certain I can at least hold that mug in my hands. When I lean forward, I close my eyes again as another wave of chills runs through me. Forgetting the tea, ignoring the background noise of water filling the tub, I crawl closer to the fire.

Then Keet is back, gently lifting me up. When I stand, it's on shaky legs. He slings an arm under my knees and another under my back, carrying me to the bathroom. Steam comes off the water in the tub, and when Keet lowers me to the ground, I grasp the edge and pull myself in, not caring that my old bra and panties are now on full display to the man I've been dreaming about. Keet lowers his eyes and turns his back, saying, "Stay there as long as you like. I'll bring the tea." He slides the door shut and I hear the echo of his footsteps on the hardwood floor. I sigh as the water's warmth reaches into my bones.

The bathroom takes up the length of the back of the house. Windows in the far wall look out into the forest, and there's a separate shower tiled in cerulean blue. I look up through the steam at the images set in the tile: a black orca swimming in a blue and green ocean. The amount of color in this room takes me by surprise; I'd thought he would live in monochromatic rooms.

Seeing a bottle of lavender bubble bath at the edge of the tub, I lean forward and open it. Another spell of shivering takes over my body, and I pour too much into the water. Keet knocks and announces he has my tea just as I'm wondering if it's possible to drown in foam.

"Come in! It's okay—I'm covered in bubbles."

The door slides open enough for the mug to lead the way, Keet's hand following before his face peers through the crack of the door.

"I think I'm going to need to buy you more bubble bath," I say, brushing the rising froth from my hair. My hair! I must look like a bedraggled mess. Keet is standing in front of me and I'm in his tub and suddenly, I just don't care. It used to irk me when friends would say, "It is what it is," thinking that was a lame way to dismiss things that ought to be paid attention to. But now I get it. Me in Keet's tub, him standing before me. It is what it is, and it will be what it will be.

Great, now I'm turning into Paul McCartney. Or was it John Lennon?

"Who wrote 'Let it Be,' Keet?" I ask.

"You must be thawing. Normally, you'd tell me The Who wrote it, instead of asking," he smiles. "The Beatles wrote it. Paul McCartney and John Lennon. But Paul says he dreamed those lines."

He glances at me and walks out, sliding the door shut. A few moments later, the piano chords to "Let it Be" thrum through a speaker in the ceiling above the tub. I slide out of my bra and panties, wring them out, and put them on the floor, then relax into the deep warmth of the tub and the soothing lyrics.

I jolt awake. The water is tepid, and I'm shivering again. The air around me is warm, and when I get out, wrapping myself in a blue towel, the floor is warm against my chilled feet too. I stand for a moment, then sit on the edge of the bathtub, breathing against the spinning in my head. Classical music's now playing through the speaker.

"Nolee?"

"Yes. I'm out of the bath."

I realize I don't know where my clothes are. The only thing between Keet and me is a door and a towel. I'd never considered myself a prudish person, but my lack of clothes was causing me to squirm.

"Keet, can you go over to my place and get some clothes for me?"

"I found some here that might fit you. I put them in the dryer, so they'd be warm. If they don't fit, I'll go get yours."

I pause before replying, thinking that in all the time I Nate and I were married, he did nothing close to that thoughtful. "Great! Hand them through the door and I'll grab them."

Again, the door cracks open, and Keet, head turned, holds the clothes in my direction. I take them with one hand, holding the towel closed with the other. When the door closes, I look down and see that everything is black. *What is it with this guy?* Still shaky, I put on the sweatpants, snugging them around my waist, then folding the waistband over to shorten them. Aside from being a little long, they mostly fit. The too-big sweatshirt and the socks warm me up when I pull them on.

I slide the door open and walk down the hallway to the living area and the warmth of the fireplace. Keet is sitting in an oversized chair, reading a book I admired, *The Hidden Life of Trees*. I grab the mug of tea, which I can now drink without scalding my mouth, and close my eyes as the ginger warms me from the inside out. Sitting cross-legged by the fire, I look up to see Keet watching me. His smile reaches all the way to his eyes, and again I wonder what those full lips feel like. Maybe he was telling the truth. Maybe he is harmless.

"I'm too cold to even think about going outside. Would you mind going over to my cabin and letting Fae out? She might want to know where I am." I sit down in front of the fire, sipping the still-warm tea.

He nods, and as he walks out the door, he turns and asks, "I should've asked this sooner. Do you know what day it is?"

"Oh, my god. How long have I been out? I think it's June third?"

He laughs. "You weren't out that long. It's still June third."

I scoot closer to the fire, staring into the orange flames.

When he comes back, Fae is close on his heels. She bounces over to me, grunting and whining. As she leans all her weight against me, I wrap my arms around her, smelling her popcorn doggy scent, and she quiets down.

"Keet, do you mind if she hangs out here with us?"

"I don't mind if she doesn't. She hasn't growled or barked at me yet, so I'd say we're off to a good start."

I smile, and watch as she sniffs around his house, her nails clicking on the floor as she goes room to room. She comes back and curls up in front of the chair Keet was sitting in. He's on the sofa now, and after watching Fae settle, he asks, "What happened out there?"

"You wouldn't believe me if I told you." I took another sip before asking him to hand me the blanket. I wrap up in it and felt truly warm for the first time in . . . "How long was I out of it?"

Keet looks at the clock by the front door. "It's about four hours since I found you. When did you take the kayak out?"

"At noon. It was a beautiful, calm day. I thought I was staying close to shore, but the sea must've changed. I looked back at the houses, and they were farther away than I wanted to be. There was this jerk in a boat going way too fast, way too close to me. I think the wake caught up with me right as I turned. I got a little off balance and freaked out, and the next thing I knew, I was in the water."

"So, it's been six hours since you almost froze to death." I can't tell from his expression if he's being funny or not, so I sip my tea and refuse to be cowed by his inscrutability. I've had a fair amount of practice with this, thanks to Silent Nate. But there is a stillness, a listening in Keet that I haven't yet figured out how to read. I notice that I'm doing it again: fitting my responses to suit someone else. I take a deep breath before saying,

"Are you being funny or . . .?"

"I didn't think I was. And I didn't find it funny to see you washed up on the beach, either."

"Why do *you* sound irritated? I was the one who almost froze out there. If it wasn't for—"

"I'm sorry, Nolee," he interrupts. "I'm also out of practice with all of this." He looks down at his hands and then looks away.

"How can you be out of practice? You talk to people all day; I've seen you. You're charming and intelligent and know so much about the Salish Sea."

Keet gives a deep laugh before saying, "Well, talking to people about what I know best is a far cry from talking to a woman I put nearly naked into my bathtub, who's now wearing my clothes and sitting in front of my fire."

I stare at him, this lean, dark man, and decide that the flips my stomach is doing aren't bad at all, but they aren't the reason for my inability to speak. I feel a catch in my throat as I realize what happened, and what could've happened.

"Please, finish what you were saying. If it wasn't for what?" His tone softer, he leans forward. His eyes are almost too kind to gaze into, but I can't look away, either.

I swallow, trying to shove down the feeling of wanting to cry. "You know that big male orca who swims around the cove sometimes?"

"Yes," he nods. He takes a deep breath and lets it out slowly.

I don't want to ruin my experience with the beautiful animal by hearing of Keet's disbelief. I also didn't want to break the tenuous intimacy that he and I seemed to share. But I have to tell him. "The orca carried me to shore. He saved me. You didn't see him? He must've been right up on the beach."

Keet shifts his gaze to the fire, running a hand through his thick hair and pushing it off his forehead. I can hear the fire popping behind me as I wait for his response. The classical music is still playing, the notes of the piano providing a quiet background for our talk.

"All I saw was you lying on the beach, shivering. I brought you in. No orca, but I do hear he's like that; here one second, gone the next."

I turn to the warmth of the fire and finish my tea. A small shiver runs through me again. Keet, was still looking at me, asks, "What was it like?"

I take a breath, and am suddenly tired again, and ready to go home to my bed.

"Unreal. I thought I was on an inner tube at first—I'm not sure how long I was in the water before he . . . before he . . ." To my horror, I burst into tears.

Keet rises from his chair and sits with me on the floor, an arm around my shoulders. I turn toward him, feeling the warmth of his skin through his t-shirt. I put my head against his chest and hear his heartbeat, slow and regular. My tears slow, and my sobs became slower too.

"It scared you. I know it scared me when I saw you lying there."

I nod, not trusting my voice. I also don't feel like moving. He's as warm as the fire burning behind me, and sleep is pulling my eyes closed. This time, I don't resist.

THIRTEEN

Keet feels her fall asleep, her body becoming pliant and heavy. Her auburn hair is drying; the strands lying over his hand are threaded through with gray and white and shimmer in the fire's light. He sits, listening to the last chords of a Mozart sonata fade away to silence, listening to Nolee breathe. The swim he planned could wait. The tremor in his hands is slight, but his need to be in the water is less than it's been in years. Here with her, he can relax. He glances at Fae, curled up on the floor in the kitchen, her amber eyes watchful.

Keet closes his eyes so he could hear the night, and Nolee, and the crackle of the fire that keeps them both warm. He brings his cheek to her hair, smelling the citrus shampoo she used. Then, folding his legs under him, he picks her up and places her, still cocooned in the blanket, on his sofa. Returning to his book, he reads until the fire and the sounds of her sleeping bring sleep to him, too.

He's awake before the ocean catches the sun's light. There are more waves today, the air is cold and wet, and the wind has picked up: a storm is on the way. He stretches before getting up from the chair and then goes over to the fireplace to start another fire. Looking over at Nolee, the only thing he can see is a tangle of rust-colored hair; she's wound herself tightly in the blanket, like a butterfly in a chrysalis. He wonders if she'll have breakfast with him or be too embarrassed to stay.

Fae is standing by the door, looking at him. *At least she isn't growling,* he thinks. As he lets her out, he hears Nolee's breathing change. He turns to the fireplace, preparing it for another fire to give her time to wake up without being watched. She yawns and hums as she stretches. He builds the fire and then hears her cursing as she tries to get out of the blanket.

"Sleep well?" he asks, holding a match to the kindling to get it to light.

"Oh, hell, yes. I'm still chilly. Mind if I shower and warm up?"

"Be my guest."

He hears her mutter, "I think I already am." He's not sure she meant for him to hear that, but he smiles as he hears her footsteps running toward the bathroom, the slide of the door as it shuts, and then the water running in the shower.

He walks back and says through the door, "As my guest, do I need to offer you tea or breakfast? Both?"

There's a long pause, and he's just about to repeat his question when she says, "Tea and breakfast sound great. I'm so hungry, I could eat all the fish in the bay!"

"I let your dog out, by the way."

"Great! I'll go over and feed her when I'm out of the shower."

He's in the kitchen when Nolee strides by and tells him she'll be right back. When she returns, she's wearing jeans and a sweater the same shade as her hair and carrying the clothes he loaned her. Her face is back to its usual color; she's no longer pale. When she smiles at him, he walks toward her, and they hug before stepping away.

"Fae all right?"

"She is. Happy to eat. She wasn't any trouble for you?"

"Not a bit. No growling or barking this time."

"She doesn't like to rush into anything. What smells so good?"

He opens the oven door, checking the frittata.

"Breakfast isn't fancy, but it will fill us up."

She steps closer, inhaling the rich aroma that steams from the skillet.

"I didn't know you could make eggs in the oven, Keet."

"Easiest way to make them."

"What else is in there?" she follows him to the table with plates.

"Rosemary. Salt and pepper. Spinach. Mushrooms, sweet potatoes, cream, and goat cheese." He sets the skillet down on a hot pad. "If you'd like some tea, there's some in the French press on the counter. I only have English Breakfast."

They eat in silence. As Keet looks at her, he realizes she's not embarrassed by yesterday, or if she is, she's hiding it well—a thought he dismisses. Nolee doesn't seem the type to hide things or cover up. She's still difficult for him to read, and she doesn't seem to trust easily, but faking how she feels? He can't see it.

"What's on your schedule for the day?"

He's surprised out of his thoughts. He puts down his fork and looks up from his plate, his breath catching at how beautiful she looks, the morning light streaming in through the windows catching the silver and warm auburn of her hair.

"You look lovely this morning, Nolee."

She gives a slight jump, and then her slow smile appears. "Not bad for an old broad who got dumped in the Salish Sea and then rescued by a killer whale, right?"

Although she laughs to herself, he doesn't join her. He picks up his fork and takes another bite. The silence stretches on until he feels her hand on his. He looks up.

"I'm sorry, Keet. I've used humor as a defense for so long that I've forgotten how to take a compliment. Hell, I've even forgotten what a compliment is." He forces a smile and gives her hand a squeeze. When he tries to release her hand, she keeps holding on.

"What I meant to say was, thank you. I'm feeling like a new woman this morning, and you're the reason for that."

Now it's his turn to start, wondering if she knows, or has remembered, anything. He dismisses this thought as well, bringing her hand to his mouth and giving it a quick kiss. She's still holding his hand, and he doesn't want to let go.

"To answer your question, I need to get *The Salish See* ready for a tour later today."

"What kind of tour?"

"Just around some islands and then back. They requested a charcuterie board and some drinks, so I'll go to the market and grab stuff before I get on the boat. Which reminds me," he lets go of her hand and gathers their empty plates. "I need to load a couple of coolers into my car."

"Can I help? With any of it?"

He stops at the sink. "Yes. If you want to meet me at the market, I'd appreciate help shopping and packing the coolers."

"Done. Just one question first?"

He nods.

"What's a charcuterie board?"

Now Keet does laugh.

The last of the coolers are stocked and loaded onto Keet's boat. I look up at the parking lot, seeing Fae's red head poking through the open car window. She's not worried, but I bet she'd like to be closer to the action. A picture like a blurry snapshot wavers into focus in my head. I see the tip of a white-and-red nose, and myself, nose and eyes and floating hair. She flattens her ears against her head and gives her best white-toothed doggie grin.

"Keet, would it be okay if Fae came down for a look before I leave?" I can feel the deck swaying gently underneath me and wish I could join the tour. Who knew a landlocked gal like me would love the water life?

"Sure. A few clients have brought their dogs. I require *them* to wear a life jacket, too."

"I don't think we need to go that far, but I wouldn't mind her getting her paws on the deck."

He waves, concentrating on his GPS and looking at the sheets Trish printed for him.

"Everything okay?" I pause on the dock, watching him.

"Yes. I was checking today's weather reports. There'll be plenty of wind, which bodes well for knocking down my fuel costs. I'd rather sail, anyway. Having a motor is insurance, but I really don't like using it." He folds up the papers and puts them in his jacket pocket.

"You know there are some pretty great weather apps you can get. I mean, if you had a phone to put them on."

Keet looks at me, his head cocked and a half-smile on his face. I laugh and he says, "You're funny today." I shrug and turn to go get Fae.

Fae wriggles when she sees me coming, then begins panting and hopping up and down.

"Just a sec, Fae, just a sec. Can you wait?"

She drops onto the seat, tucking one paw under her chest, still panting. "You are brilliant, my girl."

I open the door, grab the leash from the floor, and clip it to her harness. "Here."

She jumps down, standing at my side, her white-tipped tail wagging, her ears pointed up at me. I dig around in my pocket for a treat.

"Gently."

She takes the treat from my fingertips, her eyes crossing as she tries to look at it down the length of her short nose.

We walk down the dock, and I ask her to wait again, noticing how she's adjusting to the sensation of the floor moving. She looks around and circles. Her golden eyes investigate mine, and she pants again and wags her tail. I offer her another treat. After she takes it, we walk back to the car, and I ask her to wait again.

Walking back and forth on the dock, I repeat the same commands until I see she isn't pausing or trying to circle anymore. The lead is slack in my hand. I look up at Keet and see him watching our progress.

"Nolee, why don't you step aboard first, and then ask her on after you."

I recognize the difference between a question and an order, and smile at Fae. "Did you hear that, Fae? Sit." She drops into a sit, her paws firmly on the dock.

I step onto the boat, making sure my weight's equally distributed, and then look at Fae, holding the lead loose in my hand. "Here, Fae."

She sniffs the edge of the boat, looks at me, sniffs again, and puts one cautious paw onto the non-slip surface. Then backs away and shakes, the red of her coat shiny in the sunlight.

"Good girl! Fae, here." I'm calm, knowing she'll figure this out in her own time. My goal is to let her know I'm confident in her.

She stands up, sniffs again, and walks aboard, shaking her coat loose, then sitting by my side. I give her several treats. Still chewing, she stands up and sniffs the surrounding deck. She sees Keet, who's come near us, and the tip of her tail gives a tiny wag before she continues sniffing.

"Did you see that?" Keet has a broad smile.

"I did. You got a tail wag. This is your lucky day."

"I won't press my luck by trying to pet her."

"That's a good idea."

"I need to remember that anytime you're doing anything with Fae, it's a process. I was watching you work and noticed that you gave her a lot of breaks."

"I did. She's not only new to all of this, but still young enough to be figuring out what life as a dog means. The last thing I want to do is scare her. She's bold, and that's the part of her I'd like to encourage."

I walk with my red pup over the rest of the boat and go back to Keet.

"I think that's good for today. Have a great trip." We hug, and I feel his hand on the back of my neck, a soft touch that raises goosebumps on my bare arms. I also feel the pull of the leash as Fae finds the end of it, straining away from our embrace.

"How about a late dinner when I get back?"

"Like I'd ever turn that invitation down." I can see the outline of his eyes through his sunglasses, but it's his smile that entices me closer. I step away and pat Fae's warm head.

"It's a date. I'll call you when I get in," he says.

I walk over to Keet's place with Fae, happy to ignore my usual bedtime. She runs ahead, and then circles behind me. As Keet and I eat, we watch Fae explore his house. I hear the soft padding of her paws as she trots up and down the hallway, into the bathroom, and then into another room, where I can't hear her anymore.

"Uh-oh. When puppies go silent, it's time to investigate." I start to get up, but Keet is already on his way.

"I'll check on her. She must've found my bedroom."

I sit down abruptly. After looking at the table and empty plates, I stand and begin cleaning up. I hear the thud of a closing door, and Fae's quick steps on the floor. She finds me behind the counter and wags her tail as though she's just been on a grand adventure. Having never seen Keet's bedroom, maybe she had.

"Thanks for doing the dishes." Keet stands next to me, his arm resting against my shoulder. I lean into him.

"You're welcome. It's the least I could do."

"Well, not really," he says.

I glance up at him, not understanding. He's giving me a mischievous grin. Another wave of wanting to kiss him washes over me; if my hands weren't full of suds and dishes, I would.

"What do you mean?"

"The least you could do would be nothing."

I take a moment, during which I hear the drip and splash of the water and feel the suds dissolving in my fingers.

"I think I'm a bad influence. Was that a smart-ass remark?"

He's still smiling. "I never said you can't joke. As to the influence you're having on me, I'd say it's a good one." His voice drops a couple of registers, becoming husky and thick. He reaches up slowly, pausing with his hand near my hair. "May I?" he asks. I nod, and he threads his fingers through my ponytail, looking at me, and then back at my hair in his fingers as I feel his hand run slowly through its length.

Fae barks and I open my eyes. Keet has stepped closer, and I don't want to keep stepping away from him anymore. He takes his hand away from my hair. His bright smile is gone and in its place is a dark burning in his eyes. We're silent. Both of us are a long way down the road from being virgins or nervous kids. All the same, I *am* nervous.

He clears his throat. "I don't think Fae likes me being this close to you."

A million replies run through my head, each one reflecting my nervousness. I say the one that is pure truth. "But I do."

Time stops. We both stand still. I break my gaze away from his, setting the still soapy plate in the sink. My hands rest on its edge, and I'm unsure what comes next. Before I can look at him again and decide, he has his arms around me and lays his cheek on the top of my head. I turn, lean into him, and—soapy hands and all—hold his body next to mine as though he were the orca, carrying me back to land.

I don't know how long we've been standing here, holding each other with Fae at our feet and resigned to accepting this man. I don't know where we're going, only where I want to go, and who I want with me.

"Nolee?"

"Keet?"

"Can I walk you home?"

"I'd like that."

I finish rinsing the dishes and wipe my hands. Sensing Keet through an electromagnetic force that pulls low in my belly, I smile as he holds the door open, the night air still after a day full of wind. I hear the door thud shut and before I can stop myself, ask him, "Do you need to lock it?" When I turn, an expression of puzzlement moves across his face.

"I mean, it's important to be safe." Even I know how awkward this remark is, and know that Keet's going to put two and two together.

"I'm just walking you home and coming back. I think the house will be safe for five minutes."

As we step off the porch, Keet say, "How do you know I lock my house?"

"Because I'm nosy. Before we met, sometimes I'd see you coming and going and always pausing at your door. I guessed maybe you were locking it." The words tumble out in a rush.

When Keet takes my hand in his, I glance at him and am relieved to see that his face is thoughtful, with no trace of anger or irritation. We walk a dozen more steps before he says, "Sometimes?" I hear the smile in his voice. I have nothing useful to say, so instead, I shrug and smile. We walk side by side, the air wrapping around us, the moonlit night so bright we don't need the flashlight I brought. The warmth of his hand intertwined with mine is dizzying. I barely notice that once again, I'd forgotten to leave a light on in my house.

We climb the steps, and I turn to Keet. He steps closer to me, and I tilt my head to look up at him with an increasing sense of vertigo. I've had these moments, these times of feeling like I'm stepping close to a decision that might be a cliff's edge, wondering what would happen if I jumped. With Keet, these rusty feelings stack up, making this cliff seem higher than any I've jumped from before.

When he asks, "May I kiss you?" I feel the sweep of his breath across my cheek. I lean closer to him and whisper, "Yes." He brings his hand up to my face. The moonlight in his hair is the last thing I see before he lowers his face to mine. We step closer, and his other arm drapes around my waist, inviting me to him. As the kiss goes on, I feel my body drawn toward his, as the tide is called by the moon.

We break apart, and with my hands on his neck, I ask him "May I?" He smiles, taking one of my hands and laying it on the hair that brushes the back of his neck. We kiss again, and I sink both of my hands into his thick hair, which is coarse and soft, like the horse's manes I used to brush. I move my hands down his neck and feel the strong curve of it as it meets his shoulders.

He breaks away from the kiss and rests his head gently on my shoulder. He kisses me where my neck meets my earlobe and whispers, "Goodnight, Nolee," before stepping away and turning back to his house. Feeling drunk, spinning, and disconnected, I walk into my dark house and flip on the light. Fae trots in behind me and curls up on her bed under the stairs.

I make sure she has water in her bowl. She gets up and stands by the door, as though I'd forget that she goes out each night before going to bed. Even if she was just outside. I let her out again, and, leaning on the doorframe, check my phone for texts. A distant crunch on gravel makes me hope that Keet's coming back.

I finish a text to Abbie before looking at his house, which is now dark. I look out toward the dock. He's not there, but Fae is, standing at the edge, looking out into the bay. In this light, she's monochrome, all grays and blacks. I follow her gaze, seeing nothing but the distant lights of Vancouver, and the black sea. It surprises me that she went that far with no one out there. I whistle for her, and she trots back, stopping on the way to squat by a tree. She bounds into the house and settles into her spot again. I kneel and give her a scratch behind her ears, turn out the lights, and climb the stairs to my room.

As I'm slipping my cotton nightgown over my head, I hear a splash in the bay. Parting the curtain and looking at the moonlit silk of the water, I see an orca's dark fin—the notch tells me it's the Resident male. I think about the kiss, about Keet. I know there's a part of me that thinks I should be concerned about involving myself in another relationship, but another part, one that was thirsty for the kiss, isn't concerned at all. That part of me wants to slake my curiosity in more of those kisses with that man.

As I think the feel of his face resting gently along my neck, the heat of his breath pluming around both of us, I allow myself to imagine that maybe he's curious about me, too. I wonder why I'm going to bed alone when there's a warm, handsome man less than a hundred feet away. But before I find the courage to get dressed again and knock on Keet's door, I hear the quiet of the bay disrupted by powerful exhales.

Looking out the window, I see the male orca arc out of the black waves, flipping his white belly to the moon before crashing down and melting into the water. If I could join him in this display of joy, I would. The spring of my dry and thirsty heart is filling once more.

FOURTEEN

The next morning, the sun paints my room in gold and orange watercolor light. I roll over, stretching, then swinging my legs out of bed. The landline is ringing, and I jog down the staircase, racing the answering machine, barely aware of the chill of the floor under my feet.

"Hello?"

"Nolee? It's Keet."

I smile, the sound of his deep morning voice in my ear after I've just woken up raising goosebumps on my arms.

"I figured it was you or Ava. And you don't sound like her. Good morning."

He laughs. "Good morning to you."

I've learned to slow down when Keet and I converse, enjoying the pauses and the way he puts thought into his words. I'd gotten so used to talking at people, instead of with them, that talking with Keet feels like a master class in how to listen. But this silence is stretching out into the awkward phase. Then he breaks it.

"I wanted to ask if you had anything going on today. I thought we could take a small hike up Mt. Pelorus; Fae can come, too."

"We'd love to join you. What time were you thinking?"

"Any time, really. If we leave soon, the skies will still be clear, and there's an amazing view of the sea and her islands from the top."

"Let me grab some breakfast, and I'll be right over."

"See you then."

We hang up, I hold the handset to my chest, squeezing it tightly and grinning. Fae is standing by her food dish, wagging her tail.

"We're both going to eat and then have an activity, girlie." I kneel and she wriggles over to me, grunting as I scratch behind her ears.

Washing the breakfast dishes, I glance out the window and see Keet at his vehicle. All four doors and the hatch are open, and it looks like he's shifting things around. I was so excited to hear from him that I'd forgotten to ask if we were riding together or separately. From the stuff strewn across his porch, it looks like we're going together.

I fill a bottle with water and stuff it in the backpack, along with a collapsible dish for Fae and some granola bars. Fae dances into her harness, twirling so fast I can't get the leash attached.

"Fae, wait."

She drops with a thump, one paw tucked under her chest, looking up at me through her slanted golden eyes. She's as still as she was frenetic a moment ago, and not for the first time, or even the thousandth, I'm astounded by a herding dog's ability to go from zero to one hundred—or vice versa. She pants and smiles as I click the leash onto her harness. Then, I lift the backpack to my shoulder and we're out and on our way.

They park in a lot tucked into the shady forest. The back of the 4Runner is open, and Keet hands Nolee her backpack. She takes it from him, holding Fae's leash in her other hand. "I haven't made it over to this part of the island yet," she says. "This will be good for both Fae and me."

He pauses, shifting his own backpack to a more comfortable position. Hoping to spend more time together, he packed lunch for them; he also hopes she won't hear the clinking of the containers. He closes and locks the car, then turns to see her standing close to him. He stills, leaning in toward her. She gives him a quick kiss and says, her voice soft, "Thanks for this. I already know it's a great idea. It's also a great idea to start halfway up." She pauses as she looks at the forest around the Little Arrow parking lot. "I haven't been hiking in a while, and the thought of a thousand-plus feet elevation gain wasn't enticing."

Without thinking, he says, "I wanted to see you again, Lia, and show you more of Camas than just Osprey Bay."

"Lia?"

He fidgets with his backpack. "It's what I've called you since we first met."

"You mean like Leia from *Star Wars*?"

She doesn't know that her level green look sometimes makes him forget what he was going to say. "I don't know what *Star Wars* is. Is it a game? But it's not Lay-Ah. It's Lee-ah. Like the last three letters of Magnolia."

She stifles the laughter that bubbles in her chest and steps closer, putting her hand to his face and says, "I like it. *Star Wars* is a movie, made in 1977. And now we have to watch it one night."

Keet smiles and shrugs. "You can laugh," he said. "It's not the first time I've made that mistake."

She let the laugh out, then subsides into giggles. "How can you know this land, and the sea, and all that music and not know such a classic movie?"

"Now you know how I feel when you tell me you get The Beatles mixed up with 'those other Brit bands.'"

Nolee shrugs and says, "You've got me there."

"Besides," he says. "Any movie with the word 'war' in it isn't something I'd be interested in. Pick another one?" He turns, takes her hand, and pulls her toward him, kissing her. The wind through the trees sighs, and so does Nolee. Fae whines and pulls at her leash, and they break apart, feeling the warmth of the air between them.

"Let's get moving, is what I think that meant," Nolee says, looking down at her dog. "I'll think about your movie question."

After leaving the parking lot, they cross a small bridge. The forest is cool against their skin, the undergrowth still lush. They follow the trail, which is wide enough for Fae to trot alongside of Nolee. He hears his own sure footsteps, and her quicker, lighter ones behind him.

"There's a good picnic area close by. I thought on our way back we could stop and eat some lunch."

"You brought lunch for us?" She beams a smile at him.

"Mostly leftovers, but yes. We have lunch."

They spend the rest of the hike talking about the Lodgepole pines that Nolee spots. In between are comfortable silences, broken only by the sounds of nature. Behind her now, he catches himself admiring how she walks, then shifts his gaze to the familiar forest. Nolee stops as the forest opens onto a sweeping view of the sea, jagged mountain-tops in the distance. "What range is that, Keet?"

"Those are the Cascades. Stunning, aren't they?"

"Let's get to the top. I can't wait to see more of this view."

A few minutes later, a stone tower appears at the top of the trail. Nolee starts up-slope, her legs showing lines of muscle as she pushes against the land's steep jut.

After drinking from their water bottles, giving Fae a bowl of water, and sharing the granola bars she brought, they sit on a stone wall, and he points out the islands in front of them. They climb the steps inside the stone tower, the walls chilly against his fingertips. When they reach the top, the open air and warm sun feel good on his skin.

"So that's what Sucia Island looks like from above. It's a lot bigger than it looks from Osprey Bay," she says.

"I enjoy being up here because it reminds me how small I am in the scheme of things." He's leaning into her but looking out at the sea dotted with dark green islands, and the eagle soaring below them.

She gives him a thoughtful glance. "I get that." She reaches down and scratches Fae's head. Keet smiles, then says, "How about we head back and stop for lunch at that spot I mentioned?"

She laughs and takes his hand, giving it a gentle squeeze. "I like that you're all about the food, Keet Noland." They turn, hurrying down the steps and making their way back to the trailhead, still holding hands.

When they sit down at the table, Faye lies panting underneath and Keet unpacks his backpack.

"It's like a clown car," Nolee remarks.

"What's that?"

"Haven't you seen those videos where the doors open on a compact car and it seems like a hundred people crawl out? I think it started as a circus act."

"That would explain why I don't know what it is. Not a fan of circuses. Or zoos."

"What kind of childhood did you have?" Her tone catches him off guard. If he took the question at face value, he could interpret it as her saying that he didn't have much of a childhood without circuses and zoos. But he hears something else: curiosity. A glance tells him his hunch is right.

"Oh, a quiet one, probably, compared to most kids." He takes out a metal container that was sitting on an ice pack, removing the lid to display the remains of the salmon filet from dinner.

"You don't mind cold salmon? There's also bread and cream cheese; olives, apples, and microgreens from the farmer's market; and a couple of bars of chocolate." He spreads each on the blanket he's draped over the table. When he looks at Nolee again, she's still leaning her head on her hand, smiling at him.

"Too much?" he asks.

She shakes her head. "It's perfect. I don't think anyone has ever fed me as well as you do. Around our house when I was growing up, you fended for yourself."

"Do you have brothers and sisters?"

"There are four of us. Two brothers and a younger sister."

"The sister must have a flower name?" He glances away from her briefly to layer the bread with microgreens, cream cheese, and salmon. When he looks at her again, he's distracted from the clamoring in his stomach by the desire to kiss her. She must've seen the shift on his face because she leans across the table, meeting him halfway. The sun is warm on his head, and his mouth is warmer on hers. He can taste the sweetness of the granola bar she ate and feel the heat of her breath. He sets his food down, and places one hand on each side of her face, kissing her deeply, feeling the thrill of her responsiveness to him. When they pull away from each other, they smile, both out of breath, both speechless.

She clears her throat and sits down, her face flushed. "What did you ask me again?"

"Can I sit next to you? I feel like we're too far apart." She nods and slides over on the bench. When he sits down, he asks, "What I asked was, does your sister have a flower name too?"

She takes a drink of water. "She does. It's Lily. Lily Rachael Burnett. Rachael is after our great aunt on my dad's side. She got the better middle name."

"I don't think you told me your middle name?"

She turns her head away. "There's a reason for that. Clarke. It was my mom's mother's maiden name. Apparently, it's a thing for southern women to carry family names, or it was when I was born. What about you? Any middle name?"

"No middle name. Plain old Keet Noland."

"Noland is your father's last name?"

"It is. My mom's name was Hazel, and my dad was Charlie."

"Does Keet mean anything?"

He pauses again, feeling her thigh brushing his. He looks at her, then back down at what remains of his lunch.

"It means 'orca' or 'killer whale' in Tlingit. It was the one name my grandmother and mother agreed on when I was born."

"No wonder you have an affinity for them."

He gives her a quick smile and takes the last bite of his lunch. He brushes his hands together, and leans back, his face to the sun.

"What are your brothers' names?"

She laughs. "You remember when I said that I was lucky my mom wasn't into women outlaws, or I could've been Calamity Jane?"

He nods.

"Well, my brothers didn't get off so easily. She named the oldest Frank Hamer Burnett, and my younger brother is Maney Gault Burnett."

He shakes his head. "I'm not familiar with those names. Or Texas history. Sorry." He bumps her shoulder with his.

"They were famous Texas lawmen—Texas Rangers—and family friends. They did a bunch of stuff, but they're probably most famous for shooting Bonnie and Clyde."

"How do your brothers feel about their names?"

"They like them. Their kids grew up hearing them tell stories about their namesakes."

The wind gusts. They watch as an eagle glides through the sky and then lean toward each other. This time the kiss is slow, an exploration of taste and feel. Their arms wrap around each other, breaking apart when they people coming up behind them on the trail.

"Keet, why did you ask if you could touch my hair that first time?"

He smiles, taking her hands in his. "For my people, it has to do with the sacredness of relationships. It's an act of intimacy, because a person's hair is believed to hold their dreams and prayers, their experiences and history." She looks at him, her face serious. "So, when you touch a person's hair, you're touching all those things, too?"

He nods. "Our hair is our connection to Creator. We only cut it when we grieve, or when we are ending something and beginning something new."

"Why is your hair short? Can I ask why you cut it?"

He looks out over gray green of the sea to the jagged white peaks of the mountains in the hazy distance, the ache in his heart still clear and sharp.

"I cut it when my parents died in the car wreck." He stands up, takes another bar of chocolate out of his backpack. "Then I got used to it being short, so I've just kept it this length." Sitting down next to Nolee, Keet puts his hand on her thigh. "But sometimes, I miss it. I miss the braids."

She puts her hand on top of his and says, "I think that's a beautiful way to think about hair. For me, it's always been something of a bother. But you've given me a new perspective."

Nolee takes an olive from the container and holds it up to him, raising her eyebrows.

He nods. She feeds it to him slow, their eyes not leaving each other. He turns his head away and drops the pit into his palm, putting it in a pile with the trash he'll take back home.

"If you ever wanted to grow it out again, Keet, I'd love to see what it looks like."

He runs his hand over his neck, feeling the hairs sprouting from it. Thinks about the last time he got it cut, and how he watched the dark strands falling on the floor. How they were swept up and thrown away. How his grandmother always said that hair should be burnt with the grasses, as an offering to Creator to keep the wishes of its owner safe.

"Do you mind if Fae has that last bit of salmon?" Nolee's question pulls him back to the present.

"Go for it." He watches as she feeds Fae.

"Gentle, Fae. Gentle." She holds the salmon in her palm, her fingers curved around it. When Fae's no longer lunging for the fish, Nolee flattens her hand and lets Fae eat.

"I'm going to be gone for the next couple of days. Clients are coming in from out of the country. I'll pick them up from the marina on San Juan Island and take them up to Patos Island and come back." He opens a bar of chocolate and hands it to Nolee.

"Thanks," she says, breaking the bar in half. She hands the package back to him, and he unwraps it from the foil.

"That sounds like a long trip."

"It's not too bad. Beautiful."

"Maybe someday you could take me along."

He smiles. "I'd like that. There's nothing like sleeping on the ocean."

She laughs and shifts on the bench. "I bet there isn't."

They're quiet for a moment, and then Nolee asks, "Why don't you like movies?"

"So many of them make me feel horrible. I gave up watching them years ago." Keet scoots closer to her.

"Movies and fiction books, for me, are like being inside someone else's head. And most people's head space is unnerving. My own is crowded enough." He feels the reassuring press of her leg against his.

"It's difficult for me to separate myself from what I'm seeing and hearing, so if I see a movie that disturbs me, the images loop in my brain, almost like it happened to me. It's not entertaining. At all."

"But don't you tire of the inside of your own head? I mean, for me, it's an escape to watch movies, to see different worlds and the struggle others have and how they overcome it. YouTube has been my best friend this past year, and I don't know how I'd keep in touch with my friends without my social media accounts."

Keet turns, nodding and sweeping a dark strand of hair out of his eyes. He says, "But Lia, what do you want to escape?"

He watches her face, watches what must be a thousand replies making their way to the tip of her tongue. She looks away, sitting on her hands, her head tilted. He hears the distant laughter and loud voices of tourists as they pass by. A cry from a hawk. The rumbling motor of a Cessna as it passes by to the east. "You know what?" she says.

He shakes his head.

"I think it's a useless way of coping with a life I'm no longer living." She gives him a shaky smile, stands up, and then sits down again. "Now that you mention it, since I've been here, I'm doing a lot less movie-watching. I can't remember the last time I saw a movie when it came out. It feels good to like my life. Good, and kind of scary."

She turns back to him, the faraway expression in her green eyes returning to this day, to him. "I like my life, and I like you in it, Keet." She takes his hand in hers, and he looks down, seeing the contrast between the colors of their skin, like the strength and softness he feels in her fingers. When he looks up, her eyes are still on him and he's drawn to her, kissing her with only the sun and trees and her red dog to witness.

FIFTEEN

They drive out of the park, Keet humming a song.

"Which song, artist, and year is that one? I think I know it." Nolee asks.

He sings, his voice soft and deep, "*Slow down, you crazy child, you're so ambitious for a juvenile . . .*"

He takes her hand, still singing softly with his eyes on the road. Nolee leans her head back against the seat, closes her eyes. He feels her relaxing, and her hand warming in his.

The song ends and he's quiet. She smiles and asks, "Well? Who and when?"

Keet says, "Billy Joel, 'Vienna', 1977. The album is *The Stranger*. It's the fifth song."

"So now you know where the song is on each album?"

"Not every artist, or every album. Billy Joel is the music from my youth. The piano has always been a favorite instrument of mine."

"You must like Elton John then, too."

He nods and signals for the turn. Hearing a plane at the airport they're passing whine up the runway and take off overhead. Nolee watches as it banks and then climbs higher. Keet pulls over in a wide spot, and when she looks at him, he leans over and stops her question with a kiss.

He smiles, sits back in his seat, signals, and pulls back out on to the narrow road leading back to Osprey Bay.

"And Mozart, Beethoven, Nina Simone, Ray Charles, Tori Amos, Alicia Keys, Chopin, Omar Sharif, Eden Brent, Skip James—who was also an amazing guitar player—Pinetop Smith, Mitsuko Uchida . . ." He looks over at her, smiling. "I can go on all day, but I won't." He notices she's still grinning and then hears her laugh. "What?"

She takes his hand again, kissing the back of it. "I've done more kissing in the past two days than I have in a decade. It feels good, is what." They turn onto the dirt road, both smiling and silent.

Once they park and unload, Nolee lets Fae out and shoulders her backpack.

"Let's do that again soon," she says.

"Absolutely."

They move toward each other, and Keet looks down into her eyes and wants to pull her with him to his bed. But the pull of the sea still has him in its teeth.

After they share a long kiss, he says, "I'll call from the marina when I get back in a couple of days. May I take you to dinner at one of my favorite places in Northsound?"

Nolee nods. "It's a date."

That night I'm jarred awake by a loud bang. Fae runs up the stairs, arriving at the side of my bed, panting. Hearing the staccato pelting of rain against the window, I fumble my way to the curtains and pull them back. I see flashes of lightning out at sea, silhouetting the islands in sharp bursts of silver. The water is violent, and I hope Keet's anchored somewhere safe. Another flashbulb burst of lightning and a roar of thunder rattles the glass. The storm is unusual for this time of year; it was midsummer, and storms rarely rolled in until winter. This one is proving the weather forecasters wrong.

I make my way back to bed and turn switch on the bedside lamp, but the electricity is out. Fae trails me, her tail between her legs.

"I know, girlie, this isn't my idea of a good night's sleep either." Using my phone's flashlight, we make our way downstairs—where I find that the landline is out too. Great. I stand at the counter, tapping my fingers, then open the curtains. I'm startled to see the sea is much closer than usual. It's eaten up the beach, and the swells are mere feet from the picnic table in front of the house. Keet's house is dark and in a flash of lightning, I can see the floating dock is twisting and bucking. I find my laptop and open it, but the internet is out too.

Cursing my shortsightedness at not stocking candles, I realize there's nothing much I can do. I drink a glass of water, call Fae, and we go back upstairs, where I sit in the soft chair at the window, watching as the sea hammers everything in its path. I can't make out where the buoys are. The swells are huge, and the water is black as oil and roiling with whitecaps, tossing giant trees like toothpicks on its surface.

"Keet, I hope you're somewhere safe." I stroke Fae's head, noticing that her quivering has stopped. But then comes another window-rattling burst of thunder and lightning, and she's curling up in my lap.

I must've dozed off; when I open my eyes again, the light is gray. The thunder and lightning have moved on, but the sea is still agitated, the clouds heavy and dark. Fae is still on my lap, her red fluffy tail curled around her.

"C'mon Fae, let's get you outside before those clouds reach us."

We go downstairs, and I let her out. Standing on the wet boards of my porch in bare feet, I hear the loud crashing of sea and forest. Fae runs in circles, sniffs, does her business, and then runs back in.

"Good girl! Time for some breakfast!" The light switch gives a lonely click, and no light accompanies it. "Damn." No electricity, no stove. But there's always cereal.

After eating, I'm washing the dishes, contemplating ways to make tea when the rain starts again, sheeting down in torrents. As I bring wood in, I notice that it's getting colder. Then I search for kindling and wonder how long it would take to boil water on the woodstove once I get it going. Staring out the window again, I don't expect to see Keet's vehicle, or the male orca's large fin, but want to, all the same. It's lonely here without them and again, I worry about Keet and hope he's found a safe place to wait out the storm.

I spend the day reading by a window and teaching Fae how to play "find it." In between downpours, I bring in more wood. One book is finished and I'm contemplating another when I hear the refrigerator click on. I let out a cheer, which startles a surprised "whuff!" from Fae. To celebrate, I make a cup of tea and run warm water over her dinner. As she gulps down her food, I tell her, "Tomorrow morning, we're going to get some storm supplies, Fae. We weren't at all prepared for this weather."

The next morning, I see small windows of blue sky, but the sea is still unsettled and the wind gusts in bursts. The water has receded, and so has my nervousness, but the beach is strewn with logs and driftwood. My phone tells me that it's June 8th, Abbie's birthday. Glancing up from my phone, I see that Keet's house is still empty.

The state of the beach reminds me of Keet's kayaks. I call Fae, and we walk to his house to make sure both are still on the porch. They're filled with water, so I roll them over and dump it out. Then Fae and I walk the length of the beach; I watch Fae as she darts and cavorts with the surf. Her instinct to herd is in overdrive after being housebound for almost three days. I take a photo of Fae in the sea and text it to Abbie, along with a message wishing her a happy birthday.

Happy birthday from me and Fae! You are the most wondrous woman, and I am proud to be your mom. Did you get your birthday box? xo

She sends a text back immediately, all hearts and kiss emoji's. *Thanks, Mom! Got the box- love the pottery! I heard about the storm up there. Glad you and Fae are doing all right. Love you!*

We go back inside when it starts to rain again, and I call Keet's office to talk to Trish. The answering machine picks up. I ask her to call me when she gets in. My next call is to Andi at the shelter. The machine clicks on there, too, but halfway through my message, she answers, out of breath.

"Hey, Nolee. Made it through that freak storm?"

"Barely. That was a real gulley washer, as they'd say back home."

"It was. You need anything?"

"No, thanks. I was calling to ask y'all the same. Everyone alright?"

"Yes, there were enough people here to get all the animals tucked in and taken care of. They had extra blankets, and we fired up the woodstove."

"Me too. I'm glad we made it through. Unusual for the summer, isn't it?"

She gives a shaky laugh, and I realize she's tired. "Very. That was a February storm."

"Are you sure you don't want me to come in? You sound worn out."

Andi blows out a deep breath. "You're kind, but I was just finishing up the morning feed, and we're covered for the rest of the day."

"Promise you'll call me if you need another body."

"Promise. Thanks again, Nolee."

Four days later, late in the afternoon, I get a text from Trish. I'd left two more messages, by this time frantic and picturing the worst: Keet and his boat washed out to the ocean, lying somewhere wrecked and damaged, sunk.

Got your messages. Keet's car is still here, and his boat isn't. I haven't heard from him, but when I do, I'll let you know. He's been doing this forever. I'm sure he's okay.

I let out the breath I didn't know I was holding, and text back *Thanks so much, Trish. Hope you're okay too.*

When I don't hear from her, I decide I need to stop waiting and start doing something. Grabbing my backpack, I put Fae's harness on her and we hop in the car. Time to stock up on supplies.

The next morning, I walk down to the shore. The sun is warm and the sea's less turbulent; the waves are top-hatted with rolling whitecaps, and when I walk down on the rocks, I only see torn strands of kelp rolling through the surf. The normally clear water is murky with seaweed and kelp, dirt, and sediment. The seal is absent, probably riding out the remnants of the storm somewhere calmer—or perhaps the orca is somewhere close by.

The wind moving through the pines and the roar of the waves mimic one another, each vying to announce the last throes of the turbulent weather. At least the skies are finally blue again, instead of a dull and metallic gray. Fae helps me move the driftwood from the beach. I hand her the small branches, and I drag the logs backward, shuffling them to the side, figuring I can make a path to the sea. The bigger ones will have to wait until Keet gets back. Time to bathe, dress, and have something to eat.

Showered and waiting for the water for my tea to boil, I hear Fae whine, then the knock on my door. "Just a minute!" I turn off the heat under the kettle, wrap my robe around myself, and ask Fae to wait. She drops to the ground, still whining. I open it, torn between hoping it's Keet and wanting to pummel him if it is.

It's Keet. He's leaning on the door frame with his head lowered. I can see the jagged part, his hair rumpled as though it hasn't seen a comb in days.

"Keet?"

He looks up at me, and there are dark patches under each eye. His cheekbones are sharp in his gaunt face. I pull him inside and shut the door against the wind that enters the house in a gust behind him. Fae goes to her bed and sits on it, watching.

I guide him to the couch. "Here, sit down. Do you want some water? Tea?"

He takes a shuddering breath and leans back. "Tea would be great. Do you have anything to eat besides cereal?" He glances up at me, the trace of a smile on his weary face.

"I was going to make scrambled eggs and toast. There're fruit and scones too."

"All of it, please."

SIXTEEN

I boil water for the tea, my irritation subsiding in the wake of my sympathy. He's in no shape to withstand my wrath. Putting a bag of peppermint tea and a bag of ginger tea in a large mug, I add the hot water and some honey and take it out to Keet. His head is resting on the back of the couch, his eyes closed. Just when I decide he's gone to sleep, he says, "I don't know whether to eat or pass out."

"Your choice. I think you'll sleep better if you eat something first."

He squints at me before sitting up and taking the mug from my hands. "You're probably right." He rises, holding the mug in both hands and follows me into the kitchen. "I've been fretting about you. What happened?"

As he lowers himself down into the chair, he says, "I'll tell you once I've eaten."

I put fruit and a scone on a plate and set it on the table in front of him. He drinks his tea and watches as I take the eggs, butter, and onions out of the refrigerator. I put a thick slice of butter in the skillet and turn the heat on underneath it. Cracking four eggs into the pan, I glance over at Keet and see that the scone and fruit are gone. I add two more eggs, a little salt and pepper, and the onions, and stir.

I put four pieces of toast in the toaster oven and turn it on, then begin stirring the eggs again when Keet says, "I'll have another scone if you can spare it."

I hand him the box. "You're enjoying having me feed you for a change, aren't you?" I say.

He nods, then takes a huge bite out of his scone.

I pause long enough to lean over and kiss his cheek and whisper, "I'm glad you're okay," before heading back to the eggs. The toaster oven dings. I take the skillet off the stove and divide the food between two plates. It steams as I set it in front of him.

When his plate is clean and he's pushed back from the table, holding the still-warm mug in his hands, I ask, "You look like you haven't eaten or slept in days. Did you get caught in that storm?"

"I did. It was a monster. I didn't know whether it was night or day half the time, only that I was trying to survive."

His eyes are closing as he sits, and the mug tips. What's left of the tea is perilously near the edge of the mug, so I take it from him.

"Come on, Keet. Let's get you back on the sofa."

He grunts, then rises with my help; I have a fleeting thought that if I ever needed to move him by myself, I'd be out of luck. He lies down and I take off his shoes, give him a pillow, and cover him with a blanket. He's asleep in seconds.

Three hours later, with no sign of him waking up any time soon, I get dressed and take Fae for a walk on the beach, then into town for more groceries. Stopping at the shelter, I drop off the cat and dog food I bought before driving home.

When I open the door, I see that I didn't have to tiptoe up the steps. A bomb could've gone off and Keet wouldn't have known it; he's still in the same position he was when I left. Five more hours go by. The light slanting through the windows is mellowing from bright white to gold when I hear Keet start to wake up. The blanket rustles, then he rolls over and looks at me. I close my laptop—email can wait.

He sits up, shrugs off the blanket, shuffles to the bathroom, then comes back and lies down again. "What have you been doing?" he asks.

"Went to the market. Took Fae for a walk. Answered some email . . ." Before I've finished speaking, I see that his eyes are closed and he's asleep again. One of his arms is hanging down, and as I tuck it under the blanket, I notice a ragged gash across the back of his hand that looks like it happened recently. My little sofa is almost too small for him.

By the time I've made myself a cup of ginger tea, fed Fae, and emailed Abbie, I hear Keet stir again. He rolls on to his side and looks at me with a sleepy smile. His voice is husky when he says, "It's very warm under these blankets. Come join me?"

Leaving the mug on the counter, I walk over, sit down next to him, and run my fingers through his now even more unruly hair. It's stiff, as though he's been swimming in the sea and the saltwater has dried in it.

"I could start a fire and warm up the room for us."

"It's warmer in here." He closes his eyes, snakes his arm out from under the blanket, and wraps it around my waist. I can feel the heat coming off him, and any shyness I have about lying down with him disappears.

"First, tell me what happened out there. I thought you got stranded on Speiden island and eaten by wildebeests or something."

He gives a small smile. "The only animals left there are some sheep, deer, and the sea lions. None of which, that I know of, eat people. The simple explanation is that I got caught in the storm and had to wait it out."

"Did your GPS go out, or was your boat damaged somehow?"

Keet pauses and takes his arm away from my waist. "I disabled everything and rode out the storm until I could make my way back home. I stayed awake for almost forty-eight hours, doing my best to not get thrown into the cliffs or sunk by a wave. By the time I got to Friday Harbor, I told my clients we needed to delay their trip and tried to get back here before the storm hit." There's a long pause as his eyes close and stay closed. When I think he's fallen asleep again, he says "I didn't make it. The weather reports understated how bad the storm was."

He seems distant and tired again, drawn into himself, and I see how, even for an experienced sailor, a storm like that would be a matter of life and death. I scoot closer to him.

"Move on over."

Keet moves against the back of the sofa, and I lay down, my head against his chest and my legs curved against his. When he enfolds me in the circle of his arms, I have a sense of peace and safety that I've not felt before, not like this. Our breathing synchronizes. I sigh, shifting my hips closer to him, which tells me all I need to know about how he's feeling. I've certainly been with guys in worse places than a small sofa in a cabin at the edge of the sea.

As if he's reading my thoughts, Keet finds the hem of my pullover and puts his hand under it, cradling my belly. He kisses my neck, his hand rubbing and massaging my stomach, then tracing the line of my bra against my skin, under my breasts.

I roll toward him, and when we kiss, it's like a flare of white heat, a pulsing current going from my lips to my toes. He rolls on top of me, propped on his elbows, his hands buried in my hair. There are too many clothes between us, and I'm trying to push his sweatshirt over his head as he kisses the top of my breasts, my shirt now in a heap on the floor.

And though I can't believe I'm doing it, I stop wrangling him out of his clothes. "Keet."

He continues kissing me, his hands holding my back, lifting me toward his mouth. It won't be much longer before I rip the bra off myself, which is why I'm stopping.

"Keet."

He pauses, his breathing heavy, and looks at me, reaching for the blanket and covering us.

"Nolee?"

"I don't want to stop—"

He kisses me, moving from lips to neck to collarbone, pushing aside one of my bra straps so he can move his mouth further over my breast. "I don't want to stop either," he murmurs against my skin. A shudder runs through me.

"Keet!"

I hear my voice, the pleading in it, and wonder whether it's because I want him to keep going, or because I'm terrified—it's been a very long time since I've been with a man who brought out these feelings in me.

He pushes himself on to his hands and it seems like he's looking at me from a great distance.

"Can you get my pullover, please?"

He sits up and hands me my pullover. I sit up too, yank it back on, and run my hands over my hair, trying to smooth it down.

"What's wrong, Nolee?"

His voice is low, his eyebrows drawn together.

"There's absolutely nothing wrong. It's so right, it's terrifying. Can I tell you about a few things before you have me so far gone that I can't think straight anymore?"

"Of course you can."

I take his hands in mine.

"I don't even know where to start, so I'll just tell you it's been a very long time since I've had sex."

"Can't be any longer than me, can it?" He squeezes my hand, bringing it to his mouth so he can kiss my palm. I shiver and catch my breath before asking,

"I don't know. How long has it been for you?"

He says, "You remember me telling you about Sascha, my ex-fiancée?"

I nod.

"We broke up twelve years ago. I went a little wild after that. Probably slept with every available woman who lives on these islands, and some who don't. And some who weren't."

"How long did that last?"

"Five or six years." He runs a hand through his hair, moving it away from his eyes. "I got bored though. A lot of the women were versions of Sascha: blonde, tall, young, liked to party. I stopped that lifestyle – if it can be called anything close to a life—six years ago."

I'm not any of those things, but I'd also given up wanting to be them a long time ago. He looks at me, a question swimming in his dark eyes.

"No judgement here, Keet. I got that all out of my system before I met Nate. I know what you mean; at first, it's exciting, having sex with different people. After a while though, for me it just felt empty."

"Yes. I tired of the same old song and dance. I started swimming more, committing to my business. Then right before I met you, I was making plans to sell my cabin, sell my boat, and head out somewhere different."

"I didn't know that. Is it still an option?"

"Not anymore. Not with you here."

Searching his eyes for any signs of a half-truth, or heated words coming from a heated moment, I pause. In that split-second, I decide.

He interrupts my thoughts. "What about you? How long has it been since you had sex?"

My laugh scurries out of my throat, and look out of the window, seeing nothing but a reflection of the dimly lit living room in the dark glass, and Keet and I sitting, rumpled, together. I fidget at my pullover, pulling a loose thread from the hem, uncomfortable with the answer I'm about to give him.

"Kind of over ten years."

He's silent longer than I expect, his eyes wide, his expression incredulous.

"Ten *years*?" and then, "Kind of?"

"I'll give you the short version of a long story. Two years after Abbie was born, Nate told me he didn't want more kids. I was mostly fine with it, but that might've been because I was permanently exhausted. Things didn't feel right between the two of us. He was, and still is, a very involved father, but he was working, and I was staying home, so I was the one who got up at night to take care of Abbie when she woke up. Which was a lot."

I pause, sifting through the years of my ruined marriage. "We raised Abbie together, but he and I grew further apart. At some point, I realized that all the energy I was pouring in to getting Nate to pay attention to me—the clothes, the working out, the counseling—wasn't working. So, I decided to put that effort toward doing something that I wanted to do. I've always been good with dogs, so I started a dog day care center."

Keet glances at Fae, who's lying in her bed on her back: her lips fall away from her teeth, her white chest is raised to the ceiling, and her legs splay outward. "If you can convince that feral beast that she's safe here, I'd say your business took off."

"You're right. It did. Taking care of dogs became helping people understand their dogs, became a full-time dog-training business. The whole time, Nathan and I were raising Abbie and doing a great job. But when she went to college, I asked him to move into her old room. We hadn't so much as touched each other, by then, for over eight years."

I can hear the swells of the night sea on the beach. I clear my throat and squeeze Keet's hands with my own. He squeezes back. "I couldn't be in the same bed with someone who made it so obvious that he felt zero anything for me. I later learned that that he started his affair with Carlos not long after that, and it went on until I found out and told him we needed to divorce." My stomach is in knots, but I continue, looking into his dark eyes.

"I went to a doctor, and she ordered all kinds of tests. I'm fine, but after so many years of not feeling like I feel when I'm with you, I'm also overwhelmed."

"How come you got tested if you and Nathan hadn't had sex in so long? Is that the 'kind of' part?"

I swallow the lump that's forming in my throat.

"I . . . basically, manipulated him into having sex with me once. I was desperate. A client, a super-nice guy, was coming on to me. I had a difficult time not giving in and just going for it. I was so lonely."

Keet moves closer, letting go of my hands to wrap his arms around me. I lean into him, my heartbeat slowing to match his, and close my eyes.

"When Nathan came home one night, I was in his room, naked in his bed, and demanded that we have sex. I didn't force him, but I sure as shit guilted him into it."

Keet rubs my arm and waits for me to finish what I need to say.

"It was horrible. The next morning, Nathan told me about Carlos, and that he'd already been with him. For three years. I panicked. Booked an appointment at a clinic in another town because I couldn't stand the embarrassment of going to our family doctor to be tested for STDs at forty-nine years old. I filed for divorce the next day. So, I'll see your five or six years and raise you five more." We're both quiet.

"Have I completely spoiled the moment?" I ask.

The rumble of his laugh shivers through my ear. "Not even a little." He draws away, and I look up at him, bringing my hands to his face so I can kiss him again. He lays me down, his lips soft and yielding as he holds me. I can feel the press of his belly against mine.

We kiss, his hands stroking my hair away from my face. I wrap my arms around the broad spring of his ribcage and, where our hips come together, there's a place that's far warmer than any other parts of our meeting bodies.

"How about this, Nolee? I have to go check on my boat tomorrow, make sure she got through the storm okay," he kisses me. "Let's take the kayak out to the Point tomorrow afternoon." He kisses each eyelid. "We can have dinner together and, if you want to, I'd like it if you would stay the night with me." He kisses my neck, his warm breath sending heat through my whole body.

As I inhale his smell of musk and sea, I damn the small sofa and damn my own terror. But he's right.

"I'd like that."

As evening fades to night, we spoon on our sides. I'm sleepy, but Keet seems to be wide awake; he strokes my hair and runs his hand over my hip, humming a tune I don't recognize.

"What's that song?" I ask.

"'Life Is Better with You.' Michael Franti."

"You missed telling me the year." I can feel his deep laugh against my back.

"2013." He kisses my neck and hums the tune against my skin. I squirm, almost too aroused to resist him.

"I'd better let Fae out and get to bed myself, Keet. Before you sweet talk me into something else."

He kisses my cheek and sits up, stretching his arms and long legs out in front of him.

"I'll call you tomorrow morning then?"

"Yes; let me know how *The Salish See* came through the storm. I hope she isn't too banged up. What can I bring to dinner?"

"Why don't you pick up something chocolate for dessert?"

"You'd probably eat anything dunked in chocolate."

"Just about. It's an aphrodisiac, did you know that?"

"I did, and I don't think we need much help in that department."

He nudges me to sit up. Then he puts his arms around me again and rises, holding me close. I sigh with pleasure, and we rock together side to side. Stifling a yawn, I stand on my tiptoes so I can kiss him good night. When I open the door, Fae runs out into the dark, silent except for the jingling of the tags on her collar.

Keet is standing in front of me again. He reaches under my shirt, cradling my ribcage. He kisses me then, a long, deep kiss that draws us close together, until I'm running my hands across the bare skin of his back, warm underneath his sweatshirt.

"If you don't leave now, Keet Noland, I might just kidnap you to my bedroom." He smiles a wicked half grin and says, "Then why would I leave now?" I laugh.

Fae runs back in, curls up on her bed, and closes her eyes. Glancing at her, I say, "That's what I need to do, too."

He searches my eyes with his. "Thank you for today. I'm sorry I worried you."

I remember then I was supposed to be mad at him, to pay him back for all the hours I spent watching his house, waiting for his car to pull in—for the days I spent thinking he might have run away from me. But I can't be angry, not this close to him, not seeing and hearing the sincerity of his apology.

"Just don't do it again, okay?"

He gives me a brief kiss. "I promise. Goodnight."

I watch until he reaches his cabin and goes inside.

"Fae, what have we gotten ourselves into?" She twitches her nose, squints at me, sighs, and goes back to sleep.

"You're right. Bedtime. We'll see what the morning brings."

It isn't until I'm in bed, watching the shapes of trees move in the lingering breeze, that I realize he never told where he got caught in the storm, and how he was able to sail home.

SEVENTEEN

The kayak rolls side-to-side in the gentle sea swells. We've rounded the point on our way back to Osprey Bay and I've just dropped my gaze from the cliff that tumbles down into the water in craggy rocks and trees. We stop paddling and drift. I look over the side and see jellyfish the color of sea foam and the size of the palm of my hand.

"I wonder if our seal disappeared because the male orca is somewhere close?"

Keet's voice, deep and slow, comes from behind me. "I think she's probably hunting somewhere else, looking for fish."

"Could be. I haven't seen him in a while, though. I kinda miss the big guy."

Keet paddles again, propelling us through the water. I match his rhythm, and we're back in Osprey Bay before I want to be. There's a stillness out on the water, a primal movement and a sound below the sound level I can hear with my ears. It must resonate through my belly and bones because it feels like the echo of thunder without the lightning, or the way Keet hums against my neck.

"Can you feel that Lia?"

"Feel what?"

I'm waiting for his reply when I feel it: a soft thrumming on the underside of the kayak. It feels like hail pelting *up* from the bottom of the ocean. I'm so absorbed in looking over the side of the kayak, trying to find the source of the vibration, that I'm surprised when a black-and-white head rises out of the green water, surrounded by a halo of white bubbles.

"George!"

The baby orca blasts me full in the face with his exhale, squeaking and nudging the kayak. I wipe my face with my hand, laughing. He flips over and glides away, belly up, his white tail slapping the surface of the water. Five more dorsal fins join his small one, and the orca family is rolling and gliding around us, flashes of black and white crisscrossing underneath the kayak. I hear an exhale close by and see Nana floating toward us.

Her dorsal fin isn't as high as the big male's, but she's still a formidable presence. I see the black shine of her eye as she rolls on her side to look at us. The vibration on the bottom of the kayak begins again, a deeper and slower pulse this time. The rest of the pod rises behind her, floating and exhaling. I hear their high-pitched squeals and wonder what they are saying to each other.

"Keet, what are they doing?"

"What do you think they're doing?"

A slew of not so funny replies that come to mind disappear. It's impossible to be flippant in the presence of all this beauty. Instead, I return to my knowing place, the same place in which I can feel and see the messages of dogs.

"It feels like they're happy to have found us."

"And . . . ?"

"And I would say the feeling is mutual."

"I would agree."

I look over my shoulder and see Keet's hand in the water. Nana swims closer and glides under his hand from her pectorals to her tail, languorous and slow. I place my hand in the water too, startled by the chill. George surprises me again, rising headfirst underneath my hand so that I'm cupping his rostrum, which is larger than my head. He's warm compared to the water, and his slick firmness reminds me of the watermelons my grandma used to grow. I'd hold them in my hands when they were still on the vine, then rinse them off while they were still warm from the Texas sun. I laugh, overjoyed at being in the middle of this pod, marveling at the trust they have with us.

George moves his head so my hand is under his jaw, and I scratch lightly while gazing into his half-closed eyes.

"If he were a dog, his tail would be wagging right about now."

Keet laughs, and I keep scratching. George floats into different positions, and as I'm scratching and watching the sun reflect off his skin in bursts of light, images form in my head. It feels as though I'm dreaming with my eyes open. I see, diving into the cloudy depths, a family of orcas. They fill the sea; they're rubbing against one another, squeaking and whistling. Large dorsal fins mix with smaller, rounder ones. Baby orcas swim amongst the adults, nudging and playing, nursing and flowing in their mothers' slipstream. The black and white of their bodies is an infinite spiral, their whistles a symphony. They guide me into the middle of their pod. The only sounds I hear are the orcas' mewling and chirping and the deep thrumming heartbeat of the sea. I can't tell if the orcas are swimming in an ocean of sound, or whether the sound is swimming through the orcas.

I take a sharp inhale and open my eyes, not realizing that I'd closed them while my hand was on George. I refocus and see that my hand is now resting on his dorsal fin as he bobs by the kayak, both of us nudged by the tide.

"Lia? Are you okay?"

I swallow, my heart pounding, and stifle the tears that are on the brink of spilling over. George squeaks a note that climbs through the upper registers of my hearing and dives, the pod following him. The last I see of them is a series of white tails slapping the water. I wipe my eyes under my sunglasses. "I'm more than okay, but I don't understand what just happened."

We paddle back to the beach in silence. It isn't until we've dragged the kayak up toward his cabin that he says, "I want to hear every detail. I have a hunch I've had similar experiences."

"Yes. Of course. I'll feed Fae, then get ready for dinner. I'll meet you at your place."

He leans toward me, and I step to meet him. He takes my chilled hand in his warm one and kisses me, first on the lips, then under my jaw.

"I'll be waiting." The rasp of the stubble on his face as he lays his cheek against mine makes me close my eyes and hold him closer for a moment. As I walk away, I look over my shoulder to see Keet still watching me. I smile and put a little more sway in my hips as I climb the steps and open the door. Fae bounds beside me, circling and yipping the way coyotes do at the end of the day. I thought our morning hike would've worn her out, but she looks like she could go another five miles.

"I'm going to have to teach you about swimming, Fae." I bend down and she sniffs my nose and hair, her breath still smelling faintly puppylike.

I teeter there in the doorway, the opening between the sea and my home, enjoying the late afternoon light and the way it paints everything it touches soft peach and rose. The porch's weathered wood holds onto the heat the sun had gifted it earlier. The sea is empty of dorsal fins, the water is quiet.

I rest my hands on the porch railing and replay the vision—that's the only word for it—that George shared with me. I'm still looking at the gentle roll of the sea and the pale silhouettes of the islands when I realize that in the vision, I didn't hear any boat noise. Only ocean, and a deep bass throb, and orca sounds. I wonder if the vision was from a time before humans took to the seas. A time when orca families were robust and numerous. I close my eyes, trying to recall every detail. But holding on to a vision given to me by an orca is like trying to bottle the mist. The more I force it, the faster it evaporates. I step inside and close the door.

After she's eaten, Fae follows me up to my bedroom. Looking at the plain black cotton dress I found at the thrift store, I sigh, wondering if I needed to update my bra and panties, too. Then I realize that I'm past the age of trying to impress a man with lingerie. *Besides, he's already seen you in your underwear. It's not like it's going to be a shock.* I pick out my only matching set—also black—and toss it and the dress on the bed.

"Time for a shower, Fae."

When he hears the door open, he turns from the kitchen counter and looks up. The only thing he sees is Nolee, framed in his doorway. She's giving him the soft half-smile that makes him feel as though she sees only him, too. Her flowing black dress hugs her torso and hips, then flares out and ends above her knees. The scoop neck reveals the succulent roundness of the tops of her breasts, and he has a fleeting thought about kissing her there. Long silver earrings with turquoise insets dangle from her earlobes.

Once he's in front of her, he holds her face in both of his hands, tilts up her chin, and kisses her.

"You look stunning, Lia," he whispers.

He kisses her again, mouth, chin, and neck, until she pulls back, laughing softly. She hands him a small bag that he recognizes from the bakery.

"I think you're the first person who's said that to me in too many years. I might even believe you."

He holds her hand and leads her to the table; her face softens, and her green eyes light up at the sight of the glowing candles, the bottle of Balvenie, and the Scotch glasses he'd bought. The place settings are next to one another, the plates and bowls filled with various foods.

Burying his face in her hair, he inhales deeply. Under the shampoo and oils she's used, he detects her natural scent—earth and wind, and a mild spice that's all her.

"Keet…"

A rush of heat envelopes him and in it, his words disappear. He bends down, wraps his arms around her waist, and lifts her. She kisses him with abandon, and he feels her weight pressed against his chest. He nudges at her jaw, kissing her neck until she leans back, and he can run his tongue across the tops of her breasts. He tastes of the tang of salt and mint.

He returns her to the ground gently, but their kissing accelerates to recklessness. His hands have dropped from her waist to her hips, and he grips her to himself. She's on her tiptoes, her arms locked around his neck, and he moves his hands up the length of her back, then runs his hands through her hair before breaking away. His breath is coming sharp and quick, but before he can form any words, she says in a husky voice, "Can we have dinner later?"

He smiles, takes her hand, and she kicks off her flats and follows him down the hall. Pausing at the door to his bedroom, he kisses her slowly. "Wait here just a moment."

She nods, her green eyes sparking fire. The door slides shut, and when it opens again, he watches her as she takes in the single large candle on the wooden mantle above the gas fireplace, casting its golden light in a soft circle. The large bed has a headboard of the same dark wood as the mantle. The white duvet is turned down to show dark sheets. As Keet takes her hand and they move closer to his bed, she closes her eyes and inhales.

"What's that smell, Keet?"

"I know you like oils, so I bought a mixture called 'Passion' and put it around the room. It's not too much?"

She smiles and kisses him, pulling away so all he sees is the dancing light in her eyes.

"It's perfect. Now, let's get out of these clothes."

I'm surprised, because as rushed as we've been, when we undress each other, it's slow. Keet never takes his hands or his eyes away from me. As he removes each piece of clothing, he strokes my uncovered skin with his hand, or his lips, or his tongue. His body is close and burning. I run my hands over his chest, admiring broad shoulders that are the color of nutmeg in this dim and otherworldly light. If I were still in Texas, I would say he's rangy.

But I willingly forget my words as he slides my underwear over my hips, then strokes the back of my legs as he kneels in front of me. He kisses my thighs, pausing with his hands cradling my bottom and his cheek against my belly, against the faded cesarean scar from Abbie's birth. I run my hands through his hair, feeling the pliable curve of his earlobe, then he stands, and I run my hand down the roundness of his belly and unbutton his jeans. Mimicking him, I kneel, kissing his thighs, holding the jeans so he can step out of them. Before I can make my way up again, he takes my hands and brings me to him, kissing me with an urgency I feel tumbling deep in my pelvis.

When we both pause, I want to take my trembling hands from his face and walk out of the house on my shaky legs. He must see this hesitation because he waits, his eyes on mine, his hands warm against my bare back.

"Is this okay for you?" he whispers.

The candlelight flickers at the edge of my vision. The bed looms behind Keet. I drop my hands to his shoulders.

"Do you want to stop?" he asks, his voice still low and quiet. "We can stop if you need to."

Concern has replaced the heat in his eyes, and seeing that, I step closer. My legs stop quaking.

"I don't want to stop."

We fall into bed, me astride him as we kiss. His hips are solid between my knees. He rolls me over, and the feeling of being pinned beneath his strength causes me to wrap my arms and legs around him, bringing him closer. We are a hurricane making landfall, a storm that rushes through every trembling fortress we have each built against it. Keet kisses my neck, holds my breasts in his hands while he nuzzles each nipple before etching a tender line with his tongue down my stomach, past my belly button to the legs that I have now unlocked from around his hips. His fingers are a gentle rain, falling onto my parched skin, his touch everywhere, stroking, coaxing, exploring until he places them under each buttock, gripping, and raises me to his mouth.

There's a roaring in my ears, a rush of wind that picks me up and carries me into the clouds. My voice is lightning, my body an earthquake as it trembles against his tongue and mouth.

When he releases me, and enters me, he's a sirocco blazing through an oasis. I can see the dancing gold light glancing off the bronze of his shoulder. I loosen my grip, dimly realizing I'd sunk my nails into his back. He moans, "Do that again, Lia."

I dig my nails in, undulating underneath him as he rides through the storm I've unleashed. He grips my hair, his breath rasping against my ear. The tempest continues, a heated whirling tornado that picks us up, spins us, and drops us back down to earth.

Our breathing slows and becomes a chaste wind that blows us home. When we look at one another, though the room is dark, I feel the sun rise in my eyes, the rays refracted back through his.

∿∿∿

The smell of food entices us out of bed. Once we're back in the kitchen, I notice that the candles have burned to nubs, the pale wax pooling on the dark table. Moving with slow precision, he starts the dinner reheating, then goes to the cabin and brings Fae and her bed back with him.

"Thanks for bringing Fae over." I look at her lying on her bed, watching us. "I would've worried about her in the house alone all night."

"That didn't seem fair to me, either." As he arranges food on our plates, I pour the Scotch into two glasses, and he meets me at the table, one plate in each hand. As I look at him, the dream comes back to me in a burst: Keet hip-deep in dark water, hands raised to a bright moon.

I stand by the table, watching him, watching the flex of his arm muscles as he sets the plates down, the way the black pools of his eyes catch the candlelight. And once again, I'm moving toward him, helpless against his invisible pull. I reach up to touch the angles of his cheekbones, and kiss him, slowly, feeling the soft press of his mouth, the piquant taste of him on my tongue. His hands run across my back, around my waist, and back up to my neck.

"Do you still want to spend the night, Lia?" His forehead rests against mine, his eyes as fathomless as the sea outside.

"Yes, unless you want to kick me out."

"There are many things I'd like to do with you, and kicking you out isn't one of them."

I kiss him again, running my hand along his stubble-free cheek; I like the silk and leather of his skin.

"How about we eat before it gets cold again?"

Fae nudges my calf with her nose, and I look down to see her wagging her tail. Keet warms up some leftover salmon, then puts it in the same bowl he used when she first arrived—barking and angry—on his porch. Was that only two weeks ago? Time, once more, feels elastic. I've felt and experienced and been more of who I am in these two months since coming to Camas, than I've been most of my life.

"Fae, sit." She sits. He places the bowl in front of her. "There. Now we can eat without guilt."

"Have you started thinking dog spit isn't that bad?"

"I think Fae isn't that bad, so her spit doesn't bother me. As much."

We sit down, and Keet takes my fork, spears a bite of salad and offers it to me. The only thing I see are his almond-shaped eyes, and a shiver runs through me. The simple act of him feeding me feels as intimate as sharing our bodies.

I chew the salad and watch as he cuts a small portion from a scallop, puts it on my fork and offers it to me again. I taste the marinade and feel the slippery, meaty scallop against my tongue. This time, I can't keep my eyes open as I chew.

"I've always appreciated your enjoyment of food."

I wipe my mouth with a napkin. "How could I not enjoy anything you make, Keet?"

When I look at the table again, I see a plate with fresh rolls and a bowl of pasta primavera topped with scallops. Another bowl for the salad. In the candlelight, the gleam of dressing makes the green leaves look almost black. The large wooden cutting board holds smoked salmon flanked by three local cheeses and dried apricots and cranberries. Salt-speckled almonds nestle against dark chocolate.

"You made a charcuterie board!"

Keet smiles, kisses me, then hands me my fork. We work through our candlelit meal, the soft, honeyed light rounding the edges of our plates and catching in Keet's hair.

"You want to know something?"

I nod, my attention momentarily diverted from my meal. Keet runs his thumb along my bottom lip, catching the salad dressing that's dripped there, then licks it off, eyes closed. Without thinking about it, I lean in closer so I can taste the dressing that's now on his tongue. When we pull apart, both breathless, I ask, "What were you going to say?"

He pauses, smiles, and gathers a handful of my loose hair. "I make those meals just to watch you enjoy them."

We kiss again. This time I'm in his lap, arms around his neck, his mouth on mine. I laugh while we're still kissing, feeling better than I ever have.

"What's funny?"

"I'm not laughing because something is funny. I'm laughing because I feel so damn joyful, Keet. I feel like I'm in my twenties again, unburdened, but with all the wisdom I've gathered reaching my fifties."

He smiles, kisses the end of my nose, and shifts underneath me. I sit back down in the chair next to him, taking food from the charcuterie board.

He takes the last bite of his scallop. I can't take my eyes away from him, and he meets my look with one equally intense. A spark of candlelight flashes in the depths of his eyes. I think about looking into the eyes of the orca and am reminded of the vision I had with George.

"You said you've had experiences with the orca family, Keet?"

"Many of them. Sometimes I feel as though I could be an orca myself."

"I can almost understand that."

"When you understand it, let me know. Sometimes I feel out of my element. Like I understand nothing."

I take a sip of Scotch, watching as he sets his empty glass back on the table. He strokes my cheek, fingertips soft against my skin. Then he says, "Will you tell me what you felt out there today?"

I take a breath, then another sip of scotch, and close my eyes so I can replay the vision.

"When we were floating on the kayak, and my hand was on George's skin, pictures started flashing in front of me, like a movie. My eyes were open, but they were in my head, in black and white, like an old movie. I was in the sea, and the orcas filled it. There were mothers and babies and sisters and brothers, and they were swimming close together, touching one another, calling, floating, and playing."

Keet kisses me then, and in combination with the orca vision, my balance is skewed. It feels as though I'm falling into the night sea, one filled with mysterious possibilities. His lips on mine, the memory of the baby orca's skin, the vision of hundreds of orcas swimming in harmony—they all swirl together.

Gasping, I pull away from him.

"Lia?"

I give him a small smile. "It's nothing. Well, nothing I can explain." I touch his face, reassured by the feel of his skin. "Why don't you tell me something about your experiences?"

He pauses, blinks a few times, and reaches for my hand. I intertwine my fingers with his, hanging on to both his hand and my sanity.

"I've swum with all of them."

"Even the big male orca?"

Keet looks down, smiling. "Yes, even him."

"That didn't scare you? I know you told me they eat fish, but there are seven of them, and even George is bigger than you."

"He doesn't scare me. None of them do. By then I'd been following them and hanging out--"

I interrupt him. "By 'hanging out,' do you mean on your boat?"

He pauses a long time before giving my hand a squeeze and nodding.

"Sorry I interrupted. Please, tell me more."

He shifts in the chair, bringing his knee to rest against mine.

"When I go for a swim, or I'm not taking a tour, I'm with the orca family. I've been with them for so many years that sometimes I think we're all swimming in the same current, the same consciousness, almost."

The candlelight flickers on his skin, the color of late-summer honey. My breathing slows, and then catches again as he says, "Similar visions have come to me. My take on it is that what you saw, and what I've seen, are the oceans and seas before people. It's an ancient memory, maybe the collective memory of the orcas. Or the ocean."

I feel two parts of me at odds with each other: my healthy sceptic is rolling her eyes, and my wise one, the part who has no explanation for some of my experiences with dogs, sits in knowing silence. This part of me doesn't need to fight with the sceptic. This part of me gazes at the spiral across generations and centuries of all the people before me, seeing into time. A time when humans couldn't be out of sync with the earth around them because they were a part of it, as much as water and sky and the birds who swooped between both. I close my eyes, the schism inside me growing smaller.

When I open my eyes again, I see Keet with his eyes closed. I lean in and kiss him, and this time, it's only a kiss, and only Keet. When I pull away, his eyes are open and he's smiling.

"That sounds like a beautiful feeling. I can see why you swim so much. But I still don't understand how you do that without becoming hypothermic."

"I've been swimming in cold waters since I was a child. I guess I've adapted."

We're silent then; my eyes feel heavy, my body, warm and relaxed.

"Let's clean this up and get you to bed."

I nod then let Fae out for her last pee break of the night. When she comes back in, she settles in a tidy ball, the white tip of her tail covering her nose.

Back in the bedroom, as we pull the duvet off the floor and straighten the sheets and pillows, Keet says, "If you need anything, wake me up."

After what seems like hours of cuddling, I let Keet's breathing soothe me into sleep. I know I'm dreaming again. The silver clouds and the moonlit sky drop like curtains on a black ocean stage. Keet is standing with his back to me, the cloak floating on the surface, stirred by a wind I cannot feel or hear. The hood is pulled over his head, but the familiar shape of his torso makes me want to wade in, pull him to me. But I'm unable to move, and when I look down, my feet are stones on the shore. I call his name, and a vast echo carries beyond Osprey Bay, out into the channel, up into the sky. He turns, the cloak swirling behind him. His face in the shadow of the giant hood, his arms and torso in blackness. The hood drops away, and in a flash of white, I wake up gasping.

As soon as I sit up, disoriented, I feel Keet behind me, arms wrapped me, head resting against mine.

"Bad dream?"

I nod, breathing as though I've run a race. We lie down again, holding each other in the gray light of early morning. I'm trembling.

"I'll turn on the fireplace." He rises and flicks the switch, and I hear the clicking noise that precedes ignition—so like the orcas' clicking. It stops, but I'm still trembling.

The bed moves as Keet gets back in and rolls closer to me, gathering me to his chest. He's warm, much warmer than the sheets or the air around us.

"It wasn't a bad dream, but it scares me, and I don't know why." Not wanting to close my eyes again, I watch the orange gas flames flicker in the fireplace.

"Do you want to tell me what it is?" I feel the heat of his breath ruffle through my hair as I bury my face in his neck. I'm still debating whether to answer him when he whispers, "You don't have to," and squeezes me closer to him.

"It's about you."

His breathing changes rhythm. He sighs.

"Please tell me."

I'm fighting the trembling now, quaking against his steady chest. The dream tumbles around in my head, an endless loop with no conclusion. I kiss his collarbone, hoping to calm whatever my brain won't let me remember.

"Before I tell you, I want you to know that I've been having this dream for months, ever since I met you. Tonight was the closest I've been to seeing where it ends, or what you're trying to show me."

Keet is silent, his cheek against the top of my head, his arms around me, one leg thrown over mine, sheltering me.

"In it, I see you standing in Osprey Bay. Your back is to me and you're wearing a cloak. I can tell it's you, but the hood is up. I can't move from the rocks because my feet are stones, so I call your name. Everything is black—the sea, the islands, the sky. But you're lit by the moon, like a spotlight." Telling the dream is working; I'm not trembling, and my voice is no longer strangled.

"After you hear my voice, you turn, and the cloak floats on top of the water. It looks like you're wearing the sea. And then the hood starts to fall away. That's when I wake up. I never see your face, but I know I'm about to."

Keet shifts, tightens his grip, and kisses the top of my head. "You said you dreamed more tonight?"

I nod. And wait, closing my eyes to replay the dream.

"Tonight, the hood came off, but before I could see you, there was a flash of white. Then I woke up."

We breathe together; the soft orange light of the fire makes it feel as though we're the only two people alive. Keet strokes my hair and my back, kisses the top of my head, and I feel myself drifting off to sleep. From somewhere far away, I hear Keet's deep voice, soothing me, speaking slow and soft as though he's wrapping us both in a spell.

"Thank you for sharing your dream, Lia. Rest now. Rest. No more dreams, only sleep. There's nothing to fear, there's nothing to fight. Sleep, Lia, sleep." The last thing I feel is the vibration of his voice, singing me into a space without orca dreams.

EIGHTEEN

When I wake in the morning, it's to the smell of bacon and the sweet scent of cinnamon. I sit up, the sheet sliding from my body, and look over at the empty spot where Keet was. The fire is out, the curtains open to let in the bright light of a sunny day. I stretch, get out of bed, and hear Keet's voice.

"Lia?"

The dream washes over me, and a fuzzy memory of falling asleep to the sound of the sea. Or was it his voice? I hear a soft padding down the hall, and Fae comes in, wiggling around my feet and making her chirping bird barks.

"Good morning, little bird, good morning!" I rub her head and lower myself to the floor. She sits beside me, leaning in and panting.

"Have you eaten yet, red dog?" I'm looking into her amber eyes when I hear another set of footsteps.

"You were sleeping so soundly that I thought I'd get up and make us breakfast."

I continue to pet Fae, soothed by her weight and warmth against my bare legs.

"She hasn't eaten. She ate the last of the salmon and rice last night."

I look at Keet and smile, realizing that I'm sitting on the floor in only his t-shirt, which barely covers my hips. I use the edge of the bed to stand up, and he moves toward me, taking me in his arms and burying his face in my hair.

"Good morning, Lia."

I squeeze him tighter and say the same back to him, confused by the feeling of a wall between us. I turn my head to give him a quick kiss, hoping to knock down the barrier. The hand I have at the nape of his neck comes away damp.

"Did you go for a swim already?"

Keet laughs. "Guilty. I couldn't sleep, so I went out early this morning. Just got back a little while ago."

"Just so we're clear, Keet. I don't mind if you swim, and you don't need my permission."

There's silence then, and I feel the wall, thicker than before. I clear my throat, stepping away from him, but not able to meet his eyes.

"I'm going to dress and get Fae some breakfast. See you in ten?"

I don't wait for his answer, turning instead to gather my clothes, quick and rushed. Sliding the bathroom door shut, I strip off Keet's t-shirt and get back into my own clothes, overtaken by an urge to leave. When I slide the door open, I'm startled to see Keet standing in the doorway, frowning, his mouth a compressed straight line.

"Are you okay?" he asks.

I step back, wrapping my arms around myself. Fae is standing beside Keet, looking as confused as he does. I kneel and she comes to me, her body wriggling. I answer from the safety of her red coat where I've buried my face.

"I don't know. I'm going to feed her and shower and change, and I'll come back."

"Do you want breakfast, or to be alone for a bit?"

I notice the trembling is coming back. Fae feels it too and whines, a high-pitched sound that reverberates against my eardrums.

"Maybe it would be best if I was alone for a bit. I think I need to sort out some things."

Keet kneels, so he's at the same level as Fae and me. I lift my head and look into his eyes, hoping he doesn't notice that I'm shaking.

"Nolee, did I do something? Or not do something? Are you scared of me?"

My laugh and cry come out at the same time. "No, no, and no." I stand up, and Fae trots to the door, throwing a glance over her shoulder before looking up at it and wagging her tail.

"I think I better let her out." I stride over to the door and open it. Fae races off the porch so fast she slips, then recovers and vaults down the stairs. I turn, smiling, and look at Keet.

"Last night was perfect. You're . . ." I don't want to say perfect because I don't know what he is. "You're wonderful and it's been so long since I've felt anything, much less what I'm feeling about you. I think I'm a bit freaked out." I take a breath, noticing that I'm speaking too fast. I look out of the doorway. It's summer here on the island, and the bright green of spring is long gone.

"Okay. Call me when you feel like talking."

I stand on my tiptoes to give him a quick kiss. The smell of his skin flashes through my senses, but I pull back before he can tempt me to him. As I turn to leave, I see the table set for our breakfast. Part of me wants to join him, to share this first meal after our first time together. But that part shrinks before the trembling that won't stop until I'm back in my house. As I step off the porch, the last thing I hear is the click of a lock.

After almost running back to my cabin and shutting the door, I slide down until I'm sitting, crouched and trembling. Fae lies down beside me, her head on her paws, as the tears I've held in come trickling, then pouring, out. My broken heart is returning to me, newly mended. The fracture lines look like rivers on a map. Some are spidery and faint, traces of water fighting to flow. Some are thick, announcing their place and right to their path. As I rock back and forth, howling in misery, wanting the ache in the middle of my chest to stop, I'm also aware of a second me, the one who sits and witnesses. The one who knows.

She's the wise one who tells me dogs' secrets, the one who's wearing the gag I put on her, hoping to silence her; I only let her speak in the company of dogs, because there, her wisdom never led me astray. When she whispered that something wasn't right between me and Nate, I silenced her. When she told me it wasn't love if I contorted myself to please my parents, my lovers, my husband, I shut her into a dark room. There she stayed, kneeling, gagged and alone, until my move here. Until Keet. Until the orcas.

This whole time, when I thought I was the most *me*, I wasn't yet complete. I took her acquiescence for weakness, but now she stands before me, tall and shining, her gaze full of the strength of compassion. The gag is gone. Her hands are free. She stands, waiting for the flood of pain and grief to run itself out, a river returning to flow between its banks.

In that moment, the blade of honesty lands like a knife in my heart. Almost from the time we were married, I knew that Nate and I weren't right for each other. I knew, and I ignored my knowing. I could've been an adult and helped him find himself; instead, I tried to change who he was. It wasn't completely his fault that I felt invisible. My denial of my knowing, combined with the ridiculous thought that I could make him someone different, built the bars between us, and in myself. I was my own jailer.

I sink my hand into Fae's coat and then get up to wash my face. As I pass by the window, I see that Keet's vehicle is gone. I pick up my phone, ready to call Trish and ask if he went out but dial the shelter instead. Andi picks up the phone.

"Hi, Andi. Do you need more help? There's been a change of plans and I can come in after all." When I hear they can always use the help, I thank her and hang up. After feeding Fae, another shower, and a bowl of cereal, my red dog and I hop into the car and leave for town. I can't stand to be in that cabin one more second.

I park in the shade of a tree and open all the windows, snap Fae's lead onto her harness, and walk toward the gray-and-white-trimmed building. The glass door swings shut behind me and I wave at Andi as I stride by the desk, not sure why I'm hurrying but doing so just the same.

"Hey! I'll put Fae in the dog yard and come back, and you can tell me what I need to do today." Fae trots beside me to the dog yard, where I take off her harness. Three dogs run over, sniffing, and going into play bows. Fae darts away, outrunning all of them.

When I get back to the front desk, Andi looks up. A quiet woman with a shy smile, she has a gray bob that shows signs of the black her hair used to be, and blue eyes. I guess she's in her sixties, but her skin, light from her Irish ancestors, is clear and radiant. She files a manila folder, her long graceful fingers shutting the drawer and reaching for my hand.

"I'm so glad you've come in today, Nolee." She holds my hand briefly.

"What's going on?"

"We have a dog in quarantine. He won't let anyone near him. When he got here, he was in terrible shape, but after a few days and food, he still seemed traumatized. The vet won't come back until we can at least get a muzzle on him."

"Well, you know I always say . . ." Andi chants with me, "there aren't any dangerous dogs, just dangerous behavior." We both laugh, and I walk toward the door that says *Quarantine*. Andi calls after me, "He's not in there. We put him in one of the isolation runs. There aren't any other dogs out there now."

I step through the gate, making sure it's closed, and look out at the pen. I see a dirty shape huddled by a doghouse. The color of his coat is hard to tell, but he might be tan and white. His face has a typical husky mask;

white muzzle extending to white around his brown eyes. A bowl of water and another of untouched kibble are on the ground just inside the gate.

As soon as he sees me, he shivers. His tail wraps around his front paws, and he's hunches into himself. But his eyes never stop watching me. His ears, which are flattened against his head, look like they'd stand up if he felt better. I stop and wait, looking anywhere but directly at him. I continue to do this for the next half-hour until I am at the gate of his run. He still hasn't barked but is no longer quivering. I leave and go back into the shelter to clean the cats' litter boxes.

When I return, he hasn't moved. His ears perk up, then lay flat against his head again. This time, I get all the way to the gate, and he isn't shivering or trying to press himself through the wire of the run. I sit down, breathing deeply and studying my feet. I hear him stand, then sniff, then the pad of his feet as he takes a few steps toward me. When he retreats, he doesn't turn his back or take his eyes off me.

I sit for a few minutes longer, watching as he returns to the corner, the trembling starting again. The longer I sit, the more he blinks, then yawns. I turn away and get up in slow motion and join Andi back at the desk.

"I'll stop by every day and work with him, and if you have other work for me to do, I'll do that, too. I think he'll come around, but it might be a bit before it happens."

Andi stops typing and pushes her chair away from the computer. "It's a good thing we can get food and water in his pen. We'd be in trouble if he was aggressive."

"Did you say they found him at the top of Mt. Pelorus? By the tower?" In my mind flashes a picture of a narrow trail, the conifer woods, and the stone tower.

Andi pauses and raises her eyebrows. "I don't think I mentioned that. Let me pull his file." She returns to the computer and clicks a few times. She tilts the monitor so I can see.

"You're right. Some hikers found him and brought him in. That was two days ago." She looks up at me. "How did you know that?"

I shake my head. "I don't know. I could swear you mentioned it."

Andi laughs, "Maybe the dog told you. Do you have a name for him yet? We thought he was some sort of Husky-Labrador mix."

I give her a distracted smile in return. "Sounds about right. I don't have a name for him, but I bet one will pop up when I see him tomorrow."

After extracting Fae from her playgroup of thrashing, wagging tails and lively jumps, we drive home, winding through the shady roads, part of a stream of traffic that isn't in any rush to get where it's going. I look in the rearview mirror and see her stretched out on the back seat, panting, her eyes closed.

"Fae!" Her eyes open and she pops up to a sitting position, head tilted. "Let's go home and get some lunch. I don't know if I can handle any more of this day."

NINETEEN

Keet sails out to Patos Island. Leaving the marina, he points the bow northwest, seeing the contours of the island in his mind's eye. It's the middle of June, and though there are still plenty of tourists, the wind is in short supply. He hopes there's a mooring buoy to secure to, and later, enough wind to fill the sails for the trip home.

He sails around Active Pass, instinct telling him about the rocks that hide under its calm surface. Dark, shiny seal heads dot the water, bobbing before melting back into the sea. Nearing the narrow cove, he sees that a boat has claimed the mooring closer to shore, so he steers to starboard, to the only empty buoy. He notices that it's a slack tide with no current and is grateful; this makes picking up the mooring by himself easier.

Using his boat hook, he snags the mooring pennant, runs it through the starboard bow chock, and cleats it off. He then adds a safety line. The other boat is smaller than his, and he guesses from the kayak pulled up on the pebbled shore that its occupants are hiking.

He walks back to the cockpit, shuts down his engine, and turns off the electronics. Out of habit, he leaves his VHF tuned to channel 16 in case a fellow mariner needs help. Although sailors are a solitary lot, they rely on one another. Making sure everything is secure topside, he steps to the companionway, then descends the ladder into the cabin. Straightening the comforter on the bed, he thinks that before he and Nolee take a trip together, he needs to get new sheets. He lies down and closes his eyes, waiting for darkness.

The rolling sea and the silence lull him into semi-somnolence. Nolee drifts across the slow currents in his mind, provoking simultaneous sensations of thrill and sadness. He doesn't know what she's struggling with but empathizes with the look in her eyes. He's seen it —and has also had the same expression often enough—that it's not a shock anymore. He wonders if the vision with George and the dream she's been having got wrapped up with their lovemaking. For him, this is exactly what it was, and he wishes she were here so they could be together in the rock and sway of the boat.

Her dream doesn't surprise him, but how long she's been having it does. And if she digs a little deeper, she might find out exactly what it means. He's not worried; in fact, he's almost incapable of worry. Much of the time, worry is about things that might happen. Worry happens when life is lived in the future instead of in the present. For him, it's less of a spiritual way of thinking than it is a practical one. It's the reason he and his office manager work so well together: She takes care of his work schedule; he focuses on each day as it comes. He feels better when he concentrates about where he is instead of what may or may not happen. Still, he thought, at some point, he needs to decide whether to tell Nolee the secret he's keeping. It's this thought, swirling in a mental eddy, that prevents him from falling fully asleep.

He rolls over, trying to get comfortable in the narrow space, then gives up. His stomach rumbling, he retrieves this morning's breakfast and sits at a faded table the size of a dinner tray. Taking a bite of the now-cold bacon and following it with a bite of cinnamon roll, he looks at the leftovers of what was to have been a shared breakfast. As he chews, the urge to swim crashes inside him. Glancing through the door, he sees that it's still too light. When he walks up on to the deck, he still doesn't see any sign of the people from the other boat.

Returning to the cabin, he selects the battered copy of *The Light on the Island* from his small library and takes it up top. Lying on the deck, his legs and back warmed by the sun, he reads, hoping to be distracted until it's darker. As the sun sinks lower, the sea darkens from blue-green to navy streaked with rays of golden, end-of-day light. By the time the light finally vanishes, Keet is asleep, stretched out on his back, hands clasped across his belly. The wind is gone, and the tide is gentle.

Wakened by laughter, he props himself up on one elbow and sees the fuzzy outlines of a young couple starting a fire at one of the beach's camping sites. He smiles, glad to be awake, until his stomach growls once more. Rubbing his hand across his belly, he opens the refrigerator, wondering if he'll ever feel sated.

After eating leftover pasta and salad, he washes the dishes, pulls off his t-shirt and shorts, and walks out on to the deck. Grabbing the rail, he swings over it, lowering himself into the water in one graceful motion, then dives. He pops up, hair slicked back like the shiny head of a seal, to see where the couple went. Their tent is up, the fire burned down to embers, and he can hear their private laughter coming from inside the tent. He takes a deep breath, then dives into the sea, which is always in present tense.

I'm curled up on my sofa, checking Keet's driveway, wondering why I'm both eager and nervous about seeing him again, and about explaining my hasty departure. The seismic plates of my internal landscape are shifting, shaking up my long-held views. I'm not sure I can get used to a different vista. It's late afternoon, and he still isn't back.

My cell phone rings, and I grab it, glad of the interruption. Fae stands up, wagging her tail.

"Hey, Andi, everything okay?"

"Hi Nolee. Yes, it's good. I'm at home and I was thinking about our chat about the new dog you saw today."

"What were you thinking?" I glance back at Keet's empty driveway, then settle into the cushions.

"My mom had things happen to her like you did this afternoon."

"What things?" I grip the arm of the sofa.

"Knowing stuff without being told. She was like a human weathervane; she could've gotten a job on television."

"Really? Did she know about anything other than the weather?"

"She did, mostly about friends, and especially about us kids. She said she'd get flashes of pictures about our day, or why we were upset. We still had our secrets, but she always knew when to comfort us."

"And this was okay with her?"

"It was. Her dad, my grandpa, had the same tendencies."

"God, I'm so relieved you didn't call it a 'gift.' I'm used to these intuitions with dogs, but lately they've been showing up with other animals, and they're much clearer. It's kinda freaking me out."

"That's why I'm calling. The look on your face today told me something was going on. All I'm saying is, with me, it's no big deal. I grew up with this happening all the time."

"Do you ever get information that way?"

"Nah. It skipped all of us kids. The way I see it, though, it's like eye color or whether you're an introvert or extrovert. It's just a part of you."

Staring at Keet's empty house, I feel the seismic shift settling. "Andi, I really needed to hear this. There've been so many changes since I moved here that sometimes I don't recognize my life."

"But that's why you made the move, right? Because the life you were in wasn't the life you wanted?"

"That's it, in a nutshell," I laugh. "Seems to me that if I wanted a new life, and it's being offered to me, it would be ridiculous to reject it just because I'm nervous."

"It's not like having these hunches, or whatever you call them, is new for you, right? You said this is a common thing when you're working with dogs." I hear the bang of dishes in the background and wonder if she's having dinner.

"It is. No complaints, though. For a moment, it's like I get to enter a whole other world. I like it."

"So maybe this is you, and your new life is seeing that it doesn't just happen with dogs. Is it just animals, or are you also a weather station, like my mom?" I hear her soft laugh. "No weather station. Just animal visions."

"I'm a little jealous. Now you *have* to keep volunteering at the shelter. Plus, I like having you as a friend."

Tears come again, unexpected. "Thanks, Andi. I feel the same."

"Hey, did you come up with a name for our mystery dog?"

I pause. "His name is Wallace."

"Okay, I give up. Wallace who?"

"William Wallace, the main character in the movie *Braveheart*. A real-life Scottish hero. I think there's a very brave dog in there, and we just need to bring him out."

"I'll let everyone know and get a new card up on his pen. See you tomorrow?"

"I'll be there around noon."

We hang up, and I rest my head on my hand, staring at Keet's house, willing him to come home.

"Time to eat, Fae." Fae gets fed first, and I lean on the counter watching her, admiring her enthusiasm.

Realizing I want more than snacks for dinner, I start the pasta in one pan and dump a jar of marinara sauce into another, adding some dried garlic and basil. While I wait for both the finish up, I build a fire in the woodstove and curl up in the nearby chair. After dinner, I read until I can't keep my eyes open.

Keet's house remains dark, and the waters of the bay are almost flat, the tide rising to tug the logs out into its current once more. Before I close the curtains in my bedroom, I check for the last time. No car. No lights. If Fae weren't curled up beside my bed, this would be the most alone I've felt since I've been here.

The next morning, waking up from a mercifully dreamless sleep, I swing my legs out of bed and open the curtains, turning automatically to see if Keet's vehicle is in the driveway. It is. I pound down the stairs, Fae whining at my heels. After letting her out, letting her back in, and feeding her, I shuck off my nightdress and jump in the shower. My hair is still dripping down the back of my shirt when I grab my cell phone, take a deep breath, and close my eyes.

When I open my eyes again, I know that calling Keet is different from seeing him. Calling is what the old Nolee would've done. Had done. Returning the phone to the table, I walk to the bathroom and towel off my hair, then wind it into a bun on the top of my head. Fae pads along behind me to the kitchen. I leave her in the house with a fully stuffed treat ball and walk to Keet's front door. After knocking, I hear the click of a lock being drawn back, and the door opens.

I want to tell him why I'd acted the way I did, but all my rational plans are blown to bits when I see him. Before one word comes out of my mouth, I rush to him, put my arms around his waist, and lay my head against his chest. Wrapping his arms around me, he steps backward, drawing us both inside and shuts the door with a kick of his foot.

Neither of us speak for long minutes. Then he murmurs, "Are you okay?"

"I am. And I'm sorry I cut out of here so fast yesterday morning."

I feel him shake his head. "No apologies necessary. I understand it was a lot of new things coming at you in a short amount of time."

He leans down to kiss me, his lips firm and warm against mine. The kiss goes on. Minutes later, breathless, we stare at one another and smile. I bring my hands to his face, kiss him again, and ask, "Was that an invitation?"

"It was definitely an invitation. Assuming you don't mind going back to bed."

"I don't mind. Are there any cinnamon rolls left?"

~~~

They sit next to each other again, and Keet doesn't taste the food he's eating. He watches as Nolee makes her way through two cinnamon rolls, four strips of reheated bacon, fruit, and a cup of tea.

"What about Fae?" he asks.

"She's already been out, and she has a toy to keep her busy."

They're quiet as they clean up the table and kitchen, but they reach out and touch one another in passing. The touches are lingering . . . arms, hips, face. After she stacks the last of the dishes by the sink to dry, she turns, moving toward him. They kiss again as they maneuver down the hallway. As he lifts the shirt off over her head, he sees she isn't wearing a bra. They tumble into his unmade bed, and he takes her hard nipples in his mouth, then her breasts, lifting each one and running his tongue along the sensitive underside. He feels her squirming, hears her panting, tastes her skin.

Their bodies join and move. He feels her heels against his hips, pushing him into her. She arches her back and cries out as he keeps moving, tasting her neck, hearing her voice in his ear. Their mouths join, sharing breath, sharing a spirit that coils around them, binding them together. He loses track of time, until panting, they both relax into one another. As his breathing returns to normal, Keet rolls away, getting up to open a window.

Back in bed, Nolee moves toward him, curling under his arm, kissing his neck, throwing her leg over his. He feels the heat of her torso, the roundness of her breasts. Washed by birdsong and the sound of the sea, they both doze.

Then, voice raspy with sleep, she says, "Thank you, Keet."

"For what?"

"All of it." She kisses his jaw, running her hand through his hair.

"Can I ask what happened between yesterday morning and this morning that helped you figure things out?"

She threads his hair through her fingers, then runs her hand along his head, following the curve from forehead to ear. She pauses and shifts in bed, bringing her hand down to rest on his belly. He's lying on top of the sheets, letting the breeze cool him down. She's covered up to her waist.

He waits, eyes closed, every sense tuned to the woman beside him. He hears her laugh quietly.

"It wasn't one thing that changed. Maybe I saw that I was following a very old pattern, and that something I've always known about myself feels new because I'm able to accept it."

"What pattern, and what's new?"

"The pattern of denying that I know things without knowing *how* I know them. That's also the part that feels new. I'm seeing it's who I am, and nothing to fear."

He kisses her head, rolling over on his side to hold her to him.

"I also realized that I wanted a new life, and it would be, I don't know, contrary to toss it away when it lands right in my lap." She moves out of his arms and kisses him, breaking away to give him a soft look, "I don't think I need to run from who I am anymore."

As she watches his smiling face, he moves into her, rolling her on top of him, kissing her, wanting to fold himself into her again, wrap himself around her, breathe her into him and dive deep. They're twined together, limbs warm and languid, breathing soft and slow.

In a flash behind his closed eyes, he sees two swift currents diverge. One leads him out to the open sea, where black dorsal fins slice the surface. The other is Nolee in the kayak, turning and smiling at him. He holds her tighter, certain the day is coming when he'll have to tell her about the part of him no one outside his family knows.

She interrupts his thoughts with a nudge. He opens his eyes, gazing up at her face.

"I lost you there for a minute. You okay?"

"I am. More than okay. You inspire me."

She laughs, uncertainty written on her face.

"I was going for honesty, but I'll take inspiration." She kisses him and rolls over to lie next to him, pulling the covers up over her shoulder, placing her head on the pillow next to his.

"Why do you say 'inspire' Keet?"

"Because I still don't' accept every part of me. I admire that you've seen yourself, all of yourself, and can be all right with it. I can't, and don't know if I ever will."

She stares out the window before bringing her gaze back to his. "First, I'm a work in progress, as Abbie would say."

"And second?"

"Second, I'm not fully okay yet. But more than I was. Since I was a kid, I've had a way of seeing the world, almost like I'm seeing through it. I'm not afraid of that anymore."

He changes position, wary of hearing what it is she's about to admit. And nervous it may provoke questions about who he is as well.

"What's that?"

She smiles and takes his hand. "I know you'll understand this. You know that vision I had with George?" Keet nods, tightening his fingers around hers.

"That's not the first one. I mean, it was the first one with an orca, but I've been getting those types of pictures from animals since I was a kid. Sometimes with horses, more often with dogs. I know what to do to help them feel better. To feel safe."

He lets out the breath he wasn't aware he'd been holding.

"I never could figure out, when I was a kid, why my mom and dad would say I was as wild as the dogs I trained. The dogs and I, we knew each other. There wasn't any trouble when it was just us. They would do the things I taught them when someone else asked. But I knew they would—and did—do anything for me. And most of the time I didn't have to ask, I just knew.

"One time I was riding, and my horse was scared by a snake. He bolted, snorting and bucking, and I was cursing a blue streak trying to get off his back. I landed in the dirt, right next to a calf that didn't have the sense to run away with his momma. That cow turned, lowered her head, and charged straight toward me. I was trying to get up, and the only thought in my head was 'help!' Next thing I know, my dog Boo had cut the cow off, then bit her nose for good measure. I ran away. I called Boo off, and we went and looked for my horse. Last thing I wanted was my dad knowing I'd come off. It would've been bad news for the horse, who was just obeying his instinct. Boo never did anything like that before or after. She was a good stock dog, but not the most confident. That day, she saved me from getting really hurt.

"The funny thing is," she continues, "is that I had this 'knowing' with Nate, too. I knew he was into me, and looking back, I think I was more into him because how could I not like someone who felt that way about me? I also knew something wasn't quite right. There was always some sort of friction between us. But I ignored it because I was crazy about him being crazy about me. And then I spent eighteen years not only trying to change him but hiding from what I knew. I never admitted it to myself until yesterday, after being with you. Insane, right?"

He shakes his head. "Not insane. Perceptive."

She kisses the back of his hand. "Why do you say you don't know if you'll ever be able to accept who you are, every part of you?"

He forces himself to look into her eyes, her green, straightforward gaze, waiting for his answer.

"Ever since I left Sitka, I don't feel like I fit anywhere. As I get older, that feeling has grown. I do things, and I've built a life, but . . . it's difficult for me to feel connected. Except when I swim. When I swim, there's nothing but me and the water and the ease of that world."

The breeze and the birds singing through the open window are blended with the sound of waves greeting the shoreline.

"Lia, I should tell you something."

"I'm all ears."

"One thing I know about myself is that I'm intense in relationships. You aren't the only one whose denial caused some trouble. I thought I could convince Sascha to give up her career in LA. She was all I could see, think about, dream about, or desire for a very long time. I thought if I did all the right things, I would be enough for her, even though she was sleeping with other men. When we broke up, it about sunk me."

He sees her face shift between serious and wanting to smile. She brings a hand to her head, moving the hair behind her on the pillow.

"Intense doesn't scare me, Keet."

"You won't mind if you're the only one I want to be with?"

He hears her quick intake of breath, and then she tackles him, squeezing his shoulders, kissing his ear, wrapping her legs around him.

"I'll take that as you won't mind very much." His voice is muffled and warm against her neck.

"You can take that as I don't mind at all. Because I feel the same way."

He rolls her onto her back and kisses her, feeling the strength in her arms and the firmness of her breasts. In that moment, he feels they are each other's buttress against the world.

TWENTY

"What time is it, Keet?"

He turns his head away from her hair and looks at the bedside clock. "It's almost ten."

"I said I'd be at the shelter around noon. I'd better get dressed. They have a new dog there, and the little guy is afraid."

"You're going to use your talents on him?"

She pulls her shirt over her head and lifts her hair out from under it. "Well, I'll use whatever it is I do, hopefully *with* him. I'd like him to be a part of the conversation."

"You've named him already, haven't you?"

She grins, looking around the floor for the rest of her clothes. "Wallace, after the hero William Wallace of Scotland."

"Good choice. But before you go, I'd like to show you something."

She leans over and gives him a quick kiss. "Sure. In the meantime, where are the rest of my clothes?"

He points out the door. "You'll find them in the hallway."

I look up at Keet after slipping back into my jeans. "What did you want to show me?"

He digs in the pocket of his black hoodie and brings out a shiny black smartphone, a look of grudging amusement on his broad face.

"Is that what I think it is?"

"I don't know. What do you think it is?"

"I think you got a cell phone."

He sighs, flipping it over in his graceful hands. "I did. Trish is always talking about how easy it is to keep in touch by texting. I thought you and I could text. Keep in touch when we can't be together."

I rush to him, gripping him in a fierce hug. "Yes! I love that! I'll go get my phone and we can try it right now." I turn to leave the room, but his voice calls me back.

"Lia?"

"Yeah?" I've got the door open and am halfway out it.

"How do you turn this thing on?"

I turn around. "Did you charge it?"

"Yes. Well, Trish did. She showed me how to plug it in."

"I'll be right back, and we can go through everything."

When I get back with my phone, Fae dancing around me, I take his phone and call my number, showing him how to create a new contact. I look at him, and he's shaking his head. "I feel like my brain just melted. Can you show me how to text you, and we can do the other stuff later?"

"Of course." We play with texting for the next few minutes, and I enter Trish's number in his phone. "Anyone else you want listed?"

"How about the shelter? Just in case I can't reach you otherwise."

"Sure. Let me share the contact . . ." I look up and see the same quizzical expression cross his face. "Never mind. Who else?"

"No one else. I'll look up my grandmother's number later."

As he speaks, he's drawing slow circles on my knee; even through my jeans, I feel my skin snap to attention.

"Okay." I take his hand in mine. "If you don't stop that, I'll never get out of here."

He gives me his best innocent look. "And that's a problem because?"

"It's not. But Wallace awaits. I need to get going."

"Do you want company?"

I pause. "Yes, if that company is you."

"I'll meet you by your car in fifteen."

"Deal." We kiss, and Fae forgets to growl or circle us.

"Lia," he whispers.

"Yes, Keet?"

"Thank you. For all of it."

After introducing Keet and Andi and letting Fae out to play with the other dogs, I glance at Wallace's pen. He's in the same place he was yesterday, in the same position. The only thing that's changed is his name card on the front. I touch Keet's arm.

"Can you hang out here? I don't want to overwhelm him."

Keet nods, looking at the slobbery, dirt-encrusted ball Fae's dropped at his feet. She's put on her best pink-tongued, white-toothed, sparkly, yellow-eyed grin and is wagging her whole body. He looks at the ball, then at her, then bends down to pick it up, holding it between his thumb and forefinger.

"Dog, I must really like you." He draws his arm back and throws the ball. It flies through the sky, landing just inside the fence. I kiss his cheek and say, "Good man."

When I turn to Wallace, he hasn't moved. I stroll closer, not making eye contact, and repeat the same pattern as yesterday. This time, instead of walking directly toward him, I sidle up like I have no plan in mind. Stopping outside the gate, an idea occurs to me. I imagine a picture of me sitting beside him in his pen.

For long minutes, nothing happens. I sit down, wrap my arms around my knees, and keep Wallace in my peripheral vision. He lies down and licks around his muzzle, his eyes half-closed. Keet's still throwing the ball for the dogs. Wallace pants. I continue to replay the scene of sitting next to him inside the pen.

Wallace is still lying down. Closing my eyes, I concentrate on the picture of me sitting, him lying down, both of us sharing a quiet space. When I open my eyes, I'm surprised to see Wallace's mud-smeared muzzle inches from my face, his nose poked through the wire. I remain sitting, looking at him, not using my voice but continuing to send the picture and the feeling of peaceful coexistence.

When I meet his eyes, he gives a surprised "whuff," and moves his nose closer to me. My head lowered and taking my eyes from his, I lean in. He backs away from the fence but doesn't return to his corner. In a flash, I see a black shape looming over him while he presses himself into the ground; he has a chain around his neck and the other end is wrapped around a post. Looking at him, I close my eyes. *I see you,* I think. *I see you and that won't ever happen again. You're safe here.* When I open my eyes, he's still standing, but his ears are up, and his tail relaxes.

When I glance to see what Fae and Keet are up to, she's sitting by him, the ball in her mouth, and they're both looking in my direction. I get up and walk over to them.

I've never known what "butterflies in my stomach" felt like, but as I watch Keet watching me, I understand what that means. Putting my hand on his forearm, I bend over to take the ball from Fae. She prances backward, her front feet tap-dancing on the bare ground.

When I throw it, it goes only half as far as Keet's had. From the expression on the dogs' faces, I don't think it matters to them. I turn back to Keet.

"How'd it go?" he asks.

"Really well. He surprised me there at the end, coming up so close. I thought it was a good place to take a break."

"What were you doing?"

"My superpower stuff."

Laughing, he leans in and gives me a quick peck on the lips. From the heat on my face, I can tell I'm blushing. The dogs are back, leaping and yipping around us. We both speak at the same time, "I'm blushing, aren't I?" "Was that okay?"

"Yes! Nathan wasn't much on showing affection, in public or otherwise. But I can get used to it."

He leans in again, kissing me more slowly, our hands twining together. A solitary bark interrupts us, and I look back at Wallace's pen. He's not wagging his tail, but his large, pointy ears are still up.

"Look who's interested, Keet. I think I'll go over there and see how he feels about it." I walk up to the gate. Wallace moves to the corner and sits; his ears are still up and his tail's relaxed. I speak to him for the first time. "You have great ears, buddy." He tilts his head and starts panting. "I think this's good progress for today. I'll see you tomorrow."

We stop at the desk to chat with Andi, and I let her know I'll text her with the time I'll be back. She gives me an unusually large grin and waves before answering the phone.

We stop in Northsound for lunch, sitting outside with Fae, our conversation punctuated with stretches of companionable silence. Underneath the twin currents of excitement and newness, though, a familiar pinging alert sounds. We smile and laugh, and I watch Keet, delighting in what I see in his eyes. At the same time, another part of my brain is shuffling the pieces of a puzzle I've been looking at for months.

The swims in frigid waters, the indirect answers, the answers that might contain the truth hidden in plain sight. His orca pod, how he always sees them on the trips he takes out, his lack of friends, his grandmother and uncle his only surviving family. The small alarm continues, and this time I listen. I know I'll have to ask Keet what he's hiding, and soon. I'm nervous about the answer, but not nervous enough to repeat past mistakes.

On the drive home, he mentions that he's taking a couple out to Patos Island for a camping trip that evening. He'll overnight there and be back in the morning.

"Feel free to rummage around for leftovers at my place, Lia."

I glance at him, then back at the road. "I might take you up on that. Will the house be open, or do you have a key I can borrow?"

He pauses and then looks out the window. "I have an extra key I can give you."

I can hear something in his voice. Reluctance? Wariness?

"I'm happy to give it back, and I'll only look through the fridge, not search your entire house." I hope that joking will give us a chance to talk about whatever's causing his hesitation.

"You don't have to give it back. I hesitated because it's been a very long time since anyone but me has been in my house, and it feels new. Which then makes me nervous. But I don't have anything to hide there."

"If it makes you feel better, I'll give you a key to my cabin, too. Though I rarely lock it. Or you can leave your place open, and I'll lock up when I'm done rummaging in the fridge."

Keet smiles. Squeezes my hand. "I'll bring a key over before I leave."

After parking and letting Fae out, I look at the quiet waters of the bay. No dorsal fins, no shiny seal head, no long-tailed otter flips. Only logs, their dark shapes bobbing gently on the surface of the water.

"I wonder where that male orca has gone off to?"

I look back at Keet, who's also looking out at the bay. He turns toward me, gives me a brief kiss, and says, "Let me go get the key," before striding off. Taking Fae into the cabin, I check my phone for texts and see there's one from Abbie.

Dad is flipping out. I'll miss you at the wedding, but I'm glad you don't have to deal with his drama. xoxo

I smile and text back. *I miss you all the time. This too shall pass, my sweet girl. Love you. xoxo*

As I shove the phone in my hip pocket, I hear Keet's footsteps on the porch and look up. Fae walks over to him, wagging her tail.

"I think she might let you pet her. Hold your hand out to her first."

He looks down at her, then kneels on the floor and offers his hand. She sniffs, her tail still wagging as he gently pets her shoulder. She breaks out her best grin for him before flopping on her side and showing him her belly.

"You've totally charmed my dog. Not surprising, since you did the same with me."

He looks up and smiles, then stands and holds a small silver key in the palm of his hand. He glances at the key, then into my eyes before stepping closer and placing it gently in my hand.

"You can put that on your keyring."

I smile and kiss him. When I move away, a broad grin has replaced the trepidation on his face.

"Thank you, Keet."

In the silence that follows, I hear the sleepy afternoon sea and the distant whine of a plane. Then my phone rings, and the ringtone—an annoying beep similar to that of an alarm clock I had in college—tells me it's Nathan. I sigh, looking at Keet while deciding whether to answer it.

"Do you need to get that?"

I nod, then shake my head. "I should, but I don't want to. It's Nathan."

The phone rings again, then cuts off mid-ring, quickly followed by the ping of a text. I see the text is from Nate.

Call me. I look up at Keet.

"Everything all right?" he asks.

"I think you're a very smart man for not having a cell phone until now." I sigh. "I've no idea why Nathan wants me to call him, but I'll do it later." I run my hands up Keet's neck and into his hair, feeling the warmth of his skin. He leans down to kiss me, and we stumble over to the sofa, where we fall into each other. Hours later, I feel Keet move underneath me. "I'd better get to my boat."

"If I weren't due back at the shelter tomorrow, I'd ask about going with you. Find out what sleeping on a sailboat is like." I see his eyes dim. It's gone so quickly that I'm not sure I saw it. But the days of me denying what I know to be true are over.

"What is it?" I watch as Keet shifts to a sitting position. He shakes his head.

"There's no hiding anything from you, is there?" His eyes are clear again, looking into mine without hesitation.

"We're both allowed to have secrets. I just don't want the kind that will bite me in the ass."

He laughs and says, "Of course you can come whenever you want. And of course, I want you to spend the night with me on my boat."

"But?"

"No buts." He stands and takes my hands in his. "I've only thought about myself for a long time, which isn't really a way to live. At least, not anymore. It's no longer just me. It's us. I want it to stay that way, Lia. I'll get better at thinking—knowing—that this life now includes you and me, but I may need a little time."

I smile at him, at his earnest expression, at the slow and careful way he explains himself. I know it's not the full story, but I also know he's working his way up to that.

"Take all the time you need, Keet. I'm not going anywhere."

After a long kiss goodbye, I watch him pull out of his driveway. I look down at Fae, her red coat gleaming in the late afternoon light. "We're going to need some dinner soon, girlie." She wags her tail in agreement.

After dinner, I sit on the porch and dial Nate's number. He answers, out of breath.

"Is this a bad time?" I ask.

"No. I've just finished my run."

"What are you running from?"

"Ha ha ha." An exhale punctuates each word. I feel the vibration through the speakers in my phone and have the unpleasant sensation that he's almost here with me.

"I know you said you aren't coming to my wedding, but I wanted to see if I could change your mind. It's going to be epic."

I pull the phone away from my ear and stare at it. I've never heard Nathan use the word "epic" before.

"I'm not changing my mind."

I hear Texas birdsong and a passing car in the background.

"You're running in the neighborhood?" I ask. Abbie told me that Nathan and Carlos bought a house three blocks away from our old house.

"I am. You know me, if I can't control it, I run from it."

I'm stunned into silence by this display of self-awareness.

"Anyway, Nolee, I also called because I feel like I owe you an apology."

I'm silent so long that he says, "Hello? Are you still there?"

"Yes, still here. What are you talking about, Nate?"

"I'm talking about everything. Our whole marriage. It seems like the only thing we got right was Abbie. I'm in therapy. It's hard, but Carlos and I want to begin fresh with each other. I figured I owe you an apology, so that's what I'm trying to do. I'm sorry."

I hear the slam of a door. He must have gone inside his house. The jingling clatter of keys sounds far away, and suddenly, I get a picture of him tossing his keys on a table by the door. Instead of the smoky red ours used to be, this door is dark brown, with six small, colorful stained-glass window panels at the top. The table is wood, an antique Queen Anne end table that we'd had in our house, where it had also flanked the door. This knowledge flashes through me like heat lightning. I shake my head.

"Nolee?"

His voice sounds far away at first, then gets closer. I must've blanked out for a moment. But before I can come up with an answer that sounds sane, I hear myself asking, "Is that the end table that was in our house?"

"It is. How'd you know?"

"Your keys sound the same as I remember." I don't say the other words that come to mind— "Nice door, too"—knowing that this is getting weird, even for me. More silence. Nate clears his throat. "Anyway, that's all."

"Thank you for your apology, Nate. I owe you one too. I'm sorry about all the yelling I did. What I'm most sorry about is the way I pushed you to tell me about Carlos. That last time we were . . . together . . ."

"Nolee. Thanks, really, but I should've told you a lot sooner than I did. I'm happy, and I hope you're happy?"

I look out at the water, dark in the afternoon light, and smile. "I am. And I'm glad to hear you are, too."

It occurs to me that Nate and I are calling a truce. The amazement I feel is quickly followed by the peace that comes from laying down such a heavy, and old, resentment.

"I'll text you photos of the wedding, if that's alright?"

"I'd like that, Nate. Thank you for calling; I'm glad we talked."

"Me too. Bye, Nolee."

As I press the red button, I scratch Fae behind the ears. Judging by her half-closed eyes, she clearly approves. I think I may be able to feel the same way one day.

I text Abbie. *I just spoke with your dad. I think everything is going to be okay. It was a pleasant conversation. xo*

I wait a few moments, then get up and make Fae's dinner, which she eats without chewing. After cleaning out her bowl, she snuffles around the floor for any stray bits she might've missed. My dinner will be the leftovers from lunch with Keet. As I wait for the food to warm up, another text arrives, this time, from Abbie.

That's great, Mom! Has he calmed down about the wedding? There's a laughing emoji at the end of her question. I laugh too.

I think he's doing better with everything. A wedding is a big deal, but he's a smart guy. He and Carlos will figure it out. How are you?

Good. Doing my calc homework. How's Keet? This time an emoji with heart eyes appears. I laugh again.

He's great. We're spending a lot of time together. I'll let you get back to your homework. I add an emoji with brains exploding, hit send, and then type another message. *I'm so proud of you, Abbie, and love you even more.*

Love you too, Mom!

Walking on the beach with Fae in the grayling, end-of-day light, I see a dark shape in the channel. At first, I think it's another log floating to shore in the current. Then, standing at the water's edge, I see it again: the triangular advance of blackness through the water, followed by an exhaled cloud that hangs in the air above the swells. Fae barks once, and when I look down at her, I see that she's wagging her tail.

"You're making friends all over the place, aren't you?" I watch as the male orca dives, noticing the notch out of his dorsal fin. I wonder why the orca always shows up when Keet isn't around? It crosses my mind that I could take out the kayak and join the killer whale, but I sit, enjoying the warmth of the day caught in the rocks. He comes in close to shore, holding his head out of the water and looking at me for a long moment before blowing and diving. I think he's gone when, far out in the bay I see the white of his belly rise above the waves, his large pectoral fins splayed out as though he would take to the sky. He flips, crashing down in a shower of agitated water. I'm on my feet, clapping, glad that only Fae and I are witnessing the magic of this summer evening. He doesn't leap again. I scan the surface of the black sea but can't find his dorsal fin.

Picking up my phone, I send a text to Keet. *The big male orca came back! Wish you were here to see him with me.*

He doesn't reply.

TWENTY-ONE

Hearing a car door slam, I check my phone and see that it's just past six in the morning. Keet still hasn't answered my text. Navigating the stairs through sleep-fuzzy eyes, I let Fae out, then step onto the rough boards of the porch behind her. Keet's on his deck. He waves, and I wave back.

Smiling broadly, he climbs the steps, picks me up, and buries his head in my neck. "I missed you, Lia."

I hum with pleasure and squeeze him tighter. "I missed you, too. Did you get my text?"

"I did, though I'm not used to checking a phone. It beeped when I got close to the marina this morning."

He isn't looking at me when he says this. With his fingertips, he traces the line where my nightdress crosses my chest, over my collar bones, and around to the base of my neck. "Do you know how amazing you look right now?"

The warmth of his mouth on my neck is distracting, and I want to give in to the rush that washes over me. But warning bells are ringing, and it's time to ask him the questions that've bothered at me all night. There's a secret swimming around, but it's slippery and refuses to be caught or seen. Today is the beginning of getting to know that creature better, whatever it is. Whatever the outcome.

"Did you see the male orca?"

Keet steps away. "I didn't. But I saw the rest of his family last night. They showed up when we were close to Patos. The couple I took out there were beside themselves."

I take his hand. "Let's come inside. I need tea and clothes, in that order." He follows me inside and sits at the table while I make tea and feed Fae.

"Are you hungry?"

"Famished." His wolfish grin tells me he isn't thinking about food. I walk over to him, straddle his lap, and kiss him slow and deep. He whispers, "Bed first, then breakfast?"

"Would you mind a few questions first?"

He kisses the other side of my neck, giving a muffled "no" before edging my shirt lower.

"Keet."

He stops and looks up at me.

"Let's sit on the sofa?"

He gives me a searching look, the heat fading to . . . what? Is it fear? He follows me to the sofa and sits close as I settle into the soft cushions.

"You know that hunch I told you about, that knew Nathan and I were not quite right, but ignored it?"

He nods, his mouth set and firm.

"I've been having the same hunches. About you." Seeing him startle, I add, "What I mean is, I'm with you, one thousand percent, but I'm also wondering about a couple of things that don't add up."

He swallows. "Such as?"

"I've seen you dive off the pier at night, but I've never seen you come up."

He's staring at me without blinking. I decide to tell him everything I've been thinking about. In a rush of words, I ask him why I don't see him and the male orca at the same time. Why, even having been raised in Sitka, he can swim in the sea and not get hypothermia. Why he always dives at night. Why he sees his orca pod consistently, when I know that Southern Resident killer whales aren't in the area with even half the frequency they used to be.

"You've been learning about orcas, Nolee." His smile is tight, closed.

"I have. I want to understand them. They're important to you, and they've become important to me."

He nods, and I stay silent, waiting for him to decide. Waiting to find out if I'll get the truth.

He sits up straighter and looks at me. "There's more to me than I've shared with you."

I don't reply, searching his eyes for clues. The alarm bells aren't ringing inside me anymore.

"My family has a secret. Only my grandmother and my uncle know this about me. I've been trying to figure out when to tell you, Lia, but . . ."

He shifts, looking out of the window, his lanky frame alive with tension. If I touched him, I think he might snap like a frayed electric wire.

He takes a deep breath before he says, "I can't tell you anything, not—" he waves his hands in front of him, lost for words, "not like this. Not in spoken language." Flustered, he's speaking so quickly that his words are running into each other. He sounds like me when I first moved here. His eyes are wet, and he swipes at them with the back of his hand.

"There's something you need to know about me, something important, and I can't tell you like this!"

"Okay, Keet, okay. How *can* you tell me? I'll do my best to understand."

His breathing slows, and he moves closer. I can see uncertainty and fear moving across his face, and his resolve to not give in to it.

"You'll need to swim with the male orca."

I shake my head, not sure that I heard him correctly. "You want me to *what*?"

Keet takes both of my hands in his. "Lia, I've been swimming with him for decades. He's not always with his family, or up north. He hides here. I keep him safe. When you see me dive at night? That's me, going to meet him."

"Why do I need to swim with him?" I feel my hands, interlocked with Keet's, growing cold. "I've been in the kayak with him nearby, and he seems friendly enough, but that's not the same as intentionally getting into the water with him." I gulp and continue. "I'm grateful for that time he saved me, but I didn't know what was happening. If I swam with him now, I'd be deliberately choosing complete helplessness!"

"You wouldn't, though. You wouldn't be helpless. I can't explain it, but if you're scared, he knows it. He can read you, probably in ways even you can't imagine." I can see Keet believes this, believes that he and the orca share a special bond. For all I know, they do. But I've never seen the two of them together, and how do I know he would treat me the same way? Maybe Keet has powers I don't, and I would be at the mercy of this whale killer. I know Keet has told me the orca only eats fish, but meat is meat and, in the water, I'm way more helpless than a fish.

"Besides, what would keep me from freezing again?"

Looking into Keet's eyes, I can see I asked the question he already has an answer to. He has this planned out, and nothing I say or do will change that plan.

"I'll get a wetsuit for you. You can learn how to snorkel—it's not difficult. I'll get everything set up, I'll show you what to do, and when the time comes, you swim out to meet him and he'll bring you to where I am. We'll show you."

Keet lets go of my hands and then cradles my face. His face, inches from mine, has a yearning I've not yet seen, even during the hours we've spent in bed together. I'm losing this battle; he's convincing me by the sheer force of his belief.

"All right," I sigh, closing my eyes. "Show me what to do."

He kisses me, and then hugs me to him, nuzzling into my hair and murmuring "thank you," over and over again.

"But Keet?"

"Yes, Lia?"

"If at any point I can't do this, and I tell you that, I'll need you to back off."

"Of course. Absolutely." He moves my hair out of the way before kissing my neck, then moves to meet my mouth with his.

Breakfast was late.

My life, once spent watching the ocean for long hours or reading a book with Fae bounding along the rocks, is now full. The days are longer; a July day in the San Juan Islands lasts longer than a July day in Texas. I've got plenty to fill those long days, and the month passes in a blur.

If I'm not working at the pet store for Chena, I'm at the shelter getting to know Wallace, who is still shy but growing more confident and friendly. Each day I see him, I practice opening my mind into the space where he and I communicate. Picturing what I'd like to do with him gets easier, flowing between us like the yarn that flowed through my mother's fingers when she knitted.

Wallace is now sitting with me, letting me scratch his belly, allowing me to bathe him. It turns out he's a patchwork-colored dog, white and a soft blonde the color of winter wheat. Dark brown outlines some of the blonde patches. I never detect aggression in him, and his sweetness assures me that he's well on his way to feeling better about people.

I work with the other shelter volunteers so they know how to read Wallace, and where his strengths and weaknesses are. He's out of the isolation kennel, has been seen by the vet, and is playing with the other dogs. Although I'm tempted to keep him, and Andi is urging me to bring him home as a companion for Fae, I know one dog is enough for me. And in the back of my mind, I'm thinking, *Will I be alive to take care of him?* This is so morbid that I quickly toss it out.

When I'm not at the pet store or the shelter, Keet and I are together, sailing, sharing meals, in his bed, or practicing swimming in the sea. Keet is a natural teacher, and more than once I marvel at his patience as I splutter through the snorkeling tube after inhaling before clearing it with a strong exhale. He treads water with ease, flips and dives underneath me, lithe and graceful as the kelp that sways in underwater forests. I plug along on the surface at first, then hold my breath, going for shallow dives.

As I feel more confident, I realize that I enjoy being in the water, even though after each session I shiver so hard that Keet has to peel me out of the wet suit. In the evenings, barely able to keep my eyes open, I usually end up at Keet's place, where we eat together in front of his fireplace. The days together turn into nights together, turn into mornings together. As we synchronize with one another, for the first time in my adult life, I feel how easy a relationship can be when honesty is at the center.

For long stretches of time, I forget the orca-shaped shadow that looms over us. The dreams of Keet standing silent and cloaked by the ocean haven't visited. When I remember what all this swimming practice is leading to, I remind myself that I can stop. I don't know what makes my heartbeat stutter more: the curiosity or the fear.

TWENTY-TWO

I feel ready to snorkel on my own. I can dive and hold my breath and not lose my sense of which way is up. Although I still can't go deep, I feel good about going below the surface and being able to breathe again without sucking in half of the Salish Sea.

I come out of Keet's bathroom after a shower, smelling the seafood gumbo simmering on the stove.

"That smells amazing."

He looks up through the steam that's wafting upward from the pot.

"I hope it tastes amazing, too," he says.

Leaning against the counter, I decide it's time. "I felt good about snorkeling today. What do you think about me meeting the orca next month?"

Keet moves from the stove and stands in front of me, his fingers drumming on the counter. I wait.

"It's already the middle of August."

"Yes . . . and?" I move closer, putting my hand on top of his to quiet the agitation in his fingers.

"The water won't get much warmer than it is now. You aren't getting as chilled as you used to, but I don't think it's a good idea to wait until September." He flips his hand over, holding mine, not saying anything else.

"Well then. Let's do this tomorrow." I see him take a breath, and I can almost hear his next question.

"Before you ask me if I'm sure, Keet, the answer is yes, I am."

He moves away, grabbing his phone from the table.

"I'll check the weather. We're going to want a sunny day." He taps the screen. In the silence, I hear the slow bubble of the gumbo. I move from the counter and put a loaf of sourdough bread on a baking sheet and into the over to warm up. I feel his hand on my shoulder.

"We're good. It will be just as warm tomorrow as it was today." His smile falters.

"Keet, whatever it is you need to show me, I'm not worried about it. I mean, swimming with the male orca makes me nervous, but I trust you. We'll figure this out."

The next afternoon, Keet and I are sitting on the dock in front of his house. The day is warm and I'm sweating in the wetsuit, not entirely because of the sun. I look over my shoulder and see that the grass has turned yellow, and the beginnings of red and bright gold in the forest where the deciduous trees are preparing for a winter's sleep. Keet fidgets beside me.

My wetsuit is clinging to me in places and ways I'm still not used to. Keet's plan to share his secret with me sounds strange and more than a little dangerous, but my curiosity is practically doing backflips, and that helps drown out my doubts. I pull on my gloves, making sure that my boots are also on tight. He hands me the flippers and I adjust them to my feet.

"Remember," he says. "You'll see him stop for you on the surface. He'll come as close as he can, so you don't have to swim very far. When you get to him, hold on to his dorsal fin, and he'll do the rest. The other pod members may be there. Remember that when he lets out a big exhale, and then inhales, he'll be diving. He won't go far under. Breathe like we've practiced, and you'll be fine."

For the first time since I've known him, Keet sounds worried. Fighting my shallow breathing, my own racing heart, I'm somehow surprised at how nervous I am. Where's the excitement? Between the weight of the gear I'm wearing and the weight of my near-panic, I'll be shocked if the orca can swim at all with me holding on to him.

"Where will you be, Keet?"

"I'll be close, but you won't see me." I feel his hand on my shoulder, where it remains as the dock bobs on the gentle tide.

"I'm going to dive in. Remember—"

"To wait for the orca, got it." I turn to him, smiling, and before I can turn back, he's leaning forward and kissing me hard, his hand gripping my head, his tongue meeting mine. He stands, then dives into the sea.

Keet took off his shorts before he dove into the water; I turn around and see them in a black heap behind me. I'm halfway to shucking out of my wetsuit, gathering up his shorts, and calling this whole thing off. I don't wonder anymore if my heart is pounding because of curiosity or fear. It's fear.

Before I can give up and go back to my cabin, I see the tall, black dorsal fin dividing the water, and an exhale that's blown back out to sea by the light breeze. The orca's head appears, the rocking dorsal fin above it. I can't believe I'm willingly getting in the water, that I'm believing this story that Keet told me about some family secret. His secret, and why he can't tell me but must let the orca show me. I scan the water, looking for Keet but see only the orca.

A litany of "*I can't do this, I can't do this*" ricochets through my brain. I ignore it. Drawing the hood over my head, I pull the mask down over my eyes and nose and put the snorkel in my mouth. My hands are shaking so much that I grip the edge of the dock to stop them. The orca is waiting, bobbing in the water less than fifty feet away. His breathing matches the swell and dip of his body, relaxed in the green current. He's enormous. Beyond fear, I feel the awe that a creature this big, this intelligent, this wild is even letting me near him. Terror clawing in my chest, I close my eyes and feel the rocking of the dock and practice breathing through the snorkel.

My eyes are still closed as I lower myself into the water. If someone had told me I'd trade high-maintenance dog owners and their maladjusted dogs for the chance to freeze to death and/or be eaten by the ocean's top predator, I would've laughed in their face and called them crazy as a bull-bat. Yet here I am, swimming up to a 10,000-pound animal that could tear me to little bits before I could muster a scream. *Who's the crazy one, Nolee?*

I catch my breath and kick over to the orca. Reaching for his dorsal fin with both hands, I see that the notch is larger than I thought. *Because, girl, you're closer than you've ever been to it.* As we set off, the sheer size of his body, undulating in the water, blocks most of my vision of the channel. His black skin feels pliant under my hands.

Looking over my shoulder, I'm shocked to see that we've doubled the distance away from the dock. I turn back and, tilting my head, follow the line of his dorsal fin up to the impossibly blue sky. The notch toward the top is easily the size of my fist. He exhales and inhales deeply, then we're diving into the green and black of Osprey Bay. Before I let go and swim to the surface, the orca takes me there. My breath shudders in and out of the plastic tube. Snorkeling with Keet on a warm fall day is much different from snorkeling with the orca. I feel like a gnat, or one of those remoras that attaches itself to a shark.

The orca stretches out in front of me, his skin like shiny black silk. He tilts his head and looks at me through an eye that seems small for such a large animal. Small, but beautiful. Even through the eerie green murk, I can see that the black of his eye is ringed in white. I close my eyes, take a deep breath, then another one, and feel my body relaxing, and what Keet taught me about swimming taking over. When I open my eyes again and look through the dripping mask, the orca still has his eye on me, as we float on the surface. He's swimming again, and I inhale as much air as my lungs will hold, and we dive.

We must be only eight or ten feet deep. The water is above his dorsal fin, but not by much. I close my eyes, feeling the pressure of oxygen in my lungs. Opening my eyes again, I watch the water ahead, but there isn't much to see. Just a cloudy greenness occasionally broken by floating kelp. I also see jellyfish, and the hope that they don't sting passes through my mind.

We're rising again. My hand feels welded to the base of his dorsal fin, and I hope my grip isn't uncomfortable. The way his dorsal fin feels fascinates me. It's firm but supple, reminding me of the inner tube I'd thought I was on when he rescued me. My head breaks the surface, and we exhale at the same time. Another simultaneous inhale, and then we dive. We're going deeper this time, and my heartbeat is pounding in my ears. I close my eyes, listening instead, wanting to hear something that would help me figure this out. Hoping to feel Keet swimming beside me and letting me know everything's okay.

That's when the calling starts. I feel the power of the chirps and clicks not only with my ears, but in every atom of my body. Mewlings like kittens and notes like birdsong rattle my joints. More orcas. The thought that I might be dinner crosses my mind, but I dismiss it because at this point, there's no going back. Where *is* Keet?

We surface. This time, the orca is blowing bubbles as we ascend. My head breaks the water a moment before his does, and I look up into the blue sky. I recall how many times I'd gazed at the sky in Texas and noticed the way it came down to meet the land. Now, the land is gone and in its place is the sea's greenish-blue water. We breathe, and I have the impression that the orca is waiting for me, making sure I have enough air before taking us down again.

This time, I feel the speed of his dive, and the power he's generating. I wish he'd slow down. As that thought crosses my mind, he stops, and we hang in the water, our heads pointed down. My heartbeat has slowed, an electric jolt of pleasure erasing the fear. I'm swimming in the sea, holding on to an orca who seems to know when I need to breathe, who is here of his own free will.

The joint-rattling sensation begins again, and I realize it's his pod. Is this how they know where they are when they can't see? I close my eyes. It feels like riding down a washboard dirt road in a truck with no suspension. My body is buoyant and as relaxed as I can make it, but that sensation of my insides rattling around disconcerts me. I hear the ocean, my heartbeat, and open my eyes to see the bubbles of my breath floating to the surface. At least my breath is returning to that blue sky, even if I'm not.

A promise is a promise. I told Keet I would see this idea of his through as far as I could. Just as I'm about to let go so I can get to the surface and breathe, the orca takes me. This time I keep my eyes pointed down and breathe normally through the snorkel tube, blowing and coughing out the small amount of water I inhale.

Another mewling chorus, this time closer. Six orcas are in the water underneath us. They come into focus through the murk, like misty figures in dreams. I think this is Keet's pod, the one he said felt like family. There's baby George, and his mom Atma. I see Nana, then Belle and Poppy; circling to the other side of George is Tia. As soon as I feel I'm ready to be closer to them, the orca dives again, this time slowly, letting me float along in his wake. I look to my right and wonder if I could swing astride him like I used to ride horses. But he isn't a horse, and he isn't mine. As accommodating as he is, I'd like to stay in his good graces. I look around, listening for the pod.

The world is silent. Sunbeams slice through the water, and I have the sensation of being seen, but not by eyes. The orcas are just shapes in front of me. I can't see a gleam that would tell me whether their eyes are open or closed. My ears are full of the ocean, and my heartbeat has slowed, but although I'm holding on to the orca's fin, something is happening to my sense of who and where I am.

The sea and I are merging, its deep thrumming in my ears the only sound I need to confirm this. The thud of my heartbeat slows. Listening to the pod, I wonder if the thrumming I hear is also their heartbeat, in time with the sea. My breath is running out again, and again the orca makes his way to the surface. I increase the force of my exhale, making sure all the water leaves the snorkel. I breathe deep and slow, and in my head say to the orca, *I'm ready now.*

As we dive, I see Keet in my mind's eye. Like a blinding flash from a camera, he's emblazoned on my eyelids, my brain, and my heart. He's walking toward me wearing the black shorts I last saw him in. There's music surrounding him, though I can't tell if it comes from the picture in my mind, or the orca that surround me. The same notes repeat, slow and fast, high and low, a rhythmic phrase with no beginning and no end.

I'm enveloped in sensations: the slow bump of my heart, and the feeling of being weightless. I lie along the orca's side, hugging his dorsal fin, barely aware of anything except Keet's song. Through the hood, I hear the same notes from the male orca. They ripple through my body as though I'm lying on top of a piano. My grip tightens, my eyes open and this time I do let go and scrabble for the surface, exhaling.

When my head is above water, I tear the mask and snorkel off my face, my arms and legs moving frantically to keep me afloat. I'm hyperventilating and wonder if my face is wet with tears or seawater. *Get hold of yourself, Nolee Burnett.* I look back at our land, at our houses, and see that we aren't very far out of the bay. My breathing slows. We must have circled until the pod found us.

I feel something brush along my side, past my ribs, down my hip and leg, and then it stops. I peer through the water, seeing a flash of white. When another touch at my ribcage starts again, I see that an orca is brushing the length of my body with its flipper. It's Nana, and she's gentle, far gentler than Fae when she's excited and tries to jump all over me. The touching continues, a stroke down my ribcage, hip and thigh, as each pod member tentatively reaches out. Only George hasn't come close. Atma swims over with him, and he rolls and puts his eye close to mine, looking at me. He bumps the snorkel in my hand and nudges my shoulder. I smile. I can't help putting my hand out to touch him. He settles his round black rostrum into my palm, then rolls his head until my hand is under his jaw. I give him a light scratch, much as I do with Fae.

My breathing has returned to normal, but my heart is still tripping along like a drummer with no rhythm. The male orca rises in front of me, George sliding over his head and off the other side. This pod, this family of orcas, is so tactile; touching, rolling, and swimming together. The male orca is looking at me. I stare back, put the mask on and the snorkel in my mouth, seeing in my mind him drifting closer to me, seeing Keet holding out his hand. I reach for and hold on to his dorsal fin again, and hear his voice, low to high, squeaky to creaky door. *Let's go,* I think. I breathe, we dive, and the pod dives at the same time. When I look through my mask, they are all around us, and though there are only six, once again I remember the vision of a sea filled with killer whales. I gulp down the lump in my throat.

My oxygen runs out with a suddenness that is startling. I realize I need air immediately. The orca takes us to the surface with three powerful thrusts of his tail. I'm panting and lightheaded. The rest of the pod swim around us, and their noises sound like bird song. I wish I knew what they were saying. I wish I could talk with them. Through the water running down my mask, I see rainbows where the sun lights up their exhales. George swims over, and again Atma stays behind. As I'm looking at him, he opens his mouth and I notice he has teeth, though they are much smaller than they will be when he's an adult.

I reach out to touch him, and he takes my hand in his mouth. I freeze. When puppies try to put my hand in their mouth, I always redirect them with a chew toy. There are no chew toys for orcas—unless, of course, I turn out to be one. I feel a fizz of nervous laughter skitter in my throat, then a tremor brought on by the cold water. We are all undulating like kelp, and I have one hand around the dorsal fin of a huge orca and the other in the mouth of a baby. That baby could still rip my hand off with one flick of his head. But he doesn't. I gasp, shoving the snorkel out of my mouth again. Atma sends out a quick burst of clicks and a high-pitched whistle, and George opens his mouth.

Relieved, I take my hand back and raise it close to my mask. No indentations on the glove; even the baby orca knows how helpless I am. I can't smile, but I make eye contact and silently say *thank you.* George opens his mouth again in a broad grin and pokes his tongue out. I feel laughter in my chest and before I think about it, I'm scratching his tongue. He chirps, rotating his body so I can keep scratching, and then swims back to his mother.

I watch as the pod dives. I've been so preoccupied with George that I haven't been breathing enough to disperse the light-headedness. Through the streaming water of my mask, I once again see blue sky. But now I want to dive again, to be surrounded by this family, to be a part of their pod, more beautiful and connected than I could ever feel on my own. I move the snorkel back to my mouth, take a deep breath, and adjust my hold on his dorsal fin.

We dive, and this time, the orcas are swimming together, spiraling through the water, white bellies flashing. We're moving too, though at a sedate enough and straight enough pace that I don't worry about being twisted off.

The clicking starts, fits and stops of something that sounds like Morse code. The pod is singing, their voices mingling like their bodies, touching, leaping, disappearing, before crashing back down in a spray of white bubbles. Their songs sound much clearer underwater than they do in the air. It's like listening to a symphony with my whole body, not just my ears.

This display of joy and family and acrobatic beauty enthralls me. I don't notice that the orca is swimming again, his dorsal fin in my trembling hand undulating as he pushes his flukes through the water. We break through the surface and take in air; I wonder if he knows how much oxygen I have stored in my lungs? And then I wonder, *are we going back*? In a heartbeat, another picture flashes in my head: I see myself in the kayak, the sun sparking off my hair as I twist and paddle. A shock runs through me as I realize I'm seeing myself from Keet's point of view.

The male orca keeps swimming, his movements slow, his song beginning again. It's the same song I heard Keet singing as the pod surrounded me. And then I know. The orca whose fin I'm holding and Keet are the same . . . what? Being? This time, the thought doesn't startle me. But fear arises and steals my oxygen.

I let go and flail to the surface, my heart pounding in my ears. As I tread water, the orca slides up beside me, floating on his side, and offers me a pectoral fin that's longer and broader than I am tall. When I touch him, I feel the warmth coming through his skin, a contrast to the cool water. His eye is open, watching me. I feel a click and rattle that crawls from my feet, up my legs, through my pelvis, and into my chest. The pod breaks through the surface of the water and I see a flash of George's white belly. They circle closer as I bob on the surface, holding on to a male orca in his prime, wondering if it's Keet. The thought causes my heart to race. I put my head underwater so I can see what the rest of his pod is doing.

They stay close, circling around and beside and under us. Sometimes I feel that peculiar vibration in my joints, with my head underwater, sometimes I hear sounds that remind me of doors banging shut, or arpeggios of notes cascading up and up and up. The male orca turns, and I realize that he'd positioned himself so that I was floating between his fins, my side against his chest. I take a deep breath, and another. I close my eyes and say to him silently, *Keet, if this is you, I need to hold on to your dorsal fin again.* Before my thought is finished, the orca has rolled toward me, waiting for me to hold on. We breathe together, out, and then in, and I hold my breath as we dive.

A sense of certainty settles over me. The questions that have been weaving their way through my dreams about Keet are answered. The knife edge of fear that I'd been walking since this whole adventure began is gone. In its place is a growing warmth, an expansion of my brain and heart that feels as though they're beating in time with the ocean's pull and push. I'm not separate from anything, especially myself. I'm not alone. The orca song and their dance through the water, seem to me the only sanity that I've ever known. And once knowing it, I don't want to leave. I'm connected to something much larger than anything I could've imagined.

The orca family now swims on each side of us, and we rise together, breathe together, and dive as one. I'm lulled into the rhythm of their togetherness and the ocean that buoys us. I watch in wonder as each member of the family comes toward me again, then with a nudge or stroke of a flipper, arcs away. Atma and George are last, and I reach out my hand to him. I notice he has a strand of dull green kelp floating through his teeth. He opens his mouth, and I take it from him. He puts his eye up to my mask, blows some bubbles, and then he disappears into the cloudy water, his mother leading him. I watch the bubbles float to the surface, feeling the same effervescence bubbling in my chest. The last I see of them is Atma's large black-and-white tail flashing at me as she disappears.

We are alone together, Keet and I, as we surface. I'm now within easy swimming distance of the shore. I'm still holding on to his dorsal fin with my right hand. With my left, I take the snorkel out of my mouth, peel off the mask, and turn to look at him. His exhale and inhale are muffled; my ears must be full of water. His eye is closed. I shake my head, trying to clear my ears. I say, this time out loud, "Keet, you can look at me."

He opens a dark, purple-ringed eye and looks at me without blinking. In this moment, I realize how alive I am, and how alive Keet is, whatever form he's in. I hear his high-pitched cry, and it sounds like a question. Although the cold water is making me tremble, I take a deep breath that tastes of sea air and say to him, "I'm okay, Keet." He rolls on his side, and I swim over to him; he rolls slowly onto his back, and I lay along the length of him, listening to the vibrations of his slow, deep heartbeat, feeling his warmth through the chill of my wetsuit.

"I'm not mad, or freaked out, if that's what you're wondering." He submerges again, and I tread water. He's underneath me, only his eye-patch and the white of his jaw visible through the dark green water. When he comes back to the surface, he thrusts his head out of the water close enough for me to rest my hand along his jaw. "Well, not *too* freaked out." I smile, seeing my reflection in his watery eye.

He chirps and nudges my hand. Then, with a flash of white belly, he rolls away and dives, then rockets out of the water and cuts back in with hardly a splash. I laugh, and call out to him, "Showoff!" He comes back, and I have an image of the two of us moving closer to the dock. Splashing some water in my mask, I put it back on, put the snorkel in my mouth and exhale, then lower my head underwater. *Let's go,* I think. Holding his pectoral fin, I feel his flukes power us closer to shore. For one instant, I feel like an orca too.

Moments later, I'm treading water. Then he rises underneath me. He's too wide for me to sit astride, so I bend my knees, kneeling in front of his dorsal fin. I take off my gloves, and scratch his wide, warm back. He's still. It's just me and Keet, the sun and sea and forest, and the feeling I carry nestled inside me, like I carried Abbie for nine months. Belonging to the deep of life.

He sinks and I'm treading water again, gripping my gloves in one hand. With a last blast of air, he arcs under the waves, showing me the white underside of his tail. Then he's gone, the mist of his breath blown away by the breeze.

TWENTY-THREE

He dives deep into the black water, singing for his pod, waves of sound bouncing from familiar landmarks under sea. His tail creates whirlpools, forcing the surrounding water to fold in on itself. His dorsal fin, the arrow that heralds his arrival. He is orca, and he feels his power surge through his body and his heart.

Freed from the cage of his secret, he sounds for his family and sees, through images flashing in his brain, that they are feeding at the mouth of an inlet. The salmon are abundant, and the pod's joy sounds through their songs. Even Nana is singing, her old voice a creak and whistle that he's happy to hear. He pushes through a kelp forest, caressed by its long, slick fronds.

Increasing his speed, he points his head to the waves above him and leaps, then crashes down back into the sunlit murk. Speeding through his pod, he twists at the last moment to evade George. They play, rising and leaping, diving and splashing, spiraling around each other in swirling flashes of black and gray and white.

His belly is empty, but he rests on the surface, letting the salmon come back out from hiding. Above him he hears the drone of a helicopter hovering over them. He dives, catches a salmon, and registers the high whine of a boat motor. He circles his family and as one, they take a deep breath before diving and swimming away from boat noise. The humming in their jaws lessens, and they glide through and on top of the ocean, making for a quiet inlet where fish are plentiful, and humans are not.

The next morning, as the sun begins to slant through the trees, Keet knocks on Nolee's door. She opens it, her face somber, her smile unsure. He doesn't reach to touch her, and she seems to share his hesitancy.

"Hello, you. I was hoping to see you this morning." She moves aside so he can enter, reaching for his hand. He holds it firm in his grip.

She takes a deep breath and says, "How does it feel when you have flippers and not hands?"

Keet laughs. He knows she didn't mean to be funny, and his anxiety about seeing her now that she knows the truth about him dissipates with her question.

"Keet, I mean it!" She's laughing too but releases his hand and walks to the kitchen.

"Do you have anything for breakfast besides cereal," he asks.

"The usual. Eggs, toast, fruit. I've got ginger or green tea. I could probably find enough fixings to make a smoothie if you want it."

"All of it, plus green tea, please." He moves to the kitchen table where he stands, all awkward angles. Nolee looks at him, after turning the heat on under the kettle. She says,

"We don't have to talk about anything you don't want to talk about."

"I think it's best if we do, though, don't you?"

"I have so many questions, Keet. And you'll probably laugh your way through most of them."

"If I do laugh, it's because I'm happy that I can finally talk about it. I haven't been able to speak of what or who I am since I lived with my grandmother."

"Is Nana also your human grandmother?"

He stares at her, uncomprehending, and then realizes what she's asking.

"No, nothing like that. My orca family took me in as a gift to my human grandmother. She chose to be human when she was fifty. Before that, my mom had chosen to be human when she was twenty-eight and I was eleven. My mother left with my father. They moved to Nebraska so the ocean wouldn't tempt her. She chose my father and being human over the torment of being a woman, and orca. Being Keykwin." He smiles his thanks when she sets a mug of steaming tea in front of him. He sits as she moves back into the kitchen, pulling food out of the refrigerator.

"It felt like she abandoned her only child, but now I realize what she must've been up against. It was my grandmother who changed one last time to ask the pod to take me in."

"That's what you call yourself? A Keykwin?"

"Not 'a Keykwin.' Just Keykwin. One of the last. At least as far as I know. I was four years old when I started swimming with my orca family—the ones we named together that day on my boat."

Keet remembers the day his mother took him into the ocean, holding his small hand in hers as the water got deeper and colder. She'd said, "When you swim, you hold the blackfish in your mind, in your heart, and in your belly. Dive, headfirst and spin. It's then that the orca spirit will take you, Keet." She swam away from him, disappearing under the waves. He swam after her, diving, spinning . . . becoming orca as easy as waking up with the rising sun.

Nolee prepares their meal as she listens. After swirling the eggs and butter together in the pan, she sets the spoon down and lays four pieces of bread in the toaster oven. "What's your grandmother's name?"

"Sylvie Vent." He smiles at the thought of her, at his memories of her strength, her wisdom. "I'd better explain the legend of the orca, or the blackfish, as my grandmother's people call us."

"Aren't her people your people, too?"

"Yes, though she married a man from the Tlingit Athabascan tribes, my grandfather Jack. She told me once when I was a boy that she wasn't sure my mom would carry the Keykwin abilities."

"Is it safe to say that since you do, she did, too?"

"Yes."

"You said that your dad is white. Charlie right?"

"Yes. I can trace my heritage through my mother and grandmother to the Keykwin Nation. I was initiated through my orca family. All of my grandmother's community thought I'd take the Walk Into the Water by the time I was twenty."

"What is the Walk Into the Water? Wait," she takes a breath. "Tell me about the blackfish legend, and then I can ask more questions."

Keet shifts in the creaky chair. "There are a lot of variations, but I'll share the version told to me." He clears his throat, feeling the weight of those before him in the words.

Many years ago, when people wore cloaks of different skins, there was a clan from under the waves. They were powerful ocean singers painted in white and black, the blackfish. They struck fear into the hearts of other ocean singers, who swam far away from the land to make their own clans. But the blackfish didn't harm the people of the forest, regarding them as sisters and brothers.

Through many sunrises and sunsets, the clans of the land and the clan from under the waves were together. They danced among the trees and swam in the ocean, singing with the leaves and visiting villages underwater. As time grew longer, there were fewer celebrations among the trees, and fewer invitations from the people on the bottom of the sea. But still, the blackfish did no harm to the people of the forest.

The people of the forest moved far and wide across the earth until the spray of the ocean could no longer talk to them. The clan from under the waves spread away from the land until the wind through the trees could no longer talk with them. But still, the blackfish didn't harm the people of the land.

After more sunrises and sunsets, the people forgot their cloaks. They left them on forest floors or let them sink into the water. But there was one clan from the earth, and one blackfish clan from the water, who continued their relations. They would change skins each season, living part of the season on land, living part of the season in water.

Through generations, the people chose their cloaks, and no longer celebrated the seasons by transforming their skin. Some people feared the clan from under the waves and drove them away from their home in the water, to a place where the mountains sit next to the ocean.

But one woman, She Sings Two Worlds, came from a small clan of the blackfish people known as Keykwin, who kept the traditions of tree celebrations and visiting under the waves. They lived far away north from other earth clans, and the people from under the waves made their home there with them, too.

She Sings Two Worlds was happy walking the earth with her family, and happy under the waves. She passed her happiness on to her children, and their children, and seasons of other children. But She Sings Two Worlds first made two promises, one with land, and another with water. She vowed that only the women of the clan from under the waves could create Keykwin.

She Sings Two Worlds wound her long black hair in her hand at her neck and cut it, scattering it to the wind, letting it become the branches of trees and the peaks of mountains. She bled into the water, making it salty, letting the waves take it down to the blackness below. She raised her arms to the moon, singing it down from the sky, nursing it from her breasts, releasing it to the stars. And then she dove, drinking the sea, holding the ocean in her belly, twisting and turning until the turning and twisting water came out of her and she swam, the starlit blackfish once more.

He looks up and meets her eyes, then reaches for her hand. She takes it, and squeezes.

"That's the story of where the Keykwin came from. They have all kinds of legends explaining the animals, nature, and life."

Nolee releases his hand again and pours tea into her mug. "Can Keykwin change into other animals, or just orca?" She brings their plates over to the table.

"Only orca, as far as I know. Although, according to my grandmother, all animals are humans in different skins. The Keykwin would come out of the water to sit on land around a fire and tell stories. Sometimes they would take humans from capsized ships and escort them to the depths of their watery villages. There, the humans would also become the blackfish, but couldn't change like Keykwin."

He's silent, staring out at the sparkling morning sea. "Remember when I told you I couldn't stand being at the university? That the classes were all right, but the noise and activity were unbearable?"

She nods, tearing the crust from her toast.

"That's not the real reason I quit. The reality of that culture didn't have any room for the reality I grew up with. My grandmother raised me to see myself and others as part of the world, not the rulers of it. I got tired of the constant battle between who I was and what that world wanted me to be. That's when the feeling of being split in half began, so I left, hoping it would go away."

Pausing, he stands up and begins to pace. It's hard to breathe—it feels as though his heart has swollen or his lungs have shrunk.

"Are you okay?" he hears her ask. He nods, turns, and sits down again.

"I've never said out loud some things I need to tell you. It feels . . ." She waits for him to finish his sentence, watching him through eyes soft with understanding. He gets up again, pacing.

"Can we walk on the beach and talk about this? I'm having a hard time sitting still."

"Sure. Fae will appreciate the exercise."

It's a crisp day, the type of day when you know that summer is fading and cold weather's on its way. Keet hears the change in sound when the wind moves through the trees. The sea's rhythm soothes Keet's inner chaos.

I don't know where to start." He glances at her. They stop walking. She takes his hand.

"Start where you need to. Blurt something out, it doesn't matter. Keep talking, and I'll keep up."

He takes a deep breath and tells her the first thing that pops into his head. "Those times when you came over for dinner, and I told you the salmon was 'fresh caught'?"

She nods, her eyes never leaving his.

"It was. I caught it."

It takes a moment, but then she laughs, bending at the waist, barely able to breathe. When she stands again, she's wiping tears from her eyes.

"Of course you did! As Keykwin."

"It was the only way I could tell you who I was, without telling you."

"I thought those indentations on the fish were part of some fancy cooking method. But they were just the right size for orca teeth marks." She smiles at him. "What else?" They resume walking, making their way along the beach, following the sun, then turning to walk away from it.

"You remember that storm I got caught in a couple of months ago?"

"How could I forget?" She loops her arm through his, leaning into his shoulder.

"I took the boat out and anchored at a different marina here on Camas. So I could swim."

She frowns. Releases his arm.

"I'm sorry I lied, Nolee."

She shakes her head. "Thanks for the apology. I can understand why you did, but . . ."

He waits as she stops, looking at the kelp-slimed rocks. "No more lies, Keet. No more hiding. Deal?"

"Deal. No more lies." Fae bounces up to him with a wet ball in her mouth. He picks it up and throws it ahead of them.

"So you got caught in the storm . . ."

"Yes, I checked the weather reports, and the storm was out in the Pacific—it wasn't supposed to come this far in. But it did. I found my family in time, and we rode it out, but we couldn't eat or rest. We had to stay awake to fight the sea, to keep from being washed into the cliff, or an island, or the shallows."

"So that was true; I remember you saying something about staying awake so you could survive."

He nods.

Nolee says, "What else?"

"Only Keykwin women can give birth to other Keykwin, and they begin as human. When I'm orca, when I mate with a female orca and there's a birth, our offspring is only orca."

She stops walking again, turning, shielding her eyes against the glare of the sun with one of her hands.

"How many orca babies do you think you have?" He can see a sharpness in her eyes. He realizes that the only answer is the one that's true.

"It's a guess, but I would say six. Maybe eight. I don't know because I mated with female orcas outside of my pod. My family, my pod, is who I'm with most of the time. "

"You've never met your kids?"

"Some of them, but not all. They—we—make our homes with our mothers, aunties, and grandmothers. They stay with their own pods."

She takes her hand away from her eyes and looks down at the line of low tide, then looks at him. "Here I thought my having a daughter would be a serious deterrent for any man I was interested in dating."

In the silence that follows, she watches his face. He breaks into a slow smile that turns into a full-throated laugh, one she joins. "Oh my god, I didn't think that was going to sound as judgey as it did."

He shakes his head, leans in, kisses her, and draws away. "It's funny, and it's touching because I've never thought of it that way. The truth is, in a lot of ways, it's easier to be orca. Simpler than being human. There's family, and there's feeding together, and there's play and connection and a life spent traveling through known places."

"Is this why you said you were thinking about giving up everything here, selling your business and your house and going away? You meant going away as orca, didn't you?"

He flashes on their conversation when they began dating, and nods.

"Yes. And my answer is the same. I'm not thinking that way anymore, not with you in my life."

"Why did you think you needed to give up being human?"

"Because it feels like the knife that lives in my heart disappears when I'm orca. There's no ache or loneliness, none of the desolation that fills me up when I'm human." Despite the warmth of the day, Keet shivers.

"As orca, I'm never alone, not with my thoughts, not with my body, not with the whole of life and the enormity of the ocean. I'm part of everything. There isn't any vying for a more powerful position, or striving to be a 'better me,' or 'realizing my potential.' I'm myself, my family are each themselves, and together we live in . . ." He trails off. "Harmony is too small a word, but it hints at what it feels like. I don't think I can explain how I feel when I'm orca. After more than fifty years of living like this, it's becoming more difficult, mentally, to keep making the change from human to orca and back again."

A chilly breeze ripples across their bare arms, and Nolee shivers. Keet wants to shield her from the wind, but isn't yet sure, despite his kiss earlier, if she wants him closer. "Let's go back inside," she says, looking up at him. He watches as Fae's ears come up at the word "inside." She runs to the cabin's front door and drops the ball, looking over her shoulder, tail wagging.

Nolee pulls on a sweatshirt, starts a fire, then sits on the sofa next to him.

"I think I can understand." She runs the tips of her fingers along the length of his arm. "When you showed me who you were, after I stopped being terrified," she gives him a quick smile, "when I was with you and your orca family, there were moments of feeling as though I was one of you. It was this sense of belonging, a feeling that I've missed since I was pregnant with Abbie."

Keet reaches out to her and lays his hand on her knee. "I didn't think of that, that being pregnant would be a completely amazing experience."

She puts her hand over his. "It is. I talked to her all the time, not with my voice or even with words. I welcomed the chance to share my body so she could come into being. Maybe it was because Nate wasn't around—even when he was at home, he wasn't there—but I wasn't lonely. And I couldn't be, knowing she was with me.

"I had to have a c-section, and when they lifted her from my body, I wouldn't let them cut her umbilical cord right away. They let her lay on my chest because I was so agitated they needed to calm me down. I knew the epidural was working, but I felt it when they cut her away from me. It was a jolt, like our tether had been severed. That sense of belonging, of sharing this deep and wondrous mystery with another being, left. They gave me a sedative because as they took her away from me, I lost it. Everything in me, every shred of my being, was fighting to get up off that table and protect her. But I couldn't. I was numb from the waist down, and they strapped my arms to the table. Looking back, it was a little barbaric."

He sees the vestiges of sadness cross her face. She gets up, grabs a tissue, and wipes her eyes, blows her nose, and sits beside him.

"Nathan never believed me. Our own daughter, whom I carried and gave birth to, and he never understood that feeling." She looks at him, the green of her eyes made more intense by the tears that are still welling up. "Is that what you're telling me, Keet? That as orca, you live in that . . . belonging? That kinship?"

He nods, unable to produce words around the lump in his throat.

"You said your orca family knows you're also human?"

"They do. That pod and its ancestors have been helping my family for generations. A very long time ago we walked and swam freely between both worlds. The Walk Into the Water was a rare thing—"

She interrupts him. "Can you explain what that is?" He looks out the window.

"The Walk Into the Water is when a Keykwin leaves the human life behind to only exist as orca. The tribe has a ceremony, very much like what you think of as a funeral. He or she gives away all possessions, including the clothes they're wearing, and they walk into the ocean, shifting into orca, dying to being human."

"And this didn't happen often, and now it does?"

"My grandmother's maternal grandparents told of only one time they performed this ceremony, in the time of their own grandparents—"

Nolee holds up her hand and closes her eyes. "Wait a minute. That's a lot of grandparents."

He smiles. "Just think of it as a very long time ago."

She lowers her hand, nodding at him to continue.

"I was making plans to ask my grandmother to help me take my Walk Into the Water before I met you. She's helped three of our people make that transition. In my own time, both my grandmother and my mother have remained human."

"And is there a ceremony for that?"

"No, not really. My grandmother moved from our house by the ocean in Sitka to an apartment with her son, my uncle. She did this after she shifted for the last time, when she asked my orca family to adopt me, to look after me."

"You said your mom and dad left when you were eleven? Did she choose to stay human too?"

"She did, but she was in a state of constant suffering, torn between the ocean and the land. Most of my memories of her are helping her calm down. She lived feeling tortured, and I didn't know why. As I got older, I thought it was my fault. My dad has family in Nebraska, and she figured that was far enough inland that she wouldn't hear the call of the water."

"Did it work?"

"For a while. When I was twenty-three, they had the accident that killed them. They were driving out here to visit me. I've always wondered if something changed for her. But I'll never know."

Nolee takes his hand, moving closer to him. "They wanted to overnight in Bellingham, so they took the scenic route on the Chuckanut. An oncoming car came into their lane. They swerved and went over the edge into Samish Bay. By the time the emergency crew got there, my dad was dead, and they never found my mom's body."

His face is filled with sadness. "My grandmother thinks my mom is out there still, a matriarch in a pod. I think she would have come back and let us know she was alive. As far as I'm concerned, my mother died that day.

"And," he continues, "my grandmother also thinks the genuine conflict we face as Keykwin is between the collective and bad choices humans are making and the consistent lives of orcas. Being human seems to involve a lot of disconnection, whereas being orca, you can only live in connection."

"What do you think?"

Her question surprises him. He sits up straighter, running his hands through his hair. Looking at her, looking through her and back into his own heart. Choosing his words with care, he's surprised when a burst of anger comes out.

"Being human after being orca is like being imprisoned in a cage that's too small."

She startles, and Fae sits up with a *whuff*. She trots to Nolee, looking up at her with a small whine. Nolee rests a hand on her head, and Fae thumps down, lying across her feet.

"See that, Lia?" Keet's anger shifts. "That is what life does. It responds. It's aware of itself and of others. Being orca is thriving in a state of awareness of everything, without it cancelling out awareness of ourselves. I don't know if that's possible being human."

"Maybe you're selling humans short."

He gives her a quizzical look. She stands up, startling Fae again, who trots over to her bed and curls up and watches Nolee as she paces the small room.

"I mean, you *are* human! And look at what you can do. Hell, look at what I can do! And we're not the only ones. Others can predict things, or hear things, or see or sense things that other people don't see or hear." She pauses, but before Keet can say anything, she jumps in again.

"You can't judge one species against another, Keet. It's not fair to animals to base what we call 'intelligence,'"—she makes the air quotes sign with her fingers, jabbing in front of her like she's punching the words—"on human standards. And you can't judge humans because we can't hear or sense things like orcas, or any cetaceans. We share the same world; we are part of it. While we live in different ways, and while I know that humans aren't taking care of our planet, there are also a lot of good things happening, by good people."

Keet starts to speak, but Nolee's not done.

"And you! You get to experience two lives that are different as city and country, you get to live on land and in the water, you can hear and feel and sense things no human can imagine, *and* you can do all of this whenever you want. Seems to me there's a lot you can be thankful for. I understand the hard parts, Keet, but what about the good parts?"

She stops pacing and throws herself down on the sofa. Keet leans back, relaxed, an ankle crossed over his knee. He watches as she unwinds, the tension draining first from her face, then her body. She gives herself a small shake.

"Sorry, Fae." Her voice is softer, and the red dog walks over to her, leaning against her legs and wagging her tail.

"That was a soapbox." She gives him an embarrassed smile.

"You're not wrong. And, there isn't one thing on this planet that has benefitted from humans. On my most difficult days, the suffering of our planet at the hands of humanity sickens me. That's why I want to live out my days as orca. At least then I'll belong somewhere."

She studies him for a long moment, then says softly, "I'm too used to fighting."

The change of subject catches Keet off-guard.

"What do you mean?"

"I can feel myself getting wound up, ready to go to war for . . . what? My opinion? Really, just ready to fight to get a reaction. I need to remember that you're not Nate."

He reaches for her hand. "I'm not. But as far as I'm concerned, that wasn't a fight. I'm so deep into my split lives I can't see clearly anymore. Seeing the world through your eyes," he moves closer to her so he can touch her face, "helps me. I've been halving myself for a lot of years, not knowing who I am or where I fit. It felt like death by a million paper cuts."

She leans into his touch. "That's the perfect description of my previous marriage. I guess you and I are trying to figure out who we are on our own, and together." She leans closer, whispering before she kisses him. "It's time to heal those cuts."

TWENTY-FOUR

We're both hungry, and I suggest a meal in town. "Let's let someone else do the cooking and the dishes," I say, grabbing my backpack. "I'll treat *and* drive."

Keet laughs. His face has softened, and I wonder what kind of toll keeping his secret has taken on him. He sees me looking at him.

"What is it? Do I look too scruffy to take to dinner?" His hand rasps across his face as he rubs at it.

"You look handsome as always, Keet. I was thinking how your face has relaxed, and how heavy that secret you've been carrying must have felt."

He looks down and then back at me. "It didn't feel like it. The last three years, I've spent so much time as orca, weightless in just about every sense of that word, that when I was human, how I felt was just how I felt."

"I get that. I lived so long invisible to Nate that after a while, it became part of who I was. But when I was riding the ferry out here, I stood on the deck, and it felt like the wind was tearing things away from me, things that were no longer mine. I was glad to let the wind have them."

As we near the car, Keet steps around to my side and opens the car door for me, smiling. He pauses, unsure about the look on my face. "Do you mind?"

"No." I give him a quick kiss. "I'm surprised because it's been an age since anyone has held a door open for me."

Keet gets in and I choose a playlist, then tap "shuffle" and put the car into reverse. A twangy and bright guitar riff starts, followed by the chatter of a tambourine. More guitars join the tune, a bass, and drums. We're bumping down the dirt road, drums and guitars and bass and voices trailing behind us. *Well it's all right, riding around in the breeze, well it's all right, if you live the life you please. . ."*

Once the song ends, he says, "I didn't know you liked the Traveling Wilburys."

I turn the volume down. "Is that who that is? I have their whole CD. I kept waiting for another one, but it never happened."

"Probably because most of them died. They released two albums, by the way."

"What?" I stop my foot from hitting the brake.

He gives me a sideways glance. "Do you know who was in that band?"

"Yeah, right. Tell me, music man."

"Roy Orbison, George Harrison, Tom Petty, Bob Dylan, and Jeff Lynne." He waits for it, knowing what comes next.

"George Harrison was part of The Beatles?" I glance quickly at him, then hit a pothole and correct as we bounce down the road.

"Yup. And?"

"Bob Dylan, well, he's a legend, don't need to explain him."

"They're all legends. Roy Orbison was huge in the sixties. He was born in Texas–now you'll remember him." I rest my hand on his thigh, then stop, signal, and turn left onto the narrow road.

"Tom Petty was the lead in the band the Heartbreakers, as well as a hugely successful solo artist. Jeff Lynne was part of ELO—that's the Electric Light Orchestra." He wraps his hand around mine, explaining how the Traveling Wilburys formed ("George Harrison recruited the other four musicians to help him write a song for the B side of a single his studio wanted to release. It was so good, the studio asked them for a full album."). We're almost to Northsound before I'm aware of a long silence.

"Either you were really interested in my knowledgeable history of an iconic band and its members, or?"

"Just a sec, and I'll tell you." I navigate the short, narrow streets, looking for a place to park. After I find a spot and turned the car off, I look at Keet.

"It's always interesting to hear you talk about music. But mostly, I was listening to your voice. I like the way it sounds."

He leans over and kisses my nose. "I like the way your voice sounds too, Nolee."

"Though I wonder why your human voice is so much deeper than your orca voice. I would expect the opposite; that an animal as big as an orca would also have a deep voice, deeper than a human."

We get out of the car, and I meet him on the sidewalk. He takes my hand in his.

"Orcas don't have vocal cords."

"Really?"

"Really. They . . ." He pauses, and I can't be sure, but I think I see him blush. "We move air through a structure beneath our blowhole to make sounds. They go out through a fatty substance in our head, called the melon. We receive sounds both through our ears and our lower jaws." Keet moves to put himself between me and the street as we walk on the sidewalk.

"On the other hand, baleen whales and humpbacks do have vocal cords. And deep voices." He motions with a tilt of his head to turn right. I see the sign for the restaurant. "Casa Mariachi. Pretty bold to take a gal from Texas out for Mexican food."

"I think you'll like it."

As we wait for a table, I look at his profile. Strong nose and cheekbones, black and silver hair swept back, the stubble that gives him a dangerous, devil-may-care look. I clear my throat and lean in closer to him, taking his hand. He angles his head down so I can talk in his ear. "You hear through your jaw?"

"Excuse me? Burnett, party of two?"

I look away from Keet and nod at the young woman dressed in black. Keet interrupts my thoughts as we follow her to our table outdoors.

"I have an electric razor. Turn it on and hold it against your lower jaw." We walk to the table, and he moves behind me to pull out my chair. After he sits down, I shake my head.

"What? Why?"

"Because that's probably the closest you'll get to feeling what I feel. Those vibrations have information stored in them, and the information is a picture, like a video of what's around me as I swim. I'm not hearing with my jaw—I have an inner ear, like you do. My jaw is more like a transmitter and a booster. The sounds and clicks—some of which are beyond human hearing—are received in two places almost simultaneously."

"Welcome to Casa Mariachi! I'm Ashton. Can I get you any appetizers, or drinks?" An eager young man with curly hair and a broad grin holds his tray in front of him like a brown plastic shield. Keet orders wine, and I can't resist a blended margarita with extra salt.

After we order our drinks and an appetizer, I say to Keet, "Did I catch you blushing when you were talking about how you make sounds as an orca?" Under the table, I rest my foot against his ankle. He nudges me back.

"Maybe. It still feels awkward to talk about it openly. And I'm used to saying 'they,' not 'we.'"

Our drinks arrive, and I down two large mouthfuls of the margarita. Its flavors burst into fire as I swallow. This place doesn't skimp on their tequila.

Keet holds his wineglass, watching me with a smile. "Any good?"

When I recover my breath, I nod and take another drink, this time a sip. "Good as anything in Texas. This may become our spot. Now, back to what we were discussing earlier. Tell me something that isn't common scientific knowledge, Keet."

"What do you mean?"

"Tell me more about sending and hearing sounds, and what that's like for you."

The waiter sets a dish of *esquites* on the table, and Keet takes a bite of the spicy corn and cheese dish and closes his eyes. "Cheese is a miracle," he mumbles. He swallows, then begins talking. "The reason orca calls sound the same, or scientists only hear repeating calls, is because each orca and its call function like a single light in a dark room. If you have a giant room with a thousand chairs, and a stage, and curtains, a balcony, but it's dark, one person shining a light will only be able to see what that light is pointed at."

I nod, leaning forward, my arms on the table.

"But. Get a hundred people in there, and you'll begin to see the whole room. It will be dim, but you can get around without running into the stage. Give a thousand people a flashlight, now you've got a thousand sources of illumination and you can see the whole room, clearly. You could take a photo in there and see the details.

"Orca calls are like flashlight beams. When the calls are measured, they sound the same. Each orca call, and the information it conveys doesn't come back only to the sender, though. Other orcas who are in range benefit from the information the first orca sent, and they add their calls to the information being sent.

I hold up my hand. "Wait. You're telling me the sounds are like going to the movies?"

He rocks his head back and forth. "Yes, sort of. Put it this way. Between a small pod of six or seven, or a greater gathering of dozens, orca calls light up the ocean and give all of them accurate pictures of the topography, weather, where the salmon are gathering, where potential mates are.

Humans hear it as a consistent call without any variation. Perhaps it has an echoing quality. Perhaps there's a little rise at the end of a high note that wasn't there before. But packed within those sounds is all the information an orca is gathering about where it is, what it feels, and what it's "seeing" through echolocation. This is shared throughout the pod."

Our waiter arrives at the table holding two steaming plates of food. "Thanks, Ashton. This looks great!"

Ashton sets the plates on the table then takes off the oven mitts he wore to bring them to us. "If you want to burn yourself, touch those."

Keet and I laugh putting our hands in our laps.

We begin eating, but I haven't taken more than two bites of my meal before I look at him and ask, "Tell me more?"

He nods. "When humans look at a map, no one else knows what they're seeing. Vision is a singular experience unless you're with other people, watching the same thing." He lifts his fork in my direction. "Like you said about the movies. But sound is everywhere. What one person hears, another can as well, such as the spoken word, or music."

I scrape my fork around my plate, herding the last of the beans and rice into a neat pile. "But even with sound, we interpret it differently. Ask ten people who saw the same movie in the same theatre, and you'll probably get ten different impressions."

He nods. "True. But what is also true is that they can agree on the setting, the actors, the lighting, what dialogue they heard, the name of the director. The tangible details. What they might disagree on is the meaning. Orcas are different." He puts down his fork and knife on his empty plate. "When we send or receive sound, there's no argument about its meaning. The sounds are a true visual representation of everything around us, not what we think they mean to us individually."

"But you're individuals. You're all different."

He nods again. "Orcas are born, live out their lives, and die knowing nothing but community and shared resources. Besides food, the largest shared resource is their ability to share what they see, through sound."

We finish our meal and I have a second margarita for dessert, Keet opting for cinnamon ice cream. When I get up, the floor moves like I'm on Keet's boat. Handing my key to Keet, I tell him it would be a good idea if he drove. I loop my arm through his as we walk to the car, leaning into his steadiness.

"Man, it's been a while since I've had margaritas. Why do I always forget they make me so loopy?" I lay my head against his arm, and he shortens his long stride to match mine. He helps me into the car, and after he folds himself in and slides the seat back as far as it will go, I lean over and kiss him.

"Your place, or mine?" My eyes are close to his, so that I'm looking into two dark circles, tasting his breath as he kisses me back.

"Yours is closer."

"Your practicality is such a turn-on," I laugh. "Get driving before I crawl over there and make a public spectacle of myself."

He signals and pulls on to the road.

By the time we're back at Osprey Bay, I can barely keep my hands off Keet. I stroke his thigh, touch his face, kiss his hand, lay it against my cheek. We rush out of the car, slamming the doors. I can hear Fae in the house, yipping in excitement. I open the door and she bolts out, dancing around us, her white paws glowing in the light from the doorway.

"Good girl, Fae!" I kneel and scratch her chest. She swipes my nose with her tongue, turns, and runs off the porch, trotting along the beach with her nose to the ground.

I feel Keet behind me. He pulls me against the length of his warm body. The air is a cool contrast to the heat at my back. He turns me toward him kisses me, wrapping his arms around my waist, lifting me up. I hear the scrabble of Fae's approach, but faintly, because every sense I have is focused on the man I'm kissing. I bring my legs up around his waist, and his shifts his arms, holding me under my hips, swinging me side to side in a slow rock that leaves me breathless.

He sets me down, but I can't feel my feet. It's like I'm floating, a balloon filled with his scent, and the weight and heft of his body against mine. Panting, we step apart. I hold out my hand to him, and we walk up the steps. Fae trots in ahead of us. "I'll feed Fae first."

"I'll get the bed ready while you do that."

I nod, and we come together, our lips and bodies meeting.

"It may be the sofa if you don't go soon." There's no laughter in my voice, and no amusement as he looks at me. We're both powder kegs, ready to explode at the first spark of a match.

After putting Fae's food down, I vault up the stairs. Keet's in my bed, naked, and I can't join him quickly enough. Our coupling is urgent and quick, no words exchanged, our voices point and counterpoint to the needs of our bodies. Wrapped within our chemistry is my own acceptance of who he is, and his freedom from a heavy secret.

Afterward, as our breathing slows together, I roll away, throw off the covers, and walk over to open the window so I can feel the evening air. I look down, sure I'm steaming as a cool breeze envelops me from scalp to toes. I sigh and gather up my hair so my neck can cool, too. When I turn back, I see Keet lying on his side, watching me.

"You're beautiful, Lia. Glowing, and full like the moon."

I walk back to the bed and sit next to him. "You make me feel like some sort of goddess, Keet."

He moves a strand of hair away from my face. "You *are* a goddess, and anyone who can't see it is an idiot." I kiss his mouth, then settle down next to him, pressing my back against his chest as he curls around me.

"You said your mom showed you how to shift between human and orca when you were four?"

His answer is slow in coming, caught somewhere between breath and heartbeat. I can feel his hesitation as though it's my own.

"She did. I'd been swimming with her help since I was a baby. There's no set age for us to begin changing between forms. I guess that's when she thought I was ready."

"Were you?"

He changes position, wrapping both arms around me. "Don't know. I didn't question it. She would swim into the ocean as human and jump out of it as orca. But I knew she was my mother, and that's just the way things were. Our house was in the forest by itself, and we liked it that way because revealing ourselves as Keykwin wasn't acceptable, even within our community. Looking back, I wonder if she knew even then that she couldn't keep switching between forms. Sometimes, I think my birth may have been a way for my dad to keep her human, and a reason for her to keep trying to live two lives."

Keet sighs. "My mom used to say she felt like her spirit was in a tug of war, and that at some point it would snap. As a kid, I didn't get it. I loved swimming as orca with her, and I loved when she and I were human and cooked together."

I pull the covers up over us, but don't want to say anything, afraid of interrupting his memories as he walks through that time.

"But I get it now, Lia. I also feel the pull going in opposite directions inside of me. If I choose orca, I lose what it is to be human. If I choose to be human, I lose out on the beauty of being orca. Either way, a whole life is destroyed."

"Choices like that are terrible, aren't they?" I ask.

Keet's heartbeat pulses in my ear. "Yes, they are. You're telling me I don't have to choose anymore?"

"Not if you don't want to. Not for my sake, anyway."

We're quiet, and I watch the sunset filtering through the window, casting its orange glow onto the ocean quilt. I spot the orca, washed pale, jumping through pale ocean waves. The otter and seal are there too.

"If you want to be with your orca family for good, you can do that. Though I'd miss the hell out of you." Keet kisses my head.

"But don't make that choice on my account," I say. "If you want to be here with me, you can do that. When you want to be out there, with your family, you can do that too."

Keet sighs, and his arms tighten around me.

"I've never thought I could have both. I've spent the last five years believing that it had to be one or the other." His voice, scratchy with fatigue, is filled with relief, deep and soft. "I believed that the only way I could be in this world was as orca. Being a human man is just too . . . complicated. And it hurts. My mind and heart are bigger when I'm orca. I feel like I could hold the entire ocean and everyone in it."

"I have a hard time figuring out my own heart and mind. I think I'd explode if I had that much information coming at me."

"You might if you tried it as a person. I've come close to staying orca a few times. But the loss of my human memories was too upsetting."

"You lose your human memories? After how long?"

Keet loosens his arms around me as I roll onto my back. He says, "I don't know. It always happens after about a week. Maybe a little more. It's disconcerting enough that I return to my human form, and a human life."

I kiss him under his jaw, liking the feel of his stubble sharp on my lips. "I, for one, am glad you kept choosing to be a man."

I can hear our heartbeats increasing, synching up with one another. "Besides, I'm not here to tie you to land, and I don't believe you're here to save me. That's my job. We found each other. I have no intention of replacing the lives we already have, but we can add each other to them."

He squeezes me tighter to his chest. "That makes sense. But it'll take me a little time to get used to the idea."

"Take all the time you need, Keet. I'll be here whatever your choice is."

As I kiss him, a thought pops into my head. "I have another question for you."

He murmurs a reply against my neck. It feels very close to the bass vibration of an orca voice.

"No one has been this affectionate with me. I didn't realize how distant my family was, and how I've kept my friends distant too. I notice that your orca family is always touching each other, they're so tactile."

He murmurs what sounds like a yes, this time running his hands up and down my torso, holding the curve of my hip.

"Are you affectionate because you're also this way as an orca, or is this normal?"

"What do you mean by 'this,' Lia?"

"This. Us. I feel connected with you emotionally, of course, but also physically. I didn't realize how touch starved I've been."

His hands resume their movement across my skin. I shiver beneath his touch.

"I don't know what normal is, other than an illusion. But to answer your question, there are some...characteristics, or traits, that carry over from who I am as orca, to a human man. I've not thought about it, but maybe you're right. Maybe one does influence the other."

"Has it happened with other women?"

Keet huffs a laugh against my cheek. "That sounds like a loaded question."

I prop myself on my elbow, moving away so I can look down at him. "After all we've shared, especially the last two days, you'd think I set you up like that?"

His face turns serious. "I was physical when I was in bed with other women, after Sascha. But it began and ended there. With you, it runs deeper than our attraction to each other."

He kisses me then, his soft lips and heated breath meeting mine. I move my hand over his back, memorizing the way his muscles glide over his ribs, the knobs of his spine. My fingers run across a scar I'd noticed before but had not thought to ask about.

"What's the story behind this scar on your spine?"

I can feel a shiver run down his back, and instinctively press him closer to me, as though I could retroactively shield him from whatever happened.

"It's a bullet scar."

"A bullet? When?"

"In the eighties, when I was still young, I was full of myself, both as a man and as a blackfish. I thought I was better. It was a favorite game of mine to steal salmon from the fisherman's nets."

"I don't know whether to laugh or not."

"It's funny now, because I lived to tell the tale."

"What happened?"

"I was feeding with my orca family on a moonless night up in Sitka and broke off from them because I heard a pod of females coming close. Along the way, I encountered a fishing boat with its nets still in the water. There were salmon in them, so I ate for a while, then surfaced to taunt the fishermen, like I usually did. Swearing like a sailor has its basis in fact; they cursed me and every other killer whale."

"And then what?"

"This sailor didn't swear. He turned a spotlight on me and shot at me. It went through my dorsal fin. It hurt, but what hurt worse was the humiliation. I swam back to Sitka. My grandmother, oh, she was mad, mad, mad."

"I bet she was. What did she do?"

"Nothing. Said it served me right. Handed me a towel and told me to sleep on the floor."

He rolls toward me and tilts up my chin. His lips and touch are soft, then insistent. I wrap my arms around his torso. He moves, settling between my legs. I gasp as he enters me. Our eyes are open, watching one another. Then he buries his face in my neck and hair; I feel his hand cradle the back of my head. My hands are against his back, stroking him as we ebb and flow like the tide. Washed by silver moonlight, Keet and I make love again. I ignore the sense that this feels like the first and the last time.

After kissing Nolee in the dark hours of the morning, whispering that he'd be away for a couple of days, Keet walks naked down to the shore and wades out into the bay, its chill a welcome touch. As he swims to deeper water, he thinks how, for humans, the sea at night is a vast womb of threatening darkness. Unless a light illuminates the space around their bodies, they have neither the hearing, the sight, nor enough kinesthetic sense to recognize what's swimming around them. They have no way of knowing if they are safe or in danger. Ruled by their brains, humans have lost touch with much of their ability to sense the world they share with others—part of an everyday sadness that sometimes threatens to drown him.

The limitations of a human body don't rule Keet now. He's orca, a black-and-white bullet speeding through the sea guided by the calls of his pod, beacons that light up inside his head. Seeing with sound, he closes his eyes against the water's pressure as he goes deeper, the canary chirps, barks, and clicks leading him on. He sees each ridge in pictures behind his eyes, pictures that form as the sounds bounce from them. His large pectoral fins and flukes steering him toward the distant sounds of his family feeding, he points his nose upward and feels the cold air hit his dorsal fin before he raises his head to breathe. Inhaling the air and showing his flukes to the night sky, he dives and swims. He is the ocean, he is life, he is orca. The loneliness that gnaws at his heart when he's Keet no longer touches him.

George, his sister's baby, is first to reach him, squeaking and clicking. He bounces his small body off the large male with joy. Then they're all there, their songs a homecoming he rests in. The baby is back, rolling around with a small salmon in his mouth. He offers the salmon to the big male orca, who nudges it toward his sister, who needs it more than he does. Taking the fish, she sends a warbling gratitude before gulping it down.

Through the soft pearlescence of early morning, the pod hunts and feeds and sings, their bodies never more than a pectoral fin away, their white bellies rolling against each other. No secrets or lies are possible in a world where sound reveals each organ, and where vocal expression contains layers of meaning that only an orca can understand. He knows his pod as well as he knows himself, and in this knowing, there's contentment. He lets the tendrils of human memory slip away, floating behind him like a slick strand of kelp in the wake of a dive.

TWENTY-FIVE

"Keep 'em in the spotlights, boys!"

The pod is fleeing before speedboats in the gray hours before sunrise, the baby in the middle, the male at the rear. Seismic blasts behind them stab with a pain that obliterates any sense of where they are or where they're going. It's a noise and chaos they can't escape from. The male calls to them between these sonic booms, a song of calm and reassurance. Above them, whipping helicopter blades spray water into their blowholes when they try to breathe, frantic for air, staying at the surface precious seconds longer to expel the water.

The pod matches its speed to the baby's. Nana, after several attempts to dive or double back, leads them. As her strength ebbs, she falls to the back, and Tia takes the lead.

Through the dawn and into the day, the pod is pursued by the boats and the booming, driven into a narrow channel that ends in a cliff wall. The water is shallow here, and the orca family circles around the baby. The male feels their fear and confusion in his own heart and body. He sings again, encouraging them to rest. The booming finally stops but the boats continue to roar around them. When he brings his head up to see what they're doing, he sees nets and boats barricading the only way out. He waits with the pod, rising and falling slowly, waiting for them to match his rhythm. He doesn't approach the boats or the nets. Evening falls.

Lying on his side, he looks at the light overhead and feels the drone of blades disturbing the air and ruffling the water above them. The helicopter hovers, circles, then leaves. The boats, and the men on them, secure the nets.

"Look at that bull killer whale! He's going to make us rich."

He dives, his dorsal fin barely covered by water when he's forced to stop. He swims to his family, stroking each with his large pectorals, clicking and singing to calm them. They are tired and hungry. He sings a picture of the dawn, and of waiting for the boats and men to leave.

Dawn comes, but the men and boats don't leave. When the sun is highest in the sky, and the orcas are unable to cool themselves in the shallow water, another boat arrives and throws dead salmon into the pen. With whistles and murmurs, the male orca tells the others to eat. They will need their strength when the chance to flee arises, as he knows it will.

The orcas eat the dead fish in minutes, although George spends time playing, balancing their limp bodies on his nose, pushing them up and down through the water. After they eat, they swim in small circles, breathing. The water is too warm in the shallows. George stops playing and rises and falls with his mother.

More boats leave, their motors trailing a painful tide of sound in their wake. The male rises, his eyes above the waterline. Where the sun is descending into the sea, there's a boat with one man on it. He's wearing headphones and has his back to the orca family. The male also sees a place where the net sags lower into the water. He turns away and dives for his pod. He'll wait until dark, when he feels the man sleeping, and work on the net so they can make their escape.

At dusk, his family is swimming again, now in frantic circles. The male swims more slowly, singing of open seas and sunlight, cool waters and plentiful salmon. They hear the whine and rumble of a motor, then see another batch of dead fish being dumped into the water. This time, the family doesn't need to be convinced to eat. The male waits as they feed, and they leave a portion for him. There's no singing of thanks for the fish, of celebration. This feeding is necessity.

"They're settling down," the leader in the second boat says, a man with a graying beard and weather roughened skin. "We'll sling them up and get them into the tanker in the morning."

"What if we can't get them in slings?" the other man asks. He's wearing a black watch cap pulled nearly to his eyes. His yellowing fingers twitch for another cigarette. He wants the boss to go away so he can smoke and sleep. "The killer whales aren't going anywhere. They're docile as dogs."

"Then we shoot them. We get more money the more of them we deliver, but that big male and the baby; we want to be careful with them. They're the moneymakers." He turns the bow of his boat back to the open ocean before gunning the motor and speeding away to his camp on a nearby island.

As the sun sets behind gray storm clouds and thunder rumbles from their rostrums through their tails, the pod settles into an uneasy sleep, rising and falling and listening for the sounds they have known the whole of their lives: the sizzle of fish gathering and the cries of the gulls that follow them. The high, chattering whistles of their dolphin cousins. The pictures of familiar shorelines and ocean floor. The rumble and fizz of the ocean at the surface, and below the waves.

But beyond the feel of the night breeze on their dorsal fins, nothing is familiar. No comforting noises of home reach them. The cove, their songs, their vision, and one another are all they hear, see, and feel.

Halfway through the night, the male raises his head toward the boat and sends out a breath of quiet clicks. There's no response. He swims closer, and with a delicacy that would startle the man, rises again and glances into the boat. The human is asleep, wrapped in a blanket, the boat rocking on the ocean swell. On the other side is the sagging net, now lower in the water on the rising tide. Fog is rolling in.

Keet takes a quiet breath, dives, and swims for the edge of the net. He sings a picture for his family to wait where they are. Wait and rest, wait and rest. They dive and wait. The baby is nursing again, his mother slowing her heartbeat and rolling over so he can feed more easily. They rise as one, each exhaling quietly before another inhales, then drop to rest their bellies on the rocky ocean floor. The male tests the net with his pectoral fins, head, neck, and flukes, ascending and descending in a rhythm meant to make sure the man in the boat sleeps undisturbed.

The net is now sagging lower, and the male straddles it with his body, creating an opening through which his family can swim. Dropping beneath the waves, he clicks and for them to approach, and to escape.

As each member of his pod swims by him, they nudge his side, caress him with their flukes. The baby is first to swim to freedom, their grandmother is last. They turn as a group, waiting for him to free himself from the top of the net and join them, but he sings and clicks and squeals a high-pitched series of notes. He wants them to leave, to dive as deep as they can for as long as they can; he will follow. They'll meet far north, where the waters are icy and the fishing is abundant.

The pod circles, singing questions, singing for his safety. The male sends them pictures of cold gray skies and cool waters, fish, and their brothers and sisters of other pods. They bob on the surface, their exhales and inhales becoming erratic. The male raises his head above the waves just as the boat's spotlight hits his eye, causing him duck under the surface again.

He sends his loudest warning to his family: Away!

They dive, circle once more as the roar of the boat engine engulfs all sound, then swim for the open sea, heading to colder waters. The boat follows them until they dive and stay down, and the man loses them in the dense fog. The male feels the roar of the retreating engine, and he loses the pod's distress cries in the whirring and churning sound of the boat chasing them. The last thing he hears is the squeal of his own song, calling to them to swim far and fast.

The boat returns. The man lights a cigarette and throws the match in the water. He shines the spotlight and sees the bull killer whale floating on the surface inside the pen, no longer laying on the net. "Not so smart, are ya? You're just a big stupid fish."

Cursing, he fixes the net, then calls in on a radio filled with static. The male dives, seeking a quiet spot in the cove, but his world fills with the sound of motors and later, the roar of a helicopter that makes his skull rattle. Feeling his family growing distant, he lets the rising ocean move him. Then they're gone, and he is alone.

Two small boats flank the orca, one on each side. His dorsal fin alone is longer than either of the skiffs, but he floats quietly, not threatening the men as they work to put him in a sling. His pectorals are squeezed into round slots and his belly is forced upward. His tail hangs listlessly as they float him toward a tugboat that bobs in the dark, the throb of its engine banging against his skull. He doesn't pay attention to what the men are saying, waiting instead to let them lift his body out of his home and begin the long process of hauling him wherever his place is to be.

From the time of his chase to the time of his choice to remain in the pen, he has remained orca. First, to protect his family. Later, after they'd escaped, to keep the men focused on him as his pod swam away. He closes his eyes as they lift him from the water and a roar of thunder overrides all sound, all activity. The rain pelts down and the boat rocks in the agitated waves, listing to the side where—still suspended in mid-air—he tilts above currents he can no longer ride. He calls once, a long and mournful cry that rises past the hearing of the men, past the hearing of his family who swim on, panic silencing their singing.

Hundreds of miles away, Nolee wakes with a scream in her throat.

TWENTY-SIX

The orca is an undulating shadow floating in turquoise water. An acid taste lingers on his pale tongue. The starless-night black of his body throws sunbursts to the sky as he rises to breathe. He inhales and submerges again, remembering a green, rainy forest. His once-proud notched dorsal fin leans to the side. The water is too warm, but it provides a small shield against the hot sun.

Despite the growing dark, the male orca feels hot from the inside out. He's hungry and he's lonely, the ache around his heart a chasm too deep to sound. He surfaces, exhales, and gulps air as though he's still swimming in the currents and channels of the Salish Sea, but his fins are still. His pectorals and tail hang without life.

Noise and people have surrounded him since his capture, and he can't find a single sound that he recognizes. His memory of the transport suggests that after the boat, he was in an airplane, then a truck. He lost track of time, until he was suspended over water in a concrete tank; the reflection of a blue neon sign rippled across the water's nighttime surface. The neon flare seared into his eyes briefly when they lowered him, dripping, in his sling into the tank.

He felt the water on his flukes first, and at the edge of the tank, people rushed to free him from the sling. Rolling away from them, he yanked his pectoral fins free and was caught by a sudden riptide of dizziness. He righted himself and rose, finding the warm air with his blowhole before exhaling, gasping for breath, swimming. After only two strokes of his powerful flukes, he is forced to turn, then turn again—swimming in circles through the night and into the morning, people watching him from the edge of the tank. He didn't know where he was, but the water was too warm and the fish too cold. He'd eaten without appetite and floated without direction in the silence of the dead water.

Now, behind his eyes, he sees the twisting bodies of other orcas, towering conifers shrouded in tendrils of fog and rain, and a woman with faded auburn hair smiling at him, then turning and disappearing into the mist. The fog shifts in time with his slow, drum-deep heartbeat, until all that remains are the shadows of the trees. He casts the forest memory as a spell against amnesia and, as he slips into the in-between space of wake and sleep, he plays the memory again.

Although he can feel others of his kind in separate tanks, he's silent. His sounds bounce off the concrete and knife through his lower jaw, shooting pulses of pain through his skull. He's tried varied tones and whistles, click trains, and low-frequency calls; the information coming back is flat; like the concrete that surrounds him, the image never changes.

In the morning, he lies on his side, watching as a man—short and slim, with brown hair and sharp features—brings a large metal bucket to the edge of the pool. He sets the bucket down and, with a grin that doesn't reach his eyes, looks at the newly arrived orca.

The man, Kyle Nicks, an OceanMagic Marine Park trainer, named him Odin, for the Norse god of war and magic. Kyle likes to cast rune stones and explained to a colleague that "The blank black Odin stone portends possibilities." What he doesn't say out loud is that it also stands for death.

"Odin, you're gonna love this breakfast! We found some salmon in the freezer for you."

Although the orca can understand every word, he rolls onto his back, flicking his tail and dousing Kyle in water.

"Not gonna get rid of me that easily, my friend!" Kyle takes a handful of fish and throws them into the tank. The big male sends out a quiet pulse of clicks, beyond the hearing of the man, but the fish are as dead as the water. Still, he eats, hungrier than he realized.

"That's right, Odin. You'll fit right in. You're going to save this place, big fella, and I'm going to go right along with you."

The orca eyes Kyle, waiting for more fish.

"You're going to have to come over here if you want to eat."

The orca feels the suction of Kyle's energy, his desire for him to be closer. He pauses, and then swims to the edge of the pool, rolling on his side so he can see his captor. Kyle begins throwing the fish into the water with both hands, watching as the orca swallows them whole, then comes back up, his nose inches from the edge. Kyle reaches out to touch the magnificent head, but the orca sinks, swimming away from him.

But he can't get away. Kyle picks up the bucket and walks to the opposite side of the tank, where the orca is lying at the bottom, searching for cool water.

"You can't stay down there forever, big fella!" Kyle drops another handful of fish and laughs as the orca swims after them, gulping them down one after the other.

The orca leaves, Kyle follows. Kyle throws fish, Odin eats them.

"Odin, dude. The sooner you get with the program, the better off we'll all be. You aren't getting salmon every day, either. Too pricey, man. But once you bring in the cash, you'll be treated like a king!" Kyle picks up the now-empty bucket, checks that the gate that separates the tank from the deeper water of the show stadium is locked, and leaves.

The day passes and the evening shadows lengthen; the pool in the shade of the surrounding buildings as the sun sinks low. The orca raises his head above the water, sending loud squeaks and whistles. He rotates in place, clicking, hoping to feel information about where he is through his jaw and head.

Nothing.

Calling upon the memory of himself as human, he dives, closes his eyes and spins in place, his tail creating a whirlpool on top of the water. When he rises, he is still orca. Spinning in the opposite direction, he tries again and rises, still orca. He dives and spins, concentrating on Nolee and home. Before he is done rotating in place, he knows he is still orca. Wailing, he throws himself against the side of the tank in rage and despair as his blood stains the water red.

The spotlights flash on, temporarily blinding him. He submerges and lies at the bottom of the pool. The bleeding cut on his head, a gash in his thin skin, slows to a trickle, then stops. He opens his eyes and sees the wavering silhouettes of men walking around the pool.

"Kyle, get some fish."

"Yes, sir."

Lance West, owner of OceanMagic, has no desire to see his investment die in his first days of captivity. He watches as Kyle brings out another stainless-steel bucket of fish, dropping them into the tank.

"What about going in there with him, Kyle?"

Kyle gives his boss a quick glance. "I don't think that's such a good idea, sir. He's fresh from the wild and we don't know what he'll do. He needs months of water work."

"He's a fish-eater, for god's sake. What would he do? You scared?"

"Just playing it safe, sir. You said yourself, we need to be careful these days—public perception and all that."

West shrugs, walks over to the bucket, and throws more fish into the water. The orca ignores both the men and the fish. Pulling a white handkerchief from his pocket, West wipes his hands.

Kyle dumps the rest of the fish in the water, watching their dull scales dim as they sink toward the killer whale. "Where did you say they caught him?"

West looks away from Kyle and down at the killer whale, who still isn't eating the fish. "Iceland. Monitor him. I don't want him bashing his head in before we get him trained."

"Yes, sir, Mr. West." Kyle steps aside, close to the edge of the tank, watching as the owner stalks away, spattering water across the concrete. Looking back in the tank, wondering if Odin has eaten the fish, Kyle sees a giant mouth filled with teeth the size of his fingers rising toward his face. He stumbles back with a yell and falls, and the bucket topples into the water before he can catch it.

The orca retreats, sinking and grabbing each fish with a ferocity that Kyle wants to avoid being on the receiving end of. Tentatively, he reaches into the water and snags the bucket.

"I won't tell anyone about that little trick, Odin," he shouts into the water. The orca swims to the opposite side of the tank and surfaces before sinking to the bottom again.

The orca swims in circles, eating all the fish they give him. He learns cues to wave his pectoral fins and perform tail slaps, working out of necessity and boredom. But he won't open his mouth for Kyle; he only takes fish from the water. At night, he raises his head above the warm water and spins in slow circles, trying to understand why he can't change back to human form.

One cloudy night a week after his capture, still air vibrating with the sounds of sirens and traffic, he sees a small blinking red light. As he turns counterclockwise, he notices two more blinking red dots and wonders if they're cameras. It would make sense; if he's being watched by any eyes other than orca, he can't shift back to a man.

After two weeks, the orca has grown tired of the tank, of Kyle, of the blinking dots, of the nightly spinning nose-down in the water, and even of the rising and falling sun. On the morning of the fifteenth day of his captivity, Kyle comes in wearing a black-and-white wet suit. Instead of feeding him, he stops by a gate that separates his tank from one next to him.

"Odin, I'm gonna open this up, and you'll swim through. Then we'll work on some new tricks out where you can have more room to move."

The orca rolls on his side, away from Kyle and his falsely cheery voice. He hears the gate clang, and as he turns toward the opening, the embers of his anger burst into flame, powering him through the gate. He closes his eyes and sounds the tank with clicks and pulses, feeling its depth and its boundaries. There are concrete platforms above the tank, and as he rises to breathe, he sees that the paint is flaking into the water. He hears the whistle that means fish are coming and swims over to Kyle. As he has for the past fourteen days, the orca refuses to open his mouth. Kyle whistles again, but the orca dives, reveling in the feeling of speed and depth. Reaching the bottom too soon, he somersaults and points his nose at the surface.

When he leaps, the giant bulk of his body clearing the water, Kyle stops whistling and stands silent as five tons of orca, black skin glistening in the sun, rises above the surface like a creature taking flight. The orca comes back to the water, landing on his side and splashing Kyle, who wipes the water away from his stunned face.

The orca dives and turns again, leaping again and landing on his other side. He swims fast, his fury sending the water over the plexiglass walls, flooding the bleachers construction crews are getting ready for the crowds of people that OceanMagic is expecting.

Kyle stops blowing his whistle, stops slapping his hand on the surface of the water, watching in fascination as their new star attraction leaps and dives, speeds around the tank, first flashing his white belly and then flipping right side up. His dorsal fin cuts through the weight of the water, slicing it, making a wave in its wake. Every person working in the coliseum has stopped to watch him.

When he's calmer, the orca eyes the concrete platform opposite the stage Kyle stands on. With a powerful thrust of his tail, he rises from the water, slides on the smooth concrete, and exhales. He turns his head, orienting himself to the coliseum's layout, then pushes back into the water and swims to Kyle.

Kyle is silent, looking at the killer whale with something new in his eyes. He throws several fish into the water and watches as the orca eats them, then sits down cross-legged on the platform, bucket at his side.

The orca exhales in Kyle's face, drifting close to the bucket.

"Nope, no more fish until you let me touch you." Kyle stands up and sets the bucket away from the edge.

The orca dives, rises, and dives again, staying at the bottom of the deep pool until Kyle, cursing, takes the walkway around to Odin's holding tank and dumps the bucket of fish in it. He swims through the gate, the clang of its closing juddering through his head, eats the fish, then resumes swimming in slow, tight circles.

TWENTY-SEVEN

On the fifth day of not being able to find Keet, I drive to the marina to talk with Trish. A late summer wind whistles through the trees and the sea is a mass of rising whitecaps. To open the office door, I hold the doorknob with both hands, then scoot inside and shut it with a bang. Trish and Alex are both there, Trish behind her desk, clicking her mouse and staring at the computer and Alex, looking at his phone. I wonder if they know something I don't.

"Hey. Have y'all seen Keet?"

Trish shakes her head and continues looking at her monitor. Alex looks up, darts a glance at Trish, and shakes his head.

"It's been five days and I haven't heard from or seen him. Trish?" I say her name out of sheer exasperation, wanting some sign that she hears what I'm saying. Lowering her glasses on her thin nose, she gazes at me over the rims.

"Stop worrying, Nolee. He's done this before. He'll be back when he's ready to come back." Her chair gives a squeal that reminds me of George. But instead of making me smile, it sets off a feeling of panic rising in my chest.

"Alex, can you take me out on the boat, maybe look around at some of the other islands?"

He glances at me and then at Trish, who, absorbed by something on her screen, types with a vigorous clacking of keys. Her thin shoulders, pinched and high, lean toward the computer as though she'd like to crawl inside and show it who's boss. I can see from the part in her brown hair that she needs another dye job; her gray roots are peeking through.

"I can't, Nolee." He fidgets in his seat, adjusting the ball cap on his head. "There's a small-craft advisory for this area. The wind is coming in at over twenty knots, and the seas will get worse—up to ten feet. We can't sail. I don't think even Keet would try that."

I look from Alex to Trish and back to Alex, shifting from one foot to another. Trish gets up and leaves the room, going into the back. I can hear the metallic opening and closing of file cabinet drawers. Alex looks puzzled and then asks, "Besides, why do you want to go out on Keet's boat?"

Too late, I realize they don't know Keet's full story. In my worry I've almost given it away. Trish comes back in, and still not looking at me, opens a manila file folder and begins typing.

"It's just . . . I know he likes to keep track of a certain pod of killer whales, and if he's going to be gone, I thought we could do it."

Trish jumps in so quickly I don't have time to decide whether my excuse was believable or not. "Alex, if you take that boat out without Keet's permission, I don't care how good he thinks you are. He's going to have a problem with it."

I turn to Trish, unclenching my fists.

"I'm not asking to go out right this minute. I heard Alex when he said we can't sail in these conditions. Got it. But I wouldn't mind going out when the front has passed."

I can hear my accent thickening, a sure sign I'm getting riled up. Trish gives me an uninterested look over the frames of her glasses, then turns, her chair squealing again, and begins typing.

"Alex, I didn't mean to put you in an awkward position. Let me know if you hear from Keet, okay?"

He nods and stands up. "Gotta go. See ya, Trish."

She smiles, waves, and keeps her gaze focused on the folder.

"Me too," I say as Alex wrestles the door open. I turn back to Trish, who's still typing. "What did you mean when you said, 'he's done this before'?"

She takes off her glasses and closes the folder at the same time. Folding her glasses, she places them in the exact center of the folder, nudging them side to side before looking at me.

"Not that it's any of your business, girlfriend or not." she sighs, frowning. "But what I will tell you is occasionally, he disappears. It used to concern me too—"

The memory of panic and waking up to my own scream washes over me when I hear her use the word "concern." I'm well past concern, far closer to outright frenzy. I take a step closer and try to focus on what she's saying.

"—but now I'm used to it. For whatever reason, maybe because he's a man, or a business owner, or what have you, he has to go off somewhere by himself."

"Does he ever tell you where he goes?"

She frowns at me. "No, and it's none of my business. He told me not to worry when it happens, and to carry on as usual. I suggest you do the same."

I stare at her for a moment, then turn to leave. I can't bring myself to thank her or say goodbye.

I drive home, seeing the tops of the trees whipping back and forth, feeling my little car sway in the wind. Fae greets me with her usual yipping and full-body enthusiasm, convinced it's been years since we last saw one another instead of an hour. I kneel, rubbing her ears, asking her to sit, and then lie down and then roll over. When I stand up, I hear the chime of an incoming text and pull my phone out of my backpack. When I swipe it open, I see it's from Alex.

Hey Nolee. When this weather calms down, we can take the boat out.

I'm typing so fast that autocorrect makes my text back to him a bunch of gibberish. Taking a deep breath, I erase the whole thing and start over.

Are you sure? Trish sounded adamant.

I get an immediate reply. *I'm sure. Keet told me that if he's not here, he trusts me with his boat and to keep taking her out. Let me know when you want to go. He knows Trish can get protective, so don't worry about it.*

I smile, the first time in days. *Thanks, Alex.*

The weather remains unsettled and gray for days that feel like years. I bundle up and pace the cove's beach, looking out into the channel, hoping to see a towering black dorsal fin cutting through the turbulent sea. The weather forecasts are filled with clouds and raindrop icons. Along with wishing for Keet to return, I also try to will the sun to break through clouds that look like a steel ceiling.

The next day, I get a text from Alex.

Hey Nolee. We have a small window of decent sailing weather today. Meet me at the boat in an hour?

I smile, bouncing on the balls of my feet. Fae picks up on my happiness and circles me, panting.

Yes! Thanks, Alex!

When we arrive at the marina, I walk straight to the boat, Fae clipped into her harness at my heels. I wave to Alex and freeze when I see Trish standing next to him, her body rigid. Though since this is how I've always seen her, I can't tell if she's angry or not. I stand still, waiting.

She turns and sees me, gets off the boat, and strides toward me, the dock swaying from the force of her steps.

"I don't care who you are. This is Keet's boat. His livelihood. This is the time of year that we get it ready for winter storage, and you and Alex shouldn't be taking it out on a joy ride!"

I feel my anger rise to match hers. Fae, feeling my distress, leans against my legs, still and warm. When I look down at her, she's fixed narrowed eyes on Trish.

"Trish, this isn't a joy ride. While Keet's away, I'd like to make sure the orca pod he's kept an eye on all these years is okay. I'll deal with Keet if there's a problem."

Trish glares at me. Fae's low-pitched, rumbling growl vibrates against my legs, and I take a breath. If Trish's waiting for me to cave, she'll wait a long time.

She throws me one last glare before pushing past me. "Fine! But have that boat back before it even thinks about getting dark!"

I move toward the dock, Fae by my side, silent. We board the boat, where I snap a dog life vest on Fae and put one on myself over my jacket, then smile at Alex. "Let's go find some orcas."

He smiles back.

Despite our hopeful natures, we see nothing but a series of islands and water empty of anything except birds. No exhales pluming into the air. No joyful black-and-white leaps above the gun-metal Salish Sea. Every bay and cove are quiet, every captain we talk to on other boats assuring us that they haven't seen any orcas. Even the Transients are gone, it seems.

We motor back to the marina, and as I lower the fenders on each side of the boat, I feel my hope slipping, sinking into the dark water. The thought that Keet might be dead, that his pod might be mourning him, now comes into sharper reality and sinks its teeth into my heart and guts. Barely waving goodbye to Alex, I reach my car at a half-run, load Fae, and lean my head on the steering wheel and cry; great wracking sobs convulse in my chest, tears and saliva cover my face. I can't ignore the possibility that Keet may be gone for good.

Mopping my face with my sleeve, I start the car and head for home. I know I can't keep asking Alex to take the boat out, but decide that with the kayak, I can do some limited scouting on my own. If the weather holds, I'll begin my own search.

I take the kayak out every afternoon; sometimes I have sun and blue clouds, sometimes it's gray skies and fog. I search, paddling perpendicular to the shore, scanning the horizon for any sign of Keet or his pod. Each day, the horizon line is stubbornly unbroken. Driven by my own anxiety, I paddle farther each day, but am not confident enough to risk the channel and check the other islands.

Fae, who's learned how to ride in the front of the double kayak, comes out with me, and I watch as she cranes her neck over the side and snuffles at the water. She's my only solace on these missions, her red fur and gleaming eyes beacons in an otherwise dark occupation. Worry about what may have happened to Keet dims my usual pleasure in the bright autumn days.

TWENTY-EIGHT

It's morning, and the fall air is cooler, though the afternoons are still hot. The orca lies on the bottom of his tank. Through water lit by the morning sun, he sees the shape of someone different—a woman. Rising to take a breath, he watches her set the bucket of fish away from the side of his tank. She notices him watching her and says hello, but doesn't approach him. In that one word, he hears a familiar tone and lilt. He closes his eyes and submerges, playing the memory of a green-eyed woman with auburn hair, holding her hand out to him, and saying "Hello, you."

Nolee. The amnesia of being orca is cloaking him, but this young woman's voice has shaken him from his rage and resignation. He pops his head up closer to where she's standing and looking at something on her phone, then squeaks to get her attention.

"I thought you were more the standoffish sort, Odin?" She has curly black hair and brown eyes, and her dark brows, tilted up, make her look like someone who's just heard good news. Her skin glows with the day's heat. But it's her voice that calms some of the anger burning his belly.

As she walks around the tank, he swims slowly, following her. He squeaks again, and she laughs. He flips over, his head nearly touching the bottom of the tank, and waves his tail in the air. When he rises for a breath, she's clapping her hands.

He hears the training whistle, and then Kyle is back, scowling at the girl.

"Marissa, you know you're here as a trainee."

She looks at the ground. "Yes."

"You can't interfere with his training. We've got a lot riding on this whale, and I'm in charge of his care. Clean the buckets."

As she leaves the tank, the orca sinks to the bottom and closes his eyes, casting his memory back for Nolee. He finds her, looking over her shoulder at him as they bob on the sea in his kayak. She has water in her hair, and she's laughing. He sees her silhouette at night, her curves naked above him.

A blast of the whistle jars him from his memories. He rises at the point farthest from Kyle. The trainer is scowling.

"Odin. You're going to learn how to take fish from my hand, or you won't eat today."

But as empty as the orca's stomach is, and as determined as Kyle is, he refuses to approach the trainer for his meal. After two hours of whistles and hand signals, with the orca lying on the bottom as long as he can between breaths, Kyle gets up, shoves the bucket back into a large white cooler, and shouts "Suit yourself," before stamping away from the tank. The orca rises and hears Kyle's raised voice, berating the trainee for her work. He only understands a few words.

The day grows warmer, and the orca's skin crawls with the heat. He swims and rolls, trying to find relief. As the sun lowers in the sky, he drifts again into his memories, a tall pine forest shrouded in a mist that tendrils between the trees. He imagines the cool air. The silence. And most of all, the woman named Nolee, who brought him back to land.

It's growing dark again. There are sirens in the distance, and the loud beat of bass from music that the orca would be able name in his human form. Many things from his human life now seem like they happened in a dream. In a flash, he sees Nolee again, this time, her face as he moves to kiss her. He stops swimming, inhales and exhales slowing as he balances breathing with sleeping.

When it's more night than day, the girl named Marissa shows up by his tank again, looking both ways to make sure no one sees her. He surfaces as near to her as he can get, and blows a soft whistle, the rising and falling of the note an eerie, out-of-place sound in this concrete world. He wants to hear her voice again.

"Odin, you should just take the fish from his hand. It's not a big deal. You need to eat."

He blows an exhale, then inhales and circles the tank on the surface, rolling over to his side and waving his pectoral, longer than she is tall, in her direction.

"I would never have seen anything as amazing as you in Oklahoma. I think you're the most beautiful animal I've ever met."

He squeaks again, trying to match the cadence of her accent.

She laughs. "I'm going to throw you some fish, but don't tell Kyle, okay?" Marissa leaves, then moments later comes back with a bucket.

The orca swims up against the rough edge of his tank, places his chin there, and opens his mouth.

"Odin!" She places each fish in his mouth, and as he swallows, she's laughing.

"Now you really can't tell Kyle about this; he's been trying to get you to hand-feed for weeks!"

Keet squeaks again and blows a raspberry. Marissa is now sitting by the side of the tank, feeding him fish. Seconds later, the spotlights go on and three men in black uniforms come into the holding-tank area.

"Ma'am. You're not allowed to be back here unsupervised. Please give us that bucket and leave."

Marissa stands up, hands the bucket to the tallest man, and walks away. The orca wonders if he'll see her again.

The next morning, the dividing gate opens and the male orca swims for it, taking out his rage on the dead water. Around the coliseum tank he barrels, first one way, then another. He leaps as if to touch the clouds, dives, and somersaults until hunger pangs stop him, leading him to the surface to seek fish.

Today, though, it isn't just Kyle on the stage in front of the tank. Standing back in a suit and shiny dark shoes, is Lance West, and he's talking to Marissa.

"I saw on the security camera footage that you were hand-feeding Odin." This comes out as a statement, not a question, and the orca sees Marissa shifting from side to side, her head down. He can feel waves of worry from her.

"Yes, sir. I felt sorry for him. He didn't eat all day."

"Kyle tells me you may have interrupted his training of the killer whale, and that we're behind schedule because Odin won't let Kyle feed him."

Marissa is silent before muttering, "I'm sorry, sir. It won't happen again."

"It won't, young lady. Another stunt like that and you can go back to Oklahoma and mop the floors of that place they call an aquarium."

"Yes, sir."

The orca squeaks, then rolls on his side, raising his giant pectoral fin out of the water and waving it. The sun heats his skin in seconds, and he splashes his fin back into the water before gliding over to the platform. He puts his head out of the water near Kyle.

Kyle, looking at his boss first, brings a bucket of fish over and holds one up. Odin rests his chin on the edge, opens his mouth, and waits for its cold corpse to hit his tongue before swallowing.

He dives, flipping upside down and raising his tail out of the water to wave it. He hears the whistle, and swims to Kyle once more. Kyle gives the orca three fish and reaches out to pat his rostrum. The feel of Kyle's hand makes the orca's skin flicker with disgust.

"Well," Lance says, smiling. "Maybe you helped us out after all, Ms. Smithson." He takes a couple of steps toward the killer whale, looking down, making sure he doesn't get his shiny shoes wet, and says to Kyle, "Carry on. I think we can plan on the show we scheduled at the end of the month."

Kyle watches him walk away, then begins teaching the orca to spin in the water when he makes a circular motion with his hand. Odin gets it on the first try.

"I swear to God this whale is too smart for his own damn good," Kyle mutters. But he keeps teaching Keet tricks, and the fish are now landing in Keet's mouth like they're flowing from an Alaskan river. Marissa hangs back, saying nothing but keeping her eyes on the orca; she's sure he just saved her job.

The next day is hot, and the orca is restless, rising and falling and swimming in circles. He's disoriented by memories of someone else trying to swim to the surface of his brain. Searching the bottom of his tank for fish, he finds nothing. He's hot, he's alone, and he's ferociously hungry. Kyle arrives wearing a wetsuit and carrying a bucket of fish. The orca pokes his head out of the water but doesn't see the girl with the kind voice.

"Just you and me today, Odin." When Kyle gestures with his hand for the orca to wave his pectoral fin, he takes a breath and sinks to the bottom of his tank. Kyle walks over to the gate and opens it, but instead of moving into the larger coliseum tank, the orca rises to take a breath, then lies on the bottom, refusing to move.

Kyle sighs, takes the fish back to the cooler, and wipes his hands on his wetsuit before going to his locker and finding his phone. He scrolls through his contacts, finds Marissa's number, and taps on it.

"Marissa? Yeah, it's Kyle. I know it's your day off, but I need you to come in. Odin won't perform. I want to see if your being around makes a difference to him. Yeah. See you soon."

The orca has been dozing again, but snaps awake when he sees Marissa greet Kyle. He submerges, flips upside down, and waves his tail at her before popping back up and squeaking.

Not knowing if she should show any pleasure at his greeting, she eyes Kyle and then the orca. She's in a t-shirt, shorts, and tennis shoes today.

"You can go say hi. He wasn't this lively until you showed up. What did you do to break the ice?"

Marissa shrugs. "Don't know. Probably nothing different from y'all. I talked to him. He let me feed him fish."

"Maybe he likes women," Kyle says. He walks around to the gate, Marissa following him and Odin swimming behind Marissa, his head above the water.

The water at the bottom of the coliseum tank is cooler, and he swims upside down through the deeps for several minutes before returning to the platform. Kyle goes through all the hand signals, and the orca performs each trick for fish.

"Marissa, you want to feed him?"

"Yes!"

She grabs a handful of fish, holding them away from her body, and walks toward the killer whale who has his mouth open. Bobbing at the surface, he clicks and whistles to Marissa. She gets to the edge of the platform and drops the fish into his open mouth. He swallows and is about to dive to cool off when she slips, falls, and slides into the water next to him. He dives away from her, then floats upward from below to place his rostrum under her kicking feet. She's lost a sneaker, and he can see it slowly sinking to the bottom. He rises in slow motion, boosting her on to the platform. Kyle grabs her hand and pulls her so hard that they both slip and fall on the wet concrete.

Odin dives for the shoe, then rolls and swims to the surface. When he opens his mouth, the shoe is resting on his pink tongue. Kyle grabs it, and then gives him fish. Ignoring Marissa's excited chatter behind him, Kyle swipes back his wet hair, a slow smile spreading across his face, not quite reaching his eyes.

"Marissa, I think we have a new act for the show."

Wiping the water from her face, her eyes grow wider. Odin chins the edge of the pool, watching.

TWENTY-NINE

Odin floats through sunrises and moonsets, swimming to nowhere in the tank. Sometimes when he sleeps, he thinks he hears his pod singing him home. He sings back, only to startle fully awake when his own voice hits his body, jarring in his head. The mist has stolen his dreams of the auburn-haired woman, though the sound of Marissa's voice still comforts him. The words she speaks no longer make sense, but he feels the kindness in her lingering touch on his skin. There's a music to her speaking that gives him his only comfort.

Every night, now by habit more than because he remembers why, he puts his head out of the water, spinning slowly in place and looking for the blinking dots of light that are his only company through the dark and lonely hours. Sirens scream past and vanish in the distance, the unnatural rumble of traffic ebbs and flows—he's living in a human-made ocean that contains nothing of beauty.

Every day, he swims out to the large tank to perform. He doesn't dive and jump unless he is told to. He's hungry all the time. He nods his head or waves his pectoral fin, not understanding what is being said, only keeping his eyes on the fish that appear in Kyle's hands.

Kyle tries to teach him new tricks, but the orca is listless, unresponsive. They put vitamins and medicine into the fish, making the cold meat taste worse. Odin eats and sleeps and swims in circles and performs. His is the acceptance of a prisoner.

One day during a performance, Kyle switches places with Marissa and pretends to slip and fall into the pool. Kyle feels a tug on his ankle and looks up at the rapidly retreating surface of the water. Holding Kyle's foot in his mouth, the orca allows himself to sink. They hang there, suspended in the water's silence, the orca barely aware of the frantic man slamming his fist into his black rostrum, then clawing for the faraway surface. The orca sinks into a trance, forgetting about Kyle, forgetting that they both breathe the air that is so far above them.

Hearing the whistle, seeing the young woman's hand slapping the water above him, he comes back to his senses. With a flick of his tail, he pushes Kyle upward, releasing his foot and pushing the man up on the platform, where he sprawls, coughing. Odin hears the gate bang open, and swims into his tank. No fish are waiting for him.

The next day, they cancel the performance. The skies are gray and low, and the great male orca feels the atmosphere's changing electricity and pressure both in his body and in the water. He feels the thunder roll through him, a bang and growl bigger than his heartbeat, and spends most of the day at the bottom of his tank. Even the young woman can't coax him to eat.

Three people are now standing around his tank, looking at him. The man with the shiny shoes says, "Kyle, I've been talking with our vet, and he said Odin needs to have Tagamet medicine for ulcers. I've ordered it. It's in the break room. You can add it to the stuff he's already getting."

"Yes, sir, Mr. West. If we can get him to eat."

"The vet also said that ulcers in killer whales were common, and it wasn't a big deal."

Kyle nods, but in his mind, he sees his foot disappearing into Odin's mouth, and the two of them sinking.

"Ms. Smithson, if you can help Kyle? You seem to have a rapport with the whale. Maybe he'll eat more if you're around."

"I'll try, sir."

Kyle silently seethes at having to share his job. His failure the day before, and allowing himself to be taken under, still rankles.

Marissa breaks in on his thoughts. "Maybe we could get more salmon? He seems to like those the best."

Lance West nods, his hands behind his back. "Kyle, get those ordered, will you? Just a week's worth. Don't want the killer whale eating us out of our profits."

Kyle and Marissa shake their heads.

"I've got a board meeting. I'm trusting both of you to take care of this matter and get him back performing."

"Yes, sir," Kyle mutters.

"Oh, and no more stunts like falling in the water with him. The last thing I need is OSHA breathing down my neck. From now on, you both keep your feet on that platform and figure out an act that will bring in more people."

Without waiting for their answer, West turns away from them and walks around the puddles and out through the break-room door. They notice that Odin has risen to the surface, his dull black eye watching them.

"Do you feel sometimes like he knows exactly what we're saying?" Marissa asks.

"Don't be stupid, Ms. Smithson," Kyle mocks. "Go get his fish ready with the ulcer medication so we can feed him before he changes his mind."

At two in the morning, multiple lightning strikes from a storm charging in off the Pacific plunge the Southern California town of San Bolsa into darkness. When the orca performs his nightly vigil of looking for the blinking lights, he sees only darkness around his tank. Agitated, swimming in tight circles, he tries to remember why the lights going off is so important, then does the first thing that appears as a picture in his mind: He points his head to the bottom of the tank and spins in place.

And he is human once more. Rising in slow motion to the surface, Keet swims to the edge of the tank where, panting and out of breath, he grips concrete still warm from the day's heat. Running one trembling hand through the hair hanging in his face and pushing it out of the way, he pulls himself out of the water. At that moment, the rain starts, the cold drops pelting his naked body.

He huddles by a wall, dazed, shivering, and unsteady on his feet. Lightning arcs through the sky, and the booming thunder makes him put his hands over his ears and crouch down in fear. He's bewildered and confused. It's dark, but in the flashes of headlights from passing cars, he sees he's near the building his trainers always come through.

Keet opens the door and peers into the room. An emergency light has flicked on, illuminating the space and throwing his long shadow behind him, back to the tank. He sees a large rectangular shape and, after propping the door open, runs into the water cooler. The smells of human bodies and what must have been the last meal the employees ate before leaving make his head swim, and he sways, almost losing his balance. The words *pepperoni pizza* float across his brain. He shakes his head, shuffling on bare feet across the cool linoleum floor.

Keet sees another door across the room and goes through it. The surface changes from smooth to rough. He looks down and mutters, "Concrete," in a voice creaky from disuse. The more he moves, the more stable he feels, and he quickly realizes that he needs to find something to cover himself with. Turning around, he shuffles back into the break room and to the row of gray lockers opposite the refrigerator.

He opens each locker in the dim light, pulling out the clothes he finds. From one, he retrieves shorts that are too big for his narrow hips. These are dropped on the floor. In another, there's a pair of dark blue sweatpants. He pulls them on; they're too short, but he cinches up the drawstring, and they stay up. He continues his search, metallic clangs marking his progress as he opens and shuts each door.

In the last locker, this one smelling of body odor and aftershave, Keet finds a pair of worn-out flip-flops. He holds them up, inspecting them at eye level. They're Kyle's. Keet goes still, then drops the flip-flops on the floor. More memories rush through his brain: of Kyle's feet, of his harsh, false tones, of the black cloud that surrounded him and how it got darker when his boss was around. A sour taste floods Keet's mouth, and he bends over and retches, heaving up undigested fish. One hand braced on cold metal and the other on his knee, he's breathing as though he's just run a marathon. His hair hangs in his face, long and disheveled. Standing, he feels the weight of gravity. He slips on the flip-flops and takes a drink of water from the cooler.

In the last two lockers, he finds a stack of OceanMagic t-shirts. He paws through them until he finds a large black one. When he unfolds it, he sees a picture of an orca leaping through the O in "Ocean." Keet realizes it must be him. He bends over and retches again, but nothing comes up. His stomach unclenches and he puts on the t-shirt. The feel of the cotton on his skin first sends a shiver through him, then he begins to feel warm once more. *How long have I been in here?*

When he looks around again, he recognizes the rectangular shape. *Refrigerator.* Opening it, he finds cartons of yogurt, an apple, and a plastic container. The container has tuna in it. He eats it with his bare hands, shoveling it into his mouth, then licking his fingers clean. He does the same with two cartons of the yogurt. The apple he puts in the pocket of the sweatpants. Shutting the refrigerator door with a slam, he has another drink of water and walks out of the room. As he follows a wide brick path, he takes the apple out of his pocket and begins to eat it. There are emergency lights here as well, and as he walks through each pool of light, he looks for a way out.

His balance feels less precarious now as he reacclimates to being earth- rather than water-bound. The rain is sharp on his skin and the lightning flashes so close that he swears he can reach out and catch it. He wants to ride the lightning through the clouds, north to home.

Home. Nolee. Her name sears through his heart, and her face rises from the depths of his memory, first blurry, then clear, as though she's swimming toward him. Seeing the green of her eyes, the silver streaks that run through her auburn hair in his mind's eye, he drops to the ground, flooded with memories—memories of her warm lips on his; of her body, naked and curled around him as they fall asleep.

He stands, tilting his head back, hoping the rain will wash him clean of his time in captivity. In a flash of lightning, the planes of his face look as though they're carved from one of Sitka's red cedar trees.

Keet quickens his pace. Under an emergency light, he sees a map of the park, and studies it. The words float in and out of focus until he can make sense of them. He's looking for one word, the word that means the way out.

Exit. To his left and straight ahead. He walks, then jogs, trying to figure out where he is and how to get home. The rain slows to a soft drizzle as he comes to a white building with the OceanMagic Marine Park logo painted on it. He sweeps his hair out of his eyes and looks up at a dark sign; underneath the word "Exit" are two more words. He stares, closes his eyes and breathes, then opens them again and squints. In the dim light of an emergency lamp above the glass door he sees the words "Gift Shop."

Keet rattles the door, pushing it against the frame. It doesn't budge. He looks around, trying to find something he can use to break the glass. A hedge runs in front of a fence that ends at the gift shop, but he doesn't see any rocks. Just then, all the lights come on, and Keet covers his eyes with his arm. When he lowers it, he sees two men in black uniforms rushing through the gift shop. Keet dives for the hedge as he hears keys in the lock.

"You check on the killer whale, make sure he's okay."

The other guard rushes off, slowing from a jog to a quick walk, breath- ing as though he hasn't moved quickly in a long time.

The first guard goes back into the gift shop, sweeping his gaze up and down each aisle. Finding nothing to raise suspicion, he walks out, the glass door banging shut behind him. Keet watches as he goes down the same wet path the other guard followed. It's stopped raining.

Soaked and shivering, he comes out of the hedge and tries the gift-shop door. It opens. He walks through, looking to the right and the left before seeing another door straight ahead. He goes down an aisle of products with plush toys; the sign above them says "Take Odin home today!" Another aisle has baseball caps and more clothing, all emblazoned with the OceanMagic logo, all with his likeness jumping through the O.

Once out of the store, he knows he needs to keep going. In front of him is a dark expanse of concrete marked by straight white lines. He walks across it, the words *parking lot* appearing in his head. Reaching the street, he stops, looking around to get his bearings. To his right, a stoplight blinks yellow. A few cars are out, headlights reflecting in the shiny street. He looks to his left and sees a bus parked at the curb. Its sharp exhaust fumes burn in his nose.

He's still shivering, now more from an adrenaline rush at being free of the tank than from the cold. When he reaches the partitioned door, the bus lets out a rush of air that at first causes him to jump. When he looks up, the door is open and the smiling face of a woman beams at him, her curly black hair only precariously restrained by the headband she's wearing.

"What can I help you with, honey? Looks like you got caught in that storm. C'mon in and warm up." She motions with one hand, the other holding the large steering wheel.

"Where am I?" he asks, putting his foot on the first rubber-covered step.

"San Bolsa. You wanna go somewhere else, it'll take more than this bus to get you there." She laughs at her own joke before seeing the look of confusion on her soaking passenger's face.

"You know, San Bolsa? California?"

He nods his head, then asks her "Are we close to the ocean?"

"Honey, this line ends right on the beach. Sure you want to go down there right now? It'll be prettier in the morning."

"I'm sure. What day is it, ma'am?"

She quirks a graceful eyebrow at him; her expression of amusement and exasperation makes Keet think she may not answer him.

"It's November fourth. Not too much longer until Thanksgiving. I'm in the holiday spirit tonight. C'mon in and I'll give you a ride to the beach for free." She slaps a long lever with her hand, and Keet sees a flashing light on the dashboard. She looks at him again, and motions with her head. "Go on and sit down."

As he takes the first seat, he notices other passengers; one is asleep, others are typing on small rectangular objects. *Smartphones*, he remembers.

Three police cars rush by, sirens blasting, the red-and-blue of their flashing lights staining the inside of the bus; Keet covers his ears. The driver waits until they've passed, signals, then lumbers the big bus back on the road.

Keet must have fallen asleep, because the next thing he knows, he feels a gentle hand on his shoulder.

"Honey? Wake up. We're at the beach."

He blinks awake, sitting up straight and yawning as he watches the driver settle herself in her seat again.

"Well, go on out there if you want. I've got a schedule to keep."

"Yes, ma'am. And thank you."

"I hope to take my kids there one day." She points at his shirt. "They'd love to see that killer whale."

Keet pauses on the last step, then turns. "Take them on a whale watch instead. That's the real deal." He steps down, the door shuts, and he waves at the woman before watching the taillights disappear around a curve. The ocean is in front of him, black water frilled by whitecaps where it hits the sand. Pausing, debating whether he should try to find his way home as human with no money, or swim there as orca, he walks on to the beach, hoping the waves will give him an answer. He's hungry and tired, and both options feel like more work than he's able to do. Instead, he sits on the wet sand and rests.

The sun's first pink rays find him there, curled on his side, asleep, a small frown on his face. His feet are buried in the sand. The flip-flops are nearby, one upside down, its worn sole dull in the new day's light.

THIRTY

The same light finds Lance West, Kyle, and Marissa, along with the security guards and two local police officers, staring at the dull empty water in the orca tank. Bits of trash float on its surface. No one moves to clean the tank.

"Tell me again what you saw on the security camera footage, sir," the policewoman asks Lance. He rubs his face as if to wake up from a bad dream.

"The killer whale in his tank. I got hold of our security team about ten minutes after the power went out, and when they got to his tank, he wasn't there. Not in this tank, not in the coliseum tank, nowhere!"

"Have you noticed anyone suspicious hanging around lately?" she asks, not looking at him as she types notes one-handed into the pad she holds in the crook of her arm.

When no one answers, she looks at each person, and Marissa speaks up after looking at her bosses.

"I haven't seen anyone. Not many people are allowed back here."

"Mr. West?" the policewoman says.

"You think someone came back here, picked up ten thousand pounds of killer whale and drove away?"

The policewoman ignores his question. He stares at her, his chest inflating. "No, I don't know of anyone else being back here. I'm not here for the day-to-day operations. You need to ask Kyle."

Kyle's eyes are unfocused, and he seems to shrink into himself. He clears his throat, shakes his head, and mumbles, "No one suspicious that I saw."

"Okay," the policewoman says. Lance glances at her name badge and sees Officer Garcia.

"Ms. Garcia—"

"Officer Garcia," she corrects him, unsmiling.

He takes a moment to gather his thoughts. Then, narrowing his eyes at the police officer, he starts over. "*Officer* Garcia, when can we expect help to track down this killer whale? He's an enormous investment, and I want him back here asap."

"Mr. West, you can expect the full cooperation of our department. We'll be asking questions of all your staff and reviewing your security camera footage. A detective will meet with you later today." She looks at her pad, typing as she talks.

"Were there any backup cameras, or a generator that might have run an emergency camera?" She stops typing to look at West again.

"No. I asked our security team the same thing. Apparently, when the emergency lights were installed, they were wired on a different circuit than the cameras on the tanks. The cameras were on the main circuit with everything else. You can bet that will change." He runs his hands over his face again. "Now if you'll excuse me, I have to call the insurance company and let them know we don't have a killer whale, and we don't have his body." He shakes his head as he walks away.

The police officer finishes typing and tucks the pad into a black bag slung across one shoulder. Kyle and Marissa are silent.

"Anything else either of you care to add?" Officer Garcia asks, searching their faces.

Kyle shakes his head, and Marissa looks at him before making eye contact with the policewoman. She stands up straighter.

"Yes," she says. She notices Kyle is looking at the tank, still in shock. "A couple of days ago, during a show, Kyle and I switched places and—"

"Marissa!" Kyle grabs her arm and puts his face too close to hers. She can smell stale beer on his breath.

"Get off, Kyle! They have to know!"

"You say anything, and it will be your job." He gives her arm a shake before releasing it.

Marissa pauses, backing away from Kyle, rubbing her arm. She thinks of Odin and how she felt the first time she saw him. How gentle he was with her during performances, when she fell into the tank with him twice a day. When he carried her on his back, delivering her safely back to the stage.

"We were doing a show, and normally I'm the one who slips and falls in the water. Odin–the killer whale–comes and picks me up. I ride on his back and then he swims onto the platform, and I slide off. The crowd always goes nuts."

"Okay," the officer says. She pulls the pad out of her bag again and starts typing.

"But two days ago, Kyle wanted to be the one to fall in the water with Odin." Marissa steps away from him and warns him off with a glare of her own.

"So we do the show as normal, only now I'm playing the part of a trainer, and I pick Kyle out of the audience. He goes to feed Odin, slips, and falls in the tank. They're only supposed to be down there maybe five or ten seconds, but it seemed like a lot longer. I'm blowing my whistle, and then Odin pushes Kyle up and onto the platform."

Officer Garcia looks first at the young woman, then at Kyle, who's staring at the tank again. His face is red, his fists are clenched.

"What happened, Kyle?" The policewoman glances at her partner, who steps closer to Kyle.

"He grabbed my foot and took me down. I thought I was going to die." Both officers look at Kyle's legs. He's wearing cargo shorts and running shoes. They don't see signs of an injury.

"Were you hurt?"

Kyle crosses his arms in front of his body. Shrugs. "No. Not even a tooth mark. Damn thing was careful about trying to kill me."

"How did . . ." the policewoman pauses, thinking that what she's about to say is a first in her fifteen-year career. "How did the killer whale seem after he took you down?"

Kyle looks at her, amazed. "I don't know! I was puking up the water I swallowed!"

"Okay, sir, calm down—"

"Odin was fine," Marissa interjects. "After making sure Kyle was okay, I opened the gate to his tank, and he swam through."

"Any atypical behavior from him in his tank?"

"No, nothing. He's been a little listless lately, but we thought he was sick. He was on some vitamins and medicine."

"Were you the one who prepared his food?" Officer Garcia is typing again.

"No, I was." Kyle's swaying on his feet. "Can I sit down somewhere? I don't feel so hot."

Marissa gets a chair from the break room for him, sets it down, and walks away from it.

"Lance—Mr. West—bought the supplements. I just stuffed them in the fish we fed him and made sure he ate them."

"We'll need to take those with us," Officer Garcia glances at her partner, and he and Marissa go to the refrigerated lockers, where he retrieves two large buckets. "Officer Bruley, make sure you get Mr. West's permission to take those."

Marissa approaches the policewoman and says, "I think you need to see the break room. It looks like someone's been in there."

The first thing Keet sees when he opens his eyes is a line of white foam retreating from his vision. He sits up; his clothes are sticking to every part of his body, and sand has congealed on one side of his face. He brushes it off and looks around, blinking and shielding his eyes from the sunlight.

It's still early. In the distance, he sees a few people walking their dogs, which reminds him of Nolee and Fae. But then his stomach gives a loud grumble, and he realizes that he's ravenous. Nearby shops are still shuttered, and even if they'd been open, he has no money and no way of contacting Nolee or Trish. He's gratified to realize that his brain seems to be working better today, following each option through to a conclusion.

Stay here and beg for enough money for food and a phone call? Swim into the ocean and change to orca? The latter would be easier, but also with its own risks. Swimming from Southern California to Puget Sound could take weeks; in that time, would he forget again that he was also human? A ripple of fear clenches his belly as he wonders if at that point, he'd even know where home is. He'd never stayed in orca form for longer than a week. After so long in captivity and so short a time as human again, would he be able to change from one to the other? Or would he, like his ancestors, walk into the water and never return to land? Keet thinks it would be easier to take his chances as a human, remembering home and Nolee, than to shift to orca and battle amnesia.

He curls his toes in the cold sand and brushes off the last of the grains from his sweatpants. He could find the local police station and ask for help there. But then he remembers the look on the security guards' faces, and the wail of sirens as he sat on the bus. He doesn't know if anyone saw him or not, so he nixes the option of seeking help from the police.

Human or orca?

After watching the waves roll in and seeing more people on the beach, he decides. Yanking off the OceanMagic shirt, he picks up the flip-flops and shoves them both in a trash can. Keet walks into the surf, feeling the push and pull of the ocean, the smell of salt and fish, and the bass rumbling underneath it all. Water washes over him, and his doubt is erased. He closes his eyes and dives into a wave, then swims out to where the water is deep and cool. Sliding out of the sweatpants, he floats, eyes closed, remembering Nolee, remembering his family pod, remembering the beloved underwater landscapes of the Salish Sea. He dives, spins, and is orca once more.

He dives deeper, pushing himself away from the beach, pointing his nose to the open ocean. As he scans with clicks and high-pitched cries, he gets a picture of its depth and the shape of the unfamiliar seabed. He hears the great humpback singers in the distance, as well as the dolphins and seals passing to the west of him. Of other orcas, he feels no sound at all.

Rising for a breath, he swims on the surface and scans for fish. The whir and static of a school ahead of him catches his attention, and he dives again, putting himself between them and the surface. The orca tilts his head, sending a wave of sonar toward them, seeing their size and number. They scatter to the surface and away from him. He glides to a stop, settling at the bottom. Once the fish have slowed, he rockets straight up, catching a young fish on the first try. He swallows, relishing the taste of its meat, and twists and turns to give chase to another one. He spends most of the day feeding before he heads north, swimming in a rhythm of diving, rising, breathing—letting the ocean guide him home.

Flips and barrel rolls, rising and falling. He is at peace with the ocean that surrounds him. Pushing his tail hard against its salty coolness, diving deep, rising to breathe the warm air, he deviates only when an obstacle prevents him from swimming straight. The orca swims as he eats, swims as he sleeps. Part of a grander symphony, he is poetry without words, music without notes, a mystery without clues.

The noise of boats and their motors, the splash of people and dogs and kayaks—none of it breaks his focus on the woman with auburn hair who's the reason he's finding his way back.

THIRTY-ONE

I trudge through the mornings, aware of the heaviness of my heart and feet. Where once Fae and I walked the beach in the early watercolor light, eager to see the tall dorsal fin cut through the water, now when I'm awake, I search the internet for news about orcas.

Months ago, I read about the arrest of a captain and his crew who were thought to have captured and transported a killer whale from the waters of British Columbia. There were no leads to where the orca had been taken, and no more stories about the captain's fate.

This morning's search brings up something different, however. I read through the article so quickly that I go back and force myself to slow my eyes, and my breathing.

November 21

A killer whale, "Odin," has been missing for more than two weeks. The owner of OceanMagic Marine Park in San Bolsa, California, is concerned for his well-being. The local authorities have no leads and are urging the public to come forward with any information. Odin, the star of the local aquarium for the past two months, disappeared from his tank during a storm that left San Bolsa without power for six hours.

If anyone has seen anything suspicious in or around Ocean-Magic, please contact Detective Wayne Mills of the San Bolsa PD. OceanMagic is offering a generous reward for information leading to the safe return of their killer whale.

It can't be a coincidence. The killer whale who was captured and the killer whale who's disappeared from the Southern California aquarium must be the same. It must be Keet. The chair topples over behind me as I rocket to my feet. "Fae, here."

She rises from her bed, her slanted yellow eyes watching for signs of what our next move might be. When I put on my shoes by the door, she's warbling like a bird, her front paws dancing up and down while I lace up my shoes. Grabbing my jacket, I open the door and we jog out to the water, then stride up and down the beach. I can't take my eyes off the rippling gray expanse, willing myself to see Keet swimming to me, the sheer force of my longing thick as the winter fog.

The sun is higher, but not any warmer, by the time I sit down on our log. Fae spins twice before settling into the sand with a sigh.

I scratch her behind her ears. "Where is he, Fae? Why isn't he here?"

She blinks at me, but if she knows the answer, she's not sharing it. Neither is the sea, the morning's whitecaps slapping the rocks before slipping away. I glance at his house, and his black 4Runner, the ache in my chest cresting and crashing down. I slide down the log to sit beside Fae, tears cutting off my vision. Rocking and crying, I wrap my arms around myself as Fae whines and licks my hair. I lean toward her, and then lie down, curling into myself. Eventually, the storm of my grief passes, and I'm left empty.

Back in the cabin, I pick up my phone and see that Abbie has texted.

Hey Mom. What's up?

I smile and type back. *Nothing much. It was good to talk with you on Thanksgiving. I'm glad you, Carlos, and your dad got to spend the day together.*

Her answer comes quickly. *It was nice. I hope you can join us someday. Are you okay? You sounded sad when we talked.*

I put the phone down on the table and look out the window at the clouds settling low over the sea. I find I'm all cried out. I pick up my phone and text back. *I'm okay. There's not a lot of sun here in the winter, so it's a bit of an adjustment.*

Yeah, I'd def have a hard time without the sun too. You said Keet was on a trip? Will he be back soon?

I don't like telling my daughter half-truths, but until I know what's happened to Keet, I also don't want her fretting when her focus needs to be on school. *I hope so, sweetie. Until then, I have my work at the shelter and Chena's store!*

That exclamation point feels like some other happier woman, from a happier time, but right now, I can't talk about my wild theories. I pause, hit send, then type some more. *Are you back at the dorm?*

I am. Getting ready to go out with some friends. Have a great day, Mom. Love you!

This time, I don't have to fake the emotion. *Have fun. I love you too!*

∿∿∿

If it weren't for Fae, I'd spend my days under a blanket on the sofa. She insists on being walked and eating at regular times, and I follow her lead. I walk, I volunteer at the shelter, I reread the press release about the killer whale who disappeared from a Southern California aquarium.

The hours at Chena's store helping people with their pets are a welcome relief from wondering if Keet is still alive. I don't know what the Pacific Ocean is like this time of year, or how long it would take an orca to swim north, or even if Keet is the orca in the news articles. Hope isn't a strong enough rope to hold on to, so I focus on getting through the days, hand over hand, and diverting my now-familiar sense of helplessness into keeping busy.

It's another overcast day where four o'clock in the afternoon begins first thing in the morning. At lunchtime, I reheat the last of my Thanksgiving leftovers and share bits of turkey with Fae. As I get up to wash the dishes, I hear a thump on the porch. Fae barks, the joyful sound she makes when greeting a friend. And there are only two people she considers friends.

I throw open the door and see Keet curled on the porch, naked and shivering. The first thing I notice is how thin he is; his ribs are too close to his skin and the sharp bones of his pelvis are clearly visible. I lean down, get my hands under his arms, and pull. He stumbles to his feet, then falls on all fours, panting with the effort.

"Come on, Keet. You're home. You're going to be all right. Help me get you inside." He doesn't respond, but he does crawl, then allows me to help him stand. I guide him to the sofa, where he collapses. Covering him with a blanket, I feed more wood into the stove, warming up the room when I see he's still shivering. Fae licks the foot that is hanging off the end of the sofa.

The rest of that day, he's in and out of consciousness. He wakes up the next morning and asks for his clothes. I reach for his hand, that beautiful hand that I've ached for months to hold, but he pulls away.

"Do you want me to help you to your own house?" I barely finish asking before he's shaking his head. He turns over, his back to me, and I stare at him for a moment, then go to his house to get the clothes he needs.

After two days of one-word answers, I stop trying to coax him to talk. I also stop reaching for him, because it hurts too much when he draws away from me. He's silent, eating when I bring him food, wandering through the cabin, a wraithlike presence. Mostly, he sleeps. He won't go home, but he also won't sleep in my bed. Every night, hearing his howls shatter the quiet, I run down the stairs. Every night, he startles awake, eyes blank, and he doesn't answer me when I ask what I can do.

He's still on the sofa, still silent, his eyes dark and shuttered against the light. After kissing his head, I take Fae out for her walk.

I glance at the waves out of habit, hoping to see the joy of an orca rising to the sky. The sea laces the waves in white and they rush to shore, clattering the rocks like maracas. I keep my eyes focused on the bobbing buoys. The seal is missing, as is the otter. It's as though even the ocean has pulled into itself, the only sign of life, the waves it wears out of habit; the only movement, vestiges of an irresistible force.

I pick up the slobbery ball Fae drops at my feet and see her wide doggy grin, and the way her eyes dart between my hand and my face. When I throw the ball, I feel the rage behind it, a fiery creature who wants to burn down everything in sight. As Fae bounds away from me, I pick up all the stones I see and hurl them into the water, tears streaming down my face, a scream welling up in my throat. Finally, I stop, panting, hands on my knees. But Keet isn't there to brush it away with the gentle touch of his fingers. He's lying on my sofa, and there's nothing gentle about whatever it is he's fighting.

Abandoning the ball at my feet, Fae gives a small whine. I sit down, willing myself to breathe deeply.

"Sorry, girl. I couldn't hold it in anymore. You're okay." She lowers her head, sniffing the breeze that carries my scent to her. Since I haven't showered in at least four days, it must be rank. She approaches me slowly, wagging just the white tip of her feathery tail.

"You're okay, girl. You're okay." I pat the rocks next to me. She closes the distance between us quickly, leaning against my side, panting and snuffling in my ear. I cry again.

Finally, I swipe at my eyes with the sleeve of my jacket. I'm cold and want a cup of tea and some breakfast. I try to avoid wanting Keet back as he was; a wish like that isn't in anyone's power to grant. Standing up on shaky legs, I brush the sand off my jeans. "C'mon girl. Let's go get some breakfast." She nabs the ball and trots at my side as we walk up the beach toward the cabin that has become our home.

I'm still on the beach when I hear the exhales. I turn, watching as Fae runs out to the water, letting it lap around her paws. Her ears are cocked toward the dance of dorsal fins and breath in the morning light. I join her, seeing George and Atma, Tia and Poppy, Belle and Nana break through the water and glide back down again. There's a blank spot in their pod where a gigantic male used to swim.

"This must be the definition of bittersweet, Fae." I look down at my red dog, and she looks up at me, wagging her tail. She turns her head to look behind her, and I follow her gaze.

Keet is on the porch, watching his pod, leaning toward them, but not making any other move. At this distance, I can't tell what he's thinking. Before I can wave or call out, he turns and disappears back inside, shutting the door behind him. Fae whines when she hears me sigh. I pat her head and look at the cove, empty now of fins, the sparkling exhaled droplets gone.

$\sim\sim\sim$

Keet looks up as Nolee comes through the door, his fingers still outstretched in front of him.

"You remember asking me if having flippers felt weird after having hands?"

Nolee looks at him, surprised to hear his voice after a week of one-word answers and blank looks.

"Yes. As I also remember, we got distracted, and you didn't answer that question." She smiles at him, wanting to remind him of their conversation and the lovemaking that followed, hoping it will thaw the ice in his eyes.

Keet offers a ghost of the smile he used to beam at her. "It's not weird. Nothing about being orca is the least bit strange. I feel free, and a part of something beautiful. Held. Loved."

Looking down at her own hands, Nolee closes her eyes against the bitterness in Keet's voice.

"You know what *is* weird? After being in that tank for so long, I don't want any of those feelings. I don't want to be orca. I saw my family out

there, swimming, calling me to them, and I don't feel a fucking thing!"
His voice rises, thunderous with anger.

He stands up suddenly, and Fae shies away from him, rushing to sit by
Nolee's side.

"Nolee, I don't want to be orca and I don't want to be human. Where
does the hell does that leave me? Who am I? What am I?"

The only sound in the cabin is Keet's strained breath whooshing in and
out of his lungs. He clenches his fists and watches as Nolee's eyes meet his,
burning green lights in his colorless world. Her hand on Fae's head is soft,
but her firm voice fills the cabin.

"You're you, Keet. Keykwin. I don't know what happened to you when
you were captured, or when you were in that tank. I don't know what it
took for you to swim home and then become a man again. To come back
here, back to me. What I know is that you're not yourself right now, and
that the way back begins with a fire, a meal, and a bath. In that order. For
both of us."

Keet slumps back into the soft hollow of the sofa, holding his head in
his hands. The tears slide from his eyes and down his face in silence. He
feels the sofa settle as Nolee sits beside him, not touching, not speaking.
Fae follows her and leans against his legs. He feels the warmth from both
as his tears flow harder. The tremors that wrack his body break his voice
loose. He sobs, rocks back and forth, and shakes, the images of the net,
the rough handling of his body, and the isolation of the tank pouring out
of him, burning like venom.

Finally, exhausted, he stops crying. Nolee hands him a tissue and he
sits up and wipes his eyes and nose. He leans toward her and she's there,
wrapping him in her arms, resting her head on his as he sputters out his
story.

"They chased us in boats. We couldn't get away from them. Everything
was loud; we couldn't see where we were going. They cornered us against
a cliff, in shallow water. Being chased and captured was terrifying. I could
feel everything my family felt. Their confusion, their fear. It felt like my
heart was being ripped to shreds. But I didn't worry. I knew that if there
was a chance, I could help them escape. I would be caught, and then I
could change once no one was watching. Easy. They go free, and I would
be free again whenever I got to where they were taking me."

Nolee is silent, letting the story crash against her shoulder where he's
resting his head.

"It was uncomfortable at first. I didn't realize how heavy I am as orca," he gives a bitter laugh. "I also didn't realize how hot I would get, being out of the water. They covered me in what felt like wet towels, but the heat was burning me from the inside out. I could feel the rocking of the ocean, but I was on top of it. When I closed my eyes, I didn't know if I was on my sailboat dreaming I was orca on a ship, or if I was orca on a ship dreaming about my sailboat.

"I called for my family, but I couldn't feel them. There was only a void, and the vibrations of the ship and the rush of humans around me. Their noise was unbearable. Everything felt like nails on my skin. I could understand what they were saying, and I realized I was just a paycheck to them."

Nolee takes a deep breath and threads her fingers through his. He doesn't pull away. Fae is curled up on his feet, tail covering her nose, eyes half-closed.

"I think I blanked out most of that trip. The next thing I remember is being lowered into the tank. The air was scorching, even at night. I was looking forward to cooling down. But the water was warm, and I couldn't get deep enough to get away from the heat."

He rests his head against her again, feeling her hand stroking his hair, her breath as regular as her heartbeat. He sits up, drawing away from her, removing his hand from hers.

"The fish they fed me were dead. I was hot and hungry and lonely, and I couldn't stop thinking about how worried you were." Keet looks up and sees that Nolee's head is bowed. When she looks at him, tears are sliding down her cheeks. She wipes them away.

"When I tried to escape that night, I couldn't become human again. I tried, but I stayed orca. I bashed my head against the wall, and people showed up. Several nights later, I looked around and noticed that red dots of light were coming from structures around my tank. I could still access my human memories at that point, and knew that they were most likely security cameras, and I was being watched all the time."

"And you can't change back to being human if you're seen?"

He shakes his head. "Not by humans. I change all the time in front of my orca family. It doesn't scare them. They've also grown up with the knowledge of the Keykwin."

"But you escaped during that storm, right?" He sees Nolee then, his eyes clearer than they've been since his return. Her hair is mussed, and her hands are clasped together between her knees, as though she's afraid of touching him. Keet reaches for her hand, and she takes it, tracing the bones in his hand with one finger.

"Yes, how do you know that?"

"I spent a lot of time on the internet, looking for news of orcas. An article posted by the *San Bolsa Times* talked about a vanishing killer whale. I hoped it was you."

Keet sighs, moving to sit closer to her. "It was." He's suddenly exhausted, but even more, he's hungry. His stomach growls and Nolee smiles.

"How about the usual for breakfast?" she says.

"I'll take two of everything." He leans in and kisses her lightly, moving the hair away from her face. She pulls back, kisses his hand, and gets up and goes into the kitchen.

"Mind if I shower while you do that?" he asks.

"Shower away," she calls from behind the refrigerator door.

When he comes down the stairs, his black hair slicked out of his eyes, he sees Nolee close her laptop. There's a fire in the woodstove and the room is warm. "What were you reading?"

She sighs and opens up the laptop. "A news article. And before you ask what about, it has to do with OceanMagic aquarium."

She pauses, watching him for his reaction.

"I'm not going to explode," he says. "Please read it to me."

She takes a deep breath and reads.

December 8

Lance West, owner of OceanMagic Marine Park in San Bolsa, California, has been indicted on multiple counts of alleged illegal capture and possession of a male killer whale, endangering employees' lives, and money laundering. The killer whale is thought to be the same one stolen from the Pacific Northwest earlier this year. OSHA, the local police, the IRS, and the International Whaling Commission are continuing to investigate. Mr. West has not been released on bail and awaits trial later this month.

Nolee glances up from the screen. "There's more. Do you want me to go on?"

Keet pauses, then shakes his head. "No. I'm glad they nailed the bastard."

Nolee and Keet bring the food to the table and sit together, eating silently. Keet pauses, looking at Nolee until she catches his gaze. "Would you mind if I slept with you tonight, Lia?"

Her smile is all the answer he needs.

I don't think I expected anything, but that night, when Keet rolled away from me and dropped into an immediate sleep, the disappointment that welled up told me I *had* been expecting something after all. Chiding myself for thinking he was going to be back to himself so soon, I inched over until my back was pressed against his, closed my eyes and fell into his warmth and contact.

Now each night, I fall asleep that way, my back against his, feeling his breathing, feeling his ribs and spine pressing against his skin. He's walking up and down the beach every day for longer amounts of time, but the darkness in his eyes is only receding by millimeters. He refuses to return to his house. During the day, I go into town and come back to find him on the sofa, reading or staring into a fire he'd built in the woodstove. I text Trish updates, glad that there isn't much business during the winter months. We eat meals without tasting them, watch nature shows without seeing them. All the time, I'm waiting for him to heal. Hoping he will.

Out in the bay, after the sun slides behind the islands, his orca family appears, the blades of their fins bobbing, exhaled breaths pluming. Silent, they seem to be waiting. I have a sinking feeling that I knew who they're waiting for.

THIRTY-TWO

Keet has spent the last several nights watching Nolee sleep. Listening to her, giving himself time to change how he feels: that he needs to join his orca family and travel north. The tremor in his hands is worsening. He clenches them. He thinks about making love to her, then rolls away, gets out of bed to open the curtains and gaze at the bobbing dorsal fins in the cove.

They've been in the cove every night, swimming just outside the buoys. This night is different. He's not shaking, but as he watches his pod's exhales and hears their song floating through his head, he knows waiting is no longer an option. The moon shines a path of light on the waves, light that's crisscrossed by the dark triangular shapes and the misty breath of his family.

He turns back, sitting on the edge of the bed by Lia and memorizing her face: the soft, round curves of her cheek; the dark eyelashes; the short, slightly crooked nose. The moon's silver light shines in through the open curtains and catches in her hair, turning some of the strands a glowing white. Her face is relaxed. He leans down and kisses her forehead. She smiles and hums, squinting up at him as he strokes her hair.

"Lia, I need to go."

She smiles at him, her hair tousled, smelling of sleep. He leans down again, this time kissing her mouth, savoring her taste. In his head he sees himself remove her nightgown, sees his hands travel up her torso to her breasts, feels them joining in the night's silence. Instead, he breaks away from the kiss and stands.

She reaches for his hand. "Are you okay?" Her voice is low, still husky from sleep.

He shakes his head. "I need to go." He takes his hand away from hers.

"Go where?"

"With my orca family. I need to be with them. I need to swim."

She sits up in bed, the covers rustling. "Keet . . . don't you want to wait until—"

"I can't wait anymore!"

His outburst surprises her. She holds his eyes, swinging her legs out of bed, reaching for her robe.

"When do you think you'll be back?"

"I don't know. I don't know if I'm coming back."

He can see she's not quite awake, then watches as what he's said hits her like a blast of cold air. He talks faster, wanting her to know the plans he's put in place.

"Look, I talked with my lawyer here in town, in case I disappear." She reaches for him again, but he steps away. "Let me finish, Nolee."

"That summer storm I got caught in made me realize how unprepared I am in case something happens to me. When OceanMagic captured me, my only solace was that at least my lawyer could wrap up the details of my life."

He sees her collapse into herself. Ignoring her shock, he continues. "Alex and Trish can run the business. If I'm not back in six months, everything gets handed over to them." He's pacing now, moving back and forth in the small room that can't contain his long strides or his suffering. The memory of trying to swim in the too-small tank shudders through him. "I wrote down the lawyer's name and number. When you call, he'll know who you are." Nolee's hands are in her lap, and she's watching him; her eyes are both wet and furious. He keeps talking, hoping to make her understand.

"You can have the car and the house. I know the lease on your cabin expires in May, and I also know how much you love it here. I paid off the house years ago. It's yours if you want it. Or you can sell it. At this point, I don't much care." He stops pacing, looking out the window at the moonlit bay. The pull of the sea and his family is now beyond his ability to withstand.

He bends down and kisses her, runs his hands through her soft hair, buries his face in her neck, inhaling her scent, then breaks away and walks out of the room. She sits still and stiff, then jumps up and follows him down the stairs.

"That's it? You're going to just leave and not even give yourself a chance to recover from everything? Is this your answer? Run away? Swim away?" Her voice is shaking, and her accent is stronger. He reaches the bottom of the stairs and removes his t-shirt, letting it drop on her floor.

"You're a coward, Keet Noland—" Her voice breaks as she says his name. He turns and looks at her. She's got one hand on the banister to steady herself, and the other is covering her mouth, as though she wants to stop more words from escaping.

He strides to the front door, opens it, and walks out onto the rocky beach. He hears Fae behind him, panting in surprise at the middle-of-the-night outing. His family is closer now, and the call of the sea runs through him, a force he surrenders to. Stepping into the cold water, he feels it lap around his ankles.

"Wait!"

He turns again and sees her, hair undone, robe flying behind her. His heart aches to go to her, but the ache isn't as strong as the beckoning of the water. He puts his hand up to stop her.

"Damn you, quit telling me what to do!" Fists clenched at her side, she walks closer and stops, glaring up at him, the moonlight refracted in her eyes. "If you need to leave, then go! I promised myself I'd never beg a man for anything again, and you won't change that. Go, if that's what you want to do."

She backs away from him, arms crossed against her belly. She looks out to the mouth of the bay, where the orca pod has stilled, their warm breath floating through the air.

Fae nudges his calf, and he looks down. He kneels, petting her head. "Look after her, Fae." She wags her tail and licks his nose. He smiles, stands, and turns to the sea. In one fluid motion, he's out of his shorts and walking deeper in. When the water pools around his hips, he turns. A chill wind flutters through the trees, lifting the hair away from his neck. The water is dark, the moon shining down on it, and on him. Nolee gasps, covers her face with her hands, then removes them and looks at him once more. She stands straight, tears streaming over her pale cheeks, determined not to speak.

I wasn't awake until I heard Keet say the word "lawyer." Everything after that is bathed in unreality, a nightmare I'm only a guest in. I see his body silhouetted against the black sea and moonlit sky. His back is to me, and he's walking away. Probably for good. And the only thing I feel is rage. It pours out of me, incandescent and wild. I stop on the shore and wrap my robe around me against the frigid air biting at my legs. I see him kneel, see Fae lick his nose. Part of me is touched by this, my once feral red dog with her friend. Another part of me rages at him for abandoning her, and me, just when things were turning around. And yet another part of me never wants to see him again.

He begins his Walk Into the Water, if that is what this is, and turns. The wind comes up, blowing through the evergreens, lifting his long hair away from his face. There's no cloak, but my dream and this moment crash together, the shards realigning into the reality before me. The moonlight gilds the dorsal fins in the cove and throws Keet's high cheekbones into sharp relief.

I cover my face with my hands. I now know what was under that cloak. It was him as Keykwin, only I was too scared, or too ignorant, to see it. When I look up again, he's still there, waist-deep in dark water, but now the pod's dorsal fins and high-pitched calls fill the air and echo over the bay. He turns and looks at them, then back at me.

He smiles. "I love you, Lia." Keet turns and swims out to sea with effortless grace. The orca pod surrounds him as he dives under. Moments later, I see the giant dorsal fin appear through the surface and hear a loud exhale. The male orca turns toward me. I close my eyes and open them again to see Keet, as orca, looking at me over the water, his shiny black eye alive once more. He dives, slapping his tail on the surface as he and the pod turn as one being toward the channel, heading west.

I watch them leave, their misty breath hanging on the night air, moonlight made solid. Out in the distance, when I can no longer hear their breathing and their dorsal fins are only dark blurs, they dive, and I don't see them come up again. I sit on the log, Fae curled at my feet, and weep.

With each thrust of his tail, he releases his human memories. The farther north he travels, the closer to his home in Sitka he gets, the more he's convinced he's finished being human. But he's silent and non-responsive during the journey. He eats and swims and breathes, not sleeping even when the others in his pod need to rest. He's numb to the presence and touch of his family. Even George can't coax a response from him.

It takes the pod more than a week to reach the icy waters near Sitka, where they feed and rest. Keet watches, floating motionless as he did in the tank, while his family plays. In the time between dusk and dawn, they silently surround him. Their circle closes and they force him deeper into the black water. When he tries to surface, Nana blocks him. As she rises for air, the rest of the pod piles on top of him, wrestling him away from the surface.

At first, his response is gentle, yielding. He feels the oxygen in his full lungs and hangs in the water, letting them swarm over him until Nana reappears. She takes a fluke in her mouth, clamps down, and drags him deeper. Now, angry, he sends a hard blast of sound at them. Yanking his fluke from Nana's mouth, he feels the sting of the rake marks on his tail as he flees to the surface to breathe before they can swarm and trap him under the water again.

Seeing the flurry of tails and flukes and white frothy water, birds appear, hoping for something to eat. His rage grows, and as it does, so does his voice. The whole pod is raucous, urging him to speak, to fight, to choose. Life. Death. No longer is the choice between orca or human: His orca family forces him to fight for his life or sink beneath the waves. When he flees, they follow, capsizing him with their combined weight. When he fights, they slide away, bearing his rage with a twist of body and a staccato song that pelts him repeatedly. *Live or die. Make your choice.*

Images of Osprey Bay and Nolee play through his memory like the notes of his favorite songs. He wants to see her again, wants to make meals for her, and walk with her, and make love to her, and share a life without secrets. He feels the memories inside his body as he's fighting his family, as he strains for the surface to breathe. Finally, weak and stunned, he dives, spins, and becomes human once more. Flipping feet over head, he reaches for the surface with unsteady arms. The orca pod circles him, then closes around him. Together, they swim to a distant shore where a woman wrapped in a blanket, her gray hair in a bun on top of her head, sits looking on. They are now as silent as they were violent just moments before. The only sounds are their breathing, the gulls, and the brush of wind through the evergreen forest.

Keet rises from the water, feeling the rocks wobble under his bare feet. He's panting. The saltwater stings his eyes, and the new day's light is too intense. He squints, standing chest deep, reaching for the words his tongue needs to shape, hearing his pod exhale behind him in the ocean. He still feels the echoes of their voices in his head.

Live or die. Choose.

He shakes his head, feeling dizzy. He doesn't know why he is a man again.

"Grandmother," he croaks. "I need help."

She looks at him before rising with a grunt from her camp chair. "You need a towel and some clothes." She laughs at her own humor, her brown face glowing with mirth, before turning her back on him and going into a cabin.

When she comes back out, her arms are full of towels and clothes. Keet looks at her eyes; it's like looking into a mirror. She places the bundle on the beach before calling to him. "Get dressed, then come in."

Keet watches her walk inside, noticing the peeling paint on the small cabin revealed by the rays of the rising sun. He turns, saltwater dripping into his eyes, and sees that the dorsal fins have disappeared. Not even a flicker of feeling or thought comes from his pod. He's caught in a riptide of nothingness.

THIRTY-THREE

December had passed in waves of melancholy so deep I could barely take care of Fae, much less myself. I made it to town to ship Abbie's Christmas gifts (a blue Camas Island t-shirt, a multicolored pottery mug from the local shop) and keep myself and Fae stocked up with food, but other than that, I didn't move much.

After the new year, I woke up one morning, gazed at the wood planks over my head, and decided this was enough. Keet made his choice, and I would be damned if I was going to let it rule my life. That day the house got cleaned, Fae and I went for a hike, and I got my hair cut into what Abbie called a lob. Not having hair against my neck was a new sensation, one that made me feel both vulnerable and free.

January is a bleak month in most places, and Camas Island isn't any different. The leaden clouds match my mood, the frantic sea crowding against itself mirrors my agitation. This is the season for reading and fires and long naps, but although I'm worn out, I can't sit still. Halfway through the month, I long for some good old-fashioned Texas sunshine, then pull myself out of that reverie by splitting wood and raking pine needles out of the yard between spates of pelting rain.

Leaning on the handle of the rake, unzipping my fleece pullover, and catching my breath, I turn my eyes from the sight of Keet's empty house, the chimney that no longer has smoke rising from it, the dull windows. Instead, I admire the woodpile that's stacked high enough to get me through two island winters. I've cleared the yard of debris, the windows are clean, the picnic table and its benches are stacked against the house. A drop of rain slides down my cheek, and on the horizon, whitecaps in the channel are waving to the thick pewter clouds.

"Fae, here!" She runs around the corner, head cocked, and red ears raised. At my best guess, she's a little more than a year old now. She's been spayed and has grown into a leggy young dog, still full of puppy energy, still able to rouse me out of bed when I'd rather roll over and ignore everything. I stroke her head, then put the rake under the picnic table, and she follows me as we walk inside.

The soup I made that morning simmers. The scents of chicken and rosemary fill the cabin. I give it a stir, noticing the soft pliancy of the noodles. Grabbing a loaf of bread, I cut two slices and pop them in the toaster oven, then get out the extra chicken I cooked that morning and tear some off and put it in Fae's bowl. She eats with singular concentration. I wish I could focus like that only on what's in front of me.

The phone rings, and I lean over and pick it up, ignoring the sudden thump of my heart, the hope that it would be Keet. *He's gone, Nolee. Don't want someone who leaves at the first sign of trouble.*

"Hello?"

"Nolee, it's Ava."

"Hey, Ava, what's up?"

"Listen, Chena just called and said she needs to fly up to Alaska to help out her parents out for a couple of months."

I shiver, wondering how much colder it is up there, wondering how many layers of clothing I would need to keep warm.

"Does she need help at the store?"

"That's exactly why I'm calling, mind-reader! I figure between you and me, we can keep it open most days. Is that something you could do?"

I do a quick calculation of the money in the savings account and decide that even though I don't need the work right now, having more in the bank wouldn't be a terrible idea.

"Sure. What hours are we talking about?"

"Let me chat with Chena again and let her know, and I'll text you the hours. We can decide what works best for you and me to do."

"Sure. Thanks, Ava. It'll be good to get out of the house more often."

"I know. Pete's driving me nuts. If I have to listen to one more golf game..."

I laugh, the sound unfamiliar and startling.

"Will you also ask Chena if Fae can come along? I'd like to have her with me if it's not a problem."

"I'm sure it won't be. Thanks, Nolee! I'll text you later."

She hangs up before I can say anything else. Ladling the soup into a bowl, I butter the now-toasted bread and sit down to eat a late lunch. I allow myself a small feeling of pride that I'm able to make food without burning or ruining it.

After I've put the leftover soup in the refrigerator and washed the dishes, my phone pings with a text. I pick it up and see it's from Ava. *Chena says yes to bringing Fae. Her winter hours are Wednesday through Sunday, 10 a.m. to 5 p.m.*

I set the phone down and tap my fingers on the faded tan Formica countertop. I've been volunteering at the shelter more regularly, working with other volunteers and watching as Wallace gains more confidence. It wouldn't hurt to be away from Osprey Bay more, to replace the memories here with new ones. I began this life on my own and I can by God continue that way.

Great! I can work all day on Wednesday, Thursday, and Friday. You okay to handle weekends?

Ava's reply is immediate. *Yes. Chena will be relieved.*

My next text is to Andi at the shelter. *Hi Andi. I'm helping Chena with her store for the next couple of months, so I'll only be coming in on the weekends.*

I wait a few moments but don't see any sign she's texting back. Putting the phone on the counter and feeling lighter for the first time in months, I build a fire and sit on the sofa with the newest Ellie Griffiths novel. The rain lashes against the windows but inside, there's a fire, my belly's full of food I cooked, and my red dog is curled up and snoring lightly. *If this is what my life is going to be like from now on,* I smile to myself, *it's not a bad life.*

My phone chimes again, and I walk over to the kitchen table where I left it. I tap the screen and see it's a text from Andi. *Can you talk?* I send back a question mark.

The next moment, my phone lights up. Andi's calling. "So why all the mystery, Andi Fox?"

Her merry laughter makes me laugh too. "No mystery. I was talking with the board of directors a couple of days ago, and they wanted me to ask you to come in."

When she says nothing else, I ask, "And that's because . . ."

"Because I think they want to offer you a part-time position at the shelter, working with the animals and the volunteers."

I drop into the chair, startling Fae out of her sleep. She blinks at me slowly, her eyes narrow amber slits. I lean over and pat her.

"I just let Chena and Ava know that I'll work in the shop for the next couple of months, Wednesday through Friday. I start next week, so I guess I could come in this week sometime."

"Great. They'll be in on Friday. Does ten in the morning work for you?"

"I'll be there."

We chat a little longer, promising to go out for tea, and I hang up feeling lighter, feeling motivated, feeling as though life without Keet Noland is possible after all.

THIRTY-FOUR

He rubs his hair dry, his legs like lead as he steps onto the worn linoleum floor of the cabin. "I didn't know you kept this place, Grandmother."

She's quiet, her motions slow and deliberate as she lights a fire in the woodstove.

"It's our home. Our family started here. Even though we are all scattered like leaves from the trees, this is our beginning."

He watches her for a moment before asking, "What day is it?"

She grunts as she stands, not quite looking at him. "New Year's Day."

"Oh." She looks at him then, her expression not changing. Keet rubs his hands across his face as if to wipe away the surprise.

"When were you last human?"

"What?" He snaps back to the moment and sees her standing in front of him, her clenched fists on her round hips. She doesn't repeat her question. "Early December. I think."

The wood catches fire, crackling and orange. Face unreadable, she gives him a long look. "No trouble changing?"

He doesn't answer immediately, giving her a look of his own while thoughts churn through his mind. "None. I feel like I always do." He wonders if his time in a tank, being orca for so long, changed him. Now he had been orca for a month, and aside from feeling a little dizzy when he walked out of the water, his thoughts as a human man are clear, his mind and body as familiar as they always were. His grandmother's next question interrupts his thoughts.

"Why are you here, grandson?"

Keet lowers himself and sits cross-legged by the stove, the heat warming his back. "Is there anything to eat?" He opens his eyes to his grandmother standing as though he hasn't said anything. He sighs and put his hands

265

against his still-damp scalp. Suddenly he's twelve again, knowing he won't get what he wants until he tells her the truth.

"I'm here because I think it's time for me to take my Walk Into the Water. I've been thinking about this for a long time. And then—"

"You fell in love again." His grandmother interrupts him.

"How did you know?" He raises his head, putting his hands in his lap.

"I helped bring you into this world. Helped raise you. Being in love, grandson, is written on your face, and I can hear it in your voice. But this isn't the only reason you're here."

"No, it's not."

The fire pops and the light grows brighter. In the light and heat, he gets drowsy.

"Grandmother, is there any food?"

She remains standing, looking at him through eyes that are darker than his, though shaped and spaced just the same. They flash like the threat of heat lightning. He pushes himself off the worn rug, shivering once he's beyond the fire's warmth. As he passes her, she lays a soft hand on his arm. Her firm voice makes up for any lack of physical strength. "Sit down, Keet. Tell me why you're here."

Keet moves to the sofa with its worn green and tan fabric, most of it covered with a sheet. When he lowers himself to the spot farthest from the fire, he sinks so far down into what's left of the cushion that he wonders if he'll be able to stand up again.

His story starts with Nolee's arrival on Camas, their friendship, and his falling in love. He tells his grandmother that he revealed what he is to her, and about his capture, release, and swim home. His grandmother is silent, her face lit by the fire's dancing flames. By the time he finishes, she has fed wood into the stove three times.

Finally, Keet shimmies out of the sofa, goes to the kitchen, and takes a worn glass from the cupboard. They were in the same place they had been when he was a child, when his grandmother and grandfather reached for a glass to give him. Filling the glass with water from the tap, he takes it to his grandmother, who is still staring into the fire. He gets a second glass, fills it, and drinks until the water is gone, wiping the back of his hand across his mouth.

"Tell me why you're here, grandson." Her voice is softer, the voice of his youth.

"I thought I did."

"You've told me how you got here. I want to know why."

Keet, back on the sofa, settles again into its worn-out cushions. He's watching the rolling gray light outside, the clouds sifting through the island's trees. He knows better than to tell his grandmother that he doesn't know why he's here; that would get him nowhere. It also wasn't the truth. With a suddenness that makes his heart pound, he says to her, "I don't know who I am."

She nods and runs her hands through her hair up to her bun, adjusting it with practiced movements. She turns and looks at him for the first time since he sat down, then rises to sit on the edge of the sofa, resting her hand on his knee. He thinks it looks like a branch from a red cedar tree, burnished by weather and knotted with age. She waits for him to speak again.

"At first, helping my orca family escape being captured felt good. It felt right. I can change, and they can't. But the longer it went on, and the longer I was orca and treated like an object, the less right it felt. I thought if I escaped and swam home, if I got back to Nolee, things would be good and right again. But they aren't. When I'm human, I want to shift to orca, but when I'm orca, all I feel is darkness. My human memories refuse to die." He pauses. "Grandmother, I'm still trapped in that tank."

He gets up and puts more wood into the stove. It bursts into bright orange flames almost instantly, popping loudly when flame meets sap. When he sits again, this time on the edge of the sofa and closer to the heat of the fire, his thoughts of food are interrupted.

"I dreamt you were coming."

He looks at her, waiting, knowing she has more to say but won't be rushed.

"In the dream, you were half man and half orca, swimming through the waves with all your ancestors behind you. You breathed as a man, but swam as *kéet*, the blackfish for whom we named you."

Keet hears the waves hitting the beach. They are insistent, calling him out to their depths, enticing him. He hears his grandmother continue to speak, her voice soft and raspy.

"The blackfish dreams haven't come to me in many years. Once I made the choice to remain human and moved into town, they stopped swimming to me. They knew and respected my choice. But five nights ago, I dreamed of you. I dreamed of the ocean, and it was the blue of the sky. The blackfish were behind you, black like storm clouds, swift like rivers.

When you rose for air, it was your face. When you dived into the water, it was as *kéet*. I've been waiting in this cabin for you, grandson. The dream never came again. But you did."

She gets up and goes into the kitchen, opening the refrigerator, grunting as she lifts out a pot and sets it on the stove. Striking a match, she turns a knob, and with a touch of the match next to the burner, flames spring up. She sets the covered pot on the heat, opening the lid to peer inside.

"I hope you still like halibut stew." She smiles at him, her face soft and her eyes warm and welcoming once again.

He watches her as they eat, noticing the new lines on her face, noticing that her hands are a bit more crooked with the arthritis she's fought since she raised him. She's still strong, though she stoops now; he wonders if it's because she must, or because she's tired.

"Grandmother, how are you?"

She gives a dry laugh, her eyes sparkling once again as she looks at him. "Old." She pats his hand. "And I need a nap before we visit more." Keet looks at the clock, surprised that it's almost evening. He gets up to take their dishes, and her hand tightens around his. Arthritic or not, that hand could hold the winter wind.

"You'll be here when I wake up?"

Keet hears the statement inside the question and knows there is only one answer. "Yes, I will. I might nap too."

He kisses her cheek and helps her stand. She walks to her bedroom, and he pulls the sheet off the sofa, laying it on the floor in front of the fire. He finds another blanket in the closet, and after stoking the fire, shakes the blanket out, crawls under it, lies on his back, and closes his eyes.

Behind his eyelids, a fast-flowing flood of pictures arises. His first change from boy to blackfish, his adoption by his orca family, the first hunt of a live salmon, and the satisfying sharing of it with his pod. There is his human mother, smiling as he walks from the waves, and another of her, the years showing on her face as she cries and waves from his father's truck as he drives onto the ferry. School, friends, Nolee, Fae.

Spiraling beneath all the memories is the river of blackfish, and it is alive. Bursts of black and white, bellies and tails and fins of his orca family braid together with the smell of Nolee's skin, the wind in his face as he sails, the taste of chocolate, the vibrant colors of sunsets and sunrises. Through his dreaming, he hears the whistles and clicks of orca swimming in the ocean and through his head.

When he feels the earth under his feet and the chill of the water lapping at his ankles, he wonders for a moment if he is sleepwalking. Looking out on the flat, calm blue ocean, he sees familiar black fins grouped together, their breath becoming clouds above them as they part the water they wear as cloaks. They stop, and their heads bob on the surface, watching him. Waiting.

Without stepping away from the beach, he dives. The water is electric blue, and he uses his arms to pull him deeper. His orca family surrounds him, singing and calling with arpeggio scales that echo inside of him, a symphony in human form. He feels their lingering touch along his back, on his head, torso, and legs. He dives again, deeper, the push of his tail and the weight of his pectoral fins replacing his human body. The water gets lighter the deeper he goes, his oxygen never running out.

He pushes down, until the only thing he sees are the black outlines of the orcas around him, weaving, over and under and coiling around him, spokes to his center, twining in upward loops. When he rolls to look up, all that remains are black-and-white threads, floating in the blue sea. He rolls again and dives, where it is silent and bright. When he wakes up, it is a bright white morning in his bed in his house on Camas Island, and Nolee's head is on the pillow next to him. He reaches to touch her silvery auburn hair and yanks his hand away from her heat. He wakes up again, this time in front of the stove, where he has rolled over and touched its hot side.

He sits, staring at the dying fire, feeling a cool drip from his hair down his neck. He wipes it away as he gets up to get a drink of water, walking on legs steady and strong, finding his way through the now-dark room without need of light. The childhood home where he spent so many difficult and happy days has become a refuge, a ship that sails him to a sure and solid knowing. He will choose to live. But how?

He walks outside, his bare feet curling around the rocks on the beach. He stands, watching the dark give way to a sky that is growing lighter. He hears the door shut behind him, and his grandmother makes her way down the stairs, holding on to the railing. Keet rushes over to her, helping her to the camp chair he found her in when he came ashore.

"Can I get you anything, Grandmother?"

She coughs, then says, "Coffee. Lots of milk, and a little sugar." He smiles as he climbs the stairs. Some things never change. He's been making her coffee the same way since he was ten.

When he returns, she's staring out at the ocean where his orca family is slowly drifting. Their fins bob up and down, but they aren't going anywhere. Keet puts a blanket across her lap and hands her the mug. He sits on a log nearby, ignoring the rumbling of his stomach.

"I think you have been walking down a road that goes nowhere, Grandson."

Her quiet voice surprises him, and what she said surprises him even more. He looks at her, secure into her camp chair, the steam from the mug curling in the air.

"What do you mean?"

"I mean that sometimes you can see farther with your eyes closed. Hear more by listening without your ears. Know more without interference from your brain."

She watches the orcas in the ocean. She coughs, takes a sip of her coffee. "It's your spirit that never changes, no matter what form you find yourself in, Grandson. It is your spirit that's your home. That is unchangeable. We've handed your belief of having to choose between man or blackfish down to you, but it is not your cloak to wear. The only thing it gives you is suffering. Your mother also thought she had to choose, as did I, as did your people before you. We eased our suffering by thinking that we had no option. Choosing to be human, we thought we were taking our power back. But I know something now. Being Keykwin, changing your form, never changes who you are."

Keet feels tears running down his cheeks and raises his face to the brightening sky. He can hear his orca family out in the water, breathing together, rising and diving together, waiting for him. He wants to argue, but he knows he can't. His grandmother continues speaking.

"You can't shift from who you are. You can't run from it or swim from it, but if you let that suffering become strong enough, you will certainly die from it. It wouldn't matter if you could change into a hundred different beings, you are still you. Live or die, Grandson, that is what you said our people from under the waves asked you to choose. You make your choice with your spirit, with who you are. Whichever skin you choose to wear is only a skin. It's not you."

She turns to him, her face soft and craggy, her eyes misty. He goes to her, sits at her feet, and feels her hand on his head. "Let that cloak of suffering go, Grandson. For all of us.

"The prayers of your great grandmothers, and their great grandmothers, run through your veins. They give you power, they give you yourself, and the tribe you were born into. A long line of women, a long line of Keyk-win, ends with you but it stretches back through time, all the way to She Sings Two Worlds."

When she stops talking, he knows she's done. They sit then, part of the dawn, part of the orca pod, part of the sea and rocks and trees and wind. Keet looks at his grandmother, memorizing her in this moment, knowing she has shown him a new way to a longed-for home.

Removing his shirt and shorts at the edge of the water, he wades into the cold ocean. The six orcas form a line, waiting. He has no fear because he knows his choice. This is the same shore he walked on when he was four and changing was new, when it was exciting. He keeps walking into the same water he did when he was ten, and his grandmother changed beside him to ask the orca pod to take him in as their own, to teach him.

He swims, dives, spins, and he is orca, outracing his pod, twirling through the ocean, the weaving of black and white, bellies and backs of his family an ocean tapestry. Racing ahead of them all, his head is clear, and his memories of Nolee are crisp. He is Keet now as orca and will be Keet when he shifts back to a man. The concrete tank in his mind crumbles, falling apart as the cold, salty water of the ocean floods in. He leaps, his eyes on the shore where his grandmother stands, steady and smiling. He dives, sounding for fish. The morning passes, his family eating and playing and touching, and he knows as he watches the sun high in the sky that he has found his home. It was never gone; it will never be lost to him again.

When he walks back on land, his grandmother meets him, wrapping him in a blanket. Tears streak her round face, and her smile is brighter than the sun. He looks over his shoulder at the disappearing dorsal fins, hearing their song without his ears, seeing their graceful swimming without his eyes, knowing he is a part of them no matter how far away they are.

Turning to his grandmother, he smiles. She wraps her arms around him, her gray head resting against his chest.

"Welcome home, Grandson. Welcome home." She pats his back, steps away, and hands him his clothes.

They walk into the cabin, and he searches under the cabinet in the bathroom where the clippers used to be. When he goes into the living room where his grandmother is sitting, she looks at him, seeing the clippers in his hand. She nods and stands.

He sits in a chair in the kitchen, the buzz of the clippers as steady as his grandmother's hands, watching as dark strands float to the floor, months of suffering released. Afterward, he gathers the hair from the floor, holding it gently in one fist. Outside, the air is cold on his bare head as he wades into the water and scatters a few strands on the waves, watching them float away. Behind him, his grandmother builds a small fire with dried grass. He returns to it and drops the rest of the hair into the fire, closing his eyes as the smoke and the smell rise to the sky, gone from him now.

They go back inside. Keet showers. He's rubbing his head with a towel, smiling because he can feel Lia; she's there in the same space as his orca pod. But when he thinks about calling her, he hesitates. He dresses and goes into the kitchen to find his grandmother reheating the halibut stew. They don't talk as he sets the table. He fills their bowls and hands one to her. He realizes that many homes have had their doors open to him, and he couldn't see them. He kisses the top of his grandmother's head, closes his eyes, and gives thanks he's no longer blind.

THIRTY-FIVE

I lock the door behind the last volunteer as Andi finishes wiping off the counter with disinfectant. I'd settled into the part-time position of teaching volunteers and working with the dogs that came in, glad to have another job to look forward to when Chena comes back from Alaska next month.

Andi turns off the computers, puts away a stapler, and triple-checks that the answering machine is on. Then her eyes dart around her desk, looking for anything she might've missed.

"It's just the weekend. I'm sure it will all be here when you get back on Monday."

She looks at me and smiles. "Are you hurrying me along because you're hungry, Nolee?"

"Guilty." My answering smile falters, replaced with a frown and an unexpected jolt of pain. The picture of Keet's face after our first night together, when he admitted to going for a swim while I was asleep in his bed, catches me off-guard. I stand up straight and shove the memory down the crooked tunnel his absence has made in my heart.

Andi comes out from behind her desk and lays a soft hand on my shoulder. "You okay?"

I squeeze her hand, then turn toward the door. "Let's get my birthday dinner started so I can obliterate memories of Keet Noland with a margarita."

When I told Andi about Casa Mariachi and their legendary margaritas, I also told myself that I'd be fine going back to a place Keet and I had been to. As we walk in the door, I focus on the smells of tortillas and slow-cooked meat, the undertone of freshly made corn chips.

The server, a tall, skinny guy, glides through the double doors that

273

separate the kitchen from the dining room. Dressed in black chinos and a black button-down shirt, he wears a black apron tied at his waist.

"Where would you like to sit?" It's a slow night, and the server includes the whole restaurant in the encompassing sweep of his arm. He seems happy to have something to do.

I look at Andi and she shrugs. "You pick."

There's a table in a corner by a window, and I point at it. "That one, please."

"Right this way." With a flourish, he grabs two menus and saunters ahead of us to our table.

Andi has taken my word about the great margaritas, and our drinks are in front of us; since we're both driving, we decided to split one. I remember the last time I drank one of these, remember how I stretched my feet to touch Keet's legs. Trapped in memories.

"Okay. What's going on, Nolee?"

I startle, lifting my gaze to Andi's eyes. "Sorry. Memories."

"More Keet?"

I sigh. "Unfortunately, yes."

"Do you want to talk about them?"

"No. Yes. No. Definitely not. He brought me here once . . ." I trail off, feeling pulled in several directions.

Andi changes the subject. "You're almost a leap year baby?"

I see a glint of amusement in her blue eyes and am relieved to talk about something other than Keet. "Almost. Born at 11:18 p.m. on February 28. Just think, we could be celebrating my thirteenth birthday instead of my fifty-first."

"That would make you an underage drinker."

"Almost," I smile, taking a large sip of margarita. "Word to the wise: don't take a big mouthful of that. I'd forgotten how generous they with their tequila."

Our dinner arrives, steaming plates of pork barbacoa for me and fish tacos for Andi. I look up from my plate, watching as our waiter greets four more diners with the same air of boredom, sweeps his arm around the restaurant again, and leads them to the table Keet and I sat at the first, and last, time we were here. I take another sip of margarita, following it with a chaser of water, and look at Andi.

"Wallace is settling in well. He and Fae get along great."

"I know you'd hoped you could adopt him out. I thought you did a good job vetting the applicants, probably more than even I would've done." Andi picks up her fork, spearing the last piece of fish and popping it into her mouth.

"That retired couple was perfect for him. Quiet, loves dogs, willing to be patient with him. Did I tell you what happened when I went over there to help them get him out of his crate?"

"You didn't." She raises her glass, trickling the last of the margarita out of it and tapping the bottom with her fingers. I laugh.

"Told you they were good."

"Let's get someone else to drive us next time. I'd like a couple more of those." Andi wipes her mouth with her napkin. "You told me they could barely get Wallace out of his crate for three days, but not how you ended up with him."

I drink more water. My share of the margarita has disappeared in half the time it took her to chase hers down. The waiter walks over, giving us a half smile; someone should tell him it looks more like a simper than the superiority he's going for.

"One check or two?"

Andi jumps in before he's done talking. "One, it's mine." She looks at me. "Happy birthday, Nolee."

"It's your birthday," our waiter crows. I slide lower in my chair. He rushes away from the table, forgetting to leave the bill.

"Uh-oh. Sorry about that, Nolee." She's almost laughing, so I'm not sure how sorry she is.

"Don't worry about it. It's probably some ice cream with a candle."

Seconds later, I hear an uproar in the kitchen, then three men and a woman burst through the door, each with an instrument. Three of them are dressed in cook's whites. Our waiter is cradling a vihuela, one man has a trumpet, the woman is raising a violin to her shoulder, and the third man strums a guitar. A bowl of ice cream with a candle is nowhere in sight.

I'm mesmerized by the sombreros they all wear. The woman's is a striking velvet number embroidered with colorful threads in the shape of flowers. The three men wear matching velvet sombreros that have an intricate design in white thread around the brim and top. I gulp down the sudden thickness in my throat, wanting to forget the reminder of the Texas I had called home and instead, focus on this moment, Andi's smile as she takes in the instruments, and the joyful sounds of music and singing that fill the room.

Though there aren't many more people here than there were when we arrived, they all begin clapping along, cheering when my birthday song ends. Their joy is infectious, and because we're all cheering so loudly, the quartet launches into another song, more raucous than the last, smiling and singing and making eye contact with everyone in the room. When the last bright notes vanish in the air, I stand up, my napkin falling to the floor, clapping and cheering again. It's the happiest I've felt in months.

I look at Andi, who's also standing, her eyes wet with tears, and swipe at my own. When the band goes back into the kitchen and the room is quiet again, our waiter walks backward through the swinging doors and turns. In his hands is a bowl of cinnamon ice cream with one solitary burning candle. I feel as bright as the flame burning on top of the blue wax.

After he sets the bowl down with two spoons, a check, and an assurance not to hurry, I ask Andi, "So, was that your idea?"

She grins. "It was. The reason this place is called Casa Mariachi is that the owners are a family of mariachi musicians, from a long line of them. I called ahead and asked if they could play for you."

"They were amazing!"

"It was worth surprising you to see you so happy again. You've been pretty down since Keet left."

I run the spoon around the now-empty bowl, scraping out the last of the ice cream. I remember the joyful music and take a deep breath, refusing to sink back into the abyss of grief.

"I *am* happier. And this evening was perfect, Andi. Thank you."

"Finish your story about Wallace, Nolee. I want to hear how you ended up with a second dog."

The waiter finishes chatting with the table opposite us, sees our empty water glasses, and walks over with a pitcher. Funny how people surprise you; here I'd thought he was aloof and above all of this. Turns out, he's probably worked here a long time and he's a talented musician.

"Can I get you ladies anything else?"

When Andi shakes her head, he takes the bill with her credit card and turns to leave. Before he's out of earshot, I ask, "How long have you worked here?" The bill flutters in his hand as he turns. "Since I was thirteen. I'm a part owner with my cousin—she's the one who played the violin. I love it here." Now the smile he gives us is full and warm, his teeth white against his tanned skin.

"You're an amazing vihuela player. How long have you been playing?"

His smile grows bigger. "Since I was a kid. That's my father's instrument. I started picking the strings when I was two. He began teaching me when I was five because I wouldn't leave it alone. Still can't."

"I really loved the music. Took me right back to Texas. Mariachi music always makes me happy, even if the lyrics are sad."

He laughs. "That's right, the bitter with the sweet."

"What's your name?"

"Robert. Not Bob. Actually Roberto."

I stand and put out my hand. "Nice to meet you, Roberto not Bob. I'm Nolee, not Magnolia." He shakes my hand and laughs.

"Happy birthday, Nolee."

I sit again, looking at Andi. "So, you want to know about Wallace?"

"The suspense is killing me." She takes a large drink of water. "And I think that margarita might be, too." She places a hand on her cheek. "Hold that thought. I need to use the restroom.

When she returns and takes another drink of water, I ask her, "You okay?"

She folds the receipt around the card and places both in her wallet. "Yeah—all good. I drank a lot of fluids tonight. Had to set them free. Now, no more interruptions. Tell me about Wallace."

"When I got to the couple's house, he was in his crate, with the door open. There were so many dog toys, I thought maybe their grandkids were over or something. Turns out, not. They'd been trying to play with him for three days."

"But he didn't play, did he?"

I shake my head. "He didn't. He'd leave his crate to eat and stand by the door to the back yard when he needed to go out. That was it. I walked in the door, he opened his eyes and saw me, and I thought his tail was going to fly off his body, he was wagging it so hard. He bolted through the door behind me and sat by my car."

"Did you feel anything from him?"

"I knew you'd ask that."

"Of course! I'm not going to let you skate over the best part of the story."

I take a moment, closing my eyes, feeling the kaleidoscope of images that came rushing at me faster than Wallace's greeting.

"What was almost overwhelming was relief and happiness. After that,

I saw the faces of the man and woman, smiling. Food, toys. I caught a whiff of the trees in the back yard after it rained. All good things, not anything that felt like fear."

"That's good. So we know they're the kind of adopters we want."

"I was going to coax Wallace back into the house, but I couldn't. I sat down in the doorway and imagined him going on walks with his new people, having fun."

"What happened?" She takes another sip of water.

"Nothing. He was like a brick wall. He stayed by my car and didn't budge. I think I sat there for at least fifteen minutes. I apologized to the couple and invited them to come back to the shelter. We'll find another dog for them."

"They called and said they'd be in soon."

"Oh good. I hoped their feelings weren't hurt, and really hoped I didn't confuse them with what I was doing."

I look around, noticing that the restaurant is almost empty. "We'd better call it a night, I guess." We both stand up. I sling my backpack over my shoulder and give Andi a long hug. "Thank you. Again. This has been the best night I've had in a long time. Let's have more of them."

As Andi drives away, I sit in my car and watch her red taillights until they turn and disappear. I'm not about to let my reignited happiness do the same.

At the end of my morning shift at Chena's Doghouse, I type a grocery list on my phone. After chatting with Chena and going through the sales reports and what I'd ordered for the following week, I figured a home-cooked hot meal would be a good end to a chilly mid-April day. Stopping by the market, I say hello to Chena's husband Mike behind the meat counter, and drive home singing about perfection with Pink.

The dogs rush out of the cabin in a tumble of yips and wagging tails, nosing around my legs before galloping to the shore. As Wallace jumps back from a wave, I smile, knowing the water is still cold. Though we're all feeling the promise of spring, it's not here yet.

Humming the chorus to Pink's song, I put the groceries away, build a fire, and let the dogs back in. I sit on the sofa watching the flames, breathing in as the scent of the wood fills the room, lean my head back, and laugh when Fae and Wallace lay their heads in my lap. I stroke their heads, Fae's petite and narrow, Wallace's wide and boxy; the three of us close our eyes, listening to the lullaby of the fire, drifting.

Both dogs move from under my hand, their heads cocked at identical angles, staring at the front door.

"What is it? Visitors?" I open the door and close it again just as quickly. The night air is wet, and the forecast is for rain; patchy clouds have covered the island for months. I look out the window, and in the dim light, see the trees, the sea, and, to my delight, the seal's shiny, black head out by the buoys. She sinks, leaving behind a small circle of smaller ripples.

"Our seal is back, doggies." A look at the clock tells me it's close enough to mealtime to feed us all

The dogs are licking their muzzles and nosing around the kitchen floor for any stray bit of food as I take two chicken breasts out of the refrigerator. I preheat the oven, lay out two squares of foil, and put a breast in each. After adding potatoes, onions, carrots, and squash, I drizzle everything with olive oil and lemon juice, add salt and pepper, and make a pouch out of the foil. As I slide the cookie sheet holding the two pouches into the oven, I smile. My mother would be so proud, seeing me replicate her recipe. I feel satisfied myself, especially because I'll have leftovers.

While the chicken cooks, I put on enough clothes to keep myself warm for a short walk on the beach, including a cap and a thick scarf for my bare neck. The dogs pirouette around me, Fae emitting a high-pitched whine because she knows the exact sequence that means an excursion. Wallace stands and wags his tail, his large ears looking even larger because they're pointed up and in my direction.

"Let's walk a little, dogs. Wait, please." Wallace shimmies to a sitting position and Fae drops to the floor, one white paw tucked under her chest. I open the door and say "Okay." They race out, a tumble and flurry of feet, tails, and joyful barks, beating me to the shoreline. I follow in their wake, a ripple to their running wave.

There's a hint of spring in the air, which bites a little less when it nips at my face. The trees look a little greener, the sky a little lighter for a little longer, and the air holds the promise of all the growing things waiting to push through the dirt. Out in the cove, the otter's flipping her tail as she dives for her own evening meal. I watch to see if she's successful, and smile when I see her humped up on a beached log digging at a crab, tearing into the soft middle with her sharp teeth. I hear the crunch of shell as clearly as if she were dining beside me. The channel between the islands is quiet, with only the occasional boat motoring by toward the marina.

Although some of my friends would say my world has gotten smaller, I know with certainty that bigger isn't always better. Besides, smaller is relative. I don't need any more than the sea, the air that hovers around it, the dogs, and the meal cooking at home. My world is exactly how I want it.

At this realization, I take off my cap and let the stiff wind run its fingers along my scalp. Home, it turns out, isn't a place or the things around it. Home is a feeling, and I'm finally resting there.

THIRTY-SIX

Keet hears the roar of his grandmother's pickup coming up the road toward the cabin. The powder-blue paint job gleams as the sun catches the white of the roof. If he didn't know she'd bought it new in 1969, he'd swear it just came out of the showroom. He sees both of her hands gripping the steering wheel, and the gray roundness of her head as she peers over it. She rarely drives a straight line, but so far, there isn't a dent to be found anywhere on the truck. She either has a substantial amount of skill or an even greater amount of luck. Keet bets on both. She keeps whitewall tires on it, washes it as regular as a churchgoer, and sits on a thick cushion to see over the dash. He knows she bought it because of the step sides, but he doesn't remember ever having seen her use them.

He gives his chest a final rub with the towel, wrapping it around his waist, feeling strong in a way that's still new to him. His knows his strength is both a legacy from all those who've gone before him and his own, singular, and hard-earned. He's spent the past months in and out of the water, as orca and man, finding only an unsullied joy in each form.

He's reveled in the taste and smell of the food he fixes for himself, and sometimes for his grandmother when she visits, as well as in the immediacy of knowing his pod, seeing them inside and out, the silk and weight of their bodies as they roll with him through water lit by sun or glowing with moonlight.

It seems like eons since he swam halfway back to Camas Island with his pod, then couldn't go any farther. Keet remembers hanging motionless in the water, as though stopped by an invisible net. The human part of him hesitated. Rising to take a hurried breath, he called to his pod, the sound echoing off the sea floor far below him. They stopped, turned as one, and swam back to him. He nudged them farewell, and somersaulted in the water, a froth of bubbles trailing the powerful thrusts of his tail.

For the first time, he'd felt unsure, not ready to return to Nolee, not ready to hear what she might have to say to him. He felt his pod glide away, the companionship of their company stretching but not breaking. Their clicks and whistles grew distant, rippling through the water before fading inside his head. He swam north toward Sitka as they swam in the opposite direction, fueled by the salmon they'd fed on. He porpoised out of the water, ate, and sang to the moon all the way back to the cabin by the ocean.

Keet watches as his grandmother lowers herself from the truck and gives her a wave.

"You still here?" she says, as she has every time she visits. As if she hasn't been coming out for dinner several times a week.

"Not much longer," he replies, as if she hasn't heard the same answer for months.

They go inside, and Keet pads back to the bedroom, re-emerging in jeans and a gray pullover and rubbing a hand over his head, his hair velvet under his palm. Putting two generous slices of leftover lasagna in the oven to reheat, cheese and red sauce dripping from the layers of pasta, he asks, "How's Uncle Jerry's job search going?"

"He can't find work in Sitka. He's thinking about looking in Juneau."

"That's a long way away. Would you go with him or stay here?"

She's quiet for so long he's not sure she heard him. When he looks at her, he sees she's gazing out the window that faces the ocean. It's an early spring evening and the sky is a riot of blue and pale color that will spread into gold, pink, and orange as the setting sun paints the sky. Keet sets the table, gives his grandmother a glass of water before drinking his own, and sits down to wait for the timer to chime or his grandmother's answer, whichever comes first.

The timer wins, and he's ready to serve their dinner before he hears from her, pulled out of his reverie when she says, "I'll think about that if it happens. There's plenty for him to do here. What about you? What are you doing?"

The question, a hard counterpoint to her soft voice and face, is one he now has an answer to. After months of changing between his two forms, he knows he is the same. The black trail of clouds that seemed to follow him as a man have disappeared. His joy trebles when he's with his orca family and inhabiting his blackfish form.

His only question is how to approach Nolee after so many months of silence. Months in which, he's sure, she's moved on with her life. But staying here won't answer this question. The only way to find out if she's going to forgive him is to face her.

"I'm going back to Camas."

His grandmother nods. He mixes up a quick salad and dressing, fixes them each a plate, and sets them down on the table.

"That's what I was hoping for you, Keet."

"Can I get a ride to your apartment so I can use your phone to call Nolee, grandmother?"

She gives him an expressionless look, hauls herself up, and walks over to her purse on the counter. When she turns back to him, she's smiling that full sun smile again. In her hand is a cell phone.

I'm on the beach, lying on the warm, late-afternoon rocks when the landline rings. I get up, brushing the sand from my jeans and straightening the wrinkled t-shirt I'd pulled out of the bottom of a drawer in celebration of warmer weather. As I go through the cabin's open door, I wonder what Ava could have to say, since we had just chatted earlier that morning.

"Hello?"

The line is silent, but I think I hear the pop of a fire in the background.

"Nolee?"

His voice runs through me like a whip, and I drop to the floor as though I've been hit.

"Nolee? Are you there?"

Tears burn down my face, and I'm suddenly furious, suddenly overjoyed, suddenly wanting to hang up the phone. I stand up. "Why are you calling, Keet?"

I hear the bang of a door as it closes, and then the crunchy static of wind blowing through the phone. I'd meant to soften my voice, but the anger wouldn't let me.

"I miss you."

"Why. Are. You. Calling." I bite each word off, struggling to overcome the anger and hear him out.

"Fair enough. You have every right to be angry with me. I'm calling because I wanted to let you know that I'm flying home in a couple of days. I didn't think it'd be a good idea to just show up."

"Where are you?"

"Sitka. With my grandmother. I've been here awhile."

"And are you flying home to drop more bad news on me, or . . .?" I hear a volley of barks on the beach and look out, checking to see that everything is all right with the dogs.

"That bark sounds different. Did Fae's voice change?" he asks.

"No, that was Wallace."

"You adopted him. That's great!"

The fire that froze to glacial ice doesn't melt, even as my traitor heart ignites with joy at hearing his voice, at hearing that he's coming home. I stay silent.

"I want to come home, Nolee. To you. To Osprey Bay. I've got things figured out, and I'm more at peace than I've been since I was a kid. I know I've been gone a long time, and I know I didn't leave you . . . us . . . in a good way. Is giving me a second chance still possible?"

"Do you even know what month it is?"

In the silence between us, I feel more than hear him startle at the tone of my voice.

"It's April."

"Do you know what month you left?"

"I don't. I know I was captured in August sometime, but I never did figure out how long I was there, or when I—" I can hear him take a breath. "When I escaped."

"You showed up on my porch on November 26th. You left again two weeks later. It's now April twenty-third."

"So, more than four months."

"More than four months. You've been gone longer than we were together. For four months, I've been convinced you were gone for good. Four months of me putting my life together again, one without you in it. And I've almost succeeded. I—" my voice breaks, and I tilt the phone away from my face, looking out the door to see Wallace and Fae running through the water in tail-wagging abandon.

"I've talked with Ava, and she's willing to let me stay here past my lease term, which is up in May, while I decide what I want to do. I thought about moving back to Texas—"

"Nolee—"

"I said almost. Going back there would be like, what was it you said that time? 'Being imprisoned in a cage that's too small.'"

"The cage is gone, Nolee."

I hear him breathing, and the sound sends shivers up my pale, bare arms. I shake my head, yank a chair over, and sit down.

"When you say you want to come home, do you mean you've decided who you want to be?"

"You could say that. The short story is that I'm okay with who I am, both versions, and I'd like to be with you. If you're still interested."

"It has nothing to do with interest, Keet. I've been living as though you were never coming back. Now you say you are. I don't know how I feel right now, and I also don't know how many more of these shocks I can handle. I was just getting my feet under me. I was happy before you called."

He answers, his voice slow and measured. "Okay. I hear you. Can I call you again tomorrow?"

I stand up again, fidgeting, one arm hugging my waist. I take a deep breath, let it out. "Yes. Call in the morning. I'm at the shelter tomorrow afternoon. Bye." I pull the phone away from my ear, hear Keet say "I'll talk to you in the morning—" as I end the call, numb.

I walk out of the house, looking for the dogs. Fae and Wallace are standing side by side, fur shiny in the sun and lifted by the spring breeze. Fae barks, and out in the channel, I see six black fins gliding toward the bay. Stepping closer to the water, I call the dogs to my side, and we watch as the orcas' black heads break the surface. Their dorsal fins are easily recognizable; even without seeing their saddle markings, I know this is Keet's pod. The smallest orca does an ungainly jump out of the water, almost landing on the largest female. Despite my anger, I smile and, in that moment, realize exactly how angry I've been, and for how long. Watching George's antics as he bumps into the adults' forgiving bodies, tries to entice them into a race, and spyhops for a look around causes me to break into long-unused laughter.

Jogging over to Keet's dock and out onto its bobbing surface, I replay the memory of sitting on it in a wetsuit while Keet dove in, and of my own orca initiation. As though he's heard me—and I have no reason to doubt that he did—George swims away from his pod and comes closer to the dock. Wallace and Fae are at the edge with me, play-bowing, their noses as close to the water as they can get without falling in, tails furiously wagging. George rolls on his side and looks at us.

"Hey, George. I've missed y'all—" As soon as I say it, I sit down with a thump, tears coming slowly, pain hitting fast. I look at the dogs and at the baby orca who won't be a baby much longer, watching as he sinks into the green water and floats closer to the dock. "You're getting big so quickly, buddy." I see him through tear-filled eyes, the vision reminding me of my first sight of the pod through a wet snorkel mask.

As five familiar dorsal fins circle in the distance, George spyhops again, opens his mouth and wiggles his tongue at me. I laugh. His lighthearted playfulness washes through me. "Thanks, George. It's great to see you again." With a flash of white belly and a tail slap, George swims back to his mother's side.

During the afternoon, as I sit on the dock, my breathing slows, and the tears stop as I watch the pod alternate between relaxing and playing. Their black-and-white bellies rolling over and under, their deep exhales and bird chirps—everything they do serves to wrap me in a welcome sense of well-being. Even the dogs, now lying down, are quiet. I close my eyes, sinking into the dock's gentle rocking, listening to the calls of the orca. A clear picture of the six of them swimming together—gilded in sunlit green, undulating and graceful—forms in my mind.

Finally, my stomach tells me it's time to leave the dock and do something about a meal. On my way back to my cabin, it occurs to me I haven't checked on Keet's house in months. Grabbing his extra key from the hook by my front door, I hold it, look at it, decide. The dogs and I jog to his house; I want to get what I have in mind done and over with.

Looking around, it's much as it was the last time I was here: a little dusty, very empty. I walk to the table, running my hand along its undulating surface. I see the swipe of my hand in the dust layer, and dust motes float in the still air. The refrigerator is still cool. I flip a burner on and then off, and it works, too. Everything in the bathroom works. I open the bedroom door and pull back the curtains, then open the windows. The bed's unmade, an old, frayed sheet thrown over the mattress. Turning, I walk out of the room, opening curtains and windows as I go. A quick look outside reassures me that the dogs are still nearby, playing in the waves. As I watch, Fae outmaneuvers Wallace and snatches away the stick he was holding.

It all looks so normal. It all looks like nothing at all is wrong. The orcas are still in the bay, probably waiting for the channel traffic to die down; the dogs are playing; to the west, the sun is sinking, washing the blue sky with shades of pale yellow and orange. I'm in Keet's house, getting it ready for his return when for months, I was sure he'd never come back at all.

Shouldn't I feel grateful? Happy, even? These are questions I don't have answers to, and I never could think straight on an empty stomach. I move around his house more slowly, closing the windows but not the curtains. Locking the door behind me, I whistle for the dogs and head back to my own cabin, wondering what I can make for my dinner.

As I walk into the cabin, I take another look at the bay and see dorsal fins gliding away, moving into the setting sun. The water is orange fire and their fins are black. I close the door.

That night, despite feeling wrung out, despite a hot bath, and despite my heavy eyes, I can't sleep. After Keet left, the dream that had haunted me for months hasn't returned. *Of course it wouldn't. You know what he is now.* I throw myself on my other side and kick a foot out from under the comforter, listening to the dogs yip in their sleep. After another hour of ridiculous rolling around, I get up, bang my fists into the mattress, jam my feet into my slippers, and clomp downstairs. Looking at my phone, I see that it's 2:30 in the morning. What a useless time to be awake.

Still, I build a fire, let the dogs out, then back in, and start hot water for tea. As I'm waiting for the kettle to whistle, I glance at Keet's empty house, which looks as abandoned as I feel. After pouring the boiling water over a bag of chamomile tea, I sit down and open my laptop. Scrolling through my social media accounts doesn't work to tire me out, so I check and answer all my emails. Defeated, I snap the laptop closed and walk to the window that looks out on the bay, in which the only signs of life are the rollicking waves. Huffing with impatience, I sip my tea, enjoying the burn as it goes down, and mentally catalog my memories of Keet, jabbing at them to see if they still hurt when touched.

Resting my head in my hands, I close my eyes. The low murmur of the fire reminds me of the fires Keet and I used to build, and this memory feels warm, like his body next to mine. I stare at the flames, eyes unfocused. The fire's slow, colorful dance hypnotizes me, lulling my anger into something quieter, something less wearying.

The dogs are curled up together on Fae's bed, snoring. I take a last drink of tea, feed more wood into the stove, and lie down on the sofa. After covering myself with a blanket and pulling my knees up to my chest, I close my eyes, thinking I'll rest before I go back to bed.

I'm still there when the phone rings, and I swim up from a hard sleep to see that the light outside is diamond bright. Rubbing my eyes, I pick it up and hear Keet saying my name. "Nolee? Nolee, I'm sorry. I'm sorry for leaving like I did, and I'm sorry I've been gone so long, and I'm sorry for being so selfish."

I sit up and pull the blanket up to my chin.

"Why don't you come home, and we can talk about this in person?"

"I'll be on the next flight."

"Keet?"

"Yes?"

"I appreciate the apology."

In the space before he answers, I wonder if his hair still stands up in the morning. I wonder if he's running a hand through it. I wonder if he still smells the same.

"Nolee, I hurt you."

"Yes, and I still hurt, truth be told. I also know you were doing what you needed to for your own sanity." I hear a quiet chuckle. "I guess what I'm saying is what matters now is that both of us want to see each other again. Let's start there."

"I've never stopped thinking about you. And the way I feel about you hasn't changed either."

I feel a surge of warmth. My heart doesn't feel quite so traitorous this morning.

"I'll be home as soon as I can get there. I need to call the airport and book a flight—"

"Call me back and let me know when you get in, and I'll be there to pick you up."

"Really?"

"Really."

I hear the smile in his voice when he says, "I'm on my way."

Fae and Wallace trot into the house. I follow, closing the door behind me. After giving each of them a treat, I say, "Stay here and guard the house. I'm picking up Keet today."

I had washed the outside of my car and vacuumed the inside for the first time this spring and am hoping for a dry dirt road; it'd be nice to have a little time to enjoy a clean car. I turn, looking out into the bay as I usually do before driving away.

This time, I stop in my tracks. A large, unfamiliar black-and-white head is bobbing on the surface. I don't see any sign that others are with it. After several moments and no movement or sound, just the head's eerie bobbing, I grab my binoculars from the passenger seat and look again; the thought that perhaps it's a dead orca makes a day that was heavy feel even heavier.

But the orca is very much alive. I see its bright and blinking eye and the slight movement of its head as he (or she) looks. Looks where? I follow the line of the orca's gaze: it seems to be looking at Keet's place. I look, too, but I know all I'll see are the dusty, black 4Runner and the house's empty windows.

I put the binoculars back up to my eyes in time to see the orca blow, rising through its back before diving, and then go under, as silently as it arrived. I didn't catch sight of a saddle patch. I lower the binoculars, rubbing my eyes. It must be a female orca. Her dorsal fin is triangular-shaped, small, and upright. More than the visual cue is the sense of her, a weight low in my pelvis, where I carried Abbie. I wonder if she's a pregnant orca. But why would she be alone? I discard the idea that maybe she's a he, a young male who got lost. All the signs I got in the short amount of time looking at her tell me this orca is female.

Scanning the water in the bay and out into the channel, I don't see her again, and if I want to get to the airport on time, I need to go. The binoculars go in the glove box, and I put the car in gear.

Once at the airport, I turn the car off, and hop out. I walk closer to the terminal and see Keet sooner then I expect—smiling, in a blue t-shirt and faded jeans. His hair's been buzzed off; there's a dark shadow where it's growing back in. He's thinner than I remember. But I clearly remember sharp thrill that now explodes in the pit of my stomach. I smile and wave as we walk toward each other.

"You're a sight for sore eyes." I stop a few feet away from him, but he keeps walking toward me.

"So are you, Nolee." He opens his arms, then stops when I don't move toward him. "May I?" he asks. I nod through a haze of numbness. He steps toward me again, holding me close. The proximity makes me uncomfortable somehow, and I feel the bony curve of his ribcage against my arms before I step back and look up at him.

"Thanks for picking me up." He's smiling at me, unsure.

"Welcome home."

ACKNOWLEDGMENTS

This book began with a dream about orcas. Specifically, one very large male orca. As the months of the pandemic wore on, it became clear to me that this was not only an orca story and a love story, but also, a story about the different forms we choose to show the world. Whether we use the word "Shapeshifter," "Animagi," or another variation, the interesting thing is that the idea of humans changing form is firmly part of many cultures.

The story I have written is entirely fictional. However, I acknowledge my debt to the Indigenous cultures of the Pacific Northwest, their Oral Traditions, and Traditional Knowledge about many animals, including the blackfish. I honor and respect their cultural rights as the primary guardians of their unique Traditional Stories.

As any writer does when faced with a story but not having knowledge of some of its parts, I began researching areas inhabited by orcas. They can be found in waters all over the world. In 2019, long before the orca dream showed up, my husband and I went on a cruise to Alaska. It was seven days too long for my husband, and about a lifetime too short for me. On the seventh day, when we were docked in Victoria, Canada, a friend and I went on an orca watch trip. Assured that 90 percent of the time, killer whales were spotted on these trips, we saw nary a fin that day.

While this book is fiction, the plight of the Southern Resident killer whales is not. I understand now why my orca-less orca tour may have happened. Birth times and survival rates for young orcas are declining, and the number of females who can reproduce is in the single digits. The supply of salmon is dwindling, and Puget Sound's toxicity has been an environmental issue for decades. Increasing boat traffic and sanctioned underwater military exercises have, according to local orca experts, killed valuable members of the Southern Resident pod. Even if boats are mindful of marine life, the noise their engines make inhibits the orcas' ability to hunt and eat.

In our lifetime, we may see the disappearance of this specific culture of *Orcinus orca,* either because these factors cause them to move from waters they have inhabited for millennia or because they die off.

There's no California aquarium called OceanMagic Marine Park. It, and its practices, are fiction, although they're based on interviews I've read with trainers who have experience working with orcas in captivity. Camas Island and Osprey Bay are also fictional entities.

Orca attacks in theme parks are, from what I can tell from my research, a common occurrence. It's amazing that fatalities are as rare as they are, but that makes it no less tragic for the friends and family involved. Here in the US, trainers no longer get in the water with orcas, regardless of whether they're wild-caught or captive-bred.

The way the orca was caught and transported in my story is no longer allowed in US or Western Canadian waters, but it was the method that was used between the early 1960s and 1972. Most wild-caught orcas are taken from family groups around Russia, Iceland, and Norway; younger, smaller orcas are targeted because the larger ones weigh too much and don't adapt well. Today, there are more captive-bred orcas in tanks than those who have been caught in the wild.

Also fictionalized is the OceanMagic act in which one of the trainers "falls" into Odin's tank. After the captive orca Tilikum mauled Dawn Brancheau to death in 2010, California law prohibited trainers from getting into the water with orcas. The same law shut down SeaWorld's breeding program, which led them to rebrand their orca shows as "educational." Personally, I'd love to see the closure of marine parks, the cetaceans moved to an ocean sanctuary, and more people watching these magnificent animals in their natural environment. It's a dream I hold for the future.

Any story gets better because of a team of generous people. I owe a gigantic debt of gratitude to my husband Mark, who read this story, supported me, and was as almost as excited about the story of Keet, Nolee, and the orca as I was. To my mom, thanks for being the most excellent editor I could ask for. You've instilled in me a love of words, and the process of crafting them. Thanks to my girlfriends who have cheered me on and made suggestions that have helped this story shine brighter: Dianne, Kristin, Hunter, Anna, Morgan, Tessa, Rose, and Sara. My tribe of women friends and writers is one I rely on to keep my balance. Carissa created the artwork for the cover with skill, intuition, and heart. I feel such gratitude for our collaboration. Thank you as well to the most excellent Maryann Flett, sensitivity reader, for her guidance on writing about Indigenous Peoples with integrity and respect. Gratitude to Leslie and her husband Ric for their help with snorkeling details and to Stefan Freelan and Tim Harvey for their generosity in sharing their knowledge and love of sailing.

To researchers and orca lovers around the world, I owe a debt of gratitude as well. You have helped me understand what life among orcas, and the Southern Resident orcas means.

I have no education or formal training with dolphins and whales, boats, or the ocean, and though I've done my best to research and consult appropriate experts on these and other areas of knowledge, any mistakes in this story are mine alone.

Crissi McDonald
Colorado, 2022

READ ON FOR AN EXCERPT
FROM THE SEQUEL,
"THE CLOCK IN THE WATER."

ONE

I jab at the turn signal, making a right onto the dirt road that has barely dried out from a drenching rain. The road is lit by sunlight that reaches long fingers through the new green of the trees. In another month the forest floor will be covered with the brighter green of ferns, but April is the month of a hesitant walk between winter and spring here on Camas Island. Keet is silent throughout my talking about the lone orca I saw, staring out the window. Out of the side of my eye, I see him turn toward me.

"Are you sure it was a female orca? Alone?" Keet asks.

"Positive. I hope she's still there when we get back so you can see her." I take my foot off the accelerator approaching a pothole that yawns ahead, threatening, as it has all winter, to swallow my Honda whole.

"Tell me again what you saw."

"Only her head, bobbing on the waves. The white eyepatch was thin and long. She was spyhopping. I saw her eye through my binoculars and the strange thing is that she seemed to be looking at your house. Her stillness was eerie, actually."

"That doesn't sound normal to me either. Think she—or he—was sick?" He's holding on to the grab bar above his head, steadying himself against the onslaught of the road.

"I didn't get that feeling. I got the feeling she was watching. When she dove under, even with the binoculars, I couldn't see a saddle patch. Her dorsal fin was small and pointy, not rounded like yours. And it was short. So, I think we can safely say she might be a she."

"Huh." Keet lets go of the grab bar, running graceful hands over the dark stubble covering his head like velvet. There are more strands of gray and silver at the temples than I remember. Hell, I probably have more gray in my hair too.

"No saddle patch? No markings behind her dorsal fin at all?"

I shake my head, swerving to miss another pothole, both of my hands white-knuckling the steering wheel. I take a breath and loosen them. Other than being nervous at seeing Keet, and not being entirely clear about how I feel letting him into my life again, I don't know why I'm speeding. But I can feel the sound of his voice next to me bringing up memories, which I shove down. He keeps talking, which makes it harder to shove.

"I was thinking she might be part of a transient pod. But transients rarely come in this far, and their saddle patches are still visible. Besides, over on this side of the island, there's too much boat traffic and not enough mammals."

"I haven't seen the seal or the otter in several days. I wonder if she's been hanging around and they've found somewhere safer?"

"Or she ate them."

I throw him a look after checking to see I have a stretch of clear road.

"Let's not talk about death right away, shall we?" I can feel my hands tightening around the steering wheel again, and my breath is stuck somewhere in my chest. I clear my throat, hoping the anger that is whipping around me like a hurricane wind will thin out, at least long enough I can get home and not blow up at him in the car.

He glances at me, quick and nervous, his smile matching his glance.

"Sorry. I didn't mean to sound heartless. She doesn't sound like a resident orca, and if she's not a resident, that means she may eat other mammals."

I'm about to snap that I've already heard the spiel, but swallow the words in a gulp, remembering how Keet showed me he was from a small and ancient group of people who called themselves Keykwin. When they weren't human, they could change into an orca, the blackfish. They called this wearing a different cloak, and his shape when he wasn't a man was a very large male orca. The fish-eating kind.

Instead, I clear my throat and say, "They've kept me company and I don't like to think of them being eaten. Especially when they seem to feel safe in the cove." I see Keet look out the window, his profile familiar but his presence, not so much. I take some more deep breaths and loosen my grip, but the winds of rage are searing me from the inside. I start talking, hoping to extinguish them.

"You know what else? Besides her exhale, which wasn't that loud, I couldn't hear a thing. Not a click or a chirp. And," I add, "I didn't feel much either. She felt like a female to me, but other than that it's like she was a ghost orca or something. No pictures in my head, no feelings of light-heartedness that I usually get when your pod is around."

We make the turn down the hill, curving back toward our houses. I park in front of the A-frame cabin that has been my home for a year. Not for much longer, though. I'm going to need to decide at some point: either renew my lease or find somewhere else to be. I wasn't clear what I was going to do when I thought Keet was gone for good, so figuring out what to do while he's here is complicating the choices I was considering. This isn't the source of my anger. As I'm parking the car and opening the door, I realize I resent Keet coming back and acting as though nothing has happened. It feels like the anger I shouted at him when he made his choice to take his Walk Into the Water has been with me all along, and his arrival is the spark that has set me blazing.

We both get out. Above the clunk of the car doors shutting, I can hear Fae's yips of excitement from the cabin. I know Wallace will be right beside her, but in the two months I've had him, I have yet to hear him vocalize much. Probably because Fae does enough for both of them. I walk up the steps and turn to see Keet still standing by the car.

"Wallace is leery of strangers. Don't try to pet him and he'll be ok."

Keet nods. He can't have missed the change in my tone of voice, and I notice he's gazing at his house. I walk up the steps to my cabin and open the door asking both dogs to wait. As I open the door wider, I can see they are sitting side by side, tails wagging. I hear Fae's teeth clicking together, a staccato noise like an agitated rattlesnake.

"That'll do, dogs."

They burst from inside the house, nails scrabbling on the wood of the deck before launching themselves over the steps and blasting into the water in a white, red, cream, and tan flurry. I watch as they leave the water and race down the crescent-shaped cove's rocky beach.

Keet follows me just inside the door. I place my backpack on the table and my keys on the hook. I can see the silver glint of Keet's house key. I take it off the hook, holding it in my hand.

"Fae's not much bigger, is she?"

I turn to look at him, and for the first time see that he looks lighter. It isn't that his hair is so short. The murky look in his eyes is gone. He looks clear, and in the moment it takes for a flash of the same feeling of lightness through me, I realize he feels the same as a man as he does when he's an orca. This doesn't do anything to douse my anger.

"Nolee?"

I hold out the hand with his house key. "It's a little surreal having you back. I thought you were gone for good." I place the key in his hand. "Your other set of keys is on the table. I aired out the house and put sheets on your bed yesterday, but there isn't any food."

"Thank you for doing all that. You didn't have to."

I shrug. "No problem. And yes, Fae isn't much bigger. Wallace makes up for it though." I look out the window, seeing both dogs paddling in the shallow and sunlit sea. Wallace is twice Fae's size and will swim no matter if the weather is sunny or strewn with fog. I think to myself for the hundredth time that Wallace is part seal; I can't keep him out of the water.

As though he's read my thoughts, Keet asks, "If his head was darker, he'd look like a seal. How did you end up taking him?"

I motion for him to follow me to the water's edge. We walk out, the rocks shifting under my feet, watching the waves.

"I worked with him for a while, and he was doing great. The volunteers could interact with him, and if they were quiet and didn't make sudden movements, he was ok. He met Fae, and they played together while I was there. In February, we tried adopting him out to a nice older couple. I thought they would get along."

"Since he's here, I guess it didn't work out?"

"It didn't. He hardly left his crate for days. The couple called the shelter and when I went to pick Wallace up, he left the crate and sat by my car. He's been mine since then." I smile at the memory, feeling the tension leave my shoulders.

I listen to the breeze through the pines, watching the dancing of the water and the dogs playing in it.

Keet takes a breath before he asks me, "Do you think it's because he knows you can hear him, and he can hear you, that he gets scared if that isn't happening?"

I glance at him quickly, not wanting to look too long into his eyes. Not wanting to throw my anger at him just yet, though I know I'll have to tell him how I'm feeling at some point. "Maybe."

After a long silence he seems to realize I'm not going to offer any personal insights, he says, "I'll go check on the house. Do you need anything from the market?"

I shake my head. "No, thanks."

"Cereal?"

I smile despite trying to keep a firm grip on any show of affection. "All stocked up."

"Ok. Thanks for picking me up, Nolee."

"You're welcome." I flash a strained smile at him. He waves as he walks away.

I watch as he goes inside his house, leaving his door open. That's the third thing I notice that is different. Shaved head, a light in his eyes, an open door…all over again I feel as though I don't know him, and yet I do. And want to know more. And I don't want to get any closer than I already am.

Fae is panting beside me as I throw the ball into the bay for Wallace. I hear the 4Runner's engine, and then the loud beat of drums and bagpipes. I turn my head and focus on the dogs as Keet drives away, throwing the wet ball my wet dripping dog has brought back for me.

"Last one, Wallace, and then it's time for lunch." I whip my arm back and throw it out as far as it will go, the anger behind the throw not following it like I'd hoped but growing in intensity.

"Shit," I mutter.